Also by Boman Desai

C000055425

A GOOGLY IN THE COMPOI

This engrossing chronicle of a complicated family builds to a stunner of a conclusion.

—*Booklife*

A family's long-simmering tensions boil over during a trip to the old homestead in this literary novel.... The result is a wide-lensed meditation on power dynamics—within countries and within families.

—*Kirkus Reviews*

The tiger cub grows as dangerous as the British Raj for India. Both have tasted blood and both demand more. Desai spins a fascinating story of Parsi bloodlines, romance and intrigue, counterpointed by the events that made WWII such a watershed in the history of both India and the world.

Anjana Basu, *The Statesman*

The bare bones of the plot don't do justice to the theme, but the structure of the novel is fascinating. The entire story is wrapped around a single breakfast which takes place at the Sanjana residence at Navsari. The progress of the breakfast is broken into five sections each titled 'Day of the Tiger.' Desai skillfully closes each section with a particular character who then narrates his or her story.

Firdaus Gandavia, *Parsiana*

Boman Desai's novel pulls the reader in and doesn't let go till the end. A family secret lies at the heart of the story, but the periphery is no less exciting. Two lovers escape Stalin's Soviet Union to India and a soldier meets with tragedy during the Kut-al-amara campaign of the Great War in Mesopotamia.

—*Afternoon Despatch & Courier*

A "class" act of historical proportions, [the novel] rips into the conventional class hierarchies between British and Indians, upperclass Indians and lower.

Prasenjit Chowdhury, Deccan Herald

TRIO: a Novel Biography of the Schumanns and Brahms

<u>A Kirkus Reviews BEST BOOK OF 2016!</u>

A riveting dramatization of musical history.... Desai has produced a magisterial work, which is clearly the result of astonishingly thorough research. Although the story revolves tightly around the three main figures, there are also fascinating cameos by such musical luminaries as Richard Wagner, Franz Liszt, and Fréderic Chopin, and he memorably depicts the ego-driven rivalries between them. Each has a unique personality, and the author does a lovely job of dramatizing their quirks.

—Kirkus Reviews (starred review)

Boman Desai has dramatized the story of the Schumanns and Brahms in the form of a novel, citing their original correspondence among his sources. He writes so compellingly that it is like discovering this most romantic of stories anew. The great composers of the age make appearances when their lives intersect those of the trio, and I was glad to see that Desai presents them to us, warts and all, with the deepest sympathy and understanding. Bravo!

Zubin Mehta (Music Director: Los Angeles, Israel, and New York
Philharmonic Orchestras)

I finished reading your novel, TRIO, and found it compelling and illuminating. Would that the American (or Canadian) reading public could appreciate such a story as well told. It's a story that Tolstoy might have told in similar terms, and I do hope that it eventually gets the recognition it deserves. It is surely a tour de force.

Vernon A. Howard (Former Co-Director, Philosophy of Education
Research Centre, Harvard University)

Exhaustively researched, charming and readable, I was loath to put the novel down. It is a massive achievement and I recommend TRIO wholeheartedly not only to music lovers but to all who love to read.

Bapsi Sidhwa (Author: *The Crow Eaters, Cracking India, Water*)

I loved your book. You completely transported me. I read it through at a gallop. The love & feeling you have for the subject comes through— you disappeared & they appeared on the page, in the flesh, & I could *hear* their music. Congratulations!

Sooni Taraporevala (Screenwriter/Photographer: *Salaam Bombay, Mississippi Masala, Parsis, Yeh Bombay*)

I loved and admired this book.

Diana Athill (Author/Editor: *Instead of a Letter*, *Stet*, *Somewhere Towards the End*)

Boman Desai approached his sprawling novel, TRIO, a dramatized history of the Schumanns and Brahms, as a biography for people who hate biographies and a novel for people who hate novels. Desai does a wonderful job describing the music. The language of TRIO is so vivid it makes one want to explore the composers' repertoires which get some evocative descriptions. So do the performers themselves: Clara's meticulousness, Liszt's power and bravura, Brahms's perfection at the piano as a cocky young virtuoso and sloppiness as an old man, Mendelssohn's spot-on imitations of Liszt and Chopin. Like the music, the book is meant first and foremost to be enjoyed—and on this account, it does not fail.

Chris Spec, *Quarter Notes*

THE ELEPHANT GRAVEYARD: a *Moby Dick* for Elephants

DANA AWARD FOR BEST NOVEL OF THE YEAR

A novel set in mid-20th-century Ohio revolves around a circus troupe.

Spike Bailey, the narrator and main character of Desai's tale, is a humble trouper in the Griffin Bros. Circus in Kendall Green in 1948.... When a man named Elbo de Bleu, fleeing from the police, seeks refuge with the circus, his arrival precipitates an intricate series of events that steadily spirals out of control and results in Hero [the blackest elephant in the world, oiled to blackness to draw attention during the dreary years of the Depression] being poisoned and Spike landing in India with a guide named Prem W. Gupta. Spike narrates the tragedy at the heart of his moving story from a wiser and sadder future point: "Despise me if you will, I would think less of you if you didn't, but you couldn't despise me more than I despised myself." ...

[A] ... tale of crime, circus life, and enlightenment.

—*Kirkus Reviews*

The stunning and often changing background, the paranormal elements, the big cast and even bigger drama, contribute to an atmosphere of mystery and operatic scope and feeling.... Desai strongly captures the milieu, both its dusty grandeur and its horrors.

—*BookLife*

The novel offers the reader a leisurely, luxuriant view of the lives of joeys, bareback riders, roustabouts—and especially bullmen, those who work with elephants. Both funny and tragic, what sets Desai's work apart is the exuberance of the narrative style and the lushness of the prose, which conspire to create the sensation of a circus seen by a child for the first time.

Michael C. White (Author: *Soul Catcher*)

Part rollicking epic, part multi-generational ghost story, part disquisition on our original sins, *The Elephant Graveyard* delivers a vivid, merciless portrait of America in all its glory and monstrosity. Boman Desai has built from such ambitious material a deeply human novel, large-hearted and bold, chock full of rich characters and commentary. This is a great read, a terrific novel!

Lewis Robinson (Author: *Officer Friendly and Other Stories* and *Water Dogs*)

[A] spellbinding novel, evenly paced, that follows a circus troupe as it deals with a tragic event.... [Desai] paints a fascinating picture of a throbbing circus in Kendall Green [Ohio] in 1948, creating characters that are multifaceted and bringing to life the circus culture.... [A]n original, deft, and balanced tale that offers great entertainment. *The Elephant Graveyard* holds your attention from the jump and doesn't let go.

Christina Prescott, *The Book Commentary*

THE MEMORY OF ELEPHANTS: a Novel

Excursions into [the stories of the Parsis from Iran through India to the US] enable the author to bring into his orbit a wide geographical spread, along with fascinating scraps of literature, religion, science, anthropology, and just plain fun. Innumerable details about the most astonishingly diverse subjects crowd the pages of the novel. And that's an appropriate reason for calling it *The Memory of Elephants*.

Prabhu Guptara, review on *BBC World Service*

A big book with a baroque design. By an interweaving of narrative voices, a brilliant picture is drawn not only of individuals, but of a whole upper-class Indian family.

Adam Lively, *Punch*

India comes to life with great vividness and humor. Added to that are rewarding insights into the alien wisdom of exiles. The writing is never dull. The observations are acute; you sense a generosity of spirit in Desai's way of looking at the world and at people.

Elon Salmon, *Yorkshire Post*

Fantastical though the framework, the book is neither a fantasy nor science fiction, but a vividly realistic presentation of three generations of Parsis. A variety of strikingly life-like characters, drawn with a warm feeling of kinship, yet with much humor, and often with a penetrating satirical observation, give the novel a vibrant sense of reality.

Homai Shroff, *The Indian Post*

The charm of *The Memory of Elephants* lies in the easy naturalness with which writer Boman Desai describes life in a middle class Parsi family over three generations. It is neither pretentious nor a parody as such narratives often turn out to be.

Coomi Kapoor, *The Hindustan Times*

The characterizations are vibrant. The writing has so much drive that, once started, it is almost impossible to leave this book unfinished.

Roshni, *The Statesman Literary Supplement*

DANCING ABOUT ARCHITECTURE
(a Songwriter's Guide to the Lennon-McCartney Catalog)

A close look at the 162 Lennon-McCartney collaborations from "Love Me Do" to "The Long and Winding Road" unearths nuggets yet to be mined from their catalog. Rock music, generally speaking, is judged less for its musical value than for its performance, packaging, and delivery—less for the distribution of notes on the page than for their impact on the listener. Matters of taste cannot be questioned (those are personal), but matters of quality not only can be questioned, but must be questioned and objectively asserted. That is the business of music criticism, also the business of *Dancing About Architecture*.

It is widely known that Paul McCartney requested sole credit for just "Yesterday" from Yoko Ono (who holds Lennon's rights to the song). The song had blossomed fullblown one morning after a good night's rest, so complete in its first incarnation that Paul found it necessary to play it for others to assure himself that it was a new song. He had no lyrics and used "Scrambled eggs / Oh, my baby, how I love your legs" to sound out the melody. Yoko denied the request, but for the wrong reason. John's contribution is undeniable (as the book reveals), but Yoko doesn't know what it is, and Sir Paul himself may be amazed to find this tip of the hat to his longtime, longdead, longlovely friend. Roll over, John Lennon, and tell Paul McCartney the news!

PORTRAIT OF A WOMAN MADLY IN LOVE

BOMAN DESAI

First published as *A Woman Madly in Love* in 2004 by Roli Books for distribution only on the Indian subcontinent.

Book designed for Amazon KDP by Word-2-Kindle (www.word-2-kindle.com)

DEDICATION

I first met Manek Daver on his honeymoon with his lovely wife, Dilly (Dilnavaz), in Srinagar (Kashmir) in 1963. I was on holiday with my younger brother and mother (who was trying to start a business in Kashmiri handicrafts). We're distantly related: Manek is my mother's sister's husband's sister's husband's brother's son. I was 13 in 1963, Dilly 19, Manek 30. They kept up the friendship after we returned to Bombay, treating me and my brother to movies and dinner, teaching us how to use chopsticks at Nanking (my favorite Chinese restaurant), how to twirl spaghetti around a fork at Napoli, how to order steak at Gourdon's. I was afraid, after they had two daughters, that they would forget me and my brother, but they didn't.

Manek was a huge jazz enthusiast with a record collection stemming from the 1940s. I'm hardly in his league regarding jazz, but a friend (Anmol Vellani) was. I thought they would have much to say to each other if I introduced them—but they didn't. We were in Manek's sitting-room, they said their pleased-to-meet-you's, Manek put a jazz album on the turntable, sat crosslegged (eyes shut) on a sofa, Anmol did the same, and for the next 30 minutes neither said a word, both seeming to vibrate to the rhythm of the music as I stared goggle-eyed from one to the other.

Manek was also an enthusiast of other arts, commissioning portraits of jazz greats by unknown artists whose paintings graced their home. He also published two books of the covers of his albums. The first, *Jazz Graphics—David Stone Martin*, focused entirely on the work of David Stone Martin (1913-1991) about whom Manek said on the dust-jacket: "David Stone Martin is both the pioneer and the continuing style force of the pictorial design cover for gramophone records. From the start of the boxed 78 rpm record sets and continuing into the LP, the David Stone Martin (more simply known as DSM) style was the pace setter. A force that other illustrators found increasingly difficult to be independent of.

"DSM's pictorial covers for records started from the mid 1940's with the Asch, Disc and Stinson labels. And continued through the 1950's for the Clef, Norgran and Verve labels. As also for other record labels such as Dial, Grand Sward, Progressive. The original first issues of these records are now Collector's items—extremely hard to find." There was a great deal more about DSM who was sometimes commissioned to illustrate covers for *Time* before *Time* resorted to photographs. There were also captions from Manek and DSM (about the inspiration behind some of the covers).

His second book, *Jazz Album Covers—The Rare and the Beautiful*— continued the tradition of the first, showcasing not only the remainder of DSM's covers, not only other artists of jazz album covers, but also photographers who shortly came aboard, among them Herman

Leonard whose caption for Billie Holiday's last album cover could not be more poignant. Leonard explained: "In 1954, Norman Granz [premier jazz record producer and concert promoter, who also wrote the Foreword to Manek's book] asked me to shoot a cover for her recording session in New York; but when she arrived, I was so appalled at her appearance—so drawn and pathetic—that I said to Norman, 'I can't shoot that for a cover—it's too tragic.' He pushed me into the studio saying, 'Get in there and shoot! It may be your last chance!' and it was."

The books were published respectively in 1991 and 1994, but we had left Bombay long before, I for Chicago, they for Tokyo where his business was subsequently headquartered, but we kept up a correspondence until the mid-1990s when Manek said he didn't write letters anymore, only emails, and suggested I do the same. I had then been working on my book TRIO (a novel biography of the Schumanns and Brahms), 1,800 pages in its first draft, during which time I had quit my day job and was living off savings. I was using an Apple IIgs at the time, good enough for word processing (saving notes and manuscript on almost 100 floppy disks), but without email capability. I let Manek know that I'd get the computer after I'd finished the book and built up my bank account again. He sent me a check for $1,500 saying I should do it right away. I was overwhelmed, but stuck to my guns, only to have him send another check, this one for $2,000, saying again I should do it right away!

I worked part-time then in various capacities at the Harris Bank, sometimes running errands, hand-delivering checks from one of the bank buildings to another (there are 4 in downtown Chicago). These were checks in amounts beyond my comprehension. On one occasion, carrying two checks in two envelopes, one for $3.5 million, the other for $5 million, I stopped in the lobby of the bank to admire my own checks (from Manek) before returning to my errand, only to find a couple of blocks away that, lost in my admiration, I had left the million dollar checks in the lobby. I haven't run as fast since, but to my huge relief the envelopes with the checks were right where I had left them!

I purchased the new computer and my first email flew to Manek (of course). He and Dilly had visited Chicago on two occasions; I, Tokyo, once in 1998. True to form, when I visited, they gave me a tour of Japanese restaurants alongside an education regarding the food. Strangely, all Japanese restaurants specialize in just one kind of food: the Yakitori Torigin served nothing but varieties of grilled chicken (yakitori); Narashino Restaurant served everything (including fried eggs and shrimp) on a bed of soba (buckwheat) noodles; Shabu-Zen served wafer-thin slices of beef, pork, and vegetables prepared by the chef at our counter, each seat of which was equipped with a small pot of boiling water in which we laundered the slices (shabu-shabu being the sound of clothes being laundered in water); and Tonki served nothing but tonkatsu (breaded pork cutlets with shredded cabbage, soy, and rice).

The last time I saw Manek was later the same year. I joined him and Dilly for lunch at Chicago's O'Hare Airport. They were on their way to the Mayo Clinic. He wasn't well, leaned heavily on me as we walked, but kept a smile on his face throughout, talking as if nothing were wrong. He died a couple of months later and thinking about him chokes me up to this day. He was just 65. He had read a draft of TRIO before it was published. He would have been proud to know it was listed by *Kirkus Reviews* among their Best Books of 2016, but no less proud of my other books, among them *A Woman Madly in Love* (2004), the precursor to this new edition containing a subplot I hadn't imagined for the original (I've detailed that story in the Afterword to this book).

I don't know why he took a shine to me, but he once said he thought of me as his younger younger brother (he already had a younger brother). To get to my point: Manek found businessmen a dime a dozen. If they were worthy they would be remembered for the works they commissioned, the dedications they garnered, the charities they sponsored. Bearing that in mind, I had dedicated *A Woman Madly in Love* to him. I'm sure he doesn't need to be the dedicatee of one of my novels to be remembered, but I'm glad to be able to do at least this much—also to remember him for his kindness, not only to family and friends, but to unknown artists, myself included. It is true that a prophet remains without honor in his own country (I know this from personal experience), but not if the countrymen were of Manek's mettle. I am deeply grateful to him for his faith, generosity, understanding, and patience through some very difficult times, and it is in this spirit that I would like to rededicate this novel to:

Manek Daver
(1933-1998)
family man
businessman
jazz aficionado
patron of the arts
older older brother
and friend

ACKNOWLEDGMENTS

All writers stand on the shoulders of giants whose names need no mention, but a great many giants never step out of the shadows, never make the public record, however firmly they stand, however vital they may be to a particular writer's wellbeing. I would like to give a shout-out to those giants for the thousand and one benefits they bestowed, asking nothing in return, while I minded my solitary business: Ronnie Desai (my ever-generous and behind-the-scenes brother), the Dadabhoys and Darkis (Porus, Zerin, Abdul, Darius, Dina, and Amir), Tata-Colchesters (Shirin, Giles, Farah, & Peter), Weils (Richard & Zarine), Limbeck-Siegels (Kevin & Wendy), Suerth-Ernsts (Frank & Susanna), Diller-Ernsts (Lois & Ron), Gulyases (Stephen & Norma),

Katrak-Karkarias (Kamalrukh & Cyrus), Ghadialy-Karanjias (Rashna & Rohinton), Mehtas (Hosi & Kim), Coopers (Farobag & Ashees), Koptaks (Linda & Paul), Kennedietsches (Bill & Jeanne), Franklins (Steve & Suzanne), Davers (Minoo & Dina), Englishes (Jim & Emily), Tarapores (Erach & Silloo), Chokseys (Vera & Farhad), Tatas (Jimmy & Farida), Godrejes (Pheroza & Jamshyd), Chibbers (Homi & Maki, Percy & Yasmin, Darius & Ranjana), Taraporevalas (Kamal & Kai), Lentins (Mehernosh & Angela), Del Sestos (Xun Mei & Tony), Engineers (Rustom & Yasmin), Bapsi Sidhwa (& Noshir), Zimochs (Hank & Linda), Lalas (Sharookh & Zenobia), Mittals (Vijay & Priti), Mirzas (Parveze, Noshir, & Meher), Robin Blench, Marcia Nueske, Tom Gross, Steve Marmur, Cheryl Dority, Bina Sanghavi, Vispi Cooper, Aban Rustomji, Aban Mukherjee, Piloo Tata, Renuka Chatterjee, Kelli Hadfield Faherty (for her lovely photograph), the McArthurs (Tom & Feri, among my earliest boosters), Venkateshes (Viji [for the long-ago launch] & Venki), Anil Dharkar (editor of *Debonair*, who once requested stories saying his Boman Desai reservoir was empty), Wilma Steffes (for Alma Hall's story), Colm Hennessy (for the best jobs a writer ever had), Steve Barron (for laying so many fears to rest), Barry Birnbaum (for a cup that runneth like a river), Mom and Dad (of course)—and, again, always, Diana Athill.

If no one loved, the sun would go out.
                                                    Victor Hugo

If the fact will not fit the theory—let the theory go.

                                                    Agatha Christie

CONTENTS

EXCERPTS
TRIO
A Googly in the Compound
The Elephant Graveyard
The Memory of Elephants

PERCY FABER AND
THE MANDALAY MARKET

It was picturesque: a pretty woman, fifty years old, weeping uncontrollably. The elderly man across the desk from her chair admired her like a painting, right elbow clutched in her left hand, right hand pressed to her trembling mouth, face bowed for cover. Her hands were slender; hair black, grained with grey, thick as rope; skin the color of the beach at ebb tide; pantsuit, dull and grey. The man offered a box of Kleenex, face filling with sympathy. "My dear Ms. Cooper, please compose yourself, I beg you."

His formality, almost foreign in Chicago, from the old world more than the new, reminiscent of her Bombay childhood, brought her to her senses, and she reached for a Kleenex. She had felt from the moment they had shaken hands a strange mix of the familiar and the foreign, but been at a loss to explain it. Dabbing her face, right elbow clutched again in her left hand, she took a deep breath and crossed her arms, crumpling the Kleenex. "I'm sorry. I'm being a perfect baby."

"It's all right. Anyone can have a bad day."

She shook her head. "You don't understand." She wanted to tell him she had lost count of bad days, even bad years, after her return to Chicago, but that would not have been appropriate at a job interview—not that she had otherwise been appropriate. Suddenly, the shaking of her head grew more violent, dissolved into a giggle followed by a laugh as uncontrollable as her weeping moments earlier.

Percy Faber's eyebrows rose above the black rim of his spectacles before converging over the bridge of his nose. Finely shaped, they had been the envy of women, but now escaped their once tidy confines in tiny arcs and tendrils. His hairline, once no less fine across his brow, had slowly surrendered his scalp to a fringe of white from ear to ear, leaving his head for the most part bare, giving him the look of an Elgar or a Hardy down to the white bushy bowtie of his moustache. His eyes were his most startling feature, running through varying shades of blue even as you looked at them. A yellow tie and white shirt complemented a pale grey suit. Embarrassed by scenes, he was glad he had shut the door, but wondered if he might not have compromised himself. He had not been blind to her attractions, full face, full figure, the demeanor of a woman accustomed to command, but he had noted also the shine of her pantsuit, washed once too often, and her scuffed black patent leather shoes. There was no doubting her elegance, no doubting either that it was fading. He said nothing, but sympathy receded from his face as her giggles showed no sign of abating, falling once into a loud snort, provoking more giggles.

Taking another deep breath, she composed herself again. "I'm sorry, Mr. Faber. I'm afraid I haven't proven much of a credit to Mr. Haines's judgment."

Stacy Haines was their point of contact, Farida Cooper's former employer and Percy Faber's friend, president of Telesurveys, Inc., a market research company going out of business, precipitating Farida Cooper's resume onto Percy Faber's desk. Percy Faber was manager of Consumer Research, the market research branch of The Mandalay Market. He shook his head, smiling. "You've done no such thing. It would take a great deal more to shake my faith in Stacy's judgment. As I said, anyone can have a bad day, but we do seem to have had a misunderstanding."

She looked up, dry-eyed again and sober.

"When Stacy mentioned you were looking for a job I assumed you were looking for the same position you had at TeleSurveys, which was my rationale for granting this interview—but not, as you now say, for a market analyst position."

She was shaking her head before he had finished talking. "Not a full-fledged analyst—an assistant analyst, or a trainee. I know the business, Mr. Faber. I've been doing it for a while."

Her distinction, too fine to make a difference to his decision, revealed only her desperation. He shook his head, not without regret. "I'm afraid that is simply not good enough."

He was afraid she might erupt again into hysterics, but she remained sober, nodding her head, accepting the inevitable. "It's so ironic."

"What?"

"What you said about the job, that I would need an MBA. That seems to be my stumbling block—my *only* stumbling block. You can see from my resume that I have the necessary experience."

"But not the qualifications."

"That's what's ironic."

"Why is it ironic?"

She took another breath, shallower than before, her smile that of a beauty contestant, or morning newscaster, or gameshow host, or used car salesman, or some other such professional who smiled for a living. "Mr. Faber, what is it—I mean, what is market analysis in a nutshell? It is finding a hundred and one ways to tell your client that if his product is less expensive, lasts longer, looks better, fits the needs of more people, and comes with a guarantee, he will generate more sales than his competitors. That is *it*—the whole enchilada, as they say."

Percy Faber smiled, eyes transparent as a lagoon. "Come now, Ms. Cooper, that *is* an oversimplification, don't you think?"

Farida Cooper steepled her fingers. "No, I do not. You don't need a weatherman to know which way the wind blows—and you don't need an MBA to tell you the color of the sky."

Percy's eyes darkened, brows rising again over the rim of his spectacles. "Wouldn't you say that is just the least bit … cynical?"

Farida shook her head. "I might if it were not true—but it's true. May I give you an example?"

Percy leaned back in his chair though his eyebrows still hovered over his spectacles. "Please."

Farida brushed her hair behind her ears with her thumbs. He was aware again of grey and white tendrils rendered glossy by their thickness, long slender fingers, nails unpainted, face no less unpainted, her refreshing lack of vanity. His wife, Erica, now two years dead, had been no less sparing of makeup. He glanced at the photograph on the cabinet alongside photographs of their children. He might have slipped into a reverie if not for Farida's presence.

"In 1976, Westinghouse conducted a survey on lightbulbs. They spent one million dollars interviewing nine hundred women in nine cities. The key finding was that consumers were dissatisfied with the lifespan of a lightbulb. No lightbulb lasted long enough. Their solution was to produce a longer-lasting lightbulb and to guarantee its life. They also gave it a different shape, put it in a bright red package, and called it Turtle-Life." She leaned back in her chair, smiling again. "I read it in *The New York Times*. I could hardly believe that a vice-president at Westinghouse was citing the survey as an example of the usefulness of market analysis. I could have provided the same analysis at a fraction of the cost in a fraction of the time—and so could you, I'm sure. An hour's thought would have sufficed, a thimbleful of common sense."

Percy smiled, also relaxing his eyebrows. "Well, then, Ms. Cooper, if you find it so very obvious and unnecessary, you seem even more cynical for wanting the position at all. Wouldn't you want a position where you could make, shall we say ... a less specious contribution?"

She shook her head. "No. My point is it *can* be specious, but it doesn't have to be. It helps, for instance, to know your market. Some things you cannot expect your client to know—for example, that geography makes a difference. Here in Chicago we consume more soft drinks, New Yorkers use the most paper goods, New Englanders smoke the most cigarettes, East Central folks have a sweeter tooth, West Central folks prefer cereal ... and so on and so forth. Race makes a difference: blacks pay more than whites for durable goods; black women are more fashion-conscious than white, especially at upper-income levels." She shrugged. "That sort of thing makes a difference, and markets change continually. An analyst should be up to the mark on that sort of thing—but it doesn't take an MBA."

Percy nodded approval. "Well, now, I *am* impressed. I can see you've done your homework."

Farida shook her head. "But I haven't. That's not it at all. These are just things I picked up while working at TeleSurveys. We called people all over the country about their products—every evening except weekends from five to ten-thirty. During breaks I would glance through the magazines in the offices, *Advertisers Age, Marketing Insights, Consumer Reports, The Atlanta Economic Review*—that sort of thing." She shrugged. "I just picked things up."

Percy sighed. "You are perfectly correct in everything you say, Ms. Cooper, and if it were ten years ago I would have had no problem hiring you as a market analyst trainee. During the Seventies we hired people with degrees in Sociology, Psychology, History, English—it didn't matter. Yours is in ..." (he looked at the resume) "English, I see. What we were looking for, of course, was a basic level of education. Before that we didn't even require a Bachelor's degree, but the pool of applicants was getting too large, and we had to do something to winnow the wheat from the chaff, and however unfair it may seem we upgraded the requirement to a college degree." He shrugged. "We're following the same process again. The pool of college graduates is simply too large. We need a new bottleneck, and we've made it the MBA requirement. It indicates, if nothing else, commitment, resolve."

Farida grinned. "It might also indicate that they have money to burn, or nothing better to do with their time—but my quarrel is not with the rationale. I understand the need for bottlenecks. I just don't think the requirement should be rigid. I do think you should at least take my experience into account. High school graduates, even most college graduates, don't have this kind of experience—not even most MBAs. Don't you think my experience should count for something?"

Percy pursed his lips. "I agree with you, Ms. Cooper, but my hands are tied. I do not make the rules, but I do have to abide by them. If I were like Stacy, president of his own company, I could do what I wished, but that is not the case. I answer to Mandalay. I have to abide by their requirements."

"What you're saying then is that someone who has been to bartending school would make a better bartender than someone who has actually tended bar."

"Not quite, Ms. Cooper. If you had actual experience as an analyst that would be a different story, but I see from your resume that your experience has been strictly as an interviewer. Isn't that right?"

Farida nodded. "Yes, but that should also count for something. Having made the calls myself, I know better than most analysts how to formulate questions—how to write a smooth survey."

Percy avoided her gaze. "I can certainly appreciate that, and I can see how you would be an asset to Mandalay as an analyst—but I don't understand why, considering your experience, you weren't promoted to an analyst position at TeleSurveys, why you remained with the interviewing staff."

"Actually, I *was* asked to be an analyst, but I was in no hurry. I preferred part-time hours while I was finishing up other things—my Master's, which I'm still finishing up and … other things. I was taking one day at a time, but with TeleSurveys closing up shop my back is against the wall and I don't want to start again at the bottom of the ladder somewhere else. I want to put what I know to some use if I can."

Percy's regret showed in his eyes. "I can understand that, and I applaud you for your understanding of the business, but" (he sighed again) "I'm truly sorry."

She understood the interview was over, that he was too polite to show her the door, letting her take her time, but she remained seated, eyes dropped to the desk. She had counted on the job more than she had imagined, and considering her other disappointments the rejection became more difficult. Change was salubrious, but too many changes at once were not. Her security rested on four supports: first, a job; next, an education to improve her chances for a better job; third, a home for sanctuary when the world became unmanageable; and last, a man to share her load. As long as one of the supports was stable, preferably two, she could make changes in the others, but not in all four at once.

For the present she had no boyfriend, had not dated in years, and preferred to keep it that way. It had taken almost five years to regain her senses on the heels of the disasters with Horace and Darius. She had entertained during that time a succession of assorted men: one night stands, one month stands, six months at best, but had tired of dating men who cared no more for her than she for them, or who professed to care for her so much more than she could ever care for them, and joked that the cure for one man was another, for the second a third, and so on until she had realized that the cure for all men was no men—at least, not until she was prepared to give more of herself than externals. Meanwhile, she lived alone in a small studio, but without a job would be forced to move to cheaper lodgings in less than two months. She was two courses shy of a Master's in English, but had taken so long that Lincoln State University had not only denied her a further extension of time, but declared her previous coursework null and void—which brought her to her job. It was too important for her simply to leave Percy Faber's office without exploring alternatives.

Percy looked again at her resume. "I see you've published stories in the *Atlantic*?"

She lifted her eyes again to meet his. "Just one in the *Atlantic*, others in women's magazines, good housewives, bad careerwomen, formulaic stories—you know, the 50s mindset. My husband was an academic. He encouraged me. When we separated, I stopped." She paused, afraid she had said too much, and concluded in a hurry. "The *Atlantic* story was actually pretty bad."

He tapped the resume. "Obviously, someone disagreed with you."

She shrugged. "That's all it takes, one someone to think you're good enough to publish and everyone thinks you're good because you've been published—but I know better."

Percy laughed. "I must say cynicism appears to be the theme of the day."

Farida allowed herself a tight-lipped smile. "I know what I'm talking about. I started writing again about ten years ago, a novel from which I excerpted stories—not that anyone noticed."

She had three unpublished manuscripts to her credit, but confessing to three made her feel three times a failure. Percy's moustache bobbed with his smile. "What did your husband teach?"

"Literary theory. They like to say literary theories are more important than literature itself. They are like Joyce's Ireland, the sow that eats her farrow."

Percy smiled again. She might have guessed he found her cynical again, but neither mentioned the word. He glanced again at her resume. "You say you're finishing your Master's?"

She nodded. "In English—same as my Bachelor's." She wondered how much to say. Born and raised in Bombay, she had come to Chicago for her Bachelor's and married Horace, returned to Bombay after her marriage fell apart, returned to Chicago after the delirious days with Darius, after which she had begun working at TeleSurveys and on her Master's, dropping out of classes each time she began a novel, resuming when she finished. "I had enough stories for a thesis in Creative Writing. I thought I might as well take the courses to get a Master's. It would at least allow me to teach."

"Couldn't you do that—teach, I mean, on the strength of your published stories?"

A laugh spilled so violently from her mouth that he was afraid for a moment she had lost control again, but her smile was triumphant. "You find me cynical, but I find it all so very ironic."

"What do you mean?"

"I have published more stories than the professors who taught my courses, but they have doctorates—and those count for more than published stories. In any contest between experience and qualifications, qualifications seem to win, hands down. Don't you find that just a touch ironic?"

Percy nodded. "Touché." They were getting too far from the purpose of the interview. "I must say your plate seems rather full, Ms. Cooper. I wonder how you would find time for your coursework and your other activities even if we had a position for you."

She noticed his eyes glazing and knew she had said too much. "I would *make* time, Mr. Faber. I'm good at that. You never know how much you can do until you've done it—and I've done a lot."

Percy nodded, avoiding her gaze. "I am very impressed, Ms. Cooper and wish you all the best, but I don't know what more I can do. I wish I could be more helpful."

She understood he had tired of the interview and got up, holding out her hand. "Thank you very much for your time. I do appreciate it."

He barely gripped her hand, seeming still in a brown study. "What will you do?"

"Oh, I can always do something. I can always be a secretary. We writers make great typists—or waitresses. We're also very good at waiting."

His eyebrows rose again. "You would consider secretarial work?"

"I would consider everything within reason—but it wouldn't be my first choice."

He nodded approval. "Good. You should at least consider everything." He wished he might have finessed the interview with more success. Her sandalwood complexion reminded him of his mother—a subject he had wished to broach in tandem with something Stacy Haines had said, but the time was no longer right. It might have been the best introduction to the interview, but the requirement of the MBA had scuttled the opportunity.

She thanked him quickly again and left the office.

II

That had been Wednesday afternoon. She wished she might have been less tearful, but three setbacks delivered by the mailman the same morning had not helped. An agent had returned the manuscript of her second novel, the Illinois Fiction Prize committee had returned the manuscript of her third, and her petition for more time to complete her Master's had been denied by Lincoln State.

Any one of the setbacks would have dampened her day—but three at once, a culmination of years of such returns, in apparent collusion with the unexpected requirement of an MBA, had descended like a monsoon, leaving her too full of air and water to make a success of the interview. Such times made her wonder if she were ready to bow her head, tuck her tail between her legs, and return to the luxury that was hers for the asking in Bombay. Kaki would welcome her back without recrimination and so would her mother though her mother would luxuriate in the triumph of the parent over the prodigal.

Percy Faber had been kind, but bound no less by arbitrary requirements than Lincoln State University. She had no job, without which she would be without money for rent in two months, at which point finishing her Master's would become moot, and any man who wished to share her life under such circumstances would either be rescuing or controlling her, neither of which she wanted.

She planned to spend the rest of the day decompressing: listening to music, staring from her window, walking in the park, whatever took her fancy. She had let slip the friends from her marriage (all but Rohini), but they had always been Horace's friends, never hers, as their invisibility after the divorce had proven—and Alma Hall (her one friend in the building) was visiting friends herself in Arizona.

It was midafternoon when she climbed the stairs to her second-floor studio at Briar Place. Her apartment was entirely visible from the front door, but aside from affordability she had chosen it for one long wall, lined with windows, the jewel in her tarnished crown, framing a row of maples and honeylocusts, her picture window, providing greenery, squirrels, birds, and privacy through a lacework of branches and leaves without obstructing light.

The rest of her boxy apartment, eight by twelve by twenty, what she called her artist's cell, was strictly functional. Her belongings hugged the walls, mainly shelves bearing books and records, keeping the room snug while maintaining an illusion of space, her charcoal nude of Darius taking pride of place over the sofabed—refrigerator, stove, and sink squeezed into the far end. She had lived in the compressed apartment for almost fifteen years—though accustomed to twenty times the space, servants and drivers and chowkidars in attendance.

Letting herself into the apartment she drew the blinds, changed into a blue threadbare robe, lit sticks of sandalwood incense, stacked the record-player with Beatle records, stretched on her back on the floor and shut her eyes, rising only to turn the records over. It was seven o'clock when, curled like a fetus, music played out, she stared at a patch of wooden floor showing through the frayed heart of her carpet, crying soundlessly, only to rise moments later to fix herself a butter sandwich—dry-eyed, as if crying were akin to buying groceries or doing laundry.

Her hands told a different story, forcing themselves to butter the bread, dropping a slice so it fell on its face. She picked the fallen slice, strangling a rasp of frustration, wiping it clean of a hair and specks of dirt. She had not vacuumed in days, but counted her slices too closely to waste a single slice. Sandwiches were her staple. She ate bananas in halves, diluted soups with water, infused a single teabag into four cups, ate with a teaspoon—slowly to provide the illusion of plenty.

Finishing the sandwich she climbed into her bathtub with a well-thumbed copy of Agatha Christie's *Double Sin and Other Stories*, the bathtub empty, she fully clothed. She had lost patience for anything longer than a short story and the associations of her youth were a kiss from the past. She read in the bathroom because the light was better and she couldn't afford a brighter lamp for the living-room; the cool porcelain embrace of the tub provided a further advantage in the heat of a Chicago summer; but that evening she lacked patience even for a short story, climbed out five minutes later, pulled her bed out of the sofa, and got under the covers.

She understood her depression perfectly: she had dedicated herself to her work, snatching seconds from the sky like a magician snatched bouquets, sunlight from the day, winks from the night, to write her first novel, *Indian American*, modeled on her marriage, four hundred pages in manuscript, composed over four years, typed from start to finish from a handwritten draft, twice in the space of six months, incurring countless hours before the Sears electric, inducing constant backaches and headaches and wrist-cramps—receiving for her pains forty rejections in the space of four months from a multitude of editors, agents, and publishers, dashing in months the hopes of years. Indian-Americans were not the stuff of novels, barely even on the radar of other Americans.

She might have chosen to stop writing, but chose instead to focus on writing at the expense of publishing, on what was within her control at the expense of what was not, replicating the failure of her first novel with her second, and her second with her third. Writing, she was rejuvenated. The rest she would accept on faith, making a badge of her state of siege, the province of solitaries, losers in love, prisoners of war, the Irish of Northern Ireland, and other such long-distance runners.

FARIDA LEFT HER BED UNFOLDED, lazing through the next morning, filling the room with strains of Ella Fitzgerald singing Gershwin. Late afternoon found her walking along Belmont Harbor, watching boats, joggers, dogwalkers, groups at volleyball, basketball, softball, lacrosse, wondering how they found time. Rohini said Farida had no fun, but Rohini (husband, children, career in tow, and a split-level in Highland Park) was too pragmatic to understand the mind of an artist. Besides, in their student days, when they had roomed together, she had said Farida had too much fun.

The next day followed a similar pattern until her mail arrived, including a letter from Percy Faber. She couldn't imagine he had changed his mind, no less could she imagine what else it might be, but afraid to read the letter at once she left it unopened on her desk while she lunched on a cucumber sandwich. She sliced open the envelope finally with a dinner knife, but not before she was tucked in the embrace of her still unmade bed, and not without an acceleration of her heartbeat.

August 8, 1985
Dear Ms. Cooper:

I would like to apologize for the miscommunication we had regarding the MBA. That requirement still stands, but I am writing to say that I was very impressed with your understanding of market research, whatever your qualifications, and have a position in mind which might interest you.

It is a new position we have been thinking of creating for some time, a part-time job, four days a week. You would be responsible for organizing schedules for the surveys and acting as liaison between the analysts and survey staff. You would occasionally be required to write a survey in tandem with the analysts. You would also occasionally be required to type up surveys and letters in the absence of our regular staff secretary. The position would be neither strictly managerial nor clerical, but something in between.

As I said, it is a new position, and we are still in the process of determining its parameters. Should we come to a mutual agreement your input in the process would be invaluable. The compensation would not be as much as for a market analyst, but I don't think you would be disappointed. I am thinking as well about the extra time you would have for your scholastic and other interests.

If this prospect appeals, please call my secretary, Jane Schultz, and set up an appointment for next week.

Yours sincerely,

Percy Faber

The Mandalay Market

The corners of Farida's mouth twitched into a smile. She rose from the bed on tiptoe, stretching arms overhead like a ballerina, opening her hands like flowers releasing the letter, breaking into an impromptu waltz as the letter wafted to the floor. She danced silently for a minute before checking the time and rushing to the telephone, setting up an appointment for the following Wednesday. Nothing had been settled, but her convalescence was over. She made plans for lunch and a movie with Rohini on Sunday. The rest of the time until the interview she spent on her new manuscript, writing almost three pages daily, all of which she would later revise, but which provided for the present haven and true north, being and becoming.

III

The trappings of their second interview were the same as the first, but the second was strictly a formality and both knew it, smiling like old friends upon seeing each other. His offer had telegraphed his interest and her presence telegraphed her own. She had thought little about what terms to expect, but was relieved to learn her hourly rate would be higher than at TeleSurveys. At four days a week her weekly salary would be less, but the shortfall was compensated by time gained for personal pursuits, Wednesdays providing a mini-weekend midweek.

Cindy Anderson, one of the senior analysts, would need to interview her yet, but that too was a formality. Percy, as manager, had sung her praises in accents too lofty to refute. He was glad of the quickness with which they had conducted their business and glad that she had chosen to present herself as plainly as possible: a blue business skirt reaching below her knees, matching fullsleeved blouse buttoned to her neck, face and fingers devoid of ornamentation, pumps almost flat (placing them at the same height), the single string of costume pearls around her neck her sole concession to conventional femininity. Her lack of vanity intimated a lack of concern with trivialities, making her even more attractive. "When can you start?"

She laughed, no less pleased with her performance. "I still have another interview, Mr. Faber, don't I?"

He smiled and his eyebrows rose above the rim of his spectacles again. He had betrayed, though without embarrassment, his own eagerness. "Oh, yes, of course—with Cindy. I suppose I was wondering if you might have made other commitments?"

She was reminded again of his difference, old world concern, lilt at the end of his sentences. His eyes reminded her of Horace's, also blue, but Horace's blue was more solid, like mosaic, Percy's more chameleon, changing with the light. "No other commitments. I could start tomorrow if you wanted—and I want you to know I'm very grateful, Mr. Faber. I won't let you down."

He shook his head, raising hands as if to hold her gratitude at bay. "Nonsense. No question about that. You seemed made for the job— and, please, call me Percy. This is America, after all, you know."

She smiled. "Of course, Percy—and you must call me Farida."

He leaned back in his chair and placed his hands flat on the desk, fingers widespread. "Well, then, Farida, there is something I meant to ask you—something personal, I'm afraid."

She leaned forward, gripping the arms of her chair, black eyes widening with curiosity. "Yes?"

He sighed. "I feel now as if I have been keeping secrets from you. Believe it or not, I meant to bring this up at our first interview—but that didn't go as I had planned."

She laughed. "The best-laid plans…. Sorry. My fault."

"No, I didn't mean that at all. You see, I knew you were a Bombay Parsi. Stacy had told me. It was part of the reason he recommended you."

"He recommended me because I am a Parsi? Most Americans don't even know the word."

"Ah, but you see, my mother is also a Parsi, also from Bombay. Stacy knew that."

Farida leaned back in her chair. "No kidding? Your mother is a Parsi?"

"Yes, but she married an Englishman. My father was a lieutenant colonel in the army, which was how they met, when he was stationed in Bombay—but after Independence they returned to England, to my father's home, a small town near Cambridge called Ely, where he started a chemist's shop."

Her confusion departed: he was foreign to her American nature, familiar to her Indian; he was a Parsi, but only in part; his blue eyes had thrown her off the scent. "You didn't go with them?"

He shook his head. "I married an American girl while we were still in Bombay. Her father was a diplomat, working in the consulate at Breach Candy."

"You're married?"

"Not anymore. My wife died, cancer, two years ago."

"I'm sorry." His face seemed to fall for a moment, eyes to lose color, wings of his moustache to droop, and she wished immediately to lighten the exchange. "So, the Parsi card got me the job?"

He shook his head. "It got you the interview, nothing more. The rest you got yourself. But my curiosity was aroused by your name. You see, I think my uncle, my mother's brother, might have known your father. I think they might have spent a lot of time together at the racetrack. Are you the daughter of Nariman and Persis Cooper?"

She stiffened. "How do you know that?"

He saw her knuckles whiten as she gripped again the arms of her chair. "I'm sorry. I'm getting altogether too personal now."

She drew a deep breath; no one chose their parents, but they did choose what to do with them—and for reasons too complicated for the present she had chosen to stay away from her family. "I don't mean to be rude, but it *is* personal. You've taken me by surprise."

"No need to be surprised. You know what a small community we Parsis are—and the Cooper name is, of course, among the more prominent. Everyone knows the Coopers."

"No, you're right. Everyone knows the family. You must even know the scandals. No big secret. But I'd rather not say any more."

Her eyelids fluttered and he followed their gaze. "Of course! No need to say anything. Very rude of me to have brought it up. Please accept my apologies."

The abundance of his apologies made clear she had embarrassed him at least as much as he had embarrassed her. "No need to apologize." She got up in a hurry, holding out her hand. "I suppose I should be talking to Jane now, to set up an appointment with Cindy Anderson."

He got to his feet no less hurriedly to shake her hand. "Yes, that would be the thing to do. Yes."

"Thank you again very much. I'm looking forward to working with you."

"As am I, with you."

IV

Alma Lucinda Hall lived three floors above Farida in an apartment half a size larger, giving her twice the privacy (height and a bedroom). She was eighty-one, but her appearance and demeanor took away ten years. She had a pretty face, pudding cheeks she wished might have been leaner, and ash-blond hair she wished might have been darker (because then she would have photographed more easily). In a black and white studio portrait taken when she was twenty-five, smiling at the camera over her shoulder, she looked like a silent movie star, Lillian Gish or Vilma Banky—but her cheeks were too full, her hair was too pale. The photographer had taken awhile getting the right angle and light.

Her apartment, on the other hand, was neither too full nor too empty. The furniture was comfortable, armchairs large enough to invite sprawl. A large photograph on the wall of a rustic cottage, wooden bench on the porch, invited you into the frame. A cuckoo clock, flanked by two tall bookcases, enhanced the impression of a fairytale. She was a small woman, five-four at her peak, and seemed always to be smiling. "You won't believe what Ruth said!"

Farida sank deep into her favorite armchair, a plate of Alma's key lime pie in hand, two glasses of Zinfandel on the coffee table. "What?"

Alma clasped hands under her chin, shaking her head in wonder. "She said she didn't eat cheese because she was worried about her cholesterol."

Farida frowned. "I thought you said she had cancer."

Alma laughed, seeming to grow larger in the process. "She does! That's just it! I said I couldn't understand why she worried about her cholesterol when she has cancer."

Farida joined in the laugh, glad for Alma's return from Arizona.

"Her sister's not doing so well either. Her spine's turning to jelly. They've inserted steel rods for reinforcement—twice, I understand— very painful, I'm sure—but you know what?"

"What?"

Alma smiled, raising a didactic finger. "The body reflects the mind. She never had much backbone, she never stood up for herself, and now ..." (she shrugged) "you see what I mean?"

Farida disagreed, but understood her friend better than she understood herself. Alma was hardly as coldblooded as she sounded, but had never suffered a major illness and found it hard to understand illness in others, suspecting instead malingering or psychosomatic causes. "Well, if she didn't have a backbone before she'll have to develop one now. She's going to need all the courage she can get."

Alma still smiled, shaking her head. "That's nothing. That's just physical courage. It's spiritual courage that matters—and mental."

"I don't think you can separate them." Farida saw through her friend's rationalization. Asked to deliver the eulogy for her best friend, Abbie, Alma had panicked, delivering herself instead to a hospital, excusing herself on grounds of illness, disappointing the family of the deceased at the last minute. The hospital had given her a clean bill of health, and Farida realized her friend had been terrified of speaking in front of all those people, fooling even herself into believing she was sick, providing fodder for her theory of psychosomatic illness.

Alma looked away. "Well, anyway, it's her problem, not ours."

Farida had brought the mail she had collected while Alma had visited her friend and the two were catching up on their news. They had bonded over their similarities, both self-made orphans, both with parents beyond the pale, both without children, and Alma's successful orphanhood boded well for Farida. They had met occasionally in the lobby of the building, struck up a conversation by the mail slots, and built a friendship on evening visits, late nights over desserts and drinks.

Alma had been born in 1904, and grown up moving from town to town in Illinois. Her father had owned a team of horses, contracting himself to build roads. The family was peripatetic, progressing along the roads as they were built. When Alma was eight, her mother caught her father in an affair with a townswoman—and poisoned the horses with arsenic in their trough. When Alma was ten, her parents divorced, after which her mother supported them as a cook and cleaning woman, and her father visited once a year with a new pair of shoes for Alma. They lived in Springfield on Monumental Avenue (which led to Lincoln's tomb) with Alma's grandfather, a genial five-foot Englishman. When Alma was sixteen he introduced her to the Halls, three houses down the road—in particular, to Homer Hall, who played a honkytonk piano.

Homer was eleven years older, but the years disappeared when he played the piano. He had squeezed her elbow saying goodbye, bringing a smile to her face, sending shivers down her spine. He invited her to ride in his jalopy, and so they did every Tuesday until she turned eighteen—when they eloped.

Homer had joined the seminary at eighteen, but left seven years later, unable to reconcile the contradictions of the church—only to be confirmed in his choice when his dispensation arrived. It had taken six weeks, during which time Father Isadore had asked continually what he planned to do. He had written home regarding his decision, and had he not been welcomed back he planned to find his own way. Desperate for novices at the end of the war, Father Isadore had offered any Order he might wish, even outside the United States, and asked continually whether he had heard from home. When the dispensation arrived without any word from home, Homer planned to leave with the clothes on his back and the ten dollars the Order would give him—at which point Father Isadore brought out the letter from home which he had withheld for three weeks.

The two had moved to San Antonio, where Homer worked in a watch factory. Alma found a job in a beauty parlor only to have her mother track them down when she renewed her license. After that she visited her mother, but always got into fights with Homer on her return—and finally stopped her visits. The Depression closed the watch factory, but Homer and his brother Nathan knew enough to go into business themselves, until Nathan exhibited symptoms of schizophrenia, threatening Alma once with a kitchen knife, and Homer had him committed to an institution. Alma went to Business College, learned typing, shorthand, and quick arithmetic. They moved to Chicago because, as Homer said, Texans were still fighting the Civil War. They lived well for fifty-eight years until Homer died and Alma moved into the building on Briar, where she had lived quietly for almost five years, knowing Farida for almost three.

Farida had related her own stories, about Horace, even about Darius, and called Alma her American mother, an honorific happily borne by childless Alma. She had been pregnant once, a year after marrying Homer, but without means of support they had chosen to abort—following which she had never again wanted a child.

The two women spooned pie and sipped wine in silence until Alma shook her head in apparent disbelief. "You know, we must have got back around midnight last night. I wonder you didn't hear the altercation from your apartment. We were right outside your window."

Farida was awakened occasionally from sleep on weekend nights by madcapping teenagers on the stoop below, but had learned to blot out extraneous noises. "That was you? What happened?"

"Well, it was late, and I wanted to take a cab, but it would have been too dear all the way from the airport—so I cut a deal with two others. I said we could share a cab into the city and pay fifteen dollars each—or pay the forty or fifty dollars it would take us each individually otherwise. Everyone was satisfied until we got home. The kid sitting in front lived on our block. He argued that we should pay just ten dollars each since the cabbie was lucky enough to get two fares so close to each other. Well, they got pretty noisy and I told the kid we should stick to our agreement. We were getting a deal at fifteen dollars and there was no reason for the cabbie to share his luck—and that was that."

Farida grinned. "Look at you! The Katharine Hepburn of Briar Place!"

Alma frowned, looking past Farida. "I never cared for her! Bossy woman! Regular showoff! And what she did to that poor Spencer Tracy was beyond the pale!"

Farida's grin was sly. Alma was a man's woman, counting on her looks for attention, realizing at forty she had to smile more to gain attention, and depending all her life on men for her needs. "I think Spencer might have had something to do with that, don't you?"

Alma regained Farida's eye. "Some people may think so—but I always say the woman has control in these matters."

Farida smiled. "I would say it works both ways."

Alma nodded, looking away again. In the course of their conversations she had inveighed, to Farida's dismay, against Eleanor Roosevelt, Gloria Steinem, and Mary Tyler Moore among others. Farida had never known Alma except as a woman living alone, and it had taken her awhile to realize she disapproved of such women because they exhibited an independence unbecoming to a woman like Alma. Worse, she admired Ronald Reagan, most paternalistic of men.

V

"Ms. Frumpkin?"

The woman behind the table in the conference room stood up smiling to shake Farida's hand. "Yes. Ms. Cooper, I presume?"

She had a clear emphatic voice, sounding younger than she appeared. Farida was surprised by the apparent discrepancy, and by her handshake, as energetic as her voice. "Yes. Hello. We meet at last."

"Indeed. Please sit down."

Farida had compiled a binder of their correspondence, printing in large black letters on the cover and spine: THE CORRESPONDENCE FROM HELL. As Director of Graduate Studies at Lincoln State University, Greta Frumpkin had denied Farida's petition for an extension of time, but also requested an appointment to discuss what they might do next. She was about sixty years old and five feet tall. She had thick straight grey hair worn like a bowl over her head, a full moon of a face sporting thick rectangular lenses framing narrow grey eyes, a smile that might have been screwed in place—and red lipstick applied thick as paste, a dab on her teeth drawing attention from her other features. Her dress fell in straight lines from her shoulders as if she had been poured into a sack. She held her hands over her stomach, fingers interlaced, fingernails red as her lipstick, fingers so blunt the tips might have been chopped off by a butcher's knife. She bowed formally, not unlike a martial artist meeting his opponent.

Farida wore blue jeans patched at the knees and a light blue t-shirt. The conference room was enclosed in glass, providing the privacy of a fish tank. Greta explained as if she had read her mind. "My office is too cluttered for company. I thought this would be better."

Farida nodded sitting across the width of the table. "This is fine."

Greta tapped a file on the table, as if calling a meeting to order. "I have been looking through your records. I think we should come straight to the point. I think I have a resolution to our problem if you are amenable to the terms I have to offer."

The heart of Farida's problem was the length of her tenure. She had enrolled in the Master's program ten years earlier, but the program required all applicants to complete coursework within four years. Since her Master's was in Creative Writing she had felt justified dropping out every time she had begun a novel. Embarking on her fourth novel, she had dropped out just two courses short of graduation, but when she had reapplied for admission Greta Frumpkin had attempted to shut the door in her face with all the distaste of a Fifties housewife on a hobo with hobnailed boots threatening her newly swept kitchen floor. If Farida wished to be readmitted, she would have to take the Graduate Requirement Exams again. She had taken the exams only to find Greta unwilling to grant her the full array of credits she had earned. She leaned her elbows on the table. "Yes? What are they?"

"The problem remains, of course, that you have long exceeded the time allotted for the Master's—including two extensions—and we have rules to enforce, standards to maintain, as I'm sure you understand. If we make arbitrary exceptions for one, we make them for all, and in doing so we sacrifice integrity, credibility, accountability—we undermine our infrastructure. In short, we devalue the university itself. Now, under normal circumstances—"

Farida realized Greta had prepared a speech and was afraid she would lose her initiative if she allowed her too much momentum. She shook her head mutely.

Greta raised her chin. "Am I not being clear?"

"Perfectly clear, Ms. Frumpkin, but there is one point I would like to make regarding the rules."

"What?"

"I understand that rules and standards are necessary—but I also believe that all rules, if they are to serve their function, must be flexible. Rules should provide guidelines, not laws. Otherwise, we end up serving the very rules that are meant to serve us."

"Of course! That is why you have been granted two extensions already."

"But extensions are merely a part of the larger rule. What I am suggesting is that every problem has a unique solution and must be considered as such. If we follow rules blindly we give them too much importance, and by giving rules too much importance we reduce their effectiveness."

Greta's red smile seemed to get redder. "I disagree. That is most assuredly not the case."

"Maybe not yet—but it will assuredly be the case if we let the rules become the rulers."

"I disagree. Rules cannot become rulers unless we let them."

Farida took a deep breath. "That is precisely my point, Ms. Frumpkin. We are letting the rules become our rulers."

Greta stiffened, leaned back in her chair. "Ms. Cooper, if you wish we can debate this matter until our time is up—or we can be specific and look for a solution to your problem. Which is it going to be?"

Farida took another deep breath. "A solution."

"Good. That is at least a point on which we agree. Now, under normal circumstances, your long tenure would be grounds for termination—but your publications make your circumstances special."

"Thank you."

"Since you have continued to publish your work, I am willing to concede that you are up to date with the creative writing skills required for the degree. What is more problematic are the literature courses you took at the beginning of your tenure which are now ten years out of date. You would need to show the department that you are still proficient in these courses. You might do this by taking an examination in each of the courses in question. If you test satisfactorily, that would serve our purpose admirably—but you would need to appear for the exams within the next six months at the very latest. The question is whether you are prepared to do so."

"How many courses are we talking about?"

Greta tapped again the file before her, fingers blunt and red. "I've looked through your records, and I think we might allow all the credits except for the four earliest courses: Shakespeare Histories; Restoration Drama; the 19th Century Novel; and Contemporary American Literature. If you could show your mastery of the courses in a set of special examinations I think the department would be satisfied."

Farida remembered the courses; she had received three As and a B. "But I have already proven my proficiency in those courses. You have the record of my grades."

"Yes—but that was ten years ago. We would need to know that you retain mastery of the texts in order to graduate. If you know the texts as you say you do, that should surely not be a problem."

Greta was being facetious. The four courses comprised some forty texts. Farida could hardly remember the titles let alone the texts, but she wasn't ready to spoil her chance by saying so. "I don't understand why the years make a difference. I took the courses, you have my grades. *Henry V* and *Anna Karenina* haven't changed since I studied them, nor any of the other texts. If it were necessary for me to retain the mastery I had over ten years ago, then we would need to test everyone who has ever earned a Bachelor's or a Master's or a Doctorate to make sure they retain mastery of their material—and if not we would need to strip them of their degrees. I don't think that is what you are saying."

"No, it is not. The point is to have mastery of the subject matter within the four year span—not because the texts change, but because teaching methods change. Different pedagogical tools provide different interpretations of the texts. Their meanings change depending on when they are studied. The point is to graduate students with a harmonious rather than a haphazard set of pedagogical tools. It is the integrity of the pedagogical process that we wish to preserve."

Farida frowned. "When you talk about teaching methods, do you mean literary theory? deconstruction? that sort of thing?"

Greta nodded. "Among other things, yes—that sort of thing, as you put it, critical developments—they have gained immense precedence in the last ten years, but you have not covered it at all in your coursework, and that is a liability."

"Believe me, Ms. Frumpkin. I know a thing or two about deconstruction. I learned from a master. My teacher was Horace Fisch. Perhaps you have heard of him?"

"Of course! A brilliant man."

"Brilliance, like any gift or virtue, means nothing if it's abused—and abuse it, he did, big time."

Greta was silent, frowning. She spoke again with new respect. "Do you know him?"

"He was my husband. I was his second wife."

"Your husband?"

Farida noted, not without pleasure, Greta's eyes and lips retreat into her shrunken self. "It was a long time ago, but I know literary theory better than most people, most definitely deconstruction."

"I am sorry to hear your marriage didn't work out, Ms. Cooper, but it makes no difference to the matter at hand. Whatever you might have learned from Dr. Fisch isn't represented in your coursework. That is what matters. I'm afraid that's the best I can do. I would suggest you give my offer some thought. Otherwise, I'm afraid I have to stand by the rules."

"I shall have to think about it."

"Do—and let me know when you reach a decision, but do not take too long. The sooner this matter is settled, the better for all concerned. I think you understand that now."

Farida's eyes hardened. "Yes. I think I do."

DARIUS KATRAK AT THE DARJEELING

Returning to Bombay following the dissolution of her marriage Farida was thirty-four, but she felt a new life begin. She never walked when she could prance, never stood still when she could bounce on the balls of her feet. Entering the lobby of The Darjeeling she was aware of admiring appraisals in her wake, her cousin's just one among dozens. She could hear the strains of a combo playing "Hold Me Tight" and smiled looking over her shoulder. "I like the place already."

Ratan Cooper grinned. Farida wore a red cocktail dress, bare at the shoulders, narrow at the waist, showing six inches of thigh, hair in a beehive so black the highlights were blue among the neon lamps. She might have been oblivious to the ocean of eyes around them, but not he, particularly not of the glances he attracted himself (curious, envious) in her proximity—nothing to do with his own ensemble, he was sure, however blue his shirt, however belled his pants, however styled his hair. "I knew you would—but hold on, I say. What's the hurry? Let's get a better look at our entertainment." He led her by the arm to a showcase displaying photographs of four young men, three guitars and drums, dressed and coiffed in Edwardian suits like the early Beatles. The bill read:

THE AVENGERS

ALL BEATLES

ALL NIGHT LONG

Ratan pointed to the drummer. "That's the fellow I was telling you about, Eddie Palia. I went to school with him. I told him we were coming. He said he would stop by to say Hullo to the great Farida."

Farida elbowed his ribs. "Yes, yes. Farida the Great / born in a plate / in 1948."

Ratan staggered back a step, clutching his ribs, grinning at the nonsense rhyme from their childhood. "I swear, Farida! The things you remember."

An adjacent showcase displayed photographs of a slender redheaded woman in a long shimmering dress, arms encased in long black gloves, billed:

DANI

THE DANCER

FROM DENMARK

Ratan would have passed the showcase by, but Farida stopped him grinning. "Who is she? Someone else you know?"

Ratan shook his head, dead to her irony. "Someone new. Never saw her before." His tone stiffened, no less his face, suddenly formal. "Shall we go in?"

Farida didn't pursue the issue, but Freud was right: none so prudish as those who deny prudishness, Freud himself being the prime example, not to mention the numbers of young Indians imagining themselves sexually liberated for telling dirty jokes, overgrown boys like Ratan among them, blessed by the angel of nepotism, who gained identity, prestige, wherewithal, from the parent company of their families—but she had no right to be critical. She relied on the same company to jumpstart her own project, an art gallery. She took his arm. "Let's."

He led her into the nightclub and she felt him relax again, comforted by her touch, the pressure of her breast against his arm, her thigh against his as they walked. The Avengers followed "Hold Me Tight" with "Little Child." The maitre d' welcomed Mr. Cooper (as he called Ratan) with a smile, bowing to Farida, leading them to a table close to the stage. The houselights were dim, dimmer for the spotlit stage.

Farida walked slowly, watching the performance, eyes adjusting to the dim interior, tugging Ratan's arm, whispering in his ear. "Slow down. Now who is in a hurry? These fellows are *re*ally good!"

He chuckled. "What did I tell you? Not for nothing they are called the Bombay Beatles. Can't tell the difference, can you?"

"Instrumentally, no! Vocals, you can tell the difference—but the vocals are also excellent, so tight."

They opened menus, their intimacy cozier for the lighting and rituals of dining, their reunion so long coming. Ratan spoke conspiratorially, leaning forward to be heard over the music. "I don't want to tell you what to order, but don't order any of that sissy food. Forget about tomato soup and chicken soup and all that. You can get that out of a tin just as well. Order a good mulligatawny, something that will stick to your bones, something to remember—and order the chateaubriand. I know you can get the best steaks in the U.S., soft as butter, but not like they prepare them here, marinated in a curry and mango sauce—again, something to remember."

Farida pushed away the menu. "Sounds delicious. I'll just let you do the ordering—but no soup. The steak will be more than enough—but I'd like to start with a Beaujolais."

"Just what I was going to suggest." By the time he had ordered, the Avengers were playing "Don't Bother Me." Ratan pulled a breadstick from the breadbasket and dabbed it with butter nestled in a dish among marbles of ice. "So, tell us—what's the big diff, do you find, coming back, would you say?"

Farida smiled. The disdain in his voice was audible over the music, his smirk visible in the dim light. Familiarity bred comfort—and after the death of her marriage she wanted familiarity, predictability, not to think about what anything meant. That was the reason she had returned to Bombay, to be coddled, not challenged, as Ratan was coddling her now. Many imagined the death of her father had brought her back, to comfort no less than be comforted by a grieving mother, but her father's death was coincidental, even serendipitous, and she was happy to let others think what they wished. She said nothing, but couldn't stop smiling.

"Smiling? I said something funny?"

The tone remained, a high condescension, but the condescension of a lamb. He was older than her by two years, had traveled widely (Europe, America, Australia, Japan), but always a tourist, never a traveler, never lived anywhere except Bombay—and never would, addicted to the luxury into which he had been born. Had the luxury been portable he might have settled in England where he had graduated from the London School of Economics—or New York. Instead, like many who lived down to their expectations, achieving little because little was expected, affected playboys of the eastern world, he played his cynicism to the hilt, imagining it gave him the veneer of a rumpled man of the world, Somerset Maugham slumming. She could have pierced the veneer with a frown, brought him down with a discouraging word, but laughed instead. "No, Ratan, that is not why I am smiling. Much simpler. I am happy to be back. That is all. I am happy to see you again, happy to be dining at The Darjeeling, happy for so many things."

Even in the dim light his face seemed to brighten, features reassembling so quickly it was comical, veneer dropping like a veil. "I say, Farida, that goes double for me. It *is* good to have you back, old thing, I can't tell you enough. I do hope you plan to stay for a long while."

"Thanks, Ratan. Very sweet of you—but depends on how things go. If I can make a go of the gallery I might even settle down."

"That would be super. What's the holdup?"

"Bureaucracy, paperwork, graft—you know, the usual."

He raised his eyebrows, shaking his head. "Ah, yes, of course, the usual—signing a million forms, greasing a million palms. That alone will take forever."

"I've been warned—at least, a year. I could hardly believe it—but, of course, this is India. You were asking about differences. That's a big one. In the States it would have taken maybe a week, a month at most. India's not really geared for business at all, is it? If not for all the problems with foreign exchange I would have opened the gallery in Chicago."

"Chicago's bad luck is Bombay's good. Even the exchange problem has a silver lining if that is what keeps you here."

"Again, very sweet of you, Ratan—but enough. I get the message. No need to lay it on so thick."

He laughed. The waiter brought wine. They raised glasses to friendship. The Avengers concluded their set with "All My Loving," the rhythm guitarist announced the cabaret artist would perform next, after which the Avengers would play one more set. The spotlight vanished, houselights brightened. Ratan waved a hand for Eddie Palia's attention. "He's a good fellow, really. I think you will like him."

Eddie pointed a drumstick at Ratan to indicate he had seen him and spoke briefly with the bass player before they walked to their table, Eddie smiling, the bass player expressionless. "Hullo, Ratan."

"Hullo, Eddie, hullo. Superb, you fellows! Just superb—as usual!"

Eddie nodded modestly. "Good crowd tonight. Not too noisy."

Farida put an elbow on the table, resting her chin on the heel of her hand, smiling. "No, really! It was super! I'm enjoying it very much. Looking forward to the next set."

Both drummer and bass player smiled, Eddie spoke. "Just doing our job. I say, hullo, you must be Farida—finally!"

"What do you mean, finally?"

"I have heard nothing else from Ratan since he knew you were coming. Farida this, Farida that—and now, Farida finally! *Ve*ry pleased to meet you, I'm sure."

Ratan smiled. "Arré, where are my manners? Farida, this is Eddie, I told you about him already—and Keith Yagnik, best bass player in Bombay."

The bass player nodded, sitting at the table with Eddie at Ratan's invitation. Eddie offered Farida a cigarette, but she shook her head in deference to Ratan whom she knew didn't smoke, and waited while Eddie and Keith lit up, her eyes on the musicians. "Nice threads, I say."

Eddie touched his Beatles collar. "Part of the show—every detail counts, you know."

"I know. So how long have you fellows been playing together?"

Eddie spoke quietly. "Almost two years now. Took a little time to get the act together, you know—but now it's great fun."

"Always Beatles songs?"

"Mostly. You know—whatever's on the charts."

Farida looked from Eddie to Keith, but he only nodded, fixing his gaze on the table. Ratan leaned toward Farida, speaking confidentially, but loudly enough for the others to hear. "Keith does not talk very much—you know, typical bass player."

Farida nodded. "I know—John Entwistle, Bill Wyman, Jack Bruce."

Eddie nodded approval, leaning forward. "Seems like you know your music."

She turned to Eddie. "I've played sometimes myself, wherever there was a piano—just for fun, you know—guest sets, open mikes, that sort of thing."

"What kind of music?"

Farida sighed, hand on her breast. "Oh, my God, you have to realize this was a *very* long time ago. I did Cole Porter, some Gershwin, Irving Berlin, you know, mainly during my student days—but then I took it up again recently, just for something to do, just for fun, Beatlesongs— not the rockers, but 'And I Love Her,' 'If I Fell,' 'I'll Follow the Sun,' that sort of thing—just for fun, at parties and things."

Eddie's eyes narrowed as she spoke. "I say!"

Farida shivered, locking eyes with Eddie, anticipating his thoughts.

"I say, Farida, would you give us a song? It would be such an honor."

Keith leaned forward immediately. "I say, that would be terrific!"

Farida took a deep breath, head light as a balloon, chest housing a gaggle of birds at their bath. "Oh, my goodness, but I haven't practiced in such a long time!"

"You don't have to play, just sing. Leave the playing to us."

"Actually, you know, I could sing 'Eleanor Rigby.' I sing it a cappella sometimes. Would that be all right?"

"What are you saying? Of course! More than all right, it would be a treat! When? Now?"

"But we just ordered dinner."

Ratan pushed her gently. "Don't worry about dinner. They will keep it warm for us. Better to sing on an empty stomach, I always say."

Eddie nodded. "He's right. Bad enough playing after you've eaten, but singing is worse."

"All right! I'll do it."

Ratan clapped her shoulder lightly. "Attagirl!"

Eddie slapped the table with both hands. "'Eleanor Rigby'?"

"Yes."

"Ready?"

Farida took a deep breath. "Yes."

Eddie turned to Keith. "Lights?"

Keith got up. "I'm on it."

Eddie turned back to Farida. "Let's go. I'll announce you."

"Just announce me as Farida, please. Don't say my last name."

Eddie grinned. "Not to worry."

Farida looked at Ratan. "Wish me luck."

He squeezed her arm. "Luck."

Barely aware what she said or did, trembling with anticipation, she followed Eddie, standing by as he tapped the microphone with his finger. "Ladies and Gentlemen! May I have your attention please." He waited a few seconds as the hubbub hushed. "It gives me great pleasure to announce a very special and unexpected treat tonight. The lovely Farida, direct from the U.S., has agreed to honor us with a Beatlesong in keeping with our theme for the evening: 'Eleanor Rigby.' She will be singing a cappella. A warm welcome, please—for Far*ee*da!"

He clapped his hands in her direction, leading the applause. The houselights dimmed again; the spotlight hit the stage. She took another deep breath before entering the circle of light and commanding the microphone. "Thank you very much, Eddie, for that very kind introduction—and thank you, ladies and gentlemen. I would like to say only that I wasn't expecting to be singing tonight and I would like to thank you in advance for your indulgence and your patience. As Eddie said, I will be singing for you, in keeping with the theme of the evening, one of my favorite Beatlesongs: 'Eleanor Rigby.'"

She waited for the applause to die again. She hadn't performed in a while, but some things remained the same: she no longer saw the audience; the brighter the spotlight, the more invisible the audience. She flung her shoulders back, raised her arms, and whipped her hands back and forth, snapping her fingers on the downbeat, repeating the motion continually, bending her knees with the beat. Her voice was unsentimental, more Julie London than Paul McCartney, a cool performance in more ways than one, at once jazzy and controlled.

The applause, interspersed with whistles and cries of *Encore*, many of which she recognized from Ratan standing at their table, was bewildering at first, but gratification soon swallowed bewilderment. Eddie joined her again at the microphone. Would she like to sing another song? She agreed to one more, "And I Love Her," if the rhythm guitarist of the Avengers would accompany her, if they had sticks she could use to strike the beat herself, after which she sang "If I Fell" joined by the rest of the Avengers. Each time her phrasing was terse, laconic, suggesting a sophistication beyond the scope of the teenage lyrics, available to listeners smart enough to read between the lines. When she finally descended the stage it was with the confidence of a queen newly crowned returning to her people.

Ratan continued to applaud as she joined him at their table, grin wide as the equator. "Arré, Farida, absolutely first class! A-1 performance! You absolutely missed your calling! I am so proud!"

She sat smiling, enveloped in the good will of the room from which applause continued to crackle in snatches though the houselights had again been activated, laughing as she sat. "It was great fun! It was such great fun! I've never sung with a whole band before! I'm so glad you brought me."

Eddie and Keith had returned with her, as had the rest of the Avengers, pulling up chairs, making a hexagon of the square table, Kailash Surendranath and Ashok Muthana, lead and rhythm guitarists, all grinning like Ratan who couldn't stop, and lighting cigarettes, Farida joining them. Eddie had made quick introductions when the other Avengers had joined Farida onstage. Kailash sat on her left. "Dynamite, I say! Sheer dynamite! You should think about going professional."

Ashok, on her farther left, spoke with no less enthusiasm. "Classic moves, you've got, I swear."

Keith, directly across, grinned, snapping the fingers of one hand, mimicking her motion onstage.

Ratan looked around the table. "I say, fellows, what about a round of drinks?"

The Avengers looked at one another, but Eddie shook his head. "Very good of you, Ratan, but really, we have too little time just now. Dani will be coming out in five-ten minutes and we are playing for her also. Raincheck?"

"Of course."

"So you are from the U.S. How long are you staying?"

"Depends. At least a year. I want to start an art gallery. Maybe give drawing lessons, music lessons—just something to pass the time, you know. I hate to do nothing."

Farida was enjoying the conversation so well she wasn't aware of a woman who materialized beside her until she spoke. "Excuse me, please, but you are Farida Cooper, no?"

The woman was tall and lean, wearing a cream pleated skirt and white blouse, hair in a neat bob, spectacles on a chain around her neck. She had large grey eyes which might have been pretty had they been less flinty, had her face been less long, less bony, her smile less artificial. Farida looked up. "Yes?"

"Daughter of Nariman and Persis Cooper?"

"Yes?"

"Nariman who died only recently?"

Farida's response turned impatient. "Yes? Can I help you?"

The woman's smile widened. "No, no. Only wanted to say how much we enjoyed your performance. We are at the next table. Had to say something, it was so good."

"Thank you very much."

"And you are Ratan Cooper, no? I have seen you at weddings and navjotes."

Ratan frowned. "Do we know you?"

"No, no! We are the Dhuns." The woman pointed to the next table, party smile welded in place.

"Your last name is Dhun?"

"No, but my husband and I are both named Dhun. Our last name is Katrak."

Eddie got up. "I say, Ratan, we have to go. Farida, so very good to have met you."

Farida touched his hand, beaming around the table. "You too, Eddie—and everybody. Thank you so very much. It was such a thrill."

The other Avengers rose, Kailash winking to commiserate with Farida on the trials of fandom, the birdcage of celebrity. The woman took the chair vacated by Ashok. "May I stay for only one minute, if you don't mind?"

Ratan glowered. "If *you* don't mind, we have just ordered dinner."

The woman smiled. "We have just almost finished our own dinner."

Farida put a hand on Ratan's arm, no less annoyed, but more mindful of her fans. "We can spare a minute. What is it?"

"Nothing, really—only wanted to tell you how much we enjoyed—and to introduce myself and my family. As I was saying, over there is my husband, also named Dhun."

Ratan ignored her, buttering a bun, but Farida looked across to the woman's table. A balding man in a white bush shirt smiled, face no less lean than his wife's, eyes friendlier by far. "Hullo."

Farida returned his nod, also smiling. "Hullo, Dhun."

The man grinned. "It is our big joke. We are the Dhuns. Can get quite confusing."

Ratan spoke without looking up from his bun. "How about calling you Mr. and Mrs. Katrak?"

The woman laughed. "Of course, but no need to be so formal. Just call us Dhun. We have a knack for knowing which one is wanted—and those are the kids, twins, our pride and joy, Darius and Yasmin—but don't ask which is pride and which is joy."

Farida smiled, understanding from the girl's scowl that it was another of the family's big jokes. "We are not kids, Mummy, for God's sake—not for a long time."

Farida understood how pretty the woman might have looked had her smile been sincere. The resemblance was transparent, a handsome family, the twins alike to the clefts in their chins, the boy's hair in a high pompadour and deep sideburns, the girl's loose in a ribbon behind, the boy smiling, the girl still scowling, all plates indicating an unfinished dinner though no one ate, their interest focused on Farida.

Mrs. Katrak shook her head. "So quickly they grow up. Today is their birthday. Seventeen years old they are today. This is our celebration—for the parents. Last weekend they had their own party—with no adults allowed. You have children?"

Farida took a deep breath: the question made her uncomfortable, reminding her of what might have been until so very recently, a baby Cyrus, a baby Ruby. "No, that is a blessing I have yet to receive."

Mrs. Katrak's smile twitched momentarily. "Matter of opinion, whether it is a blessing or not—but we have brought our blessings to Darjeeling for their birthday."

Yasmin wrinkled a perfect nose. "*The* Darjeeling, Mummy—*The!* Just like in *The* Hague. It is a club, not a hill station."

Mrs. Katrak shook her head at Farida. "Kids say the darndest things, no?"

Farida waved with her fingers. "Happy birthday, you two!"

Yasmin smiled immediately, dimples twinkling in her cheeks, suddenly shy. "Thank you."

Her twin also smiled, but with more confidence, exhibiting the same dimples. "Thank you, aunty! Very much enjoyed your performance—*ve*ry much. Just super, it was."

"Oh, please, don't call me aunty. Makes me feel like I'm fifty. Call me Farida, please."

Darius's smile widened, high cheekbones lifting higher yet, cleft in his chin deepening. "Sorry. You don't look fifty—hardly even thirty."

Mr. Katrak grinned. "Hardly even twenty. Very sharp, you are looking, Farida. Very sharp."

Farida, surprised by his boldness, noted Mr. Katrak's eyes, narrow with admiration. She guessed he might have been fifty, his wife perhaps ten years younger. "Thank you, but just for the record, I am thirty-four—and no regrets about my age."

Mrs. Katrak also noted her husband's eyes. "We heard about your dad, Farida. So sorry, so sad."

"Thank you."

"But you were in the States, no? Married to an American, I think?"

Ratan continued to glower, munching his bun, his tone no friendlier than before. "How is it, Mrs. Katrak, that you know so much about us?"

Mrs. Katrak's smile tightened. "Arré, now, Ratan … you don't mind if I call you Ratan?"

"I don't know that it would make a difference if I did mind."

Mrs. Katrak laughed. "Very sorry, but you know how it is. Everyone knows everything about the Coopers, certainly in Bombay—and most certainly all the Parsis know. No big secret."

Ratan muttered in Farida's ear. "What I would like to know very much is why no one knows anything about the Katraks. *That* is what I would very much like to know."

Mrs. Katrak's laugh was less confident. "What? Sorry? My hearing is not so good anymore."

Farida laughed. "Nothing. Ratan is just being my knight in shining armor because he knows I am getting a divorce."

Mrs. Katrak took a deep breath. "Die-vorce! Ah, no, I did not know—but it is all right now, no? We Parsis are very modern about these things now. Not a problem. Love-marriages are very common also—and also die-vorces. Even here in Bombay nobody is batting an eye now."

Mr. Katrak grinned again at Farida, eyes so narrow they seemed closed. "So true. Not even an eyelash. Nothing to be ashamed of. After all, we are not living in the olden days anymore."

Mrs. Katrak ignored her husband. "So how long are you here for now? I heard you were going to teach music and drawing?"

Ratan muttered again in Farida's ear. "I thought the old battleaxe said her hearing was not so good."

Farida gripped Ratan's thigh under the table, digging her nails into the fabric, barely able to keep from laughing. "Yes, right. I want to start an art gallery, but that could take a while and in the meantime I want to do something useful. Music, art, writing—that is what I know, that is what I will teach."

"Tuitions? You will give tuitions? You will be charging?"

"Oh, no, nothing like that, no charge. I just want to pass the time in a productive way."

"Very praiseworthy."

"Thank you, but not really—very selfish."

"Very modest also, I think. Very praiseworthy also to be so modest."

Mrs. Katrak's smile felt increasingly like a shower of grease and worms. Farida wished she had taken Ratan's lead in discouraging her from the start. "Your dinner will be getting cold, Mrs. Katrak. We really mustn't keep you any longer."

"I have eaten dinner before. I will eat dinner again. More interesting talking to you."

Farida looked at Ratan who nodded vigorously. "Me too. I have also eaten dinner before, and I will also eat dinner again, but I will never let a good dinner get cold. That is the greatest sin."

Farida almost laughed again, but pointed instead at their waiter approaching with a trolley. "Look, there's our waiter with our dinner."

Mrs. Katrak's smile remained, but she got up. "I will let you two enjoy your dinner. It has been very nice talking with you. Thank you again, Farida, for your performance."

Ratan kept his eyes on the approaching trolley, but Farida returned Mrs. Katrak's attention. "Very welcome, Mrs. Katrak. Very welcome."

"Very nice talking with you also, Ratan."

Ratan's eyes remained on the trolley. "Likewise, I'm sure."

Farida allowed herself a brief laugh after Mrs. Katrak had rejoined her table and spoke under her breath. "Ratan, shame! So rude you can be."

"*Me?* What about *her?*"

"Shoo! She will hear you!"

"I don't think so. She has a hearing problem."

Farida laughed out loud, focusing on the dinner as the waiter served them, steaks an inch thick, served with casseroles of cheese and potatoes and tossed salads.

THEY HAD BARELY BEGUN TO EAT when the lights dimmed again. The stage remained unlit, but a waltz rhythm tiptoed through the dark on bass and drums, moving repeatedly from tonic to dominant and back, and they realized Keith and Eddie had begun the next performance. A dim light fell on Ashok at the microphone speaking in an undertone. "Ladies and gentlemen! It gives me great pleasure to present to you Miss Danielle, direct from Copenhagen, Denmark." Kailash, on lead, wove the first line of "Wonderful Copenhagen" into the tattoo established by bass and drums before returning to silence, spreading nervous laughter like a blanket across the room.

The light faded from Ashok and the three-step tiptoe rhythm grew more hypnotic in the dark than a symphony orchestra. Someone onstage, wearing taps, reinforced the tattoo of bass and drums in a metallic waltz, hard heel followed by two soft shoes, but the stage remained in darkness. Ratan whispered to Farida. "Dani the Dancer from Denmark must be a tap-dancer—but what a moniker!"

Farida sliced her steak, took another bite in the dark, followed with a forkful of the casserole. "I swear, the suspense is killing me. Where the hell is this Dani?"

As if in reply a long roll on the snare ended with a crash on cymbals, the spotlight illuminated the stage again, and Dani flashed into sight, appearing as she did in the photographs in the lobby, a smiling woman in a sparkling black sequined gown, red hair coiled in a nautilus on her head, ears dripping with glittering earrings, arms sheathed in long black gloves, tap-dancing to the tattoo of bass and drums which continued to stream from the stage. Kailash picked up the melody of "Wonderful Copenhagen" again, Ashok strummed the chords, all Avengers playing together as Dani began a graceful waltz, maintaining the tattoo with her feet, spotlight following her about the stage before she began to sing.

She had a pretty voice—but, as the audience was soon to discover, her voice was beside the point. Farida sang the song under her breath along with Dani and the Avengers, rising and falling with the melody as it approached its finale—only to slow down and hold back the last note. Bass and drums repeated the original tattoo, to and fro between tonic and dominant. Dani slid slowly, sinuously, out of her left glove, swung it overhead, her arm suddenly pale, and tossed it with the final cadence of the song, the last delayed word, triumphant and gleeful, into the audience.

The tiptoeing waltz leaped into three dramatic chords, during the first of which Dani tore off her second glove, during the second and third of which she tore off her dress in two quick movements. A fourth chord provided the downbeat to hurry the waltz into a quick march. Kailash throttled the neck of his guitar, squeezing the melody into a series of screams. Dani, clad in a black string bikini, surrendered to the music, augmenting the beat with taps, colored lights playing on her bare skin.

Farida was mesmerized, aroused by Dani's daring more than her nudity. It was one of the uglier verities, the very qualities which made a person an outsider made the person interesting to insiders—not unlike many in the audience she was sure, Ratan among them, who might mock Dani in public and lust after her in private. She found herself envying Dani her portability, able to make a living anywhere in the world, carrying the tools of her trade in her skin. She couldn't have done it herself, but admired Dani for standing her ground in the court of the world.

Dani finally reached behind herself to undo the string of her bikini top. Her long pale legs, caressed by color, painted with light, continued to kick and buckle, but her other hand held the bikini top in place. Her smile was at once sweet and voluptuous, young features advertising an old trade. A helix of hair fell before her eyes; Farida imagined she might toss her head to clear her vision, but instead Dani slowed down, coming to a full stop, legs apart, smile at ease, both hands holding the bikini top in place.

The music retreated to its tiptoe of bass and drums in waltz time. Dani raised her elbows slowly. A soft roll began on the snare, gradually mounting in volume. Dani flapped her elbows like wings, standing on tiptoe for flight, rising like the Swan Queen from her lake. The crescendo of drums rose to a crash on cymbals, the signal for Dani to fling her bikini top into the audience—and the death of the spotlight. Houselights were reactivated, but despite thunderous applause the stage remained bare.

Ratan was shaking his head, smirk back in place, tone dripping disdain. "Well, there you have it. I knew exactly what was going to happen. No nudity in Bombay, no sir, have no fear—cultural backwater that we are. A striptease with all tease and no strip."

Farida grinned. "What? Did you want to see her naked?"

Ratan shrugged. "What's the difference? If you've seen one naked woman you've seen them all."

Farida laughed. "You talk as if you *have* seen them all."

Ratan shrugged again, avoiding her eyes. "Not like in Chicago, I'm sure—but Bombay has its share of hippies and drugs and love-in's and what-have-you."

He was out of his league again, playing the rumpled man of the world, and she felt ungrateful. "Sorry, Ratan, very naughty of me. I was just teasing you."

He shrugged again, still avoiding her eyes. "Not a problem, but you better eat your dinner before it gets cold."

They were unaware again of Mrs. Katrak beside their table until she spoke. "Excuse me, please, but we are just leaving. Just wanted to say bye-bye."

Farida nodded, pointing to her full mouth. Ratan sliced his steak, eyes on his plate.

Mrs. Katrak smiled. "Sorry. Finish your food. What did you think about the dancer?"

Farida pointed to her mouth again. Ratan raised a forkful to his mouth.

Mrs. Katrak seemed not to notice. "Calls herself a dancer, but I knew exactly what she was when I saw her gloves. What kind of woman wears gloves in Bombay anyway?"

Mr. Katrak joined his wife, smiling no less broadly. "I would never let such a woman touch me, you know—not even touch me."

Farida swallowed her mouthful. "Well, you know, there are people who consider the naked human body a work of art."

Mrs. Katrak raised a hand in protest. "Art, of course—for art it is all right. I love your Da Vinci and your Michelangelo—but this was not art, do you think?"

"Different people have different opinions."

Mrs. Katrak seemed unconvinced—but also disinclined to disagree with Farida. "Of course, of course. Openmindedness is everything. We Parsis are very openminded about everything."

Darius spoke with a solemnity beyond his years. "It is like Mummy said before, we Parsis are very modern." Farida turned to him in surprise, only to smile when he winked, smiling himself.

Yasmin too was smiling broadly. "Yes, Mummy, we know. Parsis are very everything. There is no one like the Parsis. Best people in the world."

Mrs. Katrak shook her head. "So grown up, so fast. Talk like Americans already. Too many movies they have been seeing."

Watching them leave, Farida conceded they were an attractive family despite the flinty mother. She also conceded she liked the children as much as she didn't like the parents.

Ratan was smirking again. "Well, if you ask me, it looks like we got a show within a show."

Farida laughed again. "I was just thinking what a pity it is sometimes that children have to have parents. The twins seemed so likable, all the more amazing considering their models."

"That is the test for some people—to break away from their parents. We must all have a test."

"And what is your test?"

"Why, to have all this money and still to keep my head. Am I not the most modest, easygoing, even-tempered fellow you ever saw?"

Farida couldn't stop laughing. "Yes, Ratan, yes. I am so very glad you are my friend. You know how to make me laugh better than anyone." On impulse, she kissed his cheek.

To her surprise, he seemed almost to blush. "I say, Farida, I *am* glad to hear it. You are very special to me also, you know—*very* special. But really? You really mean it?"

"Of course, Ratan. You have to ask? You have been so good to me—you have always been so very good, since we were kids."

Ratan smirked again. "Better finish your dinner before you say something foolish."

II

Farida opened her eyes at six o'clock the next morning, but stayed in bed, inserting cassettes into the player by her bedside, stirring slowly to the Brandenburg Concertos, playing back memories of the evening before, recalling with a smile The Darjeeling, the Avengers, the Katraks, the dinner, the dancer. Blue Mansions, once her parent's house, now her mother's alone, named for the sea behind, had been painted to match its name, but monsoons had wasted the paintwork though the name remained appropriate for reasons unrelated to color.

Ratan had brought her home at one o'clock and she was surprised to have awakened so early. The thick curtains of her bedroom kept the sun at bay though her windows faced east. Her body clock had sprung eleven hours ahead into Bombay, but was still adjusting to a different pace. She had been back a week, demands of family and friends swelling to fill the days, but she needed to focus on what she wished to accomplish or, lapped by luxury, she would drift, surrender to providence, and lose the chance for a fresh start after the ugliness with Horace. Wealth provided shelter from the storm, but also chance after chance to brave the storm, and she planned to brave the storm.

The fourth Brandenburg began to play, her current favorite. She liked waking to music, but no radio station in Bombay played music she liked and she had adopted the habit of setting cassettes aside the night before. She hugged her pillow, scrambling the sheets, burying her face in the mattress, glad for the size and solitude of her bed, the smell and warmth of her body, falling in and out of slumber, reveling in the knowledge that she would not need to make her bed, prepare breakfast, launder clothes and sheets, clean the room, the flat, the house. Servants made her Bombay life voluptuous, herself a minor-league Marie Antoinette. She got up at whatever hour she wished, showered, ordered breakfast to be received in the annex to her bedroom where she read the morning news. Sashi, who had been with the family since Farida's girlhood, made her bed and swept and mopped her rooms; Dev (Sashi's brother), her driver, drove her wherever she wished; and Nergesh, her father's sister, whom she called Kaki, managed the household and prepared menus to order.

This was how she had lived her early life, the first six years on the ground floor of Blue Mansions, the rest upstairs with Kaki until she had left for Chicago, her parents continuing to live downstairs. The building housed two floors, each spacious enough to accommodate a colony. Each floor held two suites of rooms with a kitchen, sitting, and dining-room in common. The back enclosed a garden, beyond which a patch of beach separated them from the sea. Her mother and father had occupied opposing suites on the ground floor, she and Kaki on the first. Kaki had become Farida's mother more than her mother. The reason for the change was no one's business, but if anyone questioned the arrangement the answer was transparent: Kaki was otherwise alone, the Coopers were wealthy, and the wealthy were eccentric.

She liked the associations of her old room, childhood books and friends and games, richer for memories than the most luxurious hotels. She liked as well having it to herself again, not sharing it as she had with Horace during their last visit five years ago, and six years before that on their honeymoon.

The Brandenburgs came to a close, the player turned itself off, but she slept on, waking next to an insistent rap on her door, asking in a voice still drenched with sleep. "Who is it?"

Her mother came in, letting in daylight. "It's only me, sweetie. Good morning."

Farida hid her face in her pillow. "Oh, Mummy, please. I still want to sleep. We were very late last night. I'll come downstairs later. We can have breakfast."

"Sorry, sweetie, but it's nine o'clock already. I know you're on holiday, but I'm not, and I'm late for an appointment. I will only take a minute."

Farida was tempted to remind her mother she was always on holiday, her life a merry-go-round of lunches, dinners, concerts, card games, movies, shopping sprees, and visits to the club and racetrack among other Bombay entertainments, but she resisted the temptation. Her father's death and funeral, not to mention matters regarding wills and estates, so her mother said, had taken their toll on her serenity, but her mother seemed if anything sprightlier for the death. "What is it?"

Her mother flattened a sheaf of papers at her desk. "I need your signature, Farida, in four places."

"For what?"

"Just something your father wanted to ensure for your safety. You know what a worrier he was."

Farida raised her head from the pillow. She had never known her father to worry, nor her mother to joke. If anything, her mother worried and her father joked, each enough for two. "But can't you just tell me what it is?"

Her mother was smiling; she smiled more since her husband's death than Farida could remember. "Well, of course, I can, sweetie, but I simply don't want to waste time more than I have to. I have a ten-thirty with Mr. Bilimoria and I need your signature. What with everything that's happened I simply forgot. I need your signature in four places, that's all." She tapped the papers, holding out a pen. "Why not just get it over with? Then you can sleep—though it's much too nice a morning."

Farida stretched in bed, staring at her mother. She was twenty years younger than her mother, who had been twenty years younger than her father. She was more slender than Farida, brown-eyed to her black, shorter by a couple of inches, and if not for the grey in her hair they might have been sisters. In Farida's cocktail dress of the night before she might have attracted as many glances, but she was a conservative dresser. Their faces were similar, her mother's features finer, tinier, more fragile, winsome enough at the age of eighteen to attract a proposal from Mr. Nariman Cooper despite the situation of her family, the Batlivalas, as many rungs lower on the social ladder as Nariman had been older in years.

"What's the matter, sweetie? Don't you trust me?"

"Oh, Mummy, of course, I do. I just don't feel like moving."

"I'm sorry to bother you after a late night, sweetie, but I simply forgot—and now I need this for my appointment."

Farida wrenched herself from the bed. "Give me the pen."

Her mother held out the pen, pointing to where she needed her signature, and Farida signed four times, her mother turning the pages. "Thank you, sweetie." Her mother kept her eyes on the pages as she took back the pen. "Now, there is also that question about where you will stay. Have you given it any thought since we talked? It really looks rather bad, you know, if you stay upstairs when your mother is now alone. You have to think about what people will say."

She had surprised Farida, asking her to live downstairs again, mother and daughter together as they should always have been, but that was something Farida had neither considered nor wished, having lived too long and happily with Kaki. She would rather not betray Kaki, though she knew Kaki would never stand in the way of what she wanted. She flopped back in bed with a sigh. "Oh, Mummy, what will they say that they haven't said a hundred times already? I can hardly even remember when I lived … downstairs." She had almost said *when I lived with you*, but didn't wish to hurt anyone's feelings, not even her mother's. "I'm too comfortable now, Mummy … upstairs." She had been careful again not to say she was comfortable with Kaki. "It's my home. I don't see any reason to change."

"The reason is quite straightforward, sweetie. Your father has passed. People will expect you to stay with me, and they will think something is the matter if you don't—now that there's room, I mean."

Farida stared at the ceiling. "Oh, Mummy, I really don't think people care a damn where I stay—and you shouldn't either. If anyone says anything, you just send them to me. I'll take care of them."

Her mother surprised her, sounding neither cross nor aggrieved— in fact, almost amused. "Well, there really is no reason to talk about it like that. I just wanted you to think about it. You know, it really is nice to have my daughter back."

Farida turned her head, smiling to her mother. "It's good to *be* back, Mummy."

Her mother smiled. "Did you have a nice time with Ratan last night?"

"Oh, yes, Mummy—better than I expected."

"Good, I'm glad to hear it. Ratan is very fond of you, you know."

"Oh, Mummy, I didn't mean it that way. I know he is, and he's a dear sweet friend, but he's not really my cup of tea."

"What's the matter? Not American enough for you?"

"It's too complicated, Mummy. I can't explain it to you."

"Well, I don't know what you mean—but he's a whole lot better than your Horace. I never liked him, *never*—not from the start, horrible Horace. That was always how I thought about him."

Farida laughed. "Horrible Horace and rotten Ratan! What a pair!"

"Don't laugh, Farida. Look before you leap. You've been very mum about the whole thing, but he wasn't the white knight you thought he was, was he?"

Farida had said only that she was getting a divorce, nothing more. "Sorry, Mummy. I always thought you liked Horace. I'm just a little surprised."

"Well, you were in such a hurry to marry him—and I couldn't very well tell you when you were on your honeymoon—and that was the first time I met him. Sorry, sweetie, but I always felt that way—for all the difference it makes now. Anyway, what are you going to do today?"

"Make a list of everything I need to get done. Otherwise, I'll never get around to doing anything."

"Good. Making a list will keep you organized. The best thing about times of crisis is that they make you reconsider your values, what's important and what's not—and that's a good thing. It makes you realize what's really important."

"What do you mean, Mummy? Give me an example. What's important?"

"Well, take your father, for instance—you know, how he was never around?"

Her mother had once said her father was guilty of all the sins to which flesh was heir. "Yes?"

"Well, he was absent so much I got used to it. I don't miss him now that he's gone as much as I might have if he had been around more."

"Oh, Mummy, what a thing to say!"

"It's true, you know. It was a blessing in disguise."

"Still, Mummy, what a thing to say!"

"Well, I do miss him—but it's strange the things I miss about him."

"What?"

"I miss his snoring."

"But you had separate bedrooms—you lived at opposite ends of the flat!"

"I could still hear his snoring at night. It was always a comfort to me to know he was home and that was how I could tell. Did Horace snore? I always think a snoring husband is such a blessing. You always know he's there—even at the opposite end of the flat."

Farida shut her eyes again: her mother had to know better: her father's snores didn't necessarily mean he was alone.

IT WAS ELEVEN O'CLOCK WHEN FARIDA, showered and breakfasted, entered Kaki's suite with a ruler, drawing pad, pencils, watercolors, brushes, a small palette, and a mug of water. She had often been corrected as a child: a kaki was a father's brother's wife, but Kaki was her father's sister, her fooie—but fooie carried overtones of ridicule in English, and Kaki she had remained. Kaki sat with knitting in a settee in her den, Schumann's *Scenes from Childhood* on her gramophone, Monet prints framed on the wall amid early watercolors by Farida. "Kaki, may I join you?"

Kaki was a stout woman, head like a jug, capacious jaw, ears for handles, frames of her glasses thick, black, and rectangular, a character from Mother Goose, but she never seemed concerned about her appearance. She dressed sensibly, white short-sleeved blouse that morning, sky-blue skirt. "Of course, my dear. Are you going to paint something?"

Farida took for granted that others saw in Kaki what she did, a glow that illuminated her skin, brightened her face, and warmed her company. She set her things on the table. "I want to design a flier—nothing elaborate, just something to advertise the lessons I want to give."

"Piano lessons?"

"Piano lessons, painting, writing—I don't care what actually, just something to pass the time usefully until I can make a go of the gallery. I want to design something that will attract attention."

"Where will you put it?"

"The notice board of the Cathedral. I called Mr. Wheeler about it. He was very good about the whole thing, which was just what I'd hoped."

Mr. Wheeler was principal of the Cathedral and John Connon High School from which Farida had graduated eighteen years ago. "I'm not surprised. He always liked you."

"He said as an alumnus, *and* as a Cooper, I was more than welcome—but I do wish he hadn't said that. I do wish people didn't make such a fuss about Coopers."

Kaki smiled. "If they didn't, I daresay we might wish they did."

"No, Kaki, I don't think so—at least, not in my case. I think sometimes it's a curse being a Cooper. You never know if people respect you for yourself or because you're a Cooper."

"Well, of course—but it's pointless speculating, isn't it? We're Coopers, and that's that. Might as well enjoy it—and there's a lot to enjoy, don't you think?"

"I'm sure you're right, Kaki—of course, you're right. Actually, Mummy said something this morning which surprised me. She said crises make us reconsider our values—what's important."

"She's right."

"I think she was talking about marriage—relating it to my own, I mean—that it could be the very crisis to help me define my values."

"She may well be right again."

"But how can you say that, Kaki? You never married."

"But that's just another kind of crisis, isn't it—especially for a woman? I think what your mother might have been saying is that it is the crisis, not the marriage, that matters. For her, perhaps, the crisis was her marriage—for me, perhaps, the crisis is not having a marriage. In any case, the point is not even the crisis itself, but how we deal with it."

Kaki had not hurt for suitors, but refused them all, smart enough to recognize they had eyes mainly for her bank account. "What did you do, Kaki?"

"I had you."

"Oh, Kaki—but no, I mean, really."

"Arré, my dear, I'm perfectly serious. You were my own little child. I counted myself most fortunate that things turned out as they did for me."

"Oh, Kaki! *I* was the fortunate one. I had you *and* Mummy. She was always downstairs from us, but you were always right here where I needed you—where she *should* have been."

"You mustn't say that. Your mummy did the best she could."

"I'm sure she did, Kaki—of course, she did—but I *al*so had you."

"Well, then, I suppose you might say we had each other?"

"I *do* say that, Kaki—I always do."

Kaki smiled. "And so do I, my dear. So do I." She returned to her knitting as Farida prepared to paint. "My dear, wouldn't you rather have an easel than the table?"

"Not for this, Kaki. I just need a single image, something simple, not too avant-garde—a flower, maybe a lotus, maybe a lily pad, and a frog—even that might be more than I need. You know, just something colorful to catch the eye—and to show what I can do."

"Shall I call Sashi for some biscuits? I bought those strawberry centers that you like so much."

"Oh, thank you—but no, not just now. I had a late breakfast, and we're having tomato rice for lunch, my favorite, and I don't want to spoil it—but you make me feel like I'm six years old all over again. It's such a nice feeling."

Kaki smiled, keeping her eyes on her knitting. She was about to say she found Schumann's piano music perfect for a quiet session knitting when the doorbell rang. "I wonder who that could be."

Sashi answered the door, popping her head shortly into the den to address Kaki. She looked as Farida remembered from her teenage years except for her belly, bare between her choli and the waist of her sari, once tight as a drum, now slack from childbearing—a three-time mother, unlike Farida, barely four years younger, but childless, and childless to remain for the foreseeable future. She wondered how it might have been, her baby Cyrus, or Ruby, a suckling child relieving the continual pang in her nipples, raw beyond nakedness. "Bai, someone is here for Farida-bai. I have put in sitting-room."

Kaki looked at Farida. "Were you expecting someone?"

Farida put down her pencil, shaking her head. "No."

Kaki looked at Sashi. "Who is it, Sashi?"

"I don't know, bai. Someone new, one bai and one baba. She ask for Farida-bai."

"It's all right, Kaki. I'll go see who it is."

Leaving the den Farida had a premonition; arriving in the sitting-room her premonition was realized. Mrs. Katrak in a short-sleeved blouse and slacks sat in the wide sofa, Darius in a blue shirt and jeans in the adjacent club chair. Farida hesitated for a moment, unsure what the premonition meant, but they had seen her and she stepped forward with greater vigor, as if into a new dimension. Both guests rose when they saw her, Mrs. Katrak extending a hand, her smile seeming to float ahead of her hand. "There you are! Hullo, Farida! I hope we are not disturbing?"

Farida shook her hand. "Hullo, Mrs. Katrak. No, but what a surprise."

Darius seemed stiffer than she remembered from the night before, holding out his hand, but struggling it seemed for a smile. "Hullo … Farida. It is very good to see you again."

She held his hand longer, squeezing it as she had not his mother's. She liked his hesitation with her name, knowing he would have been more comfortable calling her "aunty," appreciating his effort on her behalf, smiling for him as she had not for his mother. "Hullo, Darius. Pleasure is mine."

His smile was immediate, reinforcing her impression of the night before. The Katraks were a good-looking family of greater than average height, Darius at least two inches taller than the others, perhaps five-eight with another couple of inches to grow. She preferred tall men, being five-six herself, short enough in Chicago, but in Bombay easily among the taller women, often taller than the men. Ratan was five-seven, but shorter for his slouch.

Farida spread her arms in welcome. "Please sit. Would you like some tea? coffee? lemonade?"

The guests took their seats again, Farida the club chair across from Darius, the length of the coffee table between them, Mrs. Katrak shaking her head. "No, no, wouldn't dream of imposing. We just came for a business matter, that is all."

Farida's eyebrows rose. "Business matter?"

"Yes, about our Darius—seventeen years old he is now, but still he does not know what he wants to do—very brainy fellow, IQ of 160—"

"Mummy!"

"Don't 'Mummy' me. It is true, isn't it? I am not just boasting. I am making a point here."

Darius shook his head. "It's not necessary to go into all that."

"I will decide what is necessary and what is not."

Farida leaned forward, smiling for Darius, speaking to his mother. "Please, Mrs. Katrak, go on."

"As I was saying, very brainy fellow, can do whatever he wants—but doesn't know what to do. We gave him IQ tests, 160 IQ they said, he can do sciences, arts, anything he wants—so we thought, why not architecture? It is a good mix of science and arts, also his father is an architect, my Dhun, you know?"

Mrs. Katrak held Farida's eyes and Farida nodded.

"Currently he is studying for the HSC, the 'A' levels at the Cathedral School, taking Physics and Maths and Literature and Art—the only student taking such a mixture of subjects. All the other boys are taking Physics and Maths and Chemistry; all the girls are taking Literature and Art and History."

Farida nodded. "Those were also my subjects—I mean, of course, the girls' subjects."

Mrs. Katrak's smile seemed to palpitate with the confirmation. "That is what I am saying, *all* the girls are taking the same subjects. The thing is, we want him to go to Chicago, Illinois Institute of Technology, for architecture—it has a great reputation, you must be knowing about it—their Mies van der Rohe was on the cover of *Time* magazine just now when he died—but we are also preparing, in the meantime, if, for whatever reason, money or quotas or whatever, he cannot go. He can get drafting experience in his father's office in the meantime, he can go to the Academy of Architecture here only in Bombay, all of this will make his chances better for admission to the Chicago IIT, don't you think?"

"I don't know what the requirements are, Mrs. Katrak, but I'm sure you are right—the greater his qualifications the better his chances."

"That is what we also thought. The thing is, in order to get into the Academy of Architecture he has first got to pass the Government Art exam, and his talent for painting is not very good."

Farida began to understand, but said nothing.

"Then last night you said you were thinking about giving tuitions—and when we got home I said to my Dhun that is what we should do. We should send our Darius to you for tuitions. Darius also was in agreement. We didn't have your telephone number, but we knew where you lived—everybody knows—and we live not far, in Edgewater House, just down the road in Oomer Park. You know where it is?"

Darius nodded. "Scandal Point, you know."

Farida nodded, smiling at the nickname, Bombay's lovers' lane alongside the rocky beach. She knew Edgewater House, the last building in a row seeming to rise from the sea. She remembered lashings from the monsoon when she had attended a friend's birthday party in one of the flats as a girl.

"I thought better to come sooner than later, before your time got all booked up."

Farida laughed. "I haven't even begun. I was just about to design a flier, actually, for the same reason, when you came."

"Then we are not too late?"

"If anything, too early—but you have no idea what I can do, whether I can even paint myself. What makes you so sure I can help Darius?"

Darius leaned forward, elbows on knees, wrists limp, hands dangling, speaking softly, drawing her into more than his words, pricking once more her premonition. "Actually, Farida, I *have* seen your paintings—in our studio at school. There is one of a park scene—another one of an arctic scene, with a polar bear—and my favorite is the one of a storm at sea, very Turneresque, actually. Lady Temple says you were her best student. She has kept more of your paintings than any of her other students. I thought they were also very good—nice touch, very delicate, but also very strong in the sea picture."

Farida smiled. Lady Temple was the art teacher at the Cathedral School. "Good old Lady Temple, still teaching. How is she these days?"

"She is fine, very busy, as always—but still finds time for her own work, even an exhibition once not so long ago at the Jehangir Art Gallery."

It was just the sort of exhibition for which Farida wanted her own gallery; she would have loved to have exhibited Lady Temple's paintings, shown her gratitude in the best way she could, her admiration for her teacher as much as her work. Farida leaned forward as well, elbows on knees. "I would have loved to have seen it, she was a great influence on me, but there is also another consideration. I have no idea what the Government Exam requires. I would need to find out so much about it still."

Darius's eyes never left hers, his voice remained soft, modulating to a caress. "I can tell you what you need to know. I can tell you now or later."

Farida held his eyes, leaning further into the voice. "Tell me now, if you can, in short."

"All right. In short, there are five exams. First, there is Nature Drawing, in which we have to paint from nature, flowers and leaves on a stem. Next, there is Still Life, in which we have to paint objects clumped together, a chair, shoes, clothes, books, whatever. Then there is Memory Drawing, in which we are given a subject to paint from memory. Then Geometric Design, in which we have to set a number of geometric shapes into a pattern—and finally there is Abstract Design, in which we can use any forms we want to make a pattern—you know, for a shawl or sari border or gift wrapping."

Farida frowned. "That seems like a lot—and I don't know the level of your proficiency yet. How much time do we have to prepare for the exams?"

"Nine months. Plenty of time. Exams are held every year at the J. J. School of Art."

"All right, but I would also need to see some examples of the kind of thing that's expected."

"Not a problem. I can show you past exam papers, other people's work." He shrugged. "Whatever you need, just let me know. I'm sure it won't be a problem."

"All right, then. After I have seen your work, and after I have seen what's expected, if I think I can help you—then, taking all that into consideration, let us say you have found yourself a tutor."

Darius smiled, dimples in his cheeks complementing the cleft in his chin. "Great. When can we start?"

"I will call you when I am ready, maybe in a week."

"Perfect."

They seemed almost to have forgotten Mrs. Katrak, who had clung to her smile as to a lifeline and appeared now almost to intrude on their dialogue. "Farida, you must also tell us what you will charge for tuition fees—whatever you think is fair."

"Oh, no, Mrs. Katrak. I thought I made that clear yesterday. I'm not doing this for money."

"But something you must take, no? even something nominal?"

Farida shook her head. "I don't want anything for myself, but if you feel you must give something then let me suggest you donate whatever you want to a charity instead, but *not* to a Cooper charity—and *not*, most definitely *not*, in my name. Will that be acceptable?"

"Not only acceptable, but very praiseworthy—but not fair to you."

"Mrs. Katrak, I don't want to explain myself and I don't want to defend myself. Let me say only that you would be doing me a favor, not the other way around. No need to feel badly about it."

"All right, then, if you put it like that, of course."

"That is how I put it."

Darius spoke again, softly as before. "We should exchange telephone numbers in the meantime—you know, just in case."

"Of course." Farida went to a desk against the wall behind the sofa for a pen and pad, scribbled her telephone number for the Katraks and took their number from Darius. "Now that we've got that settled, may I still offer you some tea?"

Mrs. Katrak's smile returned. "Not tea, but some water, if it is not too much trouble?"

"Of course—with ice?"

"No, just plain water from the matka, not too cold."

"Of course. What about you, Darius?"

"I'll have some tea."

Farida called Sashi for tea and water, lemonade for herself. Mrs. Katrak leaned forward, her smile leaping about the room like an obnoxious child. "So, tell us, Farida, do you find Bombay much changed?"

Everyone asked the same question and Farida replied with practiced ease. "Not really, but living in Chicago I've changed myself—and things seem different because I see things differently myself."

"Ah, yes, of course! Must be very different living in Chicago."

"Yes, it is, and that is another reason things seem different in Bombay. They are not really different, but they *seem* different because I'm now accustomed to the way things are in Chicago. I suppose what I am saying is that on the one hand I have changed myself, and on the other hand Chicago and Bombay are very different cities. It's not that Bombay has changed, but that I'm accustomed now to Chicago."

"Yes, of course! Very insightful!"

Darius spoke again, softly as before. "It must be nice to be back with old friends again."

"Yes, it is, very much, but many of my old friends are no longer in Bombay either—many are in the U.S. or the U.K." Her Chicago friends were now closer to her than her Bombay friends, but she wanted to get past the blunders of her marriage, past the guilt of her old life, and that was not something she was ready to talk about. "I'm actually leaving myself open to all possibilities for the present—of course, meeting old friends again, but also making new friends—looking forward, in fact."

"I say, then, a friend of mine, Sonu Daryanani—he's having a party on Saturday. If this is not too late notice, would you like to come?"

Farida's mouth opened, a brief gasp, and she shut it again, afraid to say a word, afraid what acceptance might mean, afraid not to accept.

Mrs. Katrak seemed to hold her breath almost as long, but spoke first. "Arré, Darius, what nonsense you are talking. They will be all kids at your party. Who is Farida going to talk to?"

Mrs. Katrak kept her eyes on Farida as she admonished her son, but Darius spoke first. "Mummy is right. At the most there will be people in their twenties, but I think you will fit in very well. I think you will find Bombay is not so far behind the times."

Farida understood there was more to be said than could be managed in Mrs. Katrak's presence, and her premonition flashed like a blade, but she nodded. "That will be all right. I think I would like that."

"Great! Then it is settled. I will pick you up at nine o'clock."

"All right."

Mrs. Katrak's eyes widened in apparent disapproval, but her smile indicated otherwise. "Arré, parents are not allowed—but perfect strangers?"

"Mummy, parents, by definition, are not allowed. It's a party, not papeti or Navroz or Christmas."

Farida smiled. "Where is the party?"

"Actually, right here at Breach Candy, in Sunita Manzil—but I will pick you up."

Breach Candy was walking distance from Blue Mansions; Edgewater House was also walking distance, but on the other side. Farida seemed aware of nothing suddenly as much as her thumping heart. She was glad for Sashi's reappearance with the water, tea, and lemonade, glad for the plate of strawberry centers which Kaki had added to the tray, glad for something to do with her hands, removing the cozy from the teapot, doily from the milk jug, pouring through a strainer, plucking sugar cubes with tongs. Mrs. Katrak seemed unable to stop talking. "He has just got his license, takes the car just to go to Kemp's Corner—just to cross the street." She laughed. "Yasmin is also learning, but she is not so good a driver. If there are no cars on the road she will hit a parked car. That is how she is."

Darius grinned. "That actually happened, but in her defense I should say at least her aim is good!"

Mrs. Katrak's smile was crooked. "Boys learn these things faster, but she also wants to drive—but I tell her, bad as she is, she will only get into an accident—but she won't listen."

"I also drive, Mrs. Katrak—and what I say is if you can drive in Bombay you can drive anywhere in the world. That is one of the big differences I find coming back, between Chicago and Bombay. The congestion in Bombay cannot be matched."

After the Katraks left Farida felt an elation not experienced in a long while. She enjoyed evenings with friends like Ratan, but felt too much in control to be truly excited—except for the night before when she had taken the stage. She was surprised at the ease with which Darius had invited her to the party, surprised with herself for accepting, but glad she was not yet too old to surprise herself.

As Sashi removed the refreshment tray from the sitting-room Kaki entered with a newspaper. "Farida, did you know you were going to be in the *Midday* today?"

"No. Whatever for?"

"Well, it says here that you performed last night at The Darjeeling. There's even a picture."

Farida looked where Kaki pointed. "Oh, God, there must have been a reporter in the restaurant—just the sort of thing I was trying to avoid."

"Why trying to avoid?"

"Well, because of daddy, and—well, you know how people think."

"Yes, but if anything the reporter seems quite sympathetic. Just read what he says."

Farida read the paragraph quickly, scanning the phrases: "Farida Cooper soldiers on"; "life must go on"; "true grit"; "genuine trouper"; "great pipes"; "bravura performance." The reporter had mentioned briefly her father's death, making of her evening a tribute to the human spirit. She nodded, smiling. "The photograph's not bad either."

III

On Saturday evening, Darius rang the Cooper doorbell just as the grandfather clock in the foyer struck nine and was let in by Sashi to wait in the sitting-room. Farida met him in a black miniskirt, wide blue belt with a brass buckle, lemon blouse, and offered him a drink, but Yasmin and her boyfriend were waiting downstairs in the car and they left the flat immediately. Descending the stairs, Darius cautioned her not to mind Yasmin's boyfriend, Arun Sarkar, saying only that he talked too much. Farida was grateful for his concern more than the warning. Her heels made them the same height, but he walked with more assurance than Ratan more than twice his age. She found herself watching him for reasons to discredit her enthusiasm, but found him instead, once more in blue jeans and white shirt, high-shouldered as a military man, loose-limbed as Elvis, easy to love as a puppy.

A jade Fiat stood in the driveway. As they walked around the car Darius was aware of Kaki's blue Buick, her mother's silver Falcon, and her father's cream Chevrolet in the open garage, each roomier than the Fiat by almost half a car, but he said nothing, opening the door of the Fiat instead for Farida. Farida waved at the couple in the back as she got in. "Hullo, everyone."

Yasmin wore a red satin dress, bright even in the shadows of the rear seat. "Hullo, Farida. Nice to see you again. This is our friend, Arun."

Arun extended a limp hand, like a tentacle, over her shoulder. "Hullo, Farida-bai. Pleased to meet you. Very many good things I have heard about you."

Yasmin lost her smile, slapping his arm, yanking it back. "Shut up, you silly! I swear I don't know what I'm going to do with you."

Arun chuckled. "Arré, what? I said I had heard good things."

Yasmin leaned forward, clutching the back of the front seat. "He thinks he's being so funny, Farida-bai and all that, letting you know he knows who you are—but he's just being stupid."

Farida smiled, remembering Darius's caution. "It's all right, Yasmin. It doesn't matter if he knows who I am or not, or if anyone knows—only that I know."

There was silence as Darius maneuvered the car onto the road toward Breach Candy. Yasmin lit a cigarette. Arun tapped Farida's shoulder extending a pack of Camels. "Cigarette?"

Farida knew the Dhun Katraks would not have approved, but understood he was testing her. She might have said something, even facetiously, but she was a guest, not a chaperone. She extracted a cigarette and lit it when Arun extended a lighter from behind. "Thanks."

Arun tapped ash from the window. "I say, Darius, is Hedvig Lingam coming to the party?"

Yasmin snapped immediately. "For God's sake, Arun, get it right. Her name is Lyngstad."

"Whatever. Everyone knows lingams are her thingums."

Yasmin stared, eyes of glass, at Arun. "I swear, Farida, sometimes I think all I ever do is apologize for Arun. Thinks he's so sophisticated, talking about lingams, so sexy he thinks he is, trying to impress you and all, but he's just being crude."

Darius glanced at Farida and she realized she needed to let them know where she stood; accepting a cigarette had been a step, but she needed to spell it out. If they worried constantly about offending her the evening would end before it had begun. "Don't worry, Yasmin. I'm having a great time already. If he gets crude with me I'll bloody well tell him to bugger off myself. I can be as crude as anyone if I want."

Arun laughed. "See? See? What did I tell you? I swear, Yasmin, about time you learned a few things about the real world. Farida has lived in Chicago. She has been married. She has managed a lingam or two in her time, I am sure."

Farida nodded, looking back at Yasmin. "Yes, of course, I have— and it has been my experience that men who talk about lingams rarely do anything else."

Yasmin laughed so suddenly she coughed. Catching her breath again she grinned. "I say, Farida, well said—right you are, dead right. Perfect description of Arun. All he can do is talk."

Arun shook his head, turning again to Darius. "So, is she coming or no, our Hedvig?"

Darius turned the car into Sophia College Lane. "Why are you asking me? How should I know?"

Farida turned her head to address Arun. "Who is this Hedvig that you are so interested in?"

Arun's eyebrows jumped. "Arré, she is only the most chikna girl in Cathedral School, sexy—from Sweden, you know, land of the chiknas. Ask Darius if you don't believe. Tell her, no, Darius?"

"Swedish by blood, maybe, but she's American. Her mum works in the consulate right here in Breach Candy."

Yasmin exhaled a cloud of smoke. "I swear, you guys have no shame, talking about her like that. What is she, a piece of meat?"

Darius brought the car to a halt. He would have come around to open the door for Farida, but she got out quickly, wanting to make it clear what she expected from the start.

Arun emerged from behind, cheeks chubbier for his grin, winking as he caught Farida's eye. "Has a rep, if you know what I mean— *Swe*dish rep."

He was shorter than her by a couple of inches, browner by a couple of shades, and the roundness of his belly was clear despite the burgundy kurta which fell across his shoulders like a sack. Farida smiled. "After that introduction I can't wait to meet her now."

Arun nodded, still grinning, eyes avoiding hers but putting her pieces together, pink toenails in black toeless pumps, black miniskirt revealing naked knees swelling into juicy thighs, trim middle swelling into the lemon blouse, twin tips of her braless nipples swollen like beestings, bifurcation of breasts in the décolletage. "Very chikna."

"So you said."

His eyebrows were jumping again. "I meant you."

Farida was not unflattered, but cautious. "Thanks, I suppose."

Arun's grin grew cheekier with each utterance. "You're welcome, I suppose."

She smiled, taking Darius's arm as he came around the front of the car. "You can look, Arun, but only Darius can touch."

Arun laughed, but no one else.

Yasmin came around the back of the car, tall as Arun in her heels, taller for her hair in a beehive, shoulders high bearing her red dress on straps slender as tendrils, the hem revealing as much thigh as Farida's, but her legs were bonier, still girlish, her torso boyish, breasts that might have passed for padding. Farida realized Yasmin was unsteady, not for her heels but the presence of a woman instead of another girl, and turned on her full smile. "You look stunning, Yasmin! Very chic!"

Yasmin smiled, losing her unsteadiness. "Really? You think so?"

"Like Janet Leigh you look, your face—and what a lovely dress!"

"Thanks. I got it just last week—birthday present." She held two packages wrapped in red with blue bows, one of which she handed Farida. "More birthday presents. This one is from you and Darius."

Farida took the package, looking at Darius. "Is it someone's birthday?"

He nodded. "Sonu's birthday, our host—also seventeen."

"Arré, Darius, you should have told me. I would have brought something."

He shook his head. "No need. This is also from you. I put your name on the tag, see?"

The tag read: *To Sonu, Happy Birthday, from Darius and Farida.* "What did we get him?"

"A shirt, same as Yasmin and Arun—same as probably just about everyone else."

Yasmin laughed. "Boys are worse than girls about clothes—they just don't like to admit it."

SOUNDS GREW AS THE LIFT ASCENDED, strains of "Aquarius" rising above a bed of party noise. Farida was less sure of herself than she had been entering The Darjeeling with Ratan, what to expect, how to behave, whether she belonged, feeling seventeen again at one of the Cathedral School socials, wondering if she might not be trying too hard to leave behind her old life, be something she was not.

The quartet was silent walking to the front door, not wishing to shout over the blare of music. The music swelled as a servant answered the doorbell. They passed through a hallway into a long dimly-lit sitting-room opening onto a verandah at the far end. A sideboard held snacks and drinks; furniture was lined against the walls to make room for dancing. Guests wore hippie patterns and colors, polka dots and stripes, girls in miniskirts, salvars, and saris, boys in kurtas and shirts, both in jeans. Cigarette smoke clouded every conversation, impressing upon Farida how easily even the appearance of censure might have redounded to her disadvantage in the car. A boy with sleepy eyes and a sleepy smile approached as they waited. "I say, Darius, good of you to come, yaar—you too, Yasmin and Arun. How is everybody?"

Darius nodded. "Fine, Sonu. Happy birthday, man!"

Yasmin and Arun wished him as well, Yasmin proffering the present, Arun looking around. "Great party, looks like, yaar."

"I say, Sonu, this is my friend, Farida. Farida, the birthday boy himself, Sonu Daryanani."

Farida smiled, offering their present. "Happy birthday, Sonu. Thanks for having me."

Sonu's grin remained sleepy. "Arré, welcome, welcome. I saw your write-up in the paper—and right after that Darius said he was bringing you. He said you were terrific. So glad you could come. You have only just come from Chicago?"

"Almost two weeks now."

"To stay?"

"Maybe—depends."

"Of course. Hope you have a good time."

Arun interrupted suddenly. "I say, Sonu, is Hedvig here yet?"

Sonu looked at the floor, sleepy smile getting sheepish. "She's coming. Jaikishen has gone to pick her up. They should be here soon." He looked up again. "I say, please, everyone, help yourselves—food, drinks, whatever you want. Can I get you anything?"

Darius shook his head. "We'll help ourselves." He turned to Farida. "Want to take a look?"

"Sure." Farida followed him gratefully, threading her way among the dancers behind him to the table laden with wafers, sandwiches, samosas, bhajias, mithai, wine, beer, Coke, Sosyo, Gold Spot.

"What will you have?"

"Maybe some Chablis. I'm not all that hungry."

Darius poured wine for two when they were approached by another boy. "Hey, Darius."

"Hey, Cisco."

"And this must be Farida."

"I say, Farida, this is my best friend, Francis Braganza. We call him Cisco, like the Cisco Kid. He lives in my building, one floor down."

Francis was taller and darker than Darius, hair a mop on his head. Farida smiled. "Hi, Cisco."

"Hullo. I say, good to meet you finally. I read your write-up in *Midday*. Wish I could have been there. Heard you were great."

Farida shook her head. "You must not believe everything you hear—and only half of what you see." Her eyes accused Darius. "I'm afraid the reports about me have been greatly exaggerated."

Darius shrugged. "Not by me. He heard nothing from me. Yasmin must have told him."

Farida slapped his arm. "Naughty boy! He *should* have heard it from you, not from Yasmin."

Arun grinned, filling his plate. "Not so naughty as he would like to be, I'm sure, hunh, Darius?"

Farida shook her head. "You know, Arun, I barely know you and already you are so predictable."

The group laughed and Arun bit into a samosa. "I say, why not go to the verandah? Less crowded—and can't beat the view."

THE VERANDAH HELD THE SPILL OF CHAIRS and dancing couples from the sitting-room. Sunita Manzil stood on a hill, the Daryanani flat on the eighteenth floor, and the panorama did not disappoint. Directly below they could see the T junction of Sophia College Lane branching up the hill from Warden Road, visible mainly for streetlamps glinting through trees. Across Warden Road the Breach Candy complex stretched like an occupation force, dubbed Little New York for its inhabitants, two decades after independence an American enclave forbidden to Indians—hospital, club, pool, residential flats, and the consulate (a majestic structure of Islamic design). Beyond Breach Candy an indigo sky met an indigo sea in a dark arc.

It was late November; days still hot, nights marginally cooler. Farida, wineglass in hand, gazed at the horizon. The talk turned to TV shows, rock concerts, power steering, none of which were available in Bombay, all of which made her the hub of the conversation. Others joined the group, friends and classmates, all interested in Farida—except a couple of Americans, offspring of diplomats, providing the hubs for other constellations of conversation. Farida realized she was the oldest person at the party. Sonu's parents were at their holiday cottage in Powai for the weekend; his brother Jaikishen was older by five years and some of his friends older yet; but none seemed older than thirty.

The music was eclectic, running through the Monkees, Stones, Cream, Herb Alpert, and Trini Lopez among others. Tom Jones was singing "Delilah" when Farida asked Darius to dance. Darius swung hips and shoulders in imitation of the singer, but Farida shook her head, pulling him into a two-step. Francis joined them on the floor with a friend; Yasmin whirled arms like helicopter blades; Arun replenished his plate and watched from a sofa. Farida whispered to Darius. "Arun doesn't like to dance?"

"Sometimes—but not like Yasmin. She can never get enough."

"She's very good, seems to know the steps—not just improvising like everyone else."

"She does, even practices at home—I say, by the way, in case you're interested, Hedvig Lingstad is right behind you, with Sonu."

Hedvig was a fat girl, even dowdy, perhaps twenty, her complexion waxy, hair so pale it seemed colorless. In her white dress, chosen perhaps ironically, she appeared like a specter in the dim light. She giggled, but her eyes seemed glazed, focusing on a point beyond the horizon, making Farida aware of a sweet smell she had overlooked before. She raised her eyebrows. "I must say I'm surprised after what Arun said. That is the most chikna girl in the school?"

Darius nodded, unsmiling. "Not for how she looks—if you know what I mean."

"Ah, I understand—Sonu's birthday present!"

"From his brother." Darius smirked. "Wonder what price Jaikishen paid for the present."

Farida was surprised by his smirk more than his words. He carried himself with such confidence it was easy to forget he was just seventeen. "Don't be a prude, Darius. I think that's sweet—I mean, as long as Hedvig fancies him, what's the harm? And even otherwise, what business is it of anyone else?"

Darius spoke warily. "No one's business."

"Exactly, no one's business—but the world will make it the business of the world—and why? Because we always make fun of what we want when we don't have the guts to get it ourselves."

Darius remained silent.

Farida had surprised herself, said more than she wished, responding to more than Darius's smirk. "Sorry. I didn't mean to go off on you like that."

"But you didn't. We had a discussion. We provided different points of view. You have given me something to think about."

Tom Jones sang "I'm Coming Home." She drew him closer, speaking with affection. "Thank you—very good of you to say so, very understanding of you. In case you haven't guessed I am going through something—what, exactly, I don't know yet myself, but I offer that as an excuse for my behavior. Call it a stage, something to do with my marriage, and … and some other things."

His arms seemed suddenly full, his body wrapped in her warmth and softness; he nodded, his cheek nuzzling her hair. "I know—your father."

She had not thought about her father; instead, she had dwelt again, however briefly, on the baby that might have been; but she nodded. "Yes, maybe, that … my father."

Darius realized her father was peripheral to her concerns. "Must be very difficult—divorce."

She shook her head. "Divorce is easy … if your marriage is difficult—but I am much more interested now in Bombay life—what people think, how they think. It is all so alien to me now. I want to know what *you* think. Would you want Hedvig to fancy you?"

Darius was surprised by her question, but he had wondered what they might talk about and was glad to follow her lead. "Not really. I don't much fancy her myself."

"And if you fancied her? Then what?"

"Then it would be a different story."

"How would it be different?"

"I don't know. I haven't thought about it—but I don't fancy her, so what's the point?"

"Maybe no point at all—but sometimes the point of a conversation becomes clear days after the conversation, don't you think?"

"Sometimes, yes."

"So what do you think about marriage?"

Again he was surprised, but grinned. "Not too much—I mean, I don't think about it too much, but maybe because I'm a boy. For girls it is different, I think. Sometimes I swear Yasmin would get married tomorrow if she had the chance."

"To Arun?"

"No. I don't think she even likes him really."

"Then why is she with him?"

"Just being rebellious, I think—because he's a Hindu." He chuckled. "My mum and dad would like nothing better than to have her settle down with a good Parsi boy—you know, good job, good family, that sort of thing—but as far as Yasmin is concerned that is the best reason to stay with Arun, even if she doesn't like him—because mummy and daddy don't like him even more."

"Does Arun know?"

"Of course, but as far as he is concerned it is also the best reason to stay with her. His parents are the same, Brahmin family. He is still too young to marry, but when he is ready I am sure they will have a good Hindu girl lined up for him." He laughed. "Who knows, maybe even with a dowry—but maybe his family is not so medieval as all that. Maybe they are past all that nonsense."

"So they are together only because their parents don't want them to be together?"

"Who knows for sure, but that is a distinct possibility—though maybe not *on*ly because. Yasmin is a very serious girl and Arun makes her laugh—though you probably couldn't tell from today. Actually, I think it's a good thing—serves both sets of parents right for being prejudiced."

Farida laughed: trouble with her parents had factored into her own marriage. "Gloria Steinem says a wife is the most expensive prostitute."

"Really? Gloria Steinem said that?"

"I'm paraphrasing—but, yes, something like that. Marriage is a form of prostitution. You've heard about Gloria Steinem?"

"Well, now, this is a big coincidence, but the only reason I know about her is that we actually met her once, long ago, when she was in Bombay—Yasmin and I were just kids. I don't even remember it, but my dad never lets us forget, not after she published her exposé about *Playboy*. He went around telling everybody he knew her—as if she was his girlfriend or something—as if he had exposed *Playboy* himself. Mummy thought it was very funny—specially since he has a subscription to *Playboy*."

Farida drew back, looking Darius in the eye. "Do you mean to say you know Gloria Steinem?"

"No, no, not know her—but it was midnight when her flight landed, and she knew nobody in Bombay, and the TWA traffic manager—a friend of my dad—felt sorry for her. He said she had great courage, so young and so pretty and in a foreign country all by herself. He took her home to stay with his family, showed her around Bombay, and brought her once to a navjote. That was where she met my mum and dad—us, also, but we were too young to remember, must have been five or six."

"Why was she in India?"

"I don't know. She was traveling on a student grant or something—broadening her horizons or something. I don't know exactly what—but my dad's friend was right about one thing. She had courage. Imagine going undercover at *Playboy*."

"I didn't know she had been in India, but her article opened a lot of eyes. Everyone thought *Playboy* was such a terrific place to work, they thought bunnies made two to three hundred bucks a week, but in fact they made less than forty bucks—and that was just the tip of the iceberg. The girls were treated pretty much like servants. Hefner was so mad at the article he commissioned a piece on Steinem himself—a hatchet job, of course. He's a real bastard."

"Really? I didn't know that."

Francis tapped Darius's shoulder. "Is it permitted?"

"Of course." Darius surrendered Farida to Francis's arms as "I'm Coming Home" segued into "Jumping Jack Flash." Farida snapped her fingers, swinging her hips—and Francis, smiling, followed her lead.

They didn't talk much, it was difficult over the din of the party, and someone shortly tapped Francis's shoulder, a boy of about fifteen who said nothing but grinned like a chimp showing all his teeth, groaning when he was tapped in turn by another grinning boy.

Farida excused herself after the next song to coax Arun to the floor. He remained stationary as he danced, moving his hands lackadaisically from the wrists. Farida shook her head in disapproval. "You should move around more, Arun. Get some exercise."

He chuckled, bobbing his eyebrows, still waggling his hands. "I would rather get the kind of exercise Lingam and Soni will soon be getting."

Farida grinned. "I swear, Arun, you are incorrigible. Is your mind always in the gutter?"

He grinned. "I'm a growing boy. Where else should it be? Dirty mind, clean body—isn't that what you said?"

"I said no such thing."

"Arré, how soon we forget." He intoned solemnly: "'Men who talk about lingams rarely do anything else.'"

Farida laughed. "I can see I shall have to be very careful what I say around you. I wonder why Yasmin puts up with you."

Arun grinned. "Just bad taste, I suppose."

THE REST OF THE EVENING PASSED WITH FEW VARIATIONS. It was long past midnight when they left, but to Farida's surprise Yasmin and Arun planned to walk home. Arun shrugged. "What to do, Farida-bai? Not the exercise I had in mind, but what to do?"

Yasmin smiled at Farida, slapping Arun's arm, shaking her head, shrugging in resignation, happy with the evening. "It was very nice to see you again, Farida—maybe again sometime—without Arun."

Arun grinned, shrugging again. Farida smiled. "I shall look forward to it. Bye for now."

Darius seemed less sure of himself in the car and so was she, both realizing the evening had been no more than a prelude to the drive home, leaving them swollen with suspense, thighs ballooning into contact across the inches of upholstery between them. Darius's voice seemed higher by an octave, rising through a constricted throat. "I hope you had a good time."

Her own voice was reedy. "Lovely time. Thanks for asking me. I enjoyed meeting your friends."

"Not too young?"

"That I expected, but I still had a lovely time. It has been so long since I danced. I can't tell you how much I needed just to let loose. I enjoyed it very much—and es*pec*ially getting to know you better."

Darius acknowledged her emphasis with a smile, but kept his attention on the road. "Good. I'm glad. I think you were quite a hit, actually—I mean, everyone knows that you are a Cooper and all that."

Her voice remained reedy, but cut like a knife. "And that makes a difference?"

"It made a difference to my mum, you know. I hate to say it, but if you were not a Cooper who knows if she would have thought of the lessons."

"And you? Does it make a difference to you?"

"I will not lie. I am glad you are an attractive woman."

The car seemed suddenly too small, stuffed with their bodies, empty of air, and her voice grew thin as a stiletto. "I did not ask that. I asked if the other things made a difference."

"About other things I couldn't care less. I'm just telling you, for me, what makes the difference."

"Why does that make a difference? I'm going to be your teacher, not your girlfriend."

"I don't know. It just does."

"And that I am a Cooper?"

"That, actually, makes no difference. I'm much happier that you are an attractive woman than that you are a Cooper."

She was glad her name meant nothing, glad he found her attractive, glad he had told her—twice—but she remained silent. She found him too bold, but no bolder than when he had invited her to the party in the presence of his mother. The invitation itself had been an act of aggression, but one she had accepted, even welcomed. It was already too late to find him too bold; she had committed herself unconscious of her commitment—but still she remained silent.

He cast a sidelong glance, brow wrinkled. "Is something wrong?"

"No. I just don't see why it makes a difference to the lessons, the way I look."

They reached Blue Mansions. Darius nodded to acknowledge the chowkidar Tukaram's salaam at the gate. She had taken his arm, called him a naughty boy, scolded him for prudishness, danced with him like a lover, spoken freely about marriage and *Playboy* and Gloria Steinem, defended Sonu and Hedvig—and he had read what he wished into the evening, reading flirtation, even seduction, into what might have been just playfulness, a wrongful reading to which he had clung perhaps since she had accepted his invitation. He had surprised himself with the invitation, but he had known she would accept. He had known something, he couldn't have said what, since the first time she had addressed him, asking him not to call her "aunty." Lacking experience in such matters he had been content to let each moment dictate the next, but it seemed the last moment had arrived. "It doesn't really make a difference. It's just a bonus."

A thought gnawed through her head: she wondered if he had engineered their ride home, asking Yasmin and Arun to walk—but wondered as well what she had wanted herself. She had lived her life conventionally for lack of an alternative, and possibly paid for it with the death of her marriage. The marriage of her parents encouraged unconventional behavior. When the rules of life failed you made new rules; when the lines drawn by society snapped you reconstructed the lines; when she had accepted his invitation she had already begun the reconstruction.

He stopped the car at the portico, beaten finally by her reserve, dimples snuffed from his cheeks, even the cleft in his chin seemed more shallow. His voice dropped to its natural depth. "Farida, I'm sorry. I think I have offended you, but I meant no such thing—quite the opposite, in fact. I'm really sorry. I have been very presumptuous."

She nodded, unsmiling. "I had a nice time. I will call you about the lessons."

He nodded, unable to hold her eyes, turning back to the wheel, shoulders slumped, face congealing in disappointment, and she felt herself weaken. "Aren't you going to kiss me goodnight?"

His eyes widened as he leaned across the seat. He barely pecked her cheek, but kept his face close. She turned her face to give him her lips, but he remained still.

Neither moved, their breaths like feathers against each other's cheeks. Five seconds seemed like five minutes before she spoke again. "What are you doing?"

He kissed her farther cheek, still chaste as a child. "Isn't this how they do it in Europe, both cheeks?"

She remained still. "Yes—and this is how they do it in America." She closed the space between their mouths, nibbling his lips with her own, puckering and pressing and probing, inducing him to follow her lead, exploring his mouth with her tongue, encouraging his own exploration. One hand cupped the back of his head, the other slid up between them to cup his jaw until she leaned over him, moaning, breathing heavily, withdrawing finally with a last lingering lick of his lips. His own hands had found their way, one to her shoulder, one to her back, taking nothing for granted after his recent presumption. His eyes remained shut, his mouth open, a low groan in his throat. She smiled: their lessons had just begun.

IV

Farida called Darius the next evening to arrange a time to discuss the requirements of the examination and acquaint herself with his work. She said nothing about the night before and neither did he, but the haste with which she had called could not have been more voluble, nor their silence on the subject more loud. Farida told him to come prepared to draw, but afraid she might have appeared too transparent set the lesson for the next Saturday morning, almost a week away, as if the longer she delayed the more she might seem professional and the less important the lessons themselves except as lessons. She had never felt this way with Horace, her skin a sheath of ice, ground trembling beneath her feet, the world no longer visible except through a veil, no more in control of herself than of a shooting star.

On Saturday morning she arranged a still life in the studio adjoining her bedroom. She withdrew the curtains and the light from the east could not have been better. She set an armchair against the wall facing the windows, draped a long coat over its back, arranged the sleeves along the arms of the chair, balanced a top hat from one of her father's costume parties on the back, and placed gumboots in front, in a parody of the invisible man. She chuckled attaching gloves to the sleeves.

Sashi called her when Darius arrived. She saw him first from behind in the sitting-room, standing before a print of Degas ballerinas, a small black portfolio leaning against the sofa. She entered quietly, standing behind the sofa, crossing her arms, admiring the colors and shapes he presented, white shirt, blue jeans (his standard attire), hands on his hips forming a hexagon with shoulders and waist, gleaming black head outlined against the shimmering white tutus of the ballerinas. "You mustn't hope for too much."

Darius had known she was behind him from her reflection in the glass of the print, but her words took him by surprise. "What?"

She grinned. "I can't teach you to paint like Degas."

He returned her grin, absorbing her hair bundled loosely in a pink ribbon, pink shirt with buttons undone revealing the swell of her breasts, tight white slacks the swell of her hips—but his grin was not without reserve. Despite her own grin she remained behind the sofa, arms crossed, when she might have shaken his hand. He had surprised himself the times he had met her, his boldness fueled by her apparent receptivity, but her later behavior had fueled only confusion. He had felt rebuked by her rebuff, punished for his precocity, found only kindness in her subsequent kiss goodnight, perhaps pity, and sobered by the light of day had determined not to presume again, not on kindness, not on pity. She was a Cooper, a grown woman, getting a divorce, living in two countries, traveling the world. His own experiences had been restricted to kisses under mistletoe at Christmas parties, moments stolen behind columns of the assembly hall during school socials, his imagination fueled by *TC*s (the pornographic *Traveler's Companion* series) and blue movies a friend had filched from his uncle's cupboard for a birthday party—but as Agatha Christie said, *Imagination is a good servant and a bad master*, and he had allowed his imagination to be too much his master.

"No fear. I just want to pass the exam."

"Good. I would hate to disappoint you." Dimples flashed again in his cheeks, but he seemed lost for a reply and she turned to the portfolio. "What have you brought to show me?"

"My drawings—also some past exam papers."

She uncrossed her arms, but remained behind the sofa, gripping its back as she leaned forward, breasts on display, eyes leashed to his, no longer grinning though her words remained mischievous. "Shall we look at them here or shall we go to my bedroom?"

His grin fluttered before disappearing as well, his eyes on his portfolio as he struggled again to reply. "Whatever is convenient."

Her mouth turned thinlipped and straight, her eyes held his tight though his own seemed stuck on the portfolio. Despite her provocation he could not have been better behaved, appearing too much a boy for the man's job she envisioned. Her reply, when it came, was not without ice. "Let me show you what I have prepared—a still life. We will have to cut across my bedroom. That's all I meant."

He nodded, congratulating himself on sidestepping her bait, convinced restraint now would serve him best. "That's what I thought you meant."

"You will take some tea, of course?"

"Sure, why not? All right. Thanks."

She called Sashi, asked her to bring tea to the studio, and led Darius toting his portfolio through her bedroom to her invisible man. "What do you think? Does that make a good still life or what?"

Darius, uncomfortable with the double entendres, especially by daylight and unsodden by drinks, leaned the portfolio against a chair, glad for a chance to laugh freely, the sheer relief of unselfconsciousness laughter. "A little too imaginative. Let me show you the kind of still lifes I mean."

She didn't laugh. "What about nudes?"

Darius stopped laughing. "Nudes?"

"For still lifes, nature drawings, whatever you want to call it. Don't they draw nudes?"

Darius shook his head, speaking patiently. "Arré, Farida, this is India, not America. No nudes, not even clothed people."

Farida had no patience with his patience, addressing her as he might a child, and raised her chin gazing down her nose. She had known there were no nudes on the syllabus, but was too mulish to surrender her attack. "We have come a long way from the Kama Sutra and Khajuraho, haven't we? We seem to be going backward, don't we?"

Darius stared, bewildered, the fire in her words quenched by the ice in her delivery. "I don't make the rules. I just want to pass the exam. Here, let me show you." He opened the portfolio, turning to a series of still-lifes consisting mainly of balls, brooms, buckets, bottles, boxes, vases, umbrellas, spectacles, shoes, fruit, and the like. "See, even the vases are empty. Flowers belong in Nature Drawing. Everything is very cut and dried. It's mainly a development of skill, not imagination—at least, where Still Life is concerned. Imagination is needed for Memory Drawing, Abstract Design, and Geometric Design."

Farida crossed her arms again. "How very boring."

Darius shrugged. "Sorry, but that's how it is."

Sashi knocked, bringing a tea tray, laden as well with Monaco and Britannia Biscuits. Darius noted she entered directly from the sitting-room; there had never been need to pass through the bedroom; but said nothing. Farida nodded toward the tray. "Help yourself. I want to look at these more closely."

"What about you? Some tea?"

"Yes, please—no milk, just one sugar."

"Ah, the American way." He poured tea, bringing Farida her cup, glad for the clarity of the domestic task.

She was looking intently at one of the still lifes: two tall slender bottles of Kalvert's Rose syrup alongside a stubbier stockier bottle of Coca Cola, all three posed among other objects behind a closed cardboard box, the bases of the bottles hidden behind the box. "Put away the tea for a minute. Something I want to show you right here."

Darius put down the cup. "I have trouble drawing glass—hard to get the transparency right—you know, the rendering."

"Yes, but I want to show you something more fundamental. This is an impossible drawing. The placement of the bottles is simply wrong. Here, I want you to do something for me." She set the drawing on the desk. "I want you to draw the bottles as if you could see them through the box—as if the box wasn't there." She gave him a pencil. "Nothing fancy, just the outlines."

He did as she asked, extending the lines of the bottles to their bases through the cardboard box. "Like that?"

"Yes, exactly like that. Do you see what you've done now?"

He stared, but said nothing.

"Look at the bases of your bottles. They overlap—the bases of the two Kalvert's bottles overlap, do you see? You have them both occupying the same space, but that's impossible. Look, if you draw it properly they also overlap the base of the box. That cannot be—physically impossible. Do you see what I mean? You've got three objects occupying the same space."

Her hand touched his as she shaded the area overlapped by the oval bases of the bottles, the rectangular base of the box. He removed his hand, but smiled with the insight. "Ah, yes, I *do* see what you mean."

"The best way to do a still life is to start at the base. Then build upward. If you get the proximity of all the items right, the rest will follow—texture and shade and everything—but if you don't get the proximity right, the rest won't matter."

"You know, I always felt there was something wrong with that picture, but I couldn't put my finger on it."

"Always start at the base."

He was still smiling, as if nothing mattered but the drawing. "Always start at the base. Such an easy thing to remember. I have learned something already."

"What else have you learned?"

"What do you mean?"

She stepped closer, rubbing her breast against his arm, standing so close he could feel her breath on his face, the warmth of her body. "Have you forgotten our first lesson—after the party? Did you learn nothing from that?"

He took a deep breath, a step back. "Farida, I didn't know what I was doing. Very presumptuous of me and I'm sorry. I said so already. I have been thinking about it and if you are going to be my teacher then maybe you should just be my teacher."

She fastened her gaze, her mouth once more a thin straight line. "When did you change your mind? What made you change?"

"No—I didn't change. I just didn't know what I wanted. I was just making it up as I went along."

"That you found me attractive?"

"No, that, I do, still—but there are so many other considerations, no?"

"Such as?"

"You are my teacher. Where will we go? What will we do? What about the exams?"

"Those are not considerations. Those are blessings. No one will question us pre*cise*ly because I am your teacher. It gives us the perfect excuse to meet."

He looked at the floor. He shook his head. "I don't know what to say."

"Well, then, let me help you. I am going to give you something that might help you to make up your mind. I shall never refer to it again, and if you have nothing to say about it we will carry on with the lessons as if none of this ever took place. Do you understand?"

He stared uncomprehendingly.

"Wait here just a minute." She left the room, returning from her bedroom with a pair of white socks. "Here, take these. When the time is right you may return them to me."

He took the socks, frowning. "Socks? You want me to draw them?"

Farida was impassive. "I am going to be your teacher, Darius, but I am not going to spoonfeed you."

"But I don't understand. What are these for?"

She spoke without humor. "For your cold feet."

His head burned with his blush, the embarrassment of a child, but he packed his portfolio. "I shall have to think about it."

She remained impassive, no longer looking at him as if she had dismissed him already. "Do."

He left without another word, without a backward look. She walked him to the front door, wordless herself. She returned to her bedroom, drew the curtains, unfastened the ribbon from her hair, pulled her blouse from her slacks, and lay on her back seemingly ready to be embalmed, her attention flitting across the dark chandeliers above, the still ceiling fan, her bed large and arid as a desert. If he didn't return the socks there would be no lessons of any kind by mutual consent. The thought left her immobile, but resolute: if he lacked courage, she lost interest. It would not be the first time she had been wrong about a man; Rohini would have said she had never been right. She couldn't have said how long she lay in virtual suspended animation, wrapped in a cold quilt, awaiting the enchanted kiss of her prince, but when the doorbell rang again she scurried like a schoolgirl, fastening again the ribbon in her hair, stuffing her blouse back into her slacks, before Sashi knocked on her door. "Bai, Baba is come back."

Baba, not *sahib* or *seth*: Farida might have winced, but only smiled. His boyhood only gave them more cover. Fugitives from Nazis had been said to disappear into recesses too small to hide babies, snatching victory from defeat. So might fugitive lovers find opportunity in the obtuseness of others, strength in their own strangeness. "Bring him here, Sashi."

The door opened slowly, letting in light, Darius popping in his head. "Hullo, Farida?"

The fluorescent light came to life over her dressing table. She sat, stiff as before, brushing her hair, talking to his reflection under the light of the mirror. "Yes?"

"I came back."

"I see. Did you forget something?"

He walked into the room, holding out the socks. "I wanted to give these back."

She let him hold the socks, still brushing her hair, no longer looking at him, not even in the mirror. "Why? What has happened in the last few minutes to make you change your mind?"

"Nothing. I was … afraid. I have never … I didn't know …"

His voice grew smaller as he talked, words breaking into air, ceasing abruptly. She turned to look at him: the hand holding the socks had dropped to his side, his face was turned as if he had been slapped, but he made the effort to return her gaze, eyes wide and wary—and her stiffness fell like a waterfall. She had been too stern, punishing him first for his aggression, then for his passivity; this was Bombay, not Chicago; he was an Indian boy, not an American man; she had expected too much from her poor mannikin, her virgin man. Her face broke, almost into a cry. "Oh, my poor darling, I should have known. Come, come to your Farida. There is nothing to be afraid of."

Darius dropped the socks, scarcely daring to breathe, unable to believe his fortune, as if a game had been concluded, a blindfold removed, a treasure made his for the taking. He remained where he stood, arms at his side, but she was suddenly before him and his arms as suddenly full. He couldn't separate the mewling sounds, slippery tongues, slippery lips, his from hers, but followed her lead, exploring her with his hands as she explored him, leading to a sudden and painful airlessness in his jeans. Her hand was massaging his crotch, but he brushed it aside, adjusting his erection more comfortably within its confines.

"What's the matter?"

"Nothing." He grinned. "Just needed more space."

She nudged him toward the bed, tripping him gently onto his back, straddling his knees, undoing his belt, the buttons of his fly. "I will give you more space. I will give you all the space you need."

HORACE FISCH, MOVIEMAKER

The younger Farida Cooper caught the eye as much as the older—more, considering the Fifties favored girls over women, prompting some women to remain girls into their forties, mincing and primping and prancing beyond their prime, unaware of the passage of time until they were themselves in their fifties, many not even then, growing gnomish of mind and body while lapsing into lisps of babyhood.

Her hair was longer at twenty-two, thick and wavy to her waist, loosely clasped in a sandalwood barrette. Her black eyes were wider and easily widened by a discouraging word. Her belly, visible in the saris she favored in Chicago, was slender to the eye, plush to the touch. She had rarely worn saris in Bombay, favoring westernwear instead, symbol of modernity and freethinking in newly independent India, particularly among the Parsi peerage from whom she drew her identity—but in Chicago some imagined she might be colored for the color of her skin and saris made her seem more exotic while highlighting her roots.

Her best friend in Chicago, Rohini Mehta, a Gujarati from Surat (a few hundred miles north of Bombay along the coast), with whom she shared an apartment, wore nothing but saris, and she enjoyed the attention they received, walking together, high-spirited, bare-bellied, brown-skinned, Farida butterscotch, Rohini chocolate, both exotic on 57th Street in what passed for the commonest garb on Bombay's Warden Road.

They were the same age, but had not shared a single class, their disciplines rarely merging, Farida's English, Rohini's Biology. A chance meeting in the cafeteria had revealed a mutual desire to let their hair down, Rohini's as thick and black as Farida's, glistening with coconut oil, descending her back in a single plait to her waist, the extremity swelling into a bushy lion's tail. Her eyes were as wide, but her arms skinnier, her frame smaller. They shared a love of silliness neither had indulged, neither in childhood nor in adolescence, and found easier to indulge with the other than with anyone else, in no small part because both were strangers in a strange world, Indians in wonderland, accountable for the first time in their lives to no one but themselves. Falling behind her friend for a moment, Farida surrendered once more to the silliness, tugging on the sash of Rohini's sari, stopping her short. "I say, wait! Hold on a sec, no? Look, there's the Rapunzel house."

Had the sash been longer she might have spun her friend around; instead, Rohini not only stopped, but staggered backward; she might have fallen had Farida not spread her arms to catch her, staggering with her friend on four legs like two clowns in a horse-suit regaining their balance. Rohini giggled, flinging the sash of her sari once more over her shoulder. "I swear, Farida, you are going to make me have an accident. I *told* you I have to go to the bathroom!"

Farida returned giggle for giggle, leaning against her friend. "Sorry, sorry. Didn't mean to pull so hard—but look! Wouldn't it be lovely to live in that tower?"

"And do what? Sit and wait for your prince all day?"

The tower of which she spoke enclosed the stairwell of the house. Farida stared, eyes glittering, bobbing on the balls of her feet as if she might jump high enough to peer into the tower, hands limp at the wrist like a dog begging. "She *sang*, Rohini. Rapunzel *sang* all day long. How do you think she attracted her prince? He heard her *sing*ing. Otherwise, he would have missed the tower altogether."

"All right, all right, if she wants to sing she can sing—but what has that got to do with me? I have got better things to do with my time."

"Oh, what do you care? You already have your prince—Prince Rohit—and what a lovely prince he is, never bothering you, always there when you need him, even giving you his carriage."

She meant, of course, his car, in which Rohini had driven them to Hyde Park. Rohit Gupta, also from Surat, was older than Rohini by six years, a medical student with little time to socialize, leaving her to attend the party on 57th Street with Farida. "Only because of his guilty conscience—easier to give me the car than to come himself—and bad enough his mother treats him like a prince, don't *you* also go calling him one now. It will only go to his head, and you can be *quite* sure I will not hesitate to hold it against you." She giggled again. "The truth is we get along so well only because he never has time to do anything with me—but what about you? What about your Benjie?"

"Benjie?!! He's no prince. That's for sure. Always bothering me when I don't need him, never there when I do—nothing like your Rohit." Benjamin Bellows, older than Farida by a year, taller by a foot, was in the final year of a Master's in aeronautical engineering. "He doesn't care about singing—only about aerodynamics. Do you know what he said? He said he was only going out with me to balance his life. Everything else in his life is streamlined, including himself— tall and thin and poky, like a needle—but not me." She thrust out her breasts, giggling again. "I knew exactly what he meant, the swine."

"Did he really say that? What a thing to say."

"His idea of a joke. Engineers have a sense of humor like a … like an aardvark."

"Why an aardvark?"

"I don't know. Did you ever see an aardvark laugh?"

"I don't think I've ever even *seen* an aardvark."

"Then don't ask so many questions. Take my word for it."

Rohini took short quick steps, legs joined at the knees. "Farida, walk fast! I *really* have to go to the bathroom—*really, really, really*!"

Farida lagged, gazing at the Robie House on their right. "Don't be silly. It would be sacrilegious to rush past the Robie House."

"It would be even more sacrilegious if I went to the bathroom in front of the Robie House!"

Farida giggled. "I never thought about it like that." She caught up with her friend. "You know, now that I think about it, if Benjie ever heard me singing in the tower he would probably just go on riding his horse, or his carriage, or whatever, to wherever he was going, most probably some aeronautics convention, or something just as silly—a whole bunch of aardvarks sitting around a table, with spectacles, smoking cigars. Can you imagine?"

Rohini giggled again, but spoke fiercely. "Farida! *SHUT! UP!* I swear, if you don't shut up you will make me go to the bathroom in my sari."

Farida took her friend by her arm. "All right, all right, all right. Sorry. I promise to be good—but how much farther do we have to go? *Why* did you have to park so far?"

"Because *you* took so long getting ready. This *al*ways happens *every*where we go. You *al*ways take your own sweet time—and parking is *al*ways a problem."

"Yes, yes, blame it on me. Seems to me you should have thought about going to the bathroom before we left. Then we wouldn't be in such a hurry now—but where exactly is this Horace fellow's house anyway?"

"We are almost there. Look, you can even see his name on the door."

Horace Fisch was an English professor, returned from a yearlong sabbatical in Paris, but his first love was travel though some said it wasn't travel he liked as much as talking about his travels. No visit was complete, not to Paris, Venezuela, Hong Kong, Damascus, Sydney, unless he had a record of the visit with which to regale his friends; the visit remained unfinished until he had shared it with the world. He shot the places he visited with 8-mm film, accompanied his efforts on his return to Chicago with a music soundtrack interspersed with commentary on reel-to-reel tapes, and coordinated film, music, and commentary for the edification of his friends. Farida squeezed her friend's hand. "Such a small house?"

"Looks smaller than it is, deceptive—very deep, actually, quite huge—four bedrooms, just so many rooms one after the other. Just wait till you see the basement, where he shows the movies—at least three times the size of our flat."

"Four bedrooms! Oh, my! Who lives with him?"

"Nobody, but they were going to have a family—before his wife left."

"Oh, poor fellow! He must feel so alone, rattling around in that big house."

"Oh, so now it's a big house?"

"Arré, of course! Four bedrooms for just one fellow? What would *you* call that?"

The driveway held a row of five cars, including a Mercedes. The front door was ajar. Rohini knocked before stepping in. They stood in a foyer, steps leading up ahead to a darkened living-room, to their left the guest bathroom beside an open door leading to the basement from which music billowed. "They are in the basement, but I can't wait. I better go right away, but you go on. I'll meet you there."

Farida recognized the strains of Debussy's *Faun*, but shook her head, pointing up the flight of stairs. "I'm not going alone. You go to the bathroom. I'll wait upstairs. We can go down together."

"All right. See you later."

The upper room was dark, curtains drawn across the windows, a clear indication it was off limits to the party though not to Farida. Artifacts in the living-room bore testament to places Horace had visited—Japanese prints, African masks, French tapestry, Dresden china—but Farida ignored everything in favor of a stack of records lying by a Telefunken radiogram. She remained oblivious, sorting through albums by Martin Denny, Dean Martin, Rosemary Clooney, Bing Crosby, Henry Mancini, until a sound, a squeak, made her aware someone else was in the room and she turned. A man faced her, his mouth open, as if he had just spoken or were about to speak, but Farida spoke first. "Did you say 'eek'?"

"What? Oh ... um."

"Well, speak up! Don't mumble! Did you say 'eek'?"

The man, perhaps in his mid-thirties, wore a beach shirt of palm trees and waves and hula girls, and white trousers. In heels, she would have matched his height. He seemed boyish for a puffiness in his cheeks and jowls—but the color of his hair, the same as his complexion, a milky blond, made him appear albinal, even balding. Additionally, the deep indigo of his eyes made the rest of him seem almost invisible. A winged moustache added panache—but he seemed under a strain, brow dipping with concentration, eyebrows arrowing into his nose. "No. I just have a high voice."

Farida grinned, accepting his answer as a game. "Oh, and why is that?"

The man spoke softly, with apparent difficulty, seeming to choke on each word, but returning her grin, wings of his moustache fluttering. "A botched tonsillectomy. My doctor had a glass eye, so they tell me, and managed to remove just half my tonsils."

Farida laughed. "Oh, that's funny. You are a funny man."

The man smiled, the moustache took flight. "What are you doing here? The party's downstairs."

"I know. I'm waiting for a friend. She's in the bathroom. I thought I'd just look through the records while I was waiting. You can tell so much about a person by his taste in music, don't you think?"

"Do you think so? What did you find out?"

"Oh, I would say this Horace fellow is a bit old-fashioned, but not completely without taste."

"Isn't that presumptuous—I mean, considering you don't know … this Horace fellow?"

Farida laughed again. "Oh, don't be such a stick-in-the-mud. Of course, it's presumptuous—but I'm not interviewing him for a job or anything. This is just between you and me."

"Well, in that case, hell, I suppose we can be as presumptuous as we want."

"Well, hell, yes!" Farida turned back to the records, flipping through a couple more.

"You won't find any Elvis Presley, if that's what you were looking for."

Farida became more thoughtful. "How did you know?"

"All the young girls, that's all they want."

"And all the boys want to *be* Elvis."

"But not the men."

"Aha! *Now* who is being presumptuous?"

The man still smiled. "Guilty as charged."

Farida saw Rohini's head bobbing into sight up the stairs and looked again at the man. "I say, you wouldn't be that Horace fellow, would you?"

The man's grin could not have been wider. "Again, guilty as charged."

"*You* are Horace? Why didn't you say something instead of letting me make a fool of myself."

"Sorry. Rude of me."

"Yes, *ve*ry rude—and also very sneaky."

"Sorry again, but it was all so very charming I didn't want to end it."

Farida smiled. "Well, then, you are forgiven—if you found it all so very charming."

Rohini remained on the top step. "I see you don't need any introductions from me."

Horace nodded to Rohini. "Hi, Rohini. So glad you could come. Where's Rohit?"

"Studying." Rohini smiled. "So how did you find Paris?"

He moved toward the stairs. "Let's go see. The movie's showing in the basement."

He looked at Farida, inviting her to join them, but Farida stood her ground, shaking her head. "Horace, I'm really sorry. I could just kick myself. I *knew* about your voice, Rohini had told me. I should have known who you were, but I had to go and stick my foot in my mouth. I'm really sorry—really!"

He shook his head, smiling. "Think nothing of it."

Rohini grinned. "Lucky for you it's such a small foot and such a big mouth." She had mentioned to Farida that Horace cast among his students for commentators to compensate for the pitch of his voice, preferring a Chinese accent for his visit to Hong Kong, an Australian for Sydney, South American for Venezuela—preferring, also, always, women. She knew him through Paresh Patel, Horace's student and Rohit's friend, whom he had asked for an Indian woman to provide commentary for his India visit. He paid generously and Rohini had enjoyed the experience. Horace had left subsequently for Paris, leaving their friendship in the lurch until the invitation to his movies of Paris and environs, for which another student, Solange Bontemp, had vocalized the commentary.

Farida fixed Horace with a glare. "What are you doing here anyway? You should be downstairs with your guests."

"I thought I heard someone."

"So you abandoned your guests?"

"Oh, they're being taken care of. Ginger knows the drill. She's seen me do it often enough."

"Who is Ginger?"

"My ex-wife."

"Your *ex*-wife is your hostess?'

"We're best friends. It's the least she could do for getting her divorce so very easily, don't you think, just to be civil?"

Farida raised her eyebrows. "*Ve*ry civil, I must say—almost *too* civil."

"She's a Cassidy now. Her new husband—Raymond Cassidy—is also downstairs. We're all good friends now."

"O brave new world, that has such people in it."

Horace smiled. "You must be an English major, but I still don't know who you are."

Rohini's eyes widened. "Oh, I say, sorry, my mistake. Horace, this is my friend, Farida Cooper."

"Cooper? You don't mean the airline people, do you?"

The Coopers had sold Indian Airways, among the first of India's domestic airlines, to the Government of India. "Not anymore. It's now a government concern—but how did you know?"

"It's more difficult *not* to know if you've visited India, wouldn't you say? Everyone knows about the Coopers."

"Of course. Silly of me—or should I say charming?"

Horace smiled again. "You know, I think you would really enjoy the movies downstairs. Have you been to Paris?"

"Three times. Twice with Kaki, my aunt—and last year with my mother."

"How did you like it?"

"I liked Japan better. I just got back from a visit with my mother—my graduation present."

"Ah, how lovely. What about your father? Doesn't he ever accompany you on your travels?"

"My father went to Japan the year before." Her father had gone with another woman and Farida preferred to make light of the matter than explain. "They're very strange, my parents. My mother always does everything my father does—but a year later. Don't even ask."

"I understand. I just told you about me and my ex-wife." He shrugged. "Don't even ask."

Farida laughed. "My father's nuts about movies too, shoots everything he sees just like you, also does music and commentary just like you—and my mother plans her own trips according to the movies of *his* trips. I don't think she even likes to travel much, but she doesn't like to be left out either. She wants to do everything my father does—but not with him."

"Really? What a coincidence—about your father's hobby, I mean."

"Not really—I mean, it's the obvious thing, isn't it, once you've got a movie, to put a soundtrack to it? My father belongs to the Cine-Society in Bombay, full of people just as nutty as himself, and every single one of them makes movies of everywhere they go, and every single one of them supplies a soundtrack with commentary—and every year we have a show, one fifteen-minute movie from every member of the society, and all the families pretend they enjoy everyone else's movies when all they want to do is talk about their own."

"That sounds like fun."

Farida shook her head. "No one is interested in the movies except their own. Most of them are bloody rubbish. They come for the food and the socializing."

Horace laughed. "I still say it sounds like fun."

"Of course, you would. You could bring all your movies."

Horace nodded, smiling, all but ignoring Rohini, as was Farida. "Maybe you could help me with a commentary sometime?"

"You've got Rohini for that already, haven't you—I mean, for your India movie?"

Rohini shook her head, implying she didn't need to be the only commentator, but Horace didn't see her. "Not about India. I still have more movies about France for which I will need a commentator."

"What about Solange Bontemp?"

"She's leaving for Paris next Wednesday."

"But I thought you wanted a French girl—I mean, for France."

Horace shook his head. "I've been thinking about it, and I don't want to be so anal anymore if I can help it. I mean, all I truly need is a more pleasant voice than my own."

"It's not such an unpleasant voice as all that."

"It's not as pleasant as yours."

Farida laughed. "Well, no, I suppose not."

Rohini shook her head. "Careful, Horace. You will give her a swelled head."

Farida flashed her friend a glance. "Too late for that. I was born with a swelled head." She turned back to Horace. "Actually, I have Rohini to thank for keeping me from getting *too* swelled a head."

Horace smiled. "And vice versa, I'm sure—not that Rohini is anything but a model of stability."

Rohini deferred the compliment with a smile. "Shouldn't we be going downstairs?"

Horace nodded. "Yes, perhaps, after all, we should."

ROHINI HELD OPEN THE BASEMENT DOOR allowing a shaft of light to lead Horace and Farida to the bottom of the stairs, seating herself on the top step. The basement, visible in the cone of light from the projector, revealed next to it a reel-to-reel tape-recorder and people in rows of chairs on either side of the beam. Farida couldn't see much else at first; even the tail end of Solange Bontemp's accented narration sounded muffled; but she recognized the opening bars of

Ravel's *La Valse* following the commentary. She recognized also the scene onscreen, a nude woman leading four uniformed men in what appeared to be a conga line on a stage, and bending forward whispered in Horace's ear. "Yvonne Menard, Folies Bergere."

Horace turned his head, smiling, nodding approval. "Very good, but watch what happens next."

The second of the men in the conga line, with his hands on the hips of the first, reached around the first to place his hands as well on the naked flanks of Yvonne Menard, upsetting the rhythm of the man in the middle. Flailing to keep his balance the first man grabbed Yvonne Menard, but she twisted out of his grasp, letting him fall, and the second man fell on top in a tangle. The third and fourth men approached Yvonne Menard, one from behind, the other from the front, attempting a clumsy sandwich while they kept the tempo, but Yvonne Menard stepped out from between them, flung her arms to the ceiling, and the orchestra played a resounding climactic chord, signaling the end of the performance. The two fallen men picked themselves up and all four made theatrical bows before Yvonne Menard kissed each goodbye escorting them off the stage.

Solange Bontemp almost giggled through her narration. "For the French, the Americans in the audience are as entertaining as the show itself. They behave like kittens with a skein of yarn or puppies with a rubber ball—or maybe they are just being American, young as only their country is young, and unsophisticated as only the young can be. Fortunately, a trouper as experienced as Yvonne Menard knows when to give them a bone and when to show them the stick."

Horace shook his head. "Americans have so much to learn."

Farida whispered again. "They were better behaved when I saw the show last year— almost too shy to do anything at all."

Horace grinned. "So were these guys when she first picked them from the audience—but I guess something happened to them when they got onstage."

The movie came to a close, timed to coincide with the last flourishes of *La Valse*. THE END zoomed into visibility from a dot in the center of the screen, drawing applause more thunderous for the reverberations in the basement. Someone switched on a light;

Horace switched off projector and tape-recorder. A woman stood by his side in a tube dress of red and white vertical stripes, hair in a bouffant. She appeared slim, but Farida could tell from her style of dress and hair that she was plump, the dress concealing the width of her waist, her hair the width of her face. "There you are, Horace. I wondered what happened to you. Now I know." She stared at Farida, her face expressionless, smiling and speaking like a professional hostess. "Very nice, but aren't you going to introduce me to your new friend?"

Horace grinned, rewinding the spool of film. "Farida, I'd like you to meet Ginger."

Farida held out her hand. "Ginger? Hullo. I love your name."

Ginger barely touched Farida's hand, her smile close-lipped, heels adding stature to a five-foot-two frame. Farida matched her height in sandals. "Thank you. I might say the same about yours. My name is actually Gloria, but we had a ginger cat with the same color hair when I was growing up." She shrugged, touching her hair. "But what about you? I thought I knew all Horace's friends."

"I came with Rohini. I don't know anyone else."

Rohini waved, getting up from her step to join them. "Hullo, Ginger. Good to see you again. We met one time—at the India movie. Maybe you remember?"

"Rohini! Of course I remember! You did the commentary! How are you?"

Rohini smiled. "Can't complain. I heard you got remarried?"

"Oh, yes! He's right around here somewhere. Raymond?"

"Also in the English Department?"

"No, honey. One of those was enough. He's a businessman—electronics or electricals or some such thing." She looked around. "Raymond!"

The basement held thirty or forty, most dressed casually, sweaters and jeans, sack-like dresses after the fashion of the time, full skirts over frilled petticoats. Some remained seated among the rows of collapsible chairs, others wandered for a refill of plates and glasses from a table at the far end of the room. They seemed to be Horace's peers from the snippets of conversation Farida overheard, members of the faculty of Chicago University. A large man, easily over six feet, towered over Ginger, glass in hand, smiling at Farida, hair gleaming in a thick black pompadour. "Yes, darling?"

Raymond Cassidy wore a pink satin shirt, narrow black tie, baggy black pants. Ginger introduced Rohini as the woman who had provided commentary for Horace's India trip, Farida as Rohini's friend. His handshake was as vigorous as Ginger's had been languid, his smile showing as many teeth as Ginger's had concealed. "That was funny, wasn't it, the way they fell all over that French poodle?"

Ginger's smile was as icy as her delivery. "She wasn't a poodle, darling. A poodle is a dog."

Raymond seemed unfazed, not even looking at his wife. "Yes, but a *French* dog." He winked at Farida. "Ginger thinks very literally, wouldn't you say?"

Farida's smile was as glacial as Ginger's. "I'm not sure I would say anything at all."

Raymond laughed, but no one said anything until Rohini turned to Horace. "I'm actually surprised you were allowed to film the sequence at all. I would have thought they might have had restrictions about such things. I mean, what is to stop you from exhibiting it commercially yourself?"

Horace was rewinding film and tape, keeping an eye on projector and recorder. "Well, it's really not the same as being there, of course—and I didn't shoot the entire revue, just enough for a taste—"

Raymond interrupted—"which serves as a commercial for the rest of the revue for us crazy American hounds."

He grinned at Ginger, daring her to contradict him, and she answered as coldly as before. "I think, darling, they might call us mongrels rather than hounds."

Raymond laughed. "Touche, darling! Touche!"

Horace placed the reel back in its canister. Someone asked him about a camera lens, someone else about Paris. Ginger asked Rohini about her boyfriend whose name she had forgotten. Raymond leaned over Farida, smiling. "Fa*ree*da, is it?"

"Yes?"

"What's a pretty girl like you doing in a place like this?"

He had not whispered the question, but leaned forward, speaking confidentially. Farida laughed, eyes widening in surprise. He was a handsome man and she smiled in reply. "Do you know something about this place that I don't?"

He grinned, taking her elbow. "Just kidding. Come on, let's get you a plate."

He was too familiar, but Farida succumbed easily, seduced by his sheer bulk, wishing not to appear a prude, particularly not in the company of adults rather than the students to whom she was accustomed. "All right. Let's go. I must say I'm famished."

She threaded her way through the company, steered by the large hand gripping her elbow, heaping a plate for herself at the makeshift buffet table with canapes, finger sandwiches, and toothpicked sausages. Someone at a bar no less makeshift than the buffet table was mixing cocktails. Someone else played a Kingston Trio record. Raymond brought her a glass of wine at her request.

"Do you think things would have been different with Stevenson?"

Crossing the room they had overheard someone criticizing Eisenhower for dragging his feet in support of the Supreme Court decision for "deliberate speed" regarding school integration. A prevalent topic of conversation that month had been the National Guardsmen in Little Rock barring black students from entering Central High School. It was an academic dogma that Stevenson would have elected intellectuals to positions of authority: poets, professors, philosophers, writers, and wits. "Don't you?"

Raymond grinned, shaking his head. "I'll tell you a secret. There's only one difference between intellectuals and nonintellectuals. Do you know what it is?"

"Why do I have the feeling you're going to tell me no matter what I say?"

Raymond's grin broadened. "Do you always answer questions with a question?"

"Wouldn't you, if it served your purpose? Now are you going to tell me the difference, or are you going to ask me another question?"

Raymond couldn't stop grinning. "The difference is this: nonintellectuals know how little they know; intellectuals don't."

Farida raised her chin. "Well, then, are you going to say Socrates was a nonintellectual?"

Raymond lost his grin, momentarily silenced, staring as if her face were changing before his eyes.

Farida grinned seeing him lose his grin. "You know what I mean. He said a wise man was wise only insofar as he knew how little he knew."

Raymond's laugh erupted like a roar over the company, drowning momentarily even the Kingston Trio. "I know what he said, Fareeda! I know what he said! I don't know why I never thought of it before myself. I suppose I would say he wasn't an intellectual. He was wise."

STEERING ROHIT'S TOFFEE DESOTO OUT OF ITS PARKING SPACE, Rohini cast a glance at Farida. "So, what did you think? Did you have a good time?"

Farida buried her face in her hands. "Oh, I had a great time, but that poor fellow, Horace—so sad, and his eyes so blue. You don't have to be Perry Mason to see he is still in love with his wife."

Rohini raised one eyebrow. "No need to be so dramatic. Did you really think so?"

"Arré, of course! Didn't you see? So obvious from the way he kept looking at her, hoping she would say something to him, begging like a dog for a bone—lighting up like a rocket when she gave him the crumbs of her attention."

Rohini kept her eyes on the road. "Hmmm. Very literary of you."

Farida giggled. "Hmmm, and very facetious of you—but I'll tell you one thing. She sure didn't do herself any favors. Did you get a good look at that Raymond fellow?"

"Why? What was wrong with him? You two seemed to get along like gangbusters."

"Shows how much you know. I thought he looked quite common, actually, didn't you?"

Rohini raised her eyebrows. "Common? I didn't think so. Quite handsome, actually—a bit like Elvis, I thought."

"That's *just* what I mean. He should act his age—like Horace. I mean, Elvis is *our* age, for God's sake. Who is he trying to impress? He should learn to accept himself for what he is."

Rohini smiled to herself. "You mean like Ginger has accepted him for what he is?"

"You are just full of facetious today, aren't you? What did you think of her anyway—Ginger? Such a cold fish I thought."

Rohini laughed. "Well, now, are you asking me what I think, or telling me what to think?"

"Asking! Of course, asking!"

"It's none of my business, Farida. She seemed all right."

"I think she should just stay away from him. What is it to her? She has her Raymond, for what he's worth, but I suppose you are right. It's really not our business, but I must say I don't understand the attraction. She seemed so plain."

"She's very rich, you know."

Farida giggled. "So am I! So what? 'The Best Things in Life Are Free.'"

Rohini laughed. "Yes, of course. The rich man's song of justification, but what about the poor man's song: 'Diamonds Are a Girl's Best Friend?'"

"Oh, Rohini, you are not being serious. I suppose it's good for her ego to have two men fussing over her—but she's not thinking about Horace at all, only about herself."

"Don't you think that's up to the two of them—or the three of them at most?"

"Of course, but Horace is in no position to bargain. They have each other, he has no one. They should just leave him alone, let him get on with his own life, but as long as she is around he will keep on pining for her, looking at her like an 'ol' houn' dog—cryin' all the time.'" She giggled again. "It's a boost to her ego, don't you see?"

"Of course, I see—but it's still up to them what they do—not any of our business."

"Yes, of course. You have your Rohit. What do you care about the troubles of others?"

"And what about you? You have your Benjie."

"Oh, Benjie. What does he know? Nothing about anything that has anything to do with anything except aeronautics."

"I thought you liked him."

"Of course, I *like* him. What is there not to *like*? But we are so different. I am an English major, and he is a … he is an aardvark." She giggled again. "Do you know what he said to me once? He said an English professor is someone who makes a living by teaching that he has no way to make a living except by teaching English. Very clever, don't you think?"

"Yes, very clever. I was there when he said it—but you a*greed* with him when he said it. That's why you got the job at Goldinger's."

Farida had been trained alongside other graduates in merchandising techniques at Goldinger & Co. "I applied because I didn't want to go straight for a Master's and I didn't know what else to do—but mainly because of Benjie. He doesn't want a wife who is bored to tears when he isn't around. First of all, if that's his idea of a proposal he's got another think coming. Secondly, it's very presumptuous of him to think my world is going to revolve around him. And thirdly, I have no desire to get married right away, maybe not even later, and certainly not to him."

"Does he know this?"

"Not in so many words."

"In how many words?"

Farida sighed. She didn't want a husband, didn't know what she wanted, perhaps just time to find out what she wanted, but she had dated Benjie for a year and assumptions seemed to have been made despite what she might have wanted. "All right. He doesn't know it, but how dare he assume it!"

"Don't you think you should talk about it?"

Farida looked straight ahead. "You know what I think? I think that when a girl is accustomed to a certain level of comfort in her life it is her prerogative to maintain it—or her husband's prerogative."

Rohini gave her friend a sharp look. "Farida, pardon my plainspeaking, but you are talking rot! That is exactly the kind of thinking that led to all those stupid men jumping off the Empire State Building after the Crash—all because they couldn't maintain their level of comfort. If you define yourself by your level of comfort you are just as stupid as them."

Farida gave her friend a pitying look. "I *don't* define myself by my level of comfort. *You're* the one who is talking rot now. All I meant is that Benjie knows something about how we live in Bombay, and he said it would be good for me to learn what it means to earn a living. It was all his idea, this job at Goldinger's. He doesn't understand at all. It's the kind of understanding that comes with maturity. Benjie's still very immature. Women mature sooner than men, you know."

"What do you mean? Do you mean you don't want the job?"

"No, I think it's a good idea—but it wasn't *my* idea. I didn't know what else to do—so I agreed."

"And what *do* you want to do?"

"I still don't know—but I want to find out be*fore* I get married."

"I think you and Benjie better have a good long talk—and better sooner than later."

Farida sighed again. "This would be so much simpler if I knew what I wanted—or if I were madly in love with Benjie—or with anyone, for that matter—someone who *real*ly needed me. That would be so nice, to be madly in love, but Benjie couldn't care less. He has no imagination. He just wants a wife, someone who will take care of him like his mummy and not embarrass him too much. That's all."

Rohini laughed. "You sound like all the romantic heroines I have ever read about, from Cinderella to Madame Bovary."

"Ah, yes, but they came to very different ends, didn't they?"

"Yes, but one of them was a fairy tale."

"Oh, Rohini, didn't you think he looked very sad?"

"Who? Horace?"

"No, King Kong! Of course, Horace!"

"Oh, yes, very sad—a real sad sack he looked."

"I swear, Rohini, if you weren't driving I would pop you one. He looks nothing like a sad sack. It is just how people look when they have been battered by life. It's a matter of maturity—something I think Horace knows about—but not you."

Rohini laughed. "Right, just what I need, a good battering."

Farida sighed yet again, shaking her head. "Oh, Rohini!" She looked out of the window, picturing Horace's moustache poised for flight and his eyes blue as a lagoon.

II

Farida adjusted the wavelength of the radio on the dashboard of the Studebaker station-wagon. Paul Anka was singing, *I'm so young and you're so old*, reminding her of the difference between her and Horace—but Horace seemed oblivious, eyes on the road. His pink shirt had surprised her, but the grey sweater covered it, and the baggy grey pants were more in keeping with her image of him. He was the oldest man she knew other than her professors and friends of her parents, and she was determined to be mature without seeming stuffy, though stuffiness seemed relentlessly to follow maturity. She sighed, rolling down the window, but he stopped her. "Would you mind very much not doing that? I catch cold easily."

She rolled the window up again. "No, I don't mind." She grinned. "You must have been one of those sickly kids."

He took a short breath. "Well, I told you about the problem with my tonsils."

She was aware once more of his voice, soft and high and choking and hesitant. "Oh, I say, I *am* sorry. I wasn't thinking. I was just joking."

His eyes remained on the road. "But you're right. I *was* sickly, still am to some extent. I almost died as a baby, not even a year old. They never did figure out what it was, but apparently I maintained a high fever for more than a week, and my breath was very strained—like a sputtering kettle, my mother used to say. It was probably related to the problem with the tonsils, but they never could be sure. She didn't sleep that entire week—and after I was well again she wanted more children—a reserve, she said, just in case something happened to me—but it never happened—no more children, I mean, no matter how they tried."

"It was the same with me, but not because I was sickly—because I was a girl, and my father wanted a male heir—but it never happened either. They were stuck with little ol' me." She giggled, more nervous than she had imagined.

"Well, then, you must know something about how it is. My mother was overprotective, and I grew up with all the defects of an overprotected child—namely, no immunity to anything. The joke in the family was that I could catch cold from staring at an ice cube."

Farida laughed, settling into her seat. They planned to record the commentary for the remainder of the Paris movies. He had picked her up from the apartment she shared with Rohini on Dearborn and Division and they were on their way to his house in Hyde Park. When she had refused payment, he had insisted on squiring her back and forth and inviting her to dinner, the very least he could do, and she had agreed. "This is such a large lovely comfortable car. I could just live in it."

Horace smiled, finally looking at her. "I'm glad you dig it."

She smiled back, imagining he was making an effort to be hip on her account, the pink shirt no less a concession to her age. "Oh, yeah, I dig it all right. It's so far gone, man, it's invisible."

Horace laughed. "Just don't get too far gone or you'll lose me. I'm old-fashioned, remember?"

"Yes, I know, but it *is* a lovely car, and I love to be driven. I like it so much I don't even care where we go."

"So what you're saying then is that you like to be taken care of. You want someone to take care of you."

Farida shook her head vigorously. "No, not at all! That is *not* what I am saying! What I'm saying is I can drive if I have to, but I like to be driven, not to have to pay attention to the traffic—so boring."

"But that's just what I'm saying—not that you can't drive, but that you would rather not. You want to be taken care of and let someone else do all the boring work."

"Well, maybe you're right, but I don't think about it like that. I want to be taken care of, but only as long as I want to be taken care of. If I wanted to be let out of the car this minute and you let me out, then I would want to stay—but if you refused to let me out, I wouldn't want to stay."

"Hmmm! Existence precedes essence."

"What?"

"Sartre—that's very existential, what you just said, isn't it?"

"Well, I don't know about that. All I know is what I want."

Horace almost laughed. "*Exact*ly! You're proving my point. Sartre is all the rage in academic circles, especially in Paris—but don't worry. If anything, it means you're more hip than you know."

Farida smiled, understanding she had been complimented though the compliment wasn't clear. She had heard of Sartre and existentialism, but knew little. She didn't care to understand more, but didn't want either to appear simple or stupid. "Well, I was just going to say that I don't care *what* you call it, but *if* I am an existentialist, I am an *in*nocent existentialist."

"Well, then, we're on the same page. What you're saying is that you want to be taken care of, but only as long as you're able to take care of yourself. If you were unable to take care of yourself, then you would no longer want to be taken care of. Am I right?"

Farida laughed. "Now you're talking. That is e*xact*ly what I mean. Taking care of me is a privilege and only I have the right to bestow that privilege on anyone. I wouldn't want just any old TomDick&Harry to take care of me—but if I were *not* able to take care of myself it would *not* be a privilege, would it? It would be charity—and who wants that?"

Horace laughed. "Spoken like a true Cooper."

"Hah! As if you would know how a Cooper speaks—but enough about me. Let's talk about you instead. Tell me about your mother. Is she still overprotective?"

"Not anymore. She's dead."

"Oh, I'm sorry. I never seem able to say the right thing."

"It's all right. It's been almost five years now—kidney failure."

"What about your father—or dare I ask?"

"He's still around—lives in Ann Arbor with his new wife—both dentists."

"Was your mother also a dentist?"

"No, she wrote."

"Wrote what?"

"Stories, for magazines—even had some published. She was more literary than my father. She named me after Horace, the poet. She had taken one of his phrases as her motto: *ut pictura poesis*—'poetry like painting.' My mother applied the phrase to prose as well. Prose must be memorable, she said, not just for what it says, but for *how* it says what it says—and poetry renders the dullest prose memorable. Even Shakespeare, for all his insights, would have remained unknown if not for his poetry."

"Your mother said that?"

"She gave examples. 'The quality of mercy is not strained' or 'Mercy is abundant in the world.' Take your pick."

Farida smiled. "'Friends, Romans, countrymen, lend me your ears' or 'I say, everybody, listen to me!'" She burst into a laugh. "'A rose by any other word would smell as sweet' or 'Romeo would smell the same even if he changed his name'—hey, that even rhymes!"

"You've got the picture."

"I like that—poetry, like painting. I wish I might have met your mother."

"I think you would have got along well. She wanted me to be a man of letters—"

"But you *are!*"

"Not really. I'm a professor—which, strictly speaking, is a man of letters, but my mother meant an artist, a poet, or a novelist. Professors, along with readers and nonreaders alike, are mere bystanders."

"Oh, but surely not."

He turned to her, pale blue eyes almost colorless. "It's all right. I'm happy enough with my choice, though she wasn't—nor my father. He wanted me to be a dentist—but I can't stand the sight of blood. I should warn you, I faint rather easily."

She spoke soberly, unsure whether he was joking. "Actually, so do I—arrhythmia." When he said nothing, she grinned. "Maybe we should swoon together sometime."

He smiled, eyes again on the road. "Indeed, maybe we should—maybe we shall."

"Dreamer! I wouldn't swoon with just any old TomDick&Harry."

His smile widened, but he said nothing. He was sorry to see, getting out of the car in his driveway, that she had pulled the sash of her sari across both shoulders, covering even her plush bare midriff, looking as demure as a model girl from India. "You must be cold in that sari."

She shook her head. "Not really, but you're right, it's pretty much the end of the season for saris—I mean, it's not winterwear. I mean, I could wear a sweater over it, but what to do with the sash? It only gets crumpled, and nobody sees it anyway. It's back to skirts and stockings and pants and blouses for me in the winter, but not for Rohini. She insists on wearing saris, even under sweaters and coats, but I just can't be bothered with all that ironing."

"It's very becoming—a sari, I mean—very elegant."

Farida smiled, turning toward the house. The Mercedes was again in the driveway, but a light in the kitchen window told her it might not belong to Horace as she had imagined. "It looks like there is someone in your house."

"Oh, it's only Ginger. She's cooking dinner."

"Ginger? Your ex-wife is cooking dinner for us?"

"Yes. I told you, didn't I? We're still good friends."

Farida raised her eyebrows. "Yes, but you didn't say *how* good. She's married to someone else, but she's cooking dinner for you?"

"And for you too."

"Yes, and for me—a bit unusual, isn't it?"

"I suppose so, but that's how we are. Our friends do find it strange, but if Raymond doesn't mind I can't see that it's anyone else's business, can you?"

"No, of course not. I'm just surprised. That's all. Raymond doesn't mind?"

He shook his head. She was disappointed to hear it, but said no more.

HORACE LED HER INTO THE HOUSE through the garage entrance, up the stairs to the living-room where he had first surprised her among his records, and into the kitchen on the right. "Yoo hoo! We're home."

"And just in time! Dinner's almost ready."

The kitchen was large, divided by a wide counter: stove, sink, refrigerator, on one side; dining table large enough for six on the other, one end set for two. Ginger faced them from the stove across the counter wearing blue jeans and an orange sweater with a crew neck the color of her hair. Farida smiled, spoke demurely, clutching the sash of her sari tightly around her shoulders. "Hi, Ginger. So good of you to cook dinner for us all. Thank you so much."

Farida's smile was irreproachable, but something in her voice betrayed her disappointment, and Ginger answered her unasked question. "Oh, you're welcome, honey—and don't worry. I won't be staying. You're just better off having me cook for you than Horace."

The sash around Farida's shoulders loosened and so did her voice. Sunk in her disappointment at finding Ginger in the house, she had been late recognizing the significance of the two table settings. "I wasn't worried—I mean, I can see the table is set for two. I was just surprised—you know, thinking about your husband and all that."

Ginger smiled. "I know. It's all very confusing, but that's what we want—and if Raymond doesn't like it he can lump it. I know he feels guilty about stealing me from Horace—but that's just silly. It wasn't anything like that. It's just that Horace is so helpless without a woman. He can't do a thing for himself. He'd lose his head if it weren't fastened to his shoulders."

Horace grinned. "Wait until you taste her Chicken Islander. You won't have any complaints."

Farida became aware of the aroma, a sweet stew, but also a competing smell, more acrid. "Oh, but I don't have any complaints. It smells heavenly. Chicken Islander?"

Ginger stirred one of two skillets on the stove before covering it again. "It's a recipe I learned when we were honeymooning in Hawaii—chicken with pineapples, tomatoes, and green peppers. It's been a favorite ever since."

The reference to the honeymoon seemed proprietary, even inappropriate considering Ginger's circumstances. Farida crossed the room to the stove. "I can hardly wait—but what is that other smell?"

"That's for Horace, grilled mutton kidneys. It's a favorite of his—but there's enough for two if you want some."

Horace smiled, raising his chin, reciting lines from memory. "'Most of all he liked grilled mutton kidneys which gave to his palate a fine tang of faintly scented urine.'"

Farida screwed her face in distaste. "What the hell are you talking about?" Horace kept his smile, his chin in the air, but offered no explanation, and Farida turned to Ginger. "Do you know what he's talking about?"

Ginger nodded. "Yes, I do, honey, but I'm sure he will want to tell you himself."

Horace hadn't moved and spoke again with the elocutionary tone. "A favorite food of the incomparable Leopold Bloom from the incomparable novel by the incomparable James Joyce."

Farida's eyes widened in comprehension. "You like Joyce? You like *Ulysses*?"

Horace shook his head. "Oh, my dear girl, 'like' is not the word."

Ginger smiled. "'Like' is, indeed, not the word."

Farida frowned, resenting the joke they seemed to share against her. "I read *Ulysses* this summer. I took it with me to Japan."

Both stopped smiling, turning to face her. Horace exhibited the most interest she had witnessed in anything yet, indigo eyes deep as an ocean. "Really? *Ulysses*? And?"

"I took a guide along, and thank God for that. I would have been completely lost otherwise."

Horace smiled again. "Of course, of course, but what a world it conjures, what vistas it reveals!"

Farida laughed. "I have to say I enjoyed the guide better than the book—more fun to read what he was trying to do than what he did—I mean, I liked the concept better than the execution. Sometimes, I don't think even the author of the guide knew what he was talking about."

Horace lost his smile. "He probably didn't, but Joyce would have said intelligibility was beside the point. The music of the words was everything. He was composing a symphony in words."

Farida grinned. "Well, if that's the case then Beethoven and Brahms have nothing to worry about. Symphonies should have melodies like novels should have stories. There is no *story* in *Ulysses*. Two people roam the city of Dublin, one is wracked with guilt about his dead mother, the other with jealousy about his cheating wife, and the climax occurs when the two meet. That is *it!*"

Ginger laughed, but Horace stiffened, standing behind the counter like a professor behind a lectern, leaning forward on his hands, blue eyes turning black. "Where is it written that every novel should have a story?"

Ginger's smile got fuller and she no longer spoke like a professional hostess, no longer seemed on guard. Farida liked her better for the difference, an ally in her sally against Horace, and kept up the attack, enjoying herself immensely. "Actually, it was Rossini who said music should have melody and fish should have sauce. It follows, then, does it not, that novels should have stories? Q.E.D."

Ginger laughed again, but Horace smirked. "Spoken like a true bourgeois."

His tone was at once hesitant and condescending, but he seemed unwilling or unable to explain himself further. Farida stopped short seeing the impasse to which she had driven him. "But I also liked some things about the book—not the intellectuality, not the cleverness, I hate showoffs, people who try too hard, but the language was sometimes very incantatory, very poetic—painting, like poetry, like your mother said—for example, when he talks about the sky at night." She closed her eyes, reciting from memory. "'The heaventree of stars hung with humid nightblue fruit.'" She opened her eyes, grinning. "See, I remember what's worth remembering—not your urine-scented kidneys."

Ginger turned narrowed eyes on Farida, but Horace laughed. "I see you are not completely without hope, Farida Cooper—and that is at least a beginning."

He might have said more, but Ginger interrupted. "It seems my work here is done. Raymond's expecting me for dinner. Horace, all you have to do is spoon the chicken and the kidneys into serving dishes whenever you're ready to eat. I'd do it myself, but it would get cold if you didn't eat right away."

Farida clasped her hands, turning to Horace. "Oh, let's eat first. The smell will otherwise drive me crazy—and, please, Ginger, why don't you stay—especially after you have gone to so much trouble?"

Ginger shook her head. "Thanks, honey, but I'd only be in the way—but don't worry. Horace will be all right now that you've put him in his place about Joyce."

"Oh, I wouldn't say I put him in his place—but can I help it if I like Joyceans more than I like Joyce?"

She turned wide bright black eyes on Horace who beamed as she had expected. Ginger smiled. "No, I suppose you can't—and I daresay Horace prefers it that way." She turned to Horace. "Pay attention now, Horace. There are two salads under foil and a bottle of Chablis in the refrigerator, also a peach souffle—and rolls in the oven. If you're going to eat first, I'll put the chicken and kidneys in serving dishes before I leave."

Horace opened his mouth, but Farida spoke first. "I'll do it. I insist. You have done enough, Ginger. Thank you so much, but I'll take it from here."

Horace looked from Farida to Ginger. "We will manage. Thank you, Ginger."

Ginger looked at Farida. "I feel better now. Horace needs someone to look after him—you know how Jewish men are. Can't do a thing for themselves."

Farida took salad bowls out of the refrigerator, removed the foil, placed them on the table, removed rolls from the oven, and spooned the chicken and kidneys into separate plates, while Horace saw Ginger to her car. She offered Horace the Chablis to open when he returned. "I can't believe you two are divorced. You seem so perfect together—even now. What happened—that is, if I am not being too nosy?"

Horace smiled, a sheep in his face. "It's no secret. She needed a manlier man—and I, as she said, needed someone to take care of me. It was that simple."

"Oh, but I cannot believe that. What do you mean, a manlier man? Someone with muscles? I cannot believe she is so shallow."

"No, not muscles, though he's got muscles—just size maybe. You've seen Raymond. He can come on like Rock Hudson when he wants to. She said he was so big she could almost live inside him like in a house—you know how tiny she is. She said he made her feel safe. The irony is, of course, that she was the one with the big apartment—and he moved in with her."

"But that is just as shallow. I cannot believe that any more than the muscles."

"We were both very young. Neither of us knew what we wanted." He shrugged. "Anyway, it's over, and we're much happier divorced than we ever were married. She has someone to take care of her, and I still have her sometimes to take care of me. Guilt probably has something to do with it, but best not analyze these things too closely." He poured the wine and they seated themselves. "But what about you? Do you have a boyfriend?"

Farida sighed. "Ah, alas, yes."

Horace's eyebrows rose. "Alas?"

Farida shook her head. "My Benjie is a very sweet boy—very tall, but skinny, not big like Raymond—but he has no notion of what makes me tick, not the slightest—no interest, not an iota, in literature, art, music. He thinks it is all just entertainment, but for me it is life itself."

Horace raised his glass in a toast. "To life itself!"

She clinked his glass almost absentmindedly. "He takes it for granted that we are going to be married, but he has never even asked me. He thinks you just get married and everything works out—automatically, just like that."

"And what do you think?"

"I think a woman needs to be won." She giggled suddenly. "No, she *yearns* to be won."

Horace passed her the rolls. "So what are you going to do?"

"I don't know. I think I'm waiting for a sign or something—almost waiting for him to do something stupid so I'll know for sure—but he's too careful to do anything stupid. He's an engineer, aeronautics. They never do anything stupid—engineers."

"Well, it seems to me that's a no-win situation. You're waiting for him to do something stupid—but you resent him for being too careful to do anything stupid. It doesn't seem to me you really want to be with him at all."

Farida's eyes widened. "You know, I think you hit the nail right on the head. See, he would never understand that because he is just a boy—but you were able to put your finger on it right away. I think it has something to do with maturity. You have it; he doesn't." She grinned. "Girls mature faster, you know—but how to tell him that?"

He nodded, offering her the kidneys, but she passed, helping herself to the chicken. "You're going to have to tell him, you know."

She sighed. "I know. Rohini says the same thing. I just don't know how."

He smiled, his voice steady. "I'm sure you'll work it out. I have faith in you."

"It's just such a bother." The kidneys sat between them, Ginger's signature on the table. She raised her head, peering into Horace's pale blue eyes. "Next time, I will do the cooking."

HORACE'S BASEMENT APPEARED LARGER for being empty, but a gooseneck lamp provided an island of light around the projector and tape-recorder when he changed reels, and the room became cozier yet when lit only by the projector beaming images on the portable screen erected midway across the room. He and Farida sat on collapsible chairs, a collapsible table before them bearing popcorn and soda, a freestanding microphone adjusted to Farida's level, Horace synchronizing projector and tape-recorder beside her.

The screen revealed the interior of a dark café, a petite, smiling, dark-haired woman dancing on a table, swishing her skirts, providing glimpses of white thighs, a gay crowd clapping in unison. Horace wished he might have had the original music to which she had danced, a gypsy band with fiddle, accordion, and tambourine, but he had compensated with a recording of Brahms's "Fifth Hungarian Dance," lowering the volume of the music to accommodate Farida's commentary. She smiled as always at the sheer exuberance of her own voice, what Horace had pronounced in his faltering tone as the sound of a waterfall, marbles pitterpattering on a marble floor, diamonds on glass, providing more *ut pictura poesis*.

"As you can plainly see, the European woman is not as buttoned down as her American counterpart. Rosie the Riveter has given way to Betty Crocker. We had more pizazz in America during the war, more of the can-do spirit, but with the return of our soldiers our women left the workforce in droves, surrendering their jobs to the men who had saved them from Hitler, and returning themselves to their time-honored roles of wives and mothers. The European woman does no less, but maintains a *joie de vivre* throughout her life which her American counterpart seems to lose upon tying the knot."

Farida had enjoyed the social and topical references, the pop philosophizing, as much as the movies themselves, and though he had written the commentary himself she had found him amenable to suggestion, making her a partner in the enterprise. Her laugh, bubbling as she read the commentary, might have seemed to contradict its theme, but as Horace had been quick to remind her: one, she wasn't married; and two, she wasn't American. Farida might have said that Indians were no more apt to dance on tables than Americans, but had been too flattered to carry the dispute further.

She had enjoyed their first session so well she had insisted on cooking for the second, preparing a lamb curry she had learned from Rohini, and enjoyed the second so much better even than the first that she had found courage to make the final break with Benjie. His response, as bankrupt of emotion as she might have expected from an aardvark, had convinced her further that she had made the right choice, down to his reply when she had suggested, following in the footsteps of Horace and Ginger, that they remain friends: *I don't think so. I think a clean break would be best.* They had been seated with chocolate malts at The Jailhouse, Elvis singing "I Want You, I Need

You, I Love You" on the jukebox. Benjie was so tall, even seated, that he appeared disapproving for his height.

She had seemed the sorrier of the two though she had initiated the break, but her regret had been minimal, reinforcing Horace's contention that she had wanted the break long before she had admitted it. Horace was the softer man, needing her more—but also the more mature man, which was what she needed herself. Benjie would bounce and spring back to life like an antelope, but Horace would break without a woman, and in his weakness she had found her utility, his maturity complementing her strength. Additionally, he was settled, lived well if not lavishly, and nothing could have suited him better than his professorship: a girl needed the kind of stability he could provide, and he needed nothing more than a girl.

The third time they met they had concluded the commentaries, celebrating with hugs and kisses, popping a champagne cork. She had told him about the break with Benjie, and driving her home he had kissed her again, more lingeringly, his hand skimming her breast, light as air, but not so she wouldn't notice. It would take him another couple of weeks synchronizing film with music and commentary, after which he wished to invite her to what might be their last session. She had breathed a little too quickly, spoken a little too soon: "I can't wait ... to see the finished product."

Piano music by Poulenc played as the camera ferried one last time across the Seine, climbed one last time the façade of Notre Dame, rising to clouds crossing the sky like an armada, and closing credits scrolled up the screen, listing music, composers, and performers, but providing as well one last unexpected credit: COMMENTARY AND EDITORIAL ASSISTANCE BY FARIDA COOPER. Her smile burst the boundaries of her face and her applause rivaled that of an auditorium. "Hurrah, Horace! Hurrah! What a fine piece of work! I do wish you could meet my father. I swear you two would get along like a house on fire. You would go ape talking about cameras and lenses and whatnot."

Horace switched on the gooseneck lamp and rewound the tape as the film spooled through the projector. "I would love to. He sounds fascinating." The end of the film unwound from its reel and whipped the projector rhythmically creating a pinwheel shadow on the floor until he set it to rewind.

"By the way, thanks for the credit. I wasn't expecting it."

"Why not? You did the work—for nothing."

"Still, I didn't expect it." Beyond the oasis of lamplight the blackness of the basement stretched like a Sahara. She smiled, lowering her voice to a whisper. "So, what shall we do now?"

The question was suggestive, but Horace kept his eyes on the rewinding reel. "Anything we want, I suppose, now that our work is done."

"So what do you want to do?"

"What would you like?"

She wanted him to take the lead. "I don't care. You're the man. You tell me."

"Well, I'll tell you what. Let me put everything away first and then we'll see."

"All right. Take your time. I'll just get comfortable." She retired from the light of the lamp to the darkness of the sofa against the wall, playing with the sash of her sari in her lap, watching him in the pool of light put reels back in their cases, the projector in its box, close the tape-recorder, dismantle the screen. The darkness gave her a point of vantage; she might have been watching him from a keyhole, under a microscope, but he finally extinguished the lamp, joining her on the sofa, and the spell was broken. In the sudden darkness she felt herself as much a specimen as she had imagined him moments before, until he put a hand on her bare midriff. "Brrrrr, Horace. Your hand is so cold."

"Sorry." He removed his hand to her haunch, rubbing her sari for warmth, inserting his other hand in her hair, clasping the back of her neck.

"Horace, your other hand is just as cold."

He laughed, removing his hand from her hair. "Sorry again."

She felt the breath of his laugh on her cheek and gave him her mouth. He was a good kisser, unlike the boys to whom she was accustomed, who imagined the harder they thrust their mouths, the more they wiggled their tongues, the more passionate they seemed and the better the kiss. She preferred the gentle touch and Horace couldn't have been more gentle, lips nibbling lips until she herself opened her mouth probing his lips with her tongue, inspiring as gentle a response from his tongue as his lips. When his hand squeezed her breast she moaned, but when the same hand, warmed now by her thigh and breast, returned to her bare midriff, she resisted. "Horace, what are you going to do?"

"Nothing that would make you uncomfortable."

"I would like us to go slow. I would like us to take it easy. I hope you don't mind. I'm still … you know … inexperienced."

Horace chose his words with care, but amusement brimmed in his tone. "Of course. I never imagined anything else. We can take it as slowly as you wish."

"Thanks, Horace. I really appreciate it. I do like you—very much, but … you know. Mustn't rush into these things."

"Of course not, but here's something to think about." He leaned away from her, putting on his elocutionary voice, staring into the blackness of the wall behind them. "'I have known many women make a difficulty of losing a maidenhead, who have afterwards made none of making a cuckold.'"

"Where is that from?"

"Sir George Etherege, *The Man of Mode; or, Sir Fopling Flutter*—a restoration play, 1676."

"Very clever, but I'm afraid I'm even more old-fashioned than that. I would still want to be married first."

Horace laughed again. "Well, then, if you're foolish enough to marry an old fart like me, maybe we should just get it over with before you come to your senses."

Farida was stunned into silence, torn between pleading he wasn't an old fart and scolding him for making her feel foolish. "Oh, my God, Horace! Is this a proposal?"

"If you want it to be."

"Don't be wishy-washy, Horace. Is it or isn't it?

"Let's just say, then, for the sake of argument, that it is."

Farida took a deep breath. "Horace, you are making me very angry. This is no time for jokes."

"Who's joking?"

"Horace, really! We hardly even know each other."

"But I *am* serious. If people thought too much about whom they married no one would get married. You have to go with your feelings in these matters—and hope for the best. Ginger thinks we make a fine couple."

"Ginger? You have talked about this with Ginger?"

"We talk about everything. I value her opinion. She knows me very well."

"Then why didn't you stay married. I swear, Horace, I still don't understand you and Ginger. It makes no sense that you still want to be friends. That is supposed to be the hardest part of a marriage, to be friends with your husband—but here you have got a divorce and you are still good friends."

Horace nodded silently, no longer looking at Farida. "It is unusual, I agree."

"Is there something else you want to tell me about her?"

"I suppose I might as well tell you now as later."

"Tell me what?"

"Actually, I alluded to it once before. The reason we are all still such good friends is guilt. The crux of it is she and Raymond became lovers while we were still married. She liked me, but she loved him, and she felt caught between the two of us. There, now you have it. That's the whole story."

Farida's eyes widened, her jaw dropped. "Horace! Oh, my God! I'm so sorry."

"It's all right. We've all come to terms with it. I'm only telling you because I would like you to understand." He caressed her arm. "*Do* you understand?"

She crossed her arms. "Horace, this is all too sudden."

He clasped his hands in his lap. "I know—but at least now you know."

"Horace, guilt for them I can understand—but why guilt for you? You did nothing wrong. Why do you keep up the friendship?"

"I question my motives for marrying her. She was a catch, you know, the only daughter of Forrest Woodrow Burnham, with a line of suitors as long as Lake Shore Drive, and she was interested in *me*. We met at a dinner at the Illinois Art Center, a function to foster art in the city—Burnham was one of the sponsors. Ginger played the Rachmaninoff "Prelude in C sharp minor"—quite splendidly, I might add—and I impressed her, so she said, with some comment about Joyce. I was different from the men she was accustomed to meeting, mostly bankers and businessmen—and, as for myself, I was just dazzled by the luxury of it all, their lifestyle, their houses, their holdings. I mean, I'm not a pauper, especially not with this house my father gave me at a time in my life when most couples are still buying their tiny little first houses—but I'm hardly in a class with the Burnhams. I was very surprised she was the least bit interested, but I supposed I was something of an experiment for her, the pre-Charles Atlas man—you know what I mean, scholarly, academic, more likely than the next to get sand kicked in his face."

"You mustn't say that. Only men with sand for brains kick sand in other people's faces."

Horace smiled. "Well, thanks for that, but I think the fact that her parents didn't entirely approve also made me something of a prize. It was the classic poor little rich girl syndrome—you know, neglected childhood, glamorous parents always on the go. I think it accounts in part for how impulsive she is. She said she was madly in love with me—but seeing how quickly she fell in love with Raymond I think now she was only in love with being in love. I was simply too weak not to find her irresistible."

Farida might have said her own childhood was similar except for Kaki. "Not weak, Horace—everyone wants to be loved. It is the universal condition. Some are rich, some are poor, some are ugly, some are beautiful—but all of us want to be loved. We are all vulnerable in that respect. Thank you for telling me all this. It helps me to understand better."

Horace nodded. "Of course. I was just too young to know better at the time—and she was very remorseful, and so was Raymond, but they were in love, and they wanted to get married." He shrugged. "What else was there for me to do?"

Farida knew about the Burnhams, bankers and industrialists, not unlike the Coopers, and was struck by a sudden thought. "Horace, you know, considering what you have just told me, I can't help wondering if the fact that I am a Cooper has any bearing on your proposal."

He shrugged again. "What can I say? I'd be lying if I said it made no difference, but it's hardly the most important thing—or even the second. It's just nice."

"Well, at least that's honest."

"But I wouldn't make the same mistake again precisely because of my first marriage. You're a very different person from Ginger."

Farida saw more similarities than differences, both of them rich, artistic, neglected, without siblings, interested in Horace, but it was enough for her that Horace saw differences. "What was that again that you quoted about maidenheads and cuckolds?"

"'I have known many women make a difficulty of losing a maidenhead, who have afterwards made none of making a cuckold.'"

She laughed. "I thought you were being a wise guy, but that makes a great deal more sense now."

Horace grinned. "I'm just a blooming cuckold who wants to make a maidenhead."

She slapped his arm. "Very clever, Mr. Blooming, but don't think I didn't get your pun."

"Never crossed my mind."

"So you have no more feelings for Ginger? She was just a mistake?"

"Yes, chalk it up to experience. Everyone is allowed at least one mistake, maybe even two or three. Look at Liz Taylor."

"*You* look at her. She may be all right as an actress, but as a wife she is a complete failure. Not even thirty, and already three marriages."

"Yes, but she keeps trying—and that's what counts. Practice makes perfect. Most people just make the best of it, however bad a marriage may be, but not her. She needed an older man. Mike Todd is twenty years older, but maybe she needed to go through younger men first to find out."

Farida spoke gently, understanding his insecurity better, wishing to reassure him it was misplaced. There was a difference of twenty years between her own parents, but that was not necessarily a recommendation; too many factors played in the mix. "Ah, Horace, so that is what this is all about. Why didn't you just come out and tell me? You are afraid you are too old for me?"

"Well, no—I mean, yes and no."

"Well, which is it? Yes or no?"

"Well, yes, I'm afraid *you* might think I'm too old for you—but no, *I* don't think I'm too old for you. You know the findings of the Kinsey Report, don't you?"

"No, I don't. What does it say?"

"Well, among other things, that a woman in her mid-thirties and a boy in his late teens are the best suited because they are both then at their sexual peak."

Farida laughed. "Fat lot of good that does. I mean, we're just the opposite, aren't we?"

"Well, again, yes and no. It also says that a man in his mid-thirties and a girl in her late teens—or early twenties, in your case—are also best suited."

"But that *is* just the opposite, isn't it?"

"Yes, but the reason is different. You see, a man is already in the dawn of his decline by then, and a girl in her late teens is better suited for him than for a boy her own age with raging hormones."

She laughed. "Are you saying you are in the dawn of your decline?"

"Not me—I mean, the words are mine, but the sentiment is Kinsey's—but I think there might be some truth in it, don't you?"

"Actually, yes, it makes sense—but what happens afterward, when the girl reaches her thirties and the man is by then in his fifties?"

"Well, ideally, I suppose, he finds a woman his own age, because in their fifties the hormone balance is about the same in men and women—and *she* finds a boy in his late teens."

Farida laughed so loudly she surprised herself. "I swear, Horace, I will just die laughing. So everyone should have at least three marriages: first to an older person, then to a younger person, and finally to a person of his or her own age."

"Precisely! And everyone takes care of everyone's children. If we accepted that as the norm, I think we might all lead much happier lives, don't you? It's only because we're brainwashed into thinking there's only one person in the world to make us happy that we remain so damn sad. Plenty of marriages end in divorce—and plenty of marriages that don't, *should*."

She laughed again. "Such a philosopher you are, Horace. In any case, tonight I just want you to take me home. You have given me a lot to think about."

"All right, but don't think too much. You know what happens then."

She stopped laughing immediately, raising her chin in the air. "Don't tell me not to think. I will think as much as I want. If you have learned nothing else about me, you should know I will always do what I think best—whatever you or anyone else may say."

He grinned. "Sorry again. Of course, you are right. Actually, that is one thing I noticed about you from the start. It's what I like best about you."

She wondered if she had been too emphatic. "All right, then. That is a good start."

III

Ginger had been playing the piano for almost two hours, part of her wedding gift, showing no sign of running out of repertory, alternating between classical and popular music. She was good enough to be on the concert circuit, and as if to showcase her ability concluded her performance with Mendelssohn's *Midsummer Night's Dream*, coaxing the piano to sing the Overture like a chorus of violins, breathe the Scherzo like a flute quartet, and announce the Wedding March like a brace of trumpets.

Once Farida had given her consent she had surprised even herself with her haste, but she wanted to honeymoon in Bombay, introduce Horace to family and friends, and they had no time to lose if they wished to keep the hot humid breath of a Bombay March from their backs. If Horace was surprised, he was no less delighted. They had planned a civil service and reception in the Hyde Park house, easier than shopping for a church and hall at short notice, inviting about sixty guests. If it were a large celebration he wanted, she promised he would get more than he bargained for in Bombay with none of the bother.

Farida had moved out of the apartment she shared with Rohini with a show of triumph at beating her friend to the altar. Rohini, disbelieving at first, had been indignant, even chiding her friend. *It is not a race! It is not a coup! This is not a question of roping a husband like a steer in a rodeo. This is for keeps, for the rest of your life. What is your hurry?*

Farida had been moving too quickly for a rational response. *Maybe not <u>just</u> like a rodeo, but the literature of marriage is full of tricks and traps and snares and stratagems. Those who play the game well get what they want; those who don't get trapped.*

She was smug, but Rohini had even less patience with her friend's literary justification. Every pro had its con, every Darcy his Lovelace, every Juliet her Lady Macbeth. The key was to examine each incident on its own merit, but Farida seemed fonder of the sound of her words than their meaning. *That is a very strange notion, I must say—but in any case, what is the hurry?*

Farida was too pleased with herself to give it more thought. *No hurry, but why wait? I want him to see Bombay at its best, before it gets too hot—and I don't want to wait a whole year for that. Now just give me your blessing like a good friend. Lectures I can get anywhere. You were, after all, the one to introduce us. Just be happy for me.*

For *me*, she had said, not for *us*. Rohini had recognized the futility of further objections. She may have introduced them, but only incidentally; she had encouraged caution and been rebuffed. She was not like Farida, but she was her friend. She knew Horace, but not as Farida knew him. She had smiled. *Of course, I am happy for you. I wish you only the best. That is why I am hesitant. This is happening so fast!*

Farida's parents had promised a reception at the Willingdon Club and telegraphed congratulations no less bewildered than Rohini's, her mother concluding: *Whatever happened to that Benjie?* Farida had soared through arrangements for the wedding, but the day itself found her subdued. She stayed with the group around the piano, Ginger suddenly a closer friend, an ally more than Rohini who stayed with Rohit knowing he was uncomfortable among large groups of Americans. Farida had organized the event and delegated so well among her friends she had nothing to do but be a bride, but felt she wasn't living up to her billing. She was relieved when Horace reentered the room, leading the applause for Ginger. "There she is, my Bronze Bombshell! Farida, darling, would you play us something? I've been singing your praises, but I need to back them up."

She was his Bronze Bombshell, he her American Albino, and she knew what to do. Her voice felt no less stiff than her body, sitting too long unused, but she smiled, glad for the invitation. She rose, once more her old self, applauding Ginger out of the piano bench, seating herself, launching her husky contralto into "Young Lovers," accompanying herself with chunks of chords much like she was strumming a guitar, large black eyes like hooks on Horace as she crooned the tune:

> *For every girl in this world*
> *There is a boy whose only joy*
> *Is that girl in his world.*

IV

Farida giggled so hard she almost choked in her effort to stay quiet. "Oh, my goodness, Horace! Have you gone crazy or what? Look at you—big hairy naked man dancing on his tiptoes like a little girl."

They were in her childhood bedroom, she still in bed, he performing an arabesque in the curtained room, a white dolphin in the morning darkness. "You hit the nail on the head, Mrs. Cooper. Mr. Fisch is crazy—stark raving bonkers about his gorgeous new wife!"

She had maintained her name, not relishing the sound of Farida Fisch. His voice was strong, as it had been since the time of their marriage less than a month past. She shook her head to mark her disapproval, but could no more stop giggling than wipe the grin from her face. "Flatterer! He is stark raving bonkers all right—but don't go blaming it on his wife. For God's sake, put on some clothes, Horace. This isn't Chicago. We are not in Hyde Park. There are other people in the house."

Horace leaped across the floor, belly jiggling, penis flopping. "Who cares? People in love are a special breed. They are not like the masses. They are not bound by the same rules. They breathe a rarer air, they feed on kisses—and they dance. Their every move is a dance." He pirouetted to her bedside, thrusting his loins in her face.

She hid under the covers to muffle her giggles. It was not the first time he had danced for her naked, what he called his Victory Dance, performed first after their first lovemaking the morning after their marriage—but the dance seemed particularly ludicrous in her childhood bedroom. "Shame-shame, poppy-shame, Horace. Kaki might be just outside. For God's sake, be quiet!"

Horace plopped on the bed beside her. "Why? We're married, aren't we? What's the problem?"

Farida raised the covers inviting him in. "No problem—just, you know, don't want to unnecessarily embarrass her."

"Oh, yes, of course, the spinster aunt."

"Don't make fun. She's my mother more than my mother. I told you."

"Yes, you did—and I must say I'm curious." He slid under the covers, cupping a breast.

"About what?"

"I don't think your mother likes me very much—I mean, your real mother."

"Oh, don't pay any attention to her. She's just jealous."

"Of what?"

"Of us—of our happiness. It's just the way she is. If she isn't happy, she doesn't want anyone else to be happy, not in the whole world."

"Why isn't she happy?"

"It's a long story."

"We've got time."

"But it's so boring."

"Not to me, it isn't."

"Oh, all right, I'll make it a *short* story—for my lord and master."

He nuzzled her neck. "Well, it's plain to see you're no Scheherazade, but make it a *good* short story. You never know. You might want to publish it some day."

"I'll do my best. My mother was a mature eighteen-year-old when she got married, but my father was an immature thirty-eight. You know what I mean. She was very serious and he was not. He was having a gay old time—as he will still tell anyone who will listen—but he needed an heir. Well, the marriage pool is small enough for Parsis in India, not to mention in the world, and smaller yet for Coopers—for whom, of course, no one is good enough—"

"Except a Fisch!"

"Rich Americans are always an exception."

"They have to be rich?"

"Of course. Will you let me get on with the story?"

"Sorry."

"All right. Now, as I was saying, my mother was very young and very pretty" (Farida laughed) "as *she* will still tell anyone who will listen."

"She is that—she is very pretty."

"It runs in the family—but anyway, the first year she had a miscarriage, and the next year she had me, but of course they wanted a boy—so she had three more miscarriages before the doctors advised against trying again. The long and the short of it is that she stopped trying, but my father didn't. I told you about his Japan trip—well, he went with someone else. Of course, my mother always says she prefers to go on her own, or with me."

"Maybe that's it! She doesn't like me because I've stolen her traveling companion."

"Don't flatter yourself, Horace. You're not that important to her and neither am I. The trouble is they should have got a divorce long ago, but my mother would never agree to it. The Cooper name is too precious to her. Besides, she pretty much burnt her bridges when she became a Cooper, thought she was too good for all the Batlivalas—her side of the family—all the *poor* relatives, and now they all think she is a snob—which she is."

"Some might say she's a very modern woman, turning a blind eye to her husband's shenanigans."

"Grinning and bearing it, you mean—but she's nothing of the kind. She has no choice. She's convinced he still wants sons, that he's still trying for heirs—at least, that's what she tells herself."

"But how would that—I mean, that would hardly be legitimate, would it?"

"Of course not. It makes no sense to anyone except Mummy—but you can't talk to her about this at all, and I don't think Daddy even tried. He's really a very easygoing fellow as long as he gets what he wants—and, being a Cooper, most of the time he does. It's a good thing the Cooper enterprises don't rely on his business acumen. We'd be in a hole so deep it would reach all the way to ..."

"Chicago?"

She laughed. "Yes, very good, Chicago. Anyway, that's my mother's story, since you asked."

"Hmmm, pity. I almost feel like I'm being forced to choose between your parents, but I'd like to be friends with both."

"Impossible—and in any case too late. You've already chosen, even before we came that was a done deal. If you think she doesn't like you, that is the more likely reason than that you have stolen her traveling companion. You have bonded with her husband."

He knew what she meant. They had been in Bombay just three days when her father had hosted an evening of his own movies and Horace's, and made plans to visit the Cine-Society with Horace that afternoon while Farida planned a reception for their friends with her mother and Kaki. "As I said, a pity. I'm closer to her in age than to your father—even to you."

"She's only five years older than you."

"That's what I mean. We might have been great friends."

"Don't kid yourself."

"All right, maybe just good friends." His hand slid to her bellybutton, following the crisscross hairs leading farther south.

"What are you doing?"

He knew she was sensitive about the hairy strip. "Following the trail of breadcrumbs home."

She giggled. "Already? Didn't you just go home? Didn't you just do your Victory Dance? I thought you said you were in the dawn of your decline."

"I am, but you have turned back time, sent planets spinning out of their orbits."

She turned to face her husband, eyes in soft focus. "As if—but so romantic you can be, my Horace, my husband."

He flexed his penis against her thigh. "You have raised a phoenix."

She giggled again, gripping his hand between her thighs, pulling on his hip. "Come, come home, my love, to your Farida."

BY THE TIME FARIDA CONVENED IN THE DINING-ROOM with Kaki and her mother to finalize plans for the reception it was three o'clock. The reception was still two weeks away, but in between she and Horace had plans to visit Goa, Mysore, and Bangalore. He had visited much of the north during his first visit, and Kashmir was at the top of their list for a summer visit. He had left at eleven in the morning with her father to visit the Cine-Society for a showing of *Cinerama in Osaka: 1955*—"a shooting of the shooting of the third cinerama film," as her father liked to say, shot by his friend Phiroz Bomanji.

The lunch dishes had been cleared, but her mother had littered the dining table with women's magazines, suggesting they might give Kaki and Farida ideas for the reception, but sitting then to one side herself, *Peyton Place* in her lap, Chopin waltzes on the gramophone. Farida was surprised her mother had lunched with them at all instead of downstairs in her own flat, but that seemed as much of a concession as she was willing to make to her daughter's visit. She didn't doubt her mother was glad to see her, but as with so much about her mother the gladness fell short, her hugs kept her at arm's length, her kisses bussed the air around her face, as if anything more robust than the lightest touch might seem vulgar.

Her father, in all things her mother's antithesis, argued that a Cooper by definition couldn't be vulgar, his mere presence transmuting lead to gold, implying that his wife, for all her affectation, would remain a Batlivala to the end of her days. He smothered Farida in a bearhug to underscore his argument, almost slurping her with kisses, holding even Horace as he might a prodigal son. They seemed to live in a gilded cage, too blinded by their own glitter to see the cage, to see even themselves as people first instead of Coopers, but in this they were no different from the public who also saw them as Coopers first.

The telephone rang, Sashi answered, calling Farida from the doorway. "It is the American sahib."

Farida excused herself but was back within minutes, face stiff with anxiety. "Something has happened to Daddy. He fainted at the Cine-Society. Horace went with him in an ambulance to Breach Candy. Everything is under control, he says, but we should get there as soon as we can."

Breach Candy Hospital was a ten-minute walk from Blue Mansions; there was no doubt the most excellent care would be taken of her father; the hospital had named a wing after Nariman Cooper in deference to the Cooper donations; but they wasted no time, taking Kaki's Buick, her driver Sunny at the wheel. Kaki was businesslike and efficient though her concern for her brother was never in doubt, but Farida would have sworn her mother had seemed almost hopeful, eyes widening, brows rising, like a child receiving an early birthday present.

Persis Cooper maintained an admirable composure at the hospital, speaking from her husband's bedside as if they were at dinner, not even touching his arm lying outside the blanket. "We came as fast as we could, Nariman. How are you feeling?"

Farida joined Horace on the other side of the bed, Kaki stood behind her mother. To Farida's surprise and relief her father was grinning, looking much as if he were waking from an afternoon rest. If anything she was surprised how young he looked—sixty-three, but seeming no older than fifty, hair as thick and full as at twenty though greying at the temples, flesh more slack around his jaw, and tiny black hairs curling untidily from brows a girl might otherwise have envied.

"Sorry, Persis, old thing, but I am afraid you will just have to wait a little longer. As you see, I am perfectly all right, good as gold."

Persis stiffened, swaying almost imperceptibly back a couple of inches. "What a thing to say, Nariman. I know that is your way of joking, but you will give Horace completely the wrong idea."

Her husband couldn't stop grinning. "Too late for that. He is now a member of the family. If he doesn't know the truth yet, he will learn it soon enough."

"Enough foolish talk, Nariman. What happened? Just tell us what happened."

Nariman lost his grin. "Nothing, absolutely nothing, just the damn arrhythmia acting up again—but try telling that to the bloody fool of a doctor. He wants to take all kinds of tests—blood tests and God knows what else. Fat bloody chance is what I say." Arrhythmia, an irregular heartbeat which caused blackouts in moments of stress, was the curse of the Coopers, a genetic affliction affecting both Nariman's father, Hormus, and his grandfather, the patriarch, the venerable Jalbhai Kekobad Cooper, fount of the Cooper enterprises. "Do you know what the bloody fool said? He said my heart doesn't beat once. He meant to say, of course, that my heart skipped a beat, but the damn fool didn't know any better. I told him I should bloody well have kicked the bucket a long time ago if my heart didn't beat once. I swear I don't know where they get these ghatis—and at Breach Candy! Bloody uneducated Indians everywhere. You wouldn't have heard such nonsense in the time of the British."

His mouth twisted, mocking the doctor's uneasy command of English. Kaki, standing behind Persis, stroked her brother's knee. "What was the incident, Nariman? What set off the seizure this time?"

Nariman grinned again. "I was sitting next to that wench of a woman, Shobha Shirodhkar—and she was giving me the eye. I think the excitement might have been too much for me."

Persis's eyes turned to marbles, but Farida slapped her father's hand. "Shut up, Daddy! What a thing to say! Stupid old man!"

For the first time Nariman was caught off guard, flinching at the slap, seeming to shrink against his will, opening his mouth to speak but saying nothing, seeming suddenly older even to Farida who had imagined him so young just moments earlier, an old man with his mouth popped open. "Sweetie, it was just a joke—just a harmless little joke."

"Well, it wasn't funny—and not that harmless either. Come on, Horace. We will wait outside."

Farida was striding out of the room when Horace raised his eyebrows, shrugged at the company, and followed her out. Kaki stroked her brother's knee again. "No need to get excited, Nariman. Let the doctors take their tests. Then come home. We could all use some rest."

Nariman frowned, looking at his sister. "Nergesh?"

"Yes, Nariman?"

"What the hell's the matter with that damn girl?"

PERCY FABER AND THE SYNCOPE

F arida?"

"Yes?" Farida looked up from a pad on which she was making notes. It was the time of day she liked best, before everyone arrived, sitting in the privacy of her cubicle, sipping coffee in between bites of a poppyseed bagel slathered with cream cheese, gathering thoughts for what needed to be done, prioritizing the work of the day. Percy Faber stood in the doorway of her cubicle. "Morning, Percy."

"May I come in?"

"Of course."

Percy sat in one of the two chairs across from her desk, head gleaming in the fluorescent light. "It's none of my business, but I've been meaning to ask you. Is everything all right?"

Farida sighed, gazing over Percy's head. More than the cold of a Chicago winter she hated the shorter days, absence of sunlight, darkness when she left her apartment at seven in the morning, darkness when she left The Mandalay Market at five in the evening, never a step in daylight. She could wear clothes against the cold, but do nothing against the darkness except wait for spring and use the brightest wattage in her apartment, but these were meager compensations. She shook her head, not knowing herself whether she meant yes or no, afraid of what Cindy Anderson might have said. "It's the season. Just dressing in the morning takes more effort and organization. I'm always more tired in the winter."

Percy nodded. "I wanted to let you know that Cindy's very happy with your work. She can't sing your praises enough."

Farida's smile was tightlipped. "Thanks, but that's mostly to Cindy's credit. She's so easy to work with. I'm very happy working with her. Just wait until spring and I'll even be able to show it."

It was a feeble joke, but she was gratified to see Percy smile. She found comfort in routine, in doing what needed to be done next, and in doing so had made herself indispensable to Cindy Anderson who had initially echoed praises back to Percy first voiced by himself. Of the four supports of her life (job, education, apartment, lover), her job remained the most dependable, allowing her to accept the disarray into which the others had fallen, but after just six months on the job she had begun making mistakes: once misaddressing outgoing mail, confusing her clients; another time matching surveys for armored crotch underwear with a list of recipients of diarrhetics, creating unintentional mirth among the interviewers, wasting the time and money of the client; and most recently confusing the demographics of two surveys, the most serious and time-consuming of her offences to correct.

She had worked late to clean up the confusion and Cindy could not have been more patient, but it bothered her that she had been so unlike herself, so stupidly careless. She understood why she had been careless, but found herself helpless to change, telling herself instead to relax, and wondered suddenly what Cindy may have told Percy. "How is everything with you?"

Percy might have said more, but his attention fastened on her lips, speckled with black dots.

"What's the matter? Why are you staring?"

"Sorry. I was just admiring your lipstick. I didn't think you wore any."

"I don't. I'm not." She touched her lips, brushing away poppy seeds. "Oh, I'm embarrassed now." She wiped the rest of the seeds from her lips with a napkin. "Poppy seeds, from my bagel."

Percy laughed. "I thought it was a new kind of lipstick—you know, like the nail polish designs."

"That's not in the polish. Those are false nails. You can buy them."

"Can you really? I know I'm behind the times, but I can see stippled lipstick taking off like a rocket—lips by Lichtenstein. It could make millions."

Farida laughed, feeling better, grateful for Percy in her life despite the other problems.

"Well, if you're sure everything's all right, I won't keep you anymore."

Farida sighed again. "Yes, everything's … all right."

"You don't seem convinced."

"It's just—it's nothing to do with work."

"If it affects your work, it's something to do with work."

She was sure then Cindy had said something. "Are you free for lunch?"

His eyebrows rose. "Not today. Tomorrow?"

She nodded. "Sure. It's not important—but it's … something—an explanation, anyway."

"All right. Tomorrow, then?"

She nodded again.

ELLA FITZGERALD SANG "ALWAYS" ON THE RADIO. Farida lounged in Alma's welcoming armchair, relieved she had made it through another workday without serious mistakes, wondering what she would say to Percy the next day at lunch. She called to Alma in the kitchen, preparing their treat for the evening. "I hate that song. It's such a lie."

"Aw, hon, you know you don't mean it. It's a pretty song."

Farida got out of the armchair to join Alma. "I *do* mean it. It has *no*thing to do with life."

Alma stayed at her task, lathering slices of apple pie with whipped cream, but not without a glance at Farida's glum face. "Hmmm! I don't know about that, but there's a story behind that song I want to tell you. Why don't you pour the cider and come to the table?"

Farida envied Alma: married to one man for fifty-eight years, she knew nothing of heartache, but knowing nothing of heartache she knew nothing of life, but knowing nothing of heartache was a blessing in itself; she lived, content to read, crochet, lunch occasionally with friends, and chat interminably on the telephone with terminally housebound friends who called themselves the Telephone Tabbies. Alma was seated when Farida poured cider from the pitcher in the refrigerator and brought the glasses to the table set with napkins and spoons. She liked Alma's stories, but wasn't in the mood for chitchat. She wouldn't have visited, feeling as she did, but it was easier than canceling.

"We were in a bar in Cicero, me and Homer."

Farida nodded, spreading whipped cream over her pie and over the sides.

"He was playing that song on the piano, but at a quicker tempo— you know, that honkytonk rhythm. He had his own way of doing everything. I never knew a man to play the piano like my Homer."

Farida kept her eyes on the pie, listening without interest.

"Anyway, this group of men came in, all in hats and coats and business suits—and they slammed cuts of meat down on the bar, telling the bartender how they wanted their steaks, and ordering drinks."

Farida's cynicism rose to the surface. "That was considerate of them, to bring their own meat."

Alma ignored her. "The leader of the group told Homer to stop playing—but Homer just went on like he never heard him."

Farida looked up, her spoon halfway to her mouth.

Alma nodded, glad for her attention. "He had a scar on his face, and this walking stick, and he pushed Homer's coat from the piano to the floor with his stick."

Alma spooned pie into her mouth, taking her time. Farida understood she was milking her attention and played along. "Then what happened?"

"Well, Homer got his coat from the floor and would have put it back on the piano and gone on playing—but I knew something was wrong and I stopped him"—her face was triumphant—"and it was a good thing I did. The man with the scar went back to his pals. It was Al Capone. If Homer had gone on playing he might have been killed." She laughed. "I never stopped telling him he owed me his life."

Farida was enthralled against her will. "Wow! Al Capone! You saw Al Capone!"

Alma laughed. "And I almost didn't live to tell the tale!"

"Always" was followed by the news. The president was being castigated because a Lebanese magazine had revealed that the U.S. government had traded arms for hostages in Iran.

Alma's eyes turned glassy as they listened. "I wish they would just leave the man alone. For once we have a president who knows what he's doing and they won't rest until they've beaten him down."

Farida would not have taken the bait, but in her ugly mood she couldn't resist. "I say this with all respect, Alma—but I wish it had come out sooner. At least, now we'll know if the great man is just a big smiling oaf or a hypocrite—but so much damage has already been done."

Alma stared so hard into the table she might have burned it to ash and seemed to grind her teeth as she spoke. "What damage has he done?"

Farida wished immediately she had said nothing. She had long accepted Alma's blind allegiance to the president out of respect for her friend, but more recently had lost the necessary fortitude. "Well, for starters, he's made a virtue of greed, he's given a national platform to groups like the Moral Majority—and then there's all that rubbish about supply-side economics: If you give the horses enough oats, the birds will also be fed."

Alma kept her eyes on the table. "Well, isn't that what matters? That everyone is fed?"

Farida shook her head, realizing Alma didn't understand what it meant for the birds to be fed. "What matters is fairness. The salary of CEOs has risen from forty times that of the average worker to almost a hundred since he took office. That's what trickle-down has done for us. The gap between the haves and the have-nots is expanding exponentially. He seems to imagine that you can motivate rich people by giving them more money, and poor people by taking it away. He has taken money from people like you and me and put it in the pockets of people like himself and his cronies. I mean, what is deregulation if not legalizing what was once considered criminal. That is what he has done."

Alma scraped her plate with her spoon, set the spoon down noisily, and sat in silence, hands a big knotted fist in her lap.

Farida squeezed her friend's arm. "I'm sorry, Alma, but he gets me so mad. In this, we're just different. You're the kind of person he loves. I'm not. You're white, you were a beautician and a secretary, both good womanly occupations, you had a husband on whom you depended, you couldn't care less about women's liberation—and I'm everything that you're not. If he saw me on the street he wouldn't even look at me. I'm not the right color. I'm not the right gender. These things make a difference to people like him. If I were rich, he wouldn't care about the rest, but I'm not."

The reference to color gave Alma pause, but her eyes remained on the table, and she spoke without irony. "He *would* see you—as a woman. He's a man—and a *gent*leman—and the man in him *would* see you—most *def*initely."

Farida looked away, not wishing to be disagreeable, but not wishing either to give up her argument. "No, he wouldn't. Why do you suppose he opposed the ERA? He doesn't see women at all—except in that ugly paternalistic way. It's that false chivalry that upsets me—the hypocrisy of it all."

"Why is it false?"

"Because for every door he opens, he closes two. For every chair he holds, he removes two. He doesn't give women a chance for true independence because there would then be less need for men like himself—men who get their worth providing for women. It's how they maintain control, don't you see?"

Alma didn't see, and Farida realized maybe she couldn't. The President's generation shared the President's myopia. Women were complacent because everything was done for them, and men because they had control. They were people of their time—but so had slave-owners been people of their time. It took major upheavals to shake people from complacency. Farida had suffered such upheavals; Alma had not. Farida was no longer that kind of woman; Alma still was. Once settled, every generation became too lazy or scared or comfortable to change—but Horace had done her a favor by behaving so reprehensibly, shaking her from the comfort of her myopia. She squeezed Alma's arm again and finished her pie.

BY FARIDA'S MEASURE, Briggs, a restaurant on the street level of their office building, provided the best fries in the Loop, and on Fridays the best pot roast. She packed a sandwich lunch every day of the week to save money, but indulged on Fridays. The waitress no longer asked what she wanted, even saved the last portion of pot roast on one occasion when Farida had been delayed. A single globe lit their booth, but so high and dim they appeared like shadows.

Percy ordered a turkey sandwich and a diet Pepsi, Farida her roast and water. They had lunched together before though not frequently and she always ordered water. He imagined it was to save money and thought no more of it, wishing she would let him pay the check, but she refused, making it a condition of the lunch, and he no longer tried, understanding it was a matter of pride, perhaps of declaring equality, and he let her choose the restaurant instead. She had become more withdrawn of late, appearing as grey and gloomy as the weather.

Farida was glad for the opportunity to unburden herself, but unsure how much to say, wishing to explain her circumstances without appearing to make excuses, and imagined the best course might be to say as little as necessary, as soon as possible, before changing the subject. Her eyes flitted around the dim restaurant while they ordered, settling finally on Percy's. "I've told you something about my difficulties with the university, my correspondence with Greta Frumpkin—the Correspondence from Hell, as I like to call it. I should show it to you sometime, it's like a page out of Kafka—but that's really all there is to it. We seem to have reached an impasse and I hate to think of all the years of study left unrecognized if they refuse to give me my degree. You know the heart of the matter. I kept dropping out to write, and they refuse to let me back into the writing program because I dropped out to write."

Percy nodded, pursing his lips, recognizing the false cheer in her voice. "If I recall correctly, that was the problem we had during our first interview—that business about experience versus qualifications."

"Yes, but you were different. You accepted my experience. You not only gave me a job, you created a new position. There are professors at the university who have never written a book teaching students how to write—but they won't allow someone who has published more than the professors even to be a student again—not only that, but I am to be discredited of the work I have done."

The false cheer dwindled to nothing, as if the effort were too much, and her voice turned flat. Percy said nothing, dropping his eyes, sipping Pepsi through a straw. Her bitterness said more than she might have wished and he remained silent out of respect.

Farida dropped her eyes as well, taking his silence for boredom. "Sorry. There's really not that much to tell. I'm probably just wasting your time by telling you how I'm wasting mine."

Her voice was quieter yet, her smile apologetic, and he was quick to correct her misimpression. "Nonsense! I need to get away as much as anyone else. I wish we might do this more often, actually—lunch, I mean—but I *really* wish Erica might have been here. She would have known better what to say." He had mentioned Erica before, his wife, a college professor of humanities herself, dead two years when he had met Farida. "So much of it has to do with money, you know. The sciences are more practical, their research attracts more funding, which makes them more glamorous. The humanities have always played stepsister to the sciences, and it makes them prickly. It makes them defensive."

Her voice strengthened with indignation. "That's *stu*pid. They're *dif*ferent, that's all. I can understand the sciences requiring students to be up-to-date, but the humanities are *ne*ver out of date. They don't change from year to year—not even from century to century. We're talking here about eternal verities. *Oliver Twist* is the same book today as it was in Dickens's time, but according to Greta Frumpkin we understand the book better now even than Dickens himself because we have superior ways of reading. I find that ridiculous."

"It *is* presumptuous."

"It *is*, isn't it? It's *stu*pid and pre*sump*tuous—*and* it's arrogant—and it's just ... *stu*pid! They're just *dif*ferent, that's all." She wrenched her gaze violently from the table. "Sorry. I guess it's affected me more than I thought."

Percy nodded again, speaking slowly. "I'm on shaky ground here, not being an academic, but Erica said much the same thing. By admitting the humanities were different they were afraid they were admitting they were inferior—which meant they weren't eligible for the same budgets and grants as the sciences. Instead, they preferred to think the humanities could be fitted into structures and paradigms and formulas just like the sciences—which may be what makes them stringent about their rules, as if the rules make them as serious as the sciences, as if the rules are no less immutable than the laws of science."

"But they're not. They're entirely arbitrary."

"Well, perhaps not entirely, but I know what you mean, and that's the source of their inferiority complex. After all, the humanities are a way of life. An understanding of the great texts comes through an understanding of life. It's not something that can be taught in a classroom, but knowing this the humanities professors feel redundant, so they teach theories of literature as if the theories make the texts clearer—as if they're teaching a scientific principle. They strain the texts through Freud and Marx and all the rest of the sages, as you know, as if they were otherwise too simple—but simplicity is what a writer aims for if he wishes to get his point across. I don't mean the simpler a text the better, but the more simply a writer is able to convey a complex thought the better he is as a writer." He would have said more, but the waitress brought their food and they busied themselves with knives and forks.

They were silent a moment before Farida looked up from her pot roast. "Thanks, Percy. It's good to know *some*one understands. I wish I might have met Erica. You must have been lovely together."

Percy took a bite of his sandwich. "Just one suggestion, if I may. If you and this Greta Frumpkin have reached an impasse you might want to go over her head. All administrators aren't such sticklers about rules, you know. I know Erica wasn't. You might have better luck with someone else."

"I was going to do just that. Thanks—and sorry about all this."

"All what?"

She hesitated. "Wallowing, I suppose."

He shook his head. "Banish the thought."

They finished in silence, Farida afraid she had focused too glaringly on herself, Percy wondering how he might help. Ascending in the elevator to the office again he invited her to a discussion of Salman Rushdie's *Midnight's Children*. "I'm not a member of the group, but Erica was. They invited me to this particular discussion because they know that I've lived in Bombay, that my mother was Indian. They need someone to untangle the Indianisms. I know you could do that better than me and I know they would love to have you. Would you like to come?"

They had talked about the book; she couldn't remember when she had found a book so exciting; also that an Indian author had received due praise and recognition; it had liberated her to write her fourth novel, *That in Some Big Houses*, as an authentic Indian, no longer a counterfeit American, but it had been ignored no less than her previous novels, accounting in no small part for her dejection, her errors at work, about which she had said nothing to Percy after all, blaming her distress instead on the weather and Greta Frumpkin. It was becoming increasingly difficult to bear, so little return for so much work, weekends sucked into her work desk, living in a state of fugue, solitary as a hibernating bear, plagued by the familiar headaches, backaches, and wrist-cramps from confronting her typewriter eight to ten hours a day. "I would like that very much. Thank you." Her words remained starchy, her gratitude that of a beggar; she was relieved still to have Percy's favor, overwhelmed by his continual kindness, a virtue to which she had been too long unaccustomed, but afraid she might use it up within days at her current rate. She remained brittle, her defense against the world, afraid to break if she did not relax, afraid to burst into tears if she did.

Percy imagined her more like an iceberg than most people, the greater part submerged, and seeing her avert her eyes in the elevator as they returned to work wondered what she was thinking. He would never have pried, preferring to let her choose her own time, but he couldn't have been more surprised when they reached their floor. She excused herself, blurting an apology, darting past him in a blur, bursting from the elevator like a horse from its box, heading for the women's room. He wondered at his own interest, afraid she might be as unstable as she had been during their first interview, but she had also been charming, proven herself capable on many fronts, personal and professional, and he was determined to be patient.

Reaching the women's room Farida dashed to the closest stall, latched herself in, and sat on the toilet, elbows on knees, hands covering her face, shaking with sobs, muffling herself as best she could. The rejections to *That in Some Big Houses* had taken her by surprise; she had imagined she had finally found her language, her theme, her voice, but no one seemed to agree or care a damn.

With the first rejections she had scheduled Friday evenings for time to cry, her cure against her longstanding depression, imagining if she were only patient she would weather the storms, but storms now came unawares, catching her by surprise, sending her scurrying to the bathroom at inopportune moments to hide her inappropriate weeping. She had been scared enough by the ocean within herself to write letters (three to Kaki, one to her mother), saying she was returning for an extended stay, only to tear the letters to pieces. Returning in so debased a state, living once more in her mother's house, childless and divorced, more foolish in age than in youth, she preferred to take her chances in Chicago—but it was more than a matter of pride. The debt she owed the Katraks for what she had done to Darius and Yasmin could never be paid. The punishment she inflicted on herself could never equal the punishment she had inflicted on them. She had earned every difficulty she encountered, deserved every rejection.

She might have found salvation in Percy's care, but felt unworthy of his attention. She found his presence almost unbearable, wishing to return his kindness but finding herself unable—worse, finding herself no longer his equal, finding herself duplicitous for talking as if she were. She was grateful for his invitation to the reading group, but afraid she would make a fool of herself. She had been too long alone, but trusting herself so little she no longer trusted men who wished her company, preferring solitude and completing the coursework for her

Master's degree, though even that appeared to have been called to a halt—worse, reversed.

Additionally, she had unnecessarily isolated herself. Parsis were a minority in India, in America a minority within a minority (Parsis among Indians among Americans), and she had distanced herself not only from the community of Parsis in America, but from all institutions that provided stability: family, religion, country. They all had their pros and cons, but in dispensing with the cons (the jingoism that came with too much pride in one's institutions), she had dispensed as well with the pros (the wellbeing provided by the same institutions). Her descent into the bowels of the proletariat, long though she had fallen, had awakened her with a thump when she had finally landed. She had been too long accustomed to luxury to accept with ease that she was now an outsider, relegated to the back door and the kindness of strangers. She had never before accepted as fully the failure of her life, but her cocoon of solitude had revealed how selfishly she had lived. She accepted that she had earned in full measure her misery and loneliness, but there were times when reality overwhelmed her.

Gradually her sobs ceased. Unfurling toilet paper by the handful, she prepared to face the world again as if nothing mattered but that she was able to maintain her face for the faces she met.

II

Percy picked her up for the discussion in a blue Volvo. She had debated the wisdom of inviting him up to her apartment and decided against it, ashamed of its proportions, the view from the wrong end of a telescope, a Cooper in distress, but almost apologized bundling herself busily into the passenger seat, taking great care her coat didn't catch in the door, speaking into the air. "Parking is impossible in this neighborhood—and with the snow it's even worse. It makes me glad I don't have a car."

She made it seem parking was the only reason she hadn't invited him, but was more transparent than she imagined. Percy may not have known what troubled her, but never doubted she was troubled, and she betrayed herself by ignoring his greeting, ignoring his smile, sparing him barely a glance, appearing to have trouble with her seatbelt. He may have been driving a cab for the attention she paid. "You're right. You don't need a car in Chicago—it's almost an affectation. The CTA is so convenient."

She gave him her first glance of the evening, wondering if he were mocking her, but he wasn't. "It really is, isn't it? The el is just three short blocks away and the bus is even closer. The only reason to have a car is if you're dating—or something like that."

She looked away immediately, afraid to imply they were dating, afraid to imply they were not, but he replied as if she could not have been more sensible. "Exactly, or an evening out with friends. It's a different kind of convenience than the CTA. I hardly use it myself—except for special occasions."

Percy lived in Sandburg Village, an apartment complex in the Gold Coast named for Carl Sandburg, poet of the people and the Illinois prairie, about twenty blocks south of Briar Place, but if Farida recognized the compliment she ignored it. "I'm looking forward to the discussion. I even read the book one more time. We lived right on Warden Road near Breach Candy, near where Rushdie himself lived. We went to the same high school. He mentions Chimalker's toyshop, Reader's Paradise, Bombelli's restaurant—all places I knew."

"That's just the sort of thing they would love to hear, unraveling the place-names, mythologies, local legends—the sort of thing no outsider might be expected to know."

Farida smiled, understanding how she might be useful. "Tell me something about them, these people we're going to see. First of all, where are we going?"

"Rogers Park. Our hosts are Joe and Nancy Shannon, brother and sister—and another sister Sheila will also be there. I know them through Nancy who was one of Erica's students. I've met some of them at other discussions, but not many, and not recently. They live in a poky little apartment, so be warned. It's going to be crowded, perhaps a dozen others, folding chairs all around, but it will be warm and cozy—and they've ordered Indian food to commemorate the occasion. It should be fun."

A gradual paralysis affected Farida's face, a blush of shame rose like mercury in a thermometer, leaving her grateful for the relative darkness of the car. If he considered an apartment poky that could hold and feed perhaps a dozen she wondered what he would say about her own, but she said nothing, shrinking further into her skin. Rohini's comment from decades earlier rebuked her again for saying it was the prerogative of a girl accustomed to a certain standard of living to maintain her standard. Rohini had cited the example of suicides in the wake of the Crash, all because they couldn't maintain their standard of living. Farida imagined she knew how the suicides might have felt: there had been nights when she had wished she might not see the morning and mornings when she had preferred the half-death of sleep, but she rallied for Percy's sake. "It sounds like fun. The food is what I miss most about India."

Mounting the narrow stairway to the Shannon residence on the third floor, Percy following behind, she felt her confidence slip like an undergarment she couldn't fix without calling attention to herself—worse, like a bodily function over which she had lost control. The house for all its warmth was modest and middleclass, barely a blot on Blue Mansions or the Hyde Park house, but neither of these had been her home, the first belonged to the Coopers, the second to Horace; her own home was considerably lower on the scale, and she no longer a Cooper except in name. She couldn't go back, not after what her mother had done. They had stopped corresponding, but she kept in touch with Kaki though flashing even for Kaki the same facade she flashed for everyone except Rohini and Alma, assailing herself with the hoariest lines: how the mighty had fallen; it never rained, but poured; false face hid what false heart knew.

Standing beside her on the landing Percy rang the doorbell, smiling encouragement, but she returned his smile at her own peril, unable to stand the falsity of her position any longer. The floor seemed to shrink beneath her feet, the walls to close in. Her head burned, her back turned greasy with sweat. She tore her hood from her head and ripped a button tearing open the front of her coat. Her head emptied so quickly of blood she could hear the drainage like a buzzing of bees, leaving her numb from the neck up, her smile a grimace. Her heart seemed first to accelerate, then to hum and whine to a close. She heard herself speak, "I'm all right, I'm all right," but her knees buckled. She put a hand against the wall to steady herself as the door opened and a woman stood before her, but the woman seemed next to rise above her before images blurred, Percy into the woman, the woman into Percy, blending all colors first into bright spots, then into white, finally into black.

When she regained consciousness she was on her back on the floor, still on the landing, people hovering like redwoods, Percy waving them into the apartment, "Give her air, let her breathe," a strange woman by his side, "Joe, call an ambulance," she still murmuring to herself, "I'm all right, I'm all right."

Percy kneeled beside her. "Of course, you are. We just want to be sure."

"What happened?"

"You fainted."

She took a deep breath. "I'm sorry to be such a bother—but I'm all right now."

"Don't be silly. We're calling an ambulance. I'm going to the hospital with you."

"Please, there's no need. I'm all right now, really."

"Just to be safe."

She felt awkward on her back on the floor, Percy by her side, two strange women standing behind him, one of whom she engaged with a smile. "I'm sorry, really, ruining the party like this."

The woman shook her head. "Don't be silly. I'm Nancy. I hope you're all right."

She had difficulty smiling and looked away. "I'm all right, but I would like to get off the floor."

"Of course. We just wanted to be sure you were all right before we moved you."

Percy helped her indoors to a sofa. A strange man brought her a glass of water. "Hi, I'm Joe."

She nodded, taking the water. "Hi. Thanks."

Sheila, the woman who had been standing with Nancy, had cleared the room, bundling everyone into the dining-room beyond. "Let her have all the air she needs. No need to crowd her."

Farida drank the water, closing her eyes, embarrassed by the trouble she had caused. Percy explained what had happened, they took her down the stairs in a stretcher and slid her into the ambulance. There was no room for more than the two paramedics and Percy followed in his car to Augustana Hospital. They administered an EKG along the way, telling her to relax, which she did as well as she could, closing her eyes, but opening them when one of the men asked the other to check what he saw on the screen. They exchanged glances, nodding at each other. Farida caught the attention of the closer paramedic, serious eyes atop a handlebar moustache. "What's the matter?"

The man shook his head, deflecting the gravity of her question. "Nothing much. You have an irregular heartbeat. It's quite common. Many people have it."

She nodded. "Ah, yes, arrhythmia, my father."

The man nodded. "That explains it. It's hereditary."

She smiled in the dark, her luck was holding: struck by the curse of the Coopers though she had long relinquished her share of their fortune. She had experienced a similar episode once as a child, but it had been so long ago she had forgotten.

She was administered an emergency battery of tests, found to be suffering only from stress, scheduled for more tests in days to come, ordered to relax, and released in Percy's cognizance. He wanted to give her his guest bedroom for the night, but she wanted to be dropped at Briar Place. It was only when he insisted on seeing her upstairs that she agreed to stay overnight at his place. She was grateful for his trouble and realized he would be seeing her apartment sooner now rather than later. It was three in the morning when they reached his apartment in Sandberg Village.

SHE WOKE THE NEXT MORNING in a double bed in a darkened room, ten o'clock by the digital clock on the nightstand, alongside a tray holding a jug of water and a glass covered by a doily. Neatly folded on a nearby chair were towels and pajamas, a bathrobe slung over the back, slippers by the bed. Getting up she saw her own clothes, blue jeans, pink blouse, and brassiere on the floor. She had meant to wear the pajamas before going to bed, but had crawled in finally in just panties.

Horrified by the lateness of the morning she nevertheless took her time, yawning, turning in bed, hugging the pillows, enjoying the luxurious expanse of a real bed instead of one that folded out of a sofa, rods and bars digging into her back, recollecting the events of the evening—before stretching, drinking water, donning the robe, shuffling barefoot with the towel through a dark hallway to the bathroom. She could hear music from the living-room and smell the coffee, but wanted first to make herself presentable.

After showering she made the bed and met Percy in the living-room, still in the bathrobe, hair turbaned in a towel, Percy's slippers on her feet, perhaps two sizes too large. Beethoven's Spring Sonata brightened the room. "Good morning, Percy."

"Hullo. Did you sleep well?"

"Like a top—or a log, or a baby. Take your pick."

He smiled. "Glad to see you're yourself again. Would you like some coffee?"

"Please. Thanks."

"It's a little late, but breakfast?"

"I'll have whatever you're having."

"Fried eggs, bacon, orange juice?"

"Perfect. Let me help you."

"Actually, there's not much to do. You can pour your own coffee if you want to be helpful."

"Okay. Thanks."

"I called the office to say I would be late, but I told them not to expect you for at least a week. You may feel well enough, but remember what the doctors said. They still want to take more tests. Do yourself a favor and just take it easy for a while."

They crossed glances before she gave way. "Maybe you're right. I must admit I feel pretty lazy."

He nodded, smiling. "Breakfast will be served in ten minutes. How do you want your eggs?"

"Over easy, please. Thanks." The carpet was thick underfoot, complementing the pale blue of the walls with a deeper shade. The furniture was dark and plush and large and comfortable. Photographs of family dotted the room alongside potted plants. Walls sported framed prints, also a commissioned portrait of his wife, recognizable from the photograph on his desk at the office. Erica rested both elbows on a table like a vase with a double-pronged base, her chin on the heels of her hands cupping her face like a calyx. Her eyes were brown and bright, suggesting mischief, not the kind of woman she would have imagined with Percy—but neither had the men in her life been the kind she would have imagined with herself. She shuffled across the room to the balcony, shut against the weather, providing a panorama of the lake, frozen and bright, the city mantled in white, and gazed in silence for a moment before sinking into a deep red armchair. "It's so peaceful here I don't ever want to leave."

"Stay. Stay as long as you wish."

"Don't tempt me." Had he not been solicitous she might have imagined he was flirting, but her own remark had been more surprising, so unexpectedly flirtatious itself. It would have been too easy to pour her problems into his shoulder, avail herself of his support, but a finger of support sometimes demanded an arm and a leg in return and she had long forsaken the role of Rapunzel singing for her prince. Her experience with princes had been instructive; she no longer suffered the need and however pauperized preferred to be her own prince. A helicopter hovered in the distance. "What floor are we on?"

"The twenty-second."

"God, it really is like heaven up here."

During breakfast he talked about his family, occasionally indicating photographs scattered around the room: English father, Parsi mother, retired from Bombay since independence to Ely, near Cambridge, retired again from running a chemist's shop; American wife, Erica, daughter of a diplomat, met and married in Bombay, with whom he had moved to Chicago; one son, a chemical engineer married to a homemaker in San Francisco, parents of a piano prodigy; another, still a bachelor, working for the EPA in New York, living with a single mother, a financial analyst, whose daughter trained for track at the Olympics. Farida said nothing about her own parents, but privy to the Parsi grapevine he had expected no less. She seemed no less reticent talking about Horace and another lover left unnamed. She said little, to his surprise, even about her novels, but spoke most, and most freely, about her friend Rohini, now living in Highland Park, Rohini's children, Sunil and Sangita—and about Alma.

It was noon when they finished breakfast. He invited her to stay though he needed to get to the office, but she insisted she had things to do herself at home. He drove her back to Briar Place and she didn't resist when he insisted on seeing her upstairs. She eyed him askance for signs of surprise when they entered her apartment, but he was surprised only by her artwork on the walls which he examined with admiration. She had said nothing about her work because she hadn't painted in a long while, not since her return to Chicago, during which time she had focused on her Master's and the novels.

He remarked next on the prettiness of her picture window, maples and honey-locusts, scurrying squirrels, the rusticity of such a scene in the heart of Chicago. He made her promise to stay in the apartment for at least that day until he returned later bringing with him a Chinese dinner, to which she agreed without resistance. Finally, he sat on the sofa-bed, his long face longer, eyebrows bobbing again on his forehead. "Farida, is there something you want to tell me—I mean, related to the stress? Are we working you too hard? I don't mean to pry, but I want you to be frank. You know, of course, that I will hold anything you say in confidence."

He had been so kind already, even before the events of the night before, she had long wished to unburden herself, but afraid to appear sorry for herself had found neither the opportunity nor the courage. She took a deep breath. "It's no secret. I've told you about my university correspondence." She picked a bound file from her desk. Under THE CORRESPONDENCE FROM HELL she had added, OR, DOWN THE RABBIT HOLE, under which she had added, OR, INTO THE BLACK HOLE, under which, OR SCREWED!!!! "Take it with you. You'll see what I mean."

Percy took the file. "Is there anything else?"

Farida took another deep breath before returning to her desk. "Nothing—except these." Her face dropped as she spoke, indicating five more files, each an inch thick. "My correspondence with editors, agents, publishers—including some awards and prizes and publications, but only rejections for all the novels, all my best work. Maybe they're right, after all, and I'm wrong. Maybe I'm just no damn good and just too damn proud to admit it—too damn *stu*pid."

Percy held her gaze, but she looked away. "I'll be the judge of that. I've never known a novelist. I would like to read one of your novels. That would tell me more than all the editors in the world. May I?"

Her eyebrows rose, lifting the rest of her face. "Of course! Nothing a writer likes better than to be read." She got on her knees, rummaging among piles of paper under her desk, pulling out *The Long Sunset,* a manuscript of about four hundred pages, and handing it to him. "I won't say a word. I don't want to make excuses. A novel should speak for itself, but I hope you like it."

WHEN PERCY RETURNED IN THE EVENING with cartons of Chinese food Farida appeared not only happier than he could remember, but giggling and girlish. He was introduced to her friend, Rohini Gupta, a plump polite smiling greying woman in a green sari with a pleasant face and firm handshake. "Very happy to meet you, Percy."

Percy liked her candid gaze. "Pleasure's mine, Rohini. Farida has talked so much about you I feel like I know you."

Farida, in t-shirt and jeans, almost jumped up and down beside her friend. "She is absolutely my best friend—and has been now for thirty years. No Rohini, no Farida. That's just the way it is. When I told her what happened she came straight away—and she's coming with me tomorrow to the hospital for my stress test. She's staying for the night. We're having a sleepover. Isn't she wonderful?"

Rohini shook her head, deflecting the praise. "For me, Farida has been one big headache after another for thirty years. Must be something very masochistic about me—but I'm very glad you are here to share this last headache with me."

Farida smiled, laying her head on her friend's shoulder. "I am her favorite headache."

Percy joined in the fun. "There are some people so charming that we willingly accept headaches on their behalf."

Rohini nodded. "She has secrets that cannot be bottled. I used to be skinnier than her, and now look at us."

Farida slapped her friend's arm. "Rohini, you have brought children into the world—oh, what a talent, to have brought children into the world. I have done nothing so very lovely—absolutely nothing."

"Rubbish, Farida! When you talk like that you are no longer my friend."

"Well, then, I won't, but let it be on your head—another headache." She grinned, turning to Percy. "What did you bring us for dinner? Did you bring enough for Rohini also? She's a big eater—as you can see. I would have warned you, but I didn't know she was coming."

Percy had brought enough for a small party, egg rolls, lemon chicken, moo shu pork, fried rice, fortune cookies, imagining Farida could use leftovers the next day. Farida pulled her tiny dining table away from the wall and they served themselves from the cartons. Percy found himself grateful for Rohini's presence, also jealous of their friendship. His family was dear to him, but scattered across the country, parents across the ocean. His acquaintanceship wasn't small, but neither was it intense. There was no one with whom he could let down his hair as did Farida and Rohini with each other, there had never been anyone besides Erica.

III

[Farida Cooper to Greta Frumpkin]
October 3, 1985
Dear Ms. Frumpkin,

I'm glad we finally met, but the question remains. What is to be done next? I would like to suggest two possible solutions to our problem. Since the qualifying paper for my Master's degree should comprise approximately eighty pages of work in fiction and poetry, I would like to suggest that I be required to submit a much longer paper, verging on two hundred pages. This would entail considerably more work than I had anticipated for the qualifying paper, but it is perhaps justified under the circumstances.

Additionally, since my biggest hurdle appears to be new approaches to the texts I studied a decade ago, it might be appropriate for me to submit a paper discussing how exactly these approaches have changed in the last decade. I can't imagine a more symmetrical arrangement. I would need to research the subject in greater depth before I could be more specific about what might be required of me, but I want to know first what you think of the suggestion. I hope you will find my proposals agreeable, and thanks again for your trouble.

Sincerely,

Farida Cooper

P.S. I would like to share a pleasanter note regarding my work that has developed since we spoke. You know, of course, that an excerpt from my new novel, <u>That in Some Big Houses</u>, was published in <u>Bits and Pieces</u>. I learned just last week that another excerpt is to be published in <u>The Other Chicago Magazine</u> next year.

She heard nothing from Greta Frumpkin in the next six weeks, and would have called but for the sensitive nature of their exchange. Instead she wrote again, twice, and received a letter finally three and a half months after her original query.

[Greta Frumpkin to Farida Cooper]

January 24, 1986

Dear Ms. Cooper:

I apologize for letting the matter of your credits slide. Somehow I had the idea that you were going to drop by the office.

I have talked with Doris Garden, the director of the writing program, and with the professors of the English courses you took ten years ago, that is Professors Brownlow, Bennett, Hale, and Handy. We have agreed that we can approve a petition to the graduate college asking that:

1) you be granted credit for the writing courses you took (on the grounds that you have kept sharp the skills you learned in the courses) and

2) *you be granted credit for the literature courses if you can pass an exam in each that would take into account developments in the field over the last decade.*

As to your proposals, I do not see how they meet the spirit, much less the letter, of the Graduate College's requirements. If you still have control over what was taught in the literature courses, then the reexamination will require you only to brush up on new developments. I have proposed what seems to me a very generous way for you to receive credit for courses taken as long as a decade ago. If you find my compromise unacceptable, I will turn the matter over to the Graduate Curriculum Committee.

I have no precedent in this matter and cannot guarantee the reaction of the Graduate college to the petition, but if you make an appointment with me to work out the form of the petition I will find out.

Sincerely,

Greta Frumpkin

cc: Professor Doris Garden

[Farida Cooper to Greta Frumpkin]

February 11, 1986

Dear Ms. Frumpkin,

Thanks for your letter of January 24. It appears we are not to have a meeting of minds after all, for which I am sorry. I do not expect to change your mind, but I would like to reiterate our differences so that we might at least be clear about our points of disagreement.

You suggest that I prepare for four exams in the four courses I took over a decade ago (Shakespeare Histories, Restoration Drama, the 19th Century Novel, and Contemporary American Literature), "only" brushing up on the new developments since that time. Surely that would mean at least being familiar with the plots and characters of the texts on which I would be brushing up. Restoration Drama alone would include Dryden's All for Love, *Otway's* Venice Preserv'd, *Etherege's* The Man of Mode, *Wycherley's* The Country Wife, *Vanbrugh's* The Relapse, *Congreve's* The Way of the World, *Farquhar's* The Beaux' Stratagem, *Cibber's* The Careless Husband, *Rowe's* The Tragedy of

Jane Shore, *Goldsmith's* She Stoops to Conquer, *and Sheridan's* The School for Scandal. *I won't bore you with the names of the texts in the other courses, but they number close to thirty, and to require me to pass examinations in each of the four courses feels punitive and repetitive. I find it unfair that you might expect ANYONE to successfully take an examination on all of these plays and novels, however well she might have known them ten years ago, unless she had either continually taught them during that time or read them frequently on her own. It is blithe of you to suggest that I need "only" brush up on them.*

You might have had a point had my emphasis been in Literature or in the Teaching of English, but it is in Creative Writing, and I can tell you with a great degree of certainty that the more a writer of fiction writes during her apprenticeship the better she gets, the sooner her style forms—but I shouldn't have to tell you this. Admittedly, my apprenticeship is long past (you know of my publications, you know my accomplishments already outstrip most of what your students will accomplish despite Master's degrees and Doctorates), but you continue to deal with my dilemma as if I were a freshman. I understand, as you say, that you have no precedent in this matter, but perhaps we should use this incident to set a precedent.

So be it. Our ways are not to converge. This is unfortunate for both of us because (for myself) I would have liked the degree to provide me with a satisfactory period to my endeavor instead of the semicolon I have at present, and (for the university) I like to think my work might some day have made you proud to count me among your graduates.

I will make no more demands on your time and I would like to thank you now for the considerable time you have already devoted to my dilemma. I will appeal instead to someone whose hands are less tied than yours appear to be.

Sincerely,

Farida Cooper

cc: Professor Doris Garden

IV

Percy didn't see Farida for the rest of the week, but called to reassure himself about her wellbeing, and was glad to learn Rohini had taken time from work to spend with her friend. The consequence of all the tests was that she had suffered a syncope, the definition of which she read, not without pride, over the telephone: "a partial or complete temporary suspension of respiration and circulation due to cerebral anemia"—related to her arrhythmia. Percy understood the cause of her anxiety, recalling her envy of Rohini's childbearing. The correspondence with the university didn't help, but the primary cause was her growing number of unpublished novels, her series of stillbirths.

He had been afraid *The Long Sunset* might not live up to his expectations, but reading evening after evening with growing interest the story of an Englishman (not unlike himself) in love with an Indian woman (not unlike herself), a study of class and racial differences during the wane of the Raj, he had found the manuscript a more subtle, mature, and profound representation of the Farida he knew in person. He had wondered what he might say to her had he not liked the manuscript, and was not only relieved but glad, even excited, that he liked it as much as he did. He wouldn't need to be polite about his assessment. Instead, he would need to moderate his praise to get her to believe him.

On Friday evening he took an Indian dinner to Briar Place. Farida's face softened with affection. "You are so good to me, Percy—*every*one is being so good. I had to literally pack Rohini off. Otherwise, she would have just moved in—but she has a *fam*ily. Oh, you also brought the manuscript back. So, what did you think?"

"We have plenty of time. Why don't we relax and talk about it over dinner?"

She took his coat. "Oh, yes. Perfect. Keep me in suspense so I can relax."

He laughed. "I didn't mean it like that. We can talk about it first if you prefer."

"No, let's talk about it over dinner—after we have relaxed. That's the key word now, isn't it? Only relax, and everything will be all right."

"We can talk about it now or later as you please—but just so there's no unnecessary suspense, let me say right off the bat that I enjoyed it immensely. We can talk about the details later."

"Thanks." She had stacked the record player with Mozart piano sonatas, set the table for two. He opened a bottle of Chablis she had chilled while she ladled food from the cartons into serving dishes: nan, tandoori chicken, mutton biryani, kulfi into a thermos. They toasted good health, friendship, Rohini. She quaffed her wine, grinning across the table. "All right. I'm relaxed now. What did you think?"

Percy drew a deep breath, picking a chicken leg with his fingers. "My mother always said that Indian food has to be eaten with your hands to be fully appreciated."

"Percy, don't play the fool with me now. Tell me what you thought."

He smiled. "All right, but you must remember I'm no expert in these matters. What I did, actually, was to apply something Erica had taught me. She said that in order to understand a book you had to ask yourself first what it was trying to say, and then how well it said what it was trying to say. She had little patience with colleagues who would push Marxist theory and Freudian theory and all the other theories at their students as if the novels had no significance on their own. Her colleagues, in turn, had little patience with her. In fact, they said she was hopelessly bourgeois—but, as she said, that was not an argument, that was name-calling, and name-calling was—and is—an admission of defeat."

Farida nodded vigorously. "Yes, exactly right. Horace was the same. If he didn't agree with something, it was bourgeois."

Percy nodded. "I'm not surprised—but getting back to the point. Using her rationale, I thought *The Long Sunset* worked very well. I think you may tighten it yet—the beginning is unnecessarily slow, for instance—but a good editor can take care of that. More to the point, it's clearly written—but I'm afraid in some circles that's not a plus. There are too many people—agents, editors, professors—who imagine the more difficult a book is to read the better it must be."

Farida laughed. "And the books you can't read at all are the best of all."

He joined her laughter, nodding again. "The more difficult a book, the smarter the person appears who pretends to understand it—but opacity is not your problem. Your problem is the American market. I'm afraid there's just not that much interest in India—not in America."

"I thought that might be the problem—but Rushdie has opened a number of doors."

"Yes, but it's still a long walk to the throne room."

Farida laughed.

"More to the point, I think I have an answer to your problem. I think you should try sending your manuscripts to England. You know, take advantage of the old colonial ties. That's how Rushdie got started. They're more interested in their old colonies than America will ever be—for reasons of nostalgia, guilt, sentiment, whatever. In any case, it's worth a try. I hope you don't mind, but I took the liberty of getting you some names and addresses from the library—British agents and publishers. I think you should try them and see what happens. What have you got to lose?"

Farida's reply was muffled, throat constricted with gratitude. "Percy, this is so very good of you. Thank you so very much."

"If anything comes of it, no one will be happier than me."

Farida said nothing, but the old world sentiment affected her more than she cared to admit. She had to look away, focus on her food, to keep her eyes from overflowing.

V

Farida leaned forward, elbows on knees, caressing Alma's wrist, kissing her hand, holding it against her cheek, looking at her friend in dismay. "I'm so sorry. I wish I might have been here for you."

Her friend slumped on the sofa, hand limp, eyes unfocused, face gaunt, a sliver of her former self, but she smiled with the kiss, and her face turned radiant for a moment. "It's not your fault, hon. You had troubles of your own."

In the two months since the friends had last spoken, Alma had lost thirty pounds, unable to keep food down. A battery of tests had revealed a form of tachycardia similar to what had killed Farida's father, and the work of digestion strained her heart. Alma could see no viable options. She had been recommended surgery, but was convinced that would kill her. She had been prescribed pills for her attacks, but they made her vomit. Farida shook her head, hating to think they had quarreled about the president the last time they had talked. "I could have called. I *should* have called. Starting tomorrow, and until you're back to your normal weight, I'm going to bring you your paper every morning before I go to work. I'll just ring your doorbell to let you know it's there. Okay?"

*Tribune*s were flung in a pile at the lobby door downstairs in plastic wraps with apartment numbers in large black letters. The daily descent for her newspaper constituted Alma's exercise regimen, but exercise was no longer a priority and the elevator was sometimes out of order. Alma shook her head. "I'm not getting back to my normal weight. I'm not taking those pills. They make me feel lousy."

Farida sighed. "They keep you alive. Alma, do you remember what you said about your friend Ruth—that she had cancer, but she wouldn't eat cheese because of the cholesterol?"

"Yes?"

"Well, you're the same. She won't eat cheese for the cholesterol, but she's dying of cancer—and you won't take your pills because they make you vomit, but you're having heart attacks. It's the *same* thing, Alma. It's *exactly* the same thing."

Alma laughed so suddenly, so hard, that Farida was afraid she would hurt herself. "You're right, hon. It's just that I feel so lousy sometimes, I don't know what I'm saying."

"I know, I know, but we've got to do what we can. The rest is not up to us, but we've got to do what we can—and I'm going to do everything I can, starting with your paper tomorrow."

Alma's eyebrows steepled as she turned to Farida. "But you're not well yourself."

"I'm weller than you!"

Alma smiled. "Thank you, hon."

"*And*, if you'll give me the key, I'll get your mail as well when I get back. Okay?"

"Thank you." She squeezed Farida's hand. "You know, I wish I knew why this was happening. If I knew why, I could do something about it."

"It's just old age, Alma. That's all."

Alma shook her head. "No, hon, the body is the servant of the mind. I've been having bad thoughts—I don't know what they are, but that's the only explanation. There's a lesson here, but I don't know what it is. God is trying to tell me something, but I don't know what it is."

Farida squeezed Alma's hand. "It's courage, Alma. God wants you to have courage."

Alma sighed. "You may be right." She held Farida's eyes in a long gaze. "You are truly the daughter I never had. I can't say it enough, how much I love you."

Farida looked away, not unembarrassed. "That makes us even. You're the mother I never had." She ignored Alma's last sentiment, not because she disbelieved her, but because she couldn't say the words herself. She would have felt disingenuous. "What I don't understand is how you turned out so well, considering the mother you had."

Alma smiled again. "That was thanks to my Homer. If not for him I would have been a bitter angry woman … just like my mother. She was a piece of work, she was. I wanted so much to be different from her that I became a pleaser—not the best thing."

"But something must have happened to make her the way she was, don't you think? I mean, your father didn't help."

"If you're talking about the affair, no, of course not—but, you know, the question is, did she turn into a hater because he had the affair, or did he have the affair because she was a hater."

The smile left her face and Alma gazed past Farida.

Farida tried to hold her friend's gaze, continuing to caress her hand, conscious of the fineness of her bones, like those of a sparrow, or the tracery of a web. "Something on your mind?"

Alma nodded. "Yes. You know how I feel about hospitals. They don't do you no good. They take the same tests over and over. They don't listen. I'm okay now, but if anything should go wrong I *don't* want to be carted off to some hospital. That'll kill me for sure and I want to die in my own apartment."

Farida took a breath as if to object, but said nothing when Alma raised a hand.

"I know what I'm doing. I called Dr. Faherty to ask her to sponsor me for hospice care. What this means is that I will be in constant contact with the hospice. I had a nurse and a social worker visit today and each of them will come once a week—or twice, if I wish—with medicines or whatever I might need. I'm telling you this so you'll know *not* to call 911 if anything happens. You have to call the hospice and I have the number—and a whole lot of other numbers here for you."

Alma handed Farida a page with the number for the Advocate Hospice, the nurse, the social worker, and her network of friends, the Telephone Tabbies. She saw her own number among the others as well. Her brow wrinkled. "Alma, is everything all right?"

Alma nodded. "Everything is as I want it to be. I'm only telling you so you will know *not* to call 911 but the hospice number. The nurse lives on Barry, just one street down, and if she's not available they'll send someone else. If I need medicine or pills or morphine or whatever, they'll bring it to me—but, whatever happens, you are *not* to call 911. I *don't* want to be taken to the hospital again. All right?"

Farida's brow remained wrinkled. "Yes, okay—but does this mean you'll be taking your pills?"

Alma smiled. "Yes, hon, I will be doing everything I can—short of going to the hospital—and thank you so much. You don't know how much I count on you."

DARIUS KATRAK, GREEN LANTERN

arida was annoyed as she joined Ratan in the back of his Plymouth and it showed in her face, brows arrowing into a flared nose, mouth narrowing to a short thin line. His tardiness had delayed their lunch by almost an hour. She might not have minded, time had less meaning in her current life, and she enjoyed letting it spread like a wash after lunch at the Willingdon Club, enjoying tea and biscuits in the Pavilion as afternoon bled into evening, gazing over a lawn splashed with bougainvillea at racehorses dotting the distant paddocks, but she had a lesson with Darius at four o'clock and much as she hated to rush would now have to hurry through lunch. "What happened to you? I'm absolutely famished. What kept you so long?"

Ratan spoke to his driver, "Abdul, Willingdon chalo," before turning to his cousin. "Sorry, old girl, but unavoidable delay. Office business. You know how it is for us poor working stiffs."

"No, I don't—and neither do you. It was very inconsiderate of you not to call. I called and called, but no one answered. Doesn't anyone at your office do any work?"

"Lunchtime—all gone to lunch."

"Except you. You were supposed to be with me. Really, Ratan, I do think you might have called."

"Sorry, but I'm telling the truth. There was no one to make the call—all gone to lunch."

"What? You're such a big shot now you can't make your own calls? I thought something might have happened. Inexcusable, what you did."

Ratan laughed and Farida relented easily, glad again for their easy camaraderie, however long she might have waited. She had long adjusted to the half day by which Bombay led Chicago, but not to the other time difference, the flexibility with which minutes ran, one into the other, expanding within seconds into hours. India was still a country ruled by daylight more than daylight savings, legend more than logic. Ratan had most likely been too lazy, not hungry enough, lost in conversation, engrossed in a magazine, or some combination of such reasons, perhaps even just having a slow tea and toast, to mind the time which had elongated beyond his calculation.

Abdul had driven the car around the driveway as they bickered and was waiting at the gate for a part in the river of traffic ahead when a tiny brown hand reached into the back window and touched Ratan's sleeve. "Seth, baksheesh?"

Ratan recoiled, suddenly petulant and harsh. "Arré, what are you doing? Who are you to touch me? Who gave you permission?"

The beggar was a tiny unwashed stick of a girl. She might have been ten or eleven though small enough to pass for seven, but her face might better have reflected someone of seventy, not just blank but hardened in blankness, not just hopeless but resigned to hopelessness, the expression of a prisoner of many years. Strands of stringy black hair were pasted with sweat to a skeletal brow. Her dress was torn, the color of dust, as was her skin, blending her with her background, making her no more than dust in motion, dust returned to dust before its time. She had touched Ratan only to get his attention, reaching into the forbidden paradise of his Plymouth, and withdrew her hand from the car, but not to her side, holding it with her other hand, brown hands turning pale palms to the light, repeating her plea, the buzz of his words no more in her ears than a buzz of flies in a drunken flight. "Seth, baksheesh, seth?"

Ratan had exhausted his interest in the girl and shouted to the driver, raising his window. "Chalo, Abdul, chalo! What are you waiting for?" He turned to Farida. "Where is that chowkidar fellow of yours? I swear, Farida, you should really give him a good talking to. A firm hand is the only thing these people understand. Otherwise, they take advantage of you. He's always salaaming when you come around, but never there when you need him—probably sleeping in his box right now."

Tukaram erupted from his box as if in response, shirt and shorts and cap of khaki, a short man of perhaps fifty years, wiry of limb, a runner's muscled calves, shooing the girl away, but she continued to tap the window. Finding a part in the traffic Abdul edged the Plymouth forward, but Farida stopped him. "Abdul, thero, wait." She rummaged in her purse. "Ratan, lower your window a sec."

"What? I thought you were in a hurry. I thought you were absolutely famished."

"I am—and the sooner you lower the window the sooner we will be on our way. Just do as I say, Ratan—before Tukaram chases her away."

She needn't have worried. Seeing Farida's activity in the car the girl held her ground, ignoring Tukaram. Ratan lowered the window, shaking his head, and Farida handed the girl a bunch of notes.

The girl's eyes bulged, her face remained otherwise expressionless. She took the money without a word, without looking at Farida, as if the money might vanish if she let it out of sight, and dashed off. Tukaram's eyes bulged no less, but he recovered in time to make a show of shooing the girl though she was no longer in sight. Abdul looked over his shoulder and Farida nodded. "Chalo, Abdul. Club chalo."

Ratan continued shaking his head. "I swear, Farida, I never took you for such a softie. One rupee would have been enough—arré, just some change would have been enough. How much did you give her? ten rupees? twenty? Did you even count?"

Farida knew she had given more than was customary, perhaps twenty to thirty times more than was customary. She was happy enough with Darius and rich enough not to measure her generosity in thimbles, but she was annoyed that her generosity had been inspired no less by her annoyance with Ratan. "What do you care? On the money we spend on lunch today she could live for a month—her whole family could live for a month."

Ratan still shook his head, still disapproving, but patronized her with a smile. "You have been away too long, Farida. That is what it is.

You have forgotten how it is. You are looking at India with the eyes of an American."

Farida looked across the front seat through the windshield ahead, but wasn't unaware of Ratan's smile. "Au contraire, mon frere, I have forgotten nothing. I know all the arguments: she will give the money to her father who will spend it on drink; she only looks miserable to play on our sympathy; if we give one of them money, we will have to give them all; if we give them money once, they will ask for it again; if we give it again, they will never learn anything except to beg; we only give them money because we feel guilty; it will make no difference in the long run whether we give them money or not. I have heard it all and it is all rubbish. If it makes no difference in the long run, it at least makes a difference in the short—and maybe if we take care of the short runs, the long run will take care of itself. If each one of us who has so much more than we need took better care of people who don't have enough, we would *all* be better off. Don't tell me I'm being a softie and don't tell me I have forgotten what it is like. If anything, I can look at India with the eyes of an Indian *and* the eyes of an American—and that is a less insular vision than someone who can see *on*ly with the eyes of an Indian. It's only our guilt and our shame that makes us treat them as you did that poor girl, more convenient to blame them for being poor than ourselves for looking away." She turned suddenly to face him, surprising him with a smile. "Now shut up, Ratan, just shut up. I don't want to quarrel with you. I just want to have a good lunch and a good conversation. When all is said and done, life is very good for us, isn't it?"

Ratan still shook his head, still smiled, but took a deep breath. "Yes, yes, I suppose it is." No one else could tell him to shut up with more charm and Ratan marveled at the alchemy that allowed her such mercurial changes of mood. He noted also, not without admiration, the colors in which she had dressed: lemon yellow blouse; milky blue jeans; hair in a silk scarf matching the color of her jeans; purse slung across her shoulder matching her blouse; black buckled belt, three inches wide, hugging her concave waist; matching black buckled sandals. He paled by comparison in a beige bush shirt, grey slacks, and black wingtips, hairline receding, waist thickening; he was hardly even taller, glad she hadn't worn heels that day. "I say, Farida, you look really super today—must be the weather or something, very agreeable."

Farida seemed unaware of his scrutiny, but knew what he meant though it had nothing to do with the weather or anything else as banal. She was a woman in love, and a woman in love lived on an exalted plane, in a world where even inanimate objects palpitated with life like the creations of spring, her very pores seemed to expand and contract with each heartbeat; her nightly dreams were full of flight, arms like rudders propelled by a helium heart, but even by day she felt unbound by gravity, every move bursting with grace, every step a leap into ether. It had been almost a month since Darius had returned with the socks, they had met three times a week for lessons, she had seen him just two days ago—but every moment away was bearable, even charming, only because she knew she would be seeing him again soon. She shuddered to think of her life once more without him, a lacerated landscape bearing beings of cracked skin and brittle bones, a world lacking a center not knowing what it lacked, the pulsing oceanic galactic radiant heart of love. She held her smile. "Thank you, Ratan. Sorry to snap at you like that, but you see we shall have to hurry through lunch now because you were late. I have someone coming for a drawing lesson at four o'clock. I *told* you."

"I know, but can't you just let her wait for a bit?"

"First of all, it's a him, not a her—and second, no, I can't."

"Farida, I was really looking forward to a nice leisurely lunch with you. Can't you call him to postpone or reschedule—or just say you are going to be a little late?"

"No."

"Why not?"

Farida grinned. "Because that would be inconsiderate—something you wouldn't understand."

Ratan scowled. "I think you are doing me an injustice. Who is this fellow anyway? Anyone I know?"

"Actually, yes. His name is Darius Katrak. We met him the night we saw the Avengers—the son at the next table. You remember the family?"

"Oh, my God, yes! *We are the Dhuns.* How could anyone forget? However did that come about?"

Farida laughed, explaining the circumstances. By the time she was finished they had reached the avenue of palms leading to the driveway of the Willingdon. They entered through the wide entrance hall, signed themselves in, and went directly to the dining-room, seating themselves under a fan reaching down from the high ceiling on a long spindle, he ordering a saddle roast and Coke, she veal medallions and a Mangola, tomato soup and salads for both. "I just love this old place. It's been a home away from home for me. Sometimes, when things weren't going well between Mummy and Daddy, Mummy would come upstairs to talk to Kaki, and I would call one of my friends—Bucky or Threaty or Shobha or Vera—and Ramesh would drive me to pick them up, and we would all come here, and everything would be all right again. We would have such a good time just talking and snacking and drinking Cokes that we never wanted to go home. In fact, I used to wish that time would just stop right then and there."

The Willingdon Club had also been the site of the wedding reception for Horace, to show him off to her friends, but she said nothing about that. The waiter, uniformed in white, brought their soups and salads. Ratan smiled, passing her the breadbasket and butter. He knew the girls she mentioned, highschool friends. "You know, Farida, I have to tell you how much I admire you, how you always speak your mind—in particular, how you never stay mad for long. If something upsets you, you just let it out—but once it's out, it's out, and you can carry on as if nothing had happened."

Farida smiled, but shook her head. "What in the world brought this on? What the hell are you talking about? Why should I stay mad—do you mean at you?"

Ratan nodded. "I am sure you are the same with everyone—but, yes, for instance, take what happened with me just now. I was almost an hour late, and then that beggar girl—and look at you now, cool as a cucumber."

Farida laughed. "Arré, Ratan, how can I stay mad at you? I understand you too well. You are like a little boy who has had all the advantages of travel and money and all the rest of it, but none of the responsibilities. You know everything, but understand nothing. It's not your fault if you don't know better. It's a pity, but you pay a price without even knowing it. It would be so stupid of me to stay mad at you. Much better to enjoy what you have to offer, don't you think?"

"You see, that is just the sort of thing I'm talking about. I'm not sure you haven't taken me down a peg, but you did it so very nicely I would have to be a fool to object."

Farida laughed. "And, of course, you are no fool."

He laughed in response though he recognized her laughter was grained with irony. "Actually, I am, for you—but only for you."

Farida squeezed his hand. "Dear Ratan. Don't think I don't appreciate it."

"I know you do—in fact, I've been giving it a lot more thought these days—I mean, since you've come back."

She still grinned, but her eyes narrowed, cautious. "What? About being a fool for me?"

"Yes, if you want to put it like that—but, I mean, seriously, Farida, I am very fond of you—but you know that, of course."

She knew she infatuated him. They had been to the movies twice since The Darjeeling, but he had never imposed his affection. She might once have welcomed his interest out of curiosity if nothing else, but not since she had met Darius. She turned her attention to her salad. "Of course, I do—and so am I of you, dear Ratan. Why else do you think I put up with you?"

He shook his head. "Farida, I am trying to be serious. Just be serious for a moment."

"But I don't want to be serious. There is too much seriousness in the world—and I have had too much of it in my life. I want to enjoy my life. I want to have some fun for a change. I just want to play the fool—like you."

"You think I play the fool?"

"No more than anyone else in the family—I mean, we might be Coopers, and we might act like big shots, but we are still big fish in a very small pond."

"Bombay is a small pond?"

"On the stage of the world, it is—that is, if you can have a pond on a stage." She laughed again. "What I mean is that by international standards, it is. It's not New York or London or Paris or Rome. It's not even Chicago—and, in any case, if we weren't Coopers we would amount to very little even in Bombay."

"But why think of it like that? We *are* Coopers, after all."

"Yes, but there are Coopers and there are Coopers. There are the Coopers who made us Coopers, and there are the Coopers who were merely born Coopers. The former were entrepreneurs, the latter merely caretakers. The former add to the Cooper fortune, the latter subtract. We are among the latter and very fortunate, but we mustn't let it go to our heads."

"I'm afraid I don't see that it matters—I mean, what does it matter as long as we are Coopers?"

"Well, I suppose what I mean to say is that if we hadn't been born Coopers we might have had more incentive to become like the people who made us Coopers."

Ratan opened his mouth, but let it hang without a word, finally once more shaking his head. "You know, I don't know how we got onto this subject. It's so far from what I wanted to discuss."

"We weren't discussing anything. We were just talking."

He shook his head. "What I started to say, it's really quite simple. We have known each other all our lives. We have both just confessed to being fond of each other. I think we should ratchet it up to the next level."

"Oh, but I'm very happy with this level."

"Don't be silly, Farida. This level has run its course. We have to move forward. Otherwise, we simply move back."

"But why ruin a good thing?"

Ratan leaned forward. "To make it better—only to make it better."

Farida shook her head. "Ratan, please don't spoil it. This is really not the time."

"Don't tell me you have never thought about it."

"Not in a long time, Ratan—and this is most definitely *not* the time."

He was silent for a moment before leaning back in his chair again. "Sorry, of course, your dad. Sorry, sorry. I was thinking only about myself."

"I know you were—but there's also Horace, you know. I'm not divorced yet."

"Right, right, of course, of course, I'm sorry—but just tell me one thing. I'm not pressing you or anything, just asking. Is there anyone else?"

"Ratan, really!"

"Just asking."

"Don't ask."

Their meals arrived, and Ratan leaned back allowing the waiter to take their soup bowls. "All right, I won't—just so long as you know."

"I know. Now let's talk about something else."

"What do you want to talk about?"

"Just any old rubbish you can think of—nothing serious."

Ratan looked at Farida, but focused over her head. "I say, I think I'm about to be preempted."

"What do you mean?"

"Isn't that your old pal, Bucky Bharucha, coming to join us?"

Farida turned her head. "Oh, my God, you're right—speak of the devil. I say, Bucky, your ears must have been burning. I was just talking about you, about the good times we used to have in this very dining-room."

A plump smiling woman, wearing a baggy blue blouse and black slacks which might have been painted onto her legs, stood beside their table. "I *thought* it was you. I heard from Shobha you were back. I was out of the country myself—just got back three days ago."

Farida got up to embrace her friend. "What a treat to see you. Can you sit? or are you with someone?"

"Just Hoshang—Jubro, we call him, because he's so big, my cousin's boy—wasn't even born when you left—but sure, I can sit for a minute or two. He's just finishing his ice cream."

"What about your own kids?"

"In school. Jubro is recuperating from measles and his Bucky Aunty is taking him to the cinema after lunch. We are going to see *The Parent Trap*."

"How nice—you know Ratan, of course."

"Of course." Bucky nodded to Ratan, sitting down.

Ratan returned the nod, never standing up. "Hullo, Bachamai. Good to see you again."

He had used her formal name, knowing she didn't like it, in an attempt at humor. Farida ignored him, gripping her friend's wrist. "So, where did you go?"

"The Netherlands, Belgium, Luxembourg, all the little countries— just me and Jhangu. Never been before, but we loved them all, especially the Netherlands—planning to go back already. We were only there ten days. The people were just so lovely—also the food, the country, everything. You really must go sometime."

"Actually, I *have* been, when I was eleven years old, the whole summer—with Kaki."

"That's right, of course. I had forgotten. How is Kaki?"

"The same, thank God—still my rock of Gibralter. No matter what happens I can always count on her. How is Jhangu? How are the kids, Burjor and Roshni? Must be all grown up now."

"Burjor is eight, and Roshni will be seven next month. We almost didn't go because of them—both got over the chicken pox only just before we left. Thank God they were all right—stayed with my mother while we were gone."

"And how is Jhangu?"

"Doing *very* well, I'm happy to say. He is now the bank president."

"At the State Bank, really? I say, that is a bit of first class. I think I had heard something, actually. Please convey my congratulations."

"Thanks—but I must say it's gone to his head. Likes to boss everybody around in the house just like in the office now. I have to keep telling him: in the house, *I* am the president."

Farida grinned. "Good for you. Tell him if he gets too bossy, I shall come and give him a piece of my mind as well."

Ratan nodded meaningfully at Bucky. "She's not just whistling dixie—as they say in Chicago. She will do what she says. She's very good at it."

Farida patted Ratan's arm. "I think what my dear cousin is trying to tell you ever so politely is that I have given him a piece of my mind so very often that he speaks with a great deal of experience."

Bucky laughed. "Poor Ratan."

Farida smiled. "Don't worry about Ratan. He takes care of himself very well—but what about you? Any thoughts about going back to work?"

"Are you joking or what? I stopped working before I had the kids. Why go back now?"

"But don't you miss it, having something to do—specially now with the kids growing up?"

"Arré, what is there to miss? I was an accountant, boring as all hell. Why do you think I quit?"

"Ah, yes, of course. I remember now." Farida had been on her honeymoon with Horace in India, when Bucky and Jhangu had been on theirs in the States, the reverse directions ringing peals of laughter at the time. Bucky had quit her job with TELCO to the consternation of all her friends, most of all her husband. *I only got the degree to get married. Otherwise, he would not have married me. Said from the start he wanted a double income—but too late now. What is he going to do? Divorce me? He has to take care of me. I wouldn't have quit if we needed the money—but he makes enough.* At the time it had seemed a victory, deception the handicap women were allowed against the economic power of men.

"I really should let you finish your lunch before it gets cold—but come to dinner sometime, no? Then we will talk. Jhangu will also like to see you. I'll give you a ring, okay?"

"That will be lovely."

"Bring Ratan also if you want. I heard about you and Horace. So sorry."

"No need. The good thing about divorce is it allows you to right the wrongs of marriage."

"Maybe in America. Here, thank God, marriage is pretty much for keeps—only choice is, like it or lump it."

Ratan addressed his next remark directly to Bucky. "I think it's best to marry within the community, don't you think? Less chance of a bad marriage that way. Everyone knows what to expect from the start. Bad enough we have to account for personal differences and family differences, but when we marry outside the community we also have cultural differences—and the more the differences the more difficult the marriage."

Bucky winked. "Farida, I think Ratan is trying to tell you something. Maybe you should listen?"

Farida grinned. "I only listen to Ratan when I feel like it—and he only listens to me when he feels like it. That is part of the privilege of friendship. If we listened to each other all the time, that might just be the end. So much of our friendship is based on ignoring each other."

Bucky and Ratan both laughed, Bucky taking her leave shortly, prompting a remark from Ratan. "God, how fat she is getting. No wonder she and her husband are fighting."

Farida shook her head, poking his soft stomach, bulging over his belt. "Look who's talking. It's a pity, Ratan, but wit simply doesn't become you."

"I wasn't trying to be witty, just honest. Maybe if you were more honest with her yourself you could save her marriage."

"What rubbish are you talking now?"

"You heard her, no? Marriage is for keeps, like it or lump it. I think she's lumping it—but if she lost some weight, if she gave her Jhangu some incentive to come home, she might start liking it again."

"If what you say is true, then they have a lot more to worry about than her weight."

"Agreed, agreed—but it would at least be a step in the right direction."

"Maybe, maybe not."

"What about you and Horace? You never said anything—just that it was over."

"I can tell you it wasn't my weight that was the problem."

"I didn't mean that—but what happened?"

"Someday I will tell you—but I'm not ready to talk about it yet."

"Of course. I wasn't prying or anything. You can call me anytime—day or night. That is what friends are for—and like it or lump it, I am your friend."

Farida smiled, patting his arm. "Dear Ratan."

The affectionate gesture gave him courage to open his suit again. "Farida, just tell me one thing. *If* you had a beau—and I'm not saying you have one, but *if* you had a beau—would you tell me?"

Farida sighed. Her parents might have talked about a "beau," so might her Bombay friends, but as a Chicagoan she found it ludicrous, preferring "boyfriend" or "partner" or "lover," but couldn't explain the difference to Ratan. She had more in common with both cultures than either an Indian or an American, but less in common with either culture than a native of either country. "It would depend."

"On what?"

"Whether you would approve or not."

"What do you mean? If he was a blackie or something?"

"Yes, precisely. You have answered your own question simply by asking it. I'm not saying it's your fault, Ratan, that you are prejudiced. You don't know any better. You are like so many of us Parsis, talking about how liberated we are, but when faced with the truth, when faced with the prospect of a mixed marriage, whether with a white or a black or a yellow or a Hindu or Muslim or Christian or whatever, they revert to the old conservative arguments: we only want what's best for you; we are only looking out for your best interest—but what they're really doing is fighting for a way of life that is vanishing, a reality that should never have been a reality, but one with which they have now grown too comfortable to part. They make it seem as if it's compassion, as if they care about you, but it's really just selfishness. The old order always fears the new: the old is threatened by the new because the new reminds the old that it is dispensable—that it is on its way out."

"Wow! I never took you for a philosopher, but you and I are surely of the same order. I am only two years older than you, you know."

She didn't feel like explaining. "I know. Forget it. I was just jabbering."

"No, it's actually very interesting. Divorce is making you more philosophical. It happens that way, they say."

"Maybe you're right. It makes you ask Why, it makes you less complacent—but you better hurry now. I don't want to be late for my lesson."

Ratan had finished about half his roast, but put down his knife and fork slowly. "Farida, I am having such a good time with you. I would still like to have some pudding. Why rush? The fellow will wait if it is that important. I mean, after all, what is he? Just a student—not the bloody Aga Khan that we have to rush through our lunch for him. I mean, he's not your beau or anything. So what's the problem?"

Farida felt blood rush like a geyser to her face. Her eyes lashed into his like hooks. "I swear, Ratan, sometimes you can be a real shit. I begin to see why you have never married."

Her appeal was undeniable, appalling and attractive at once, raw and romantic. Ratan wanted to say she was never more beautiful than when she was angry, but a glimmer of light held his tongue: he knew that would upset her further though he couldn't have said why. It was perhaps the difference between the old and new orders she had mentioned, he unfortunately of the old. "I say, Farida, take it easy. It was just a bloody joke. You seem so ... I don't know—perfect, sometimes—that I forget your divorce is still very new. Sorry."

Farida buried her gaze in her veal. "No, I'm the one who should be sorry. You are right. I am overreacting to everything. Must be the divorce—and I don't even know it. Thank you for your patience. I really appreciate it."

"Don't mention it. My pleasure."

She laughed. "I don't see how it can be your pleasure—but really, I'm sorry. I had no right to go off on you like that."

"That's what friends are for."

"Dear Ratan."

IT WAS NOT QUITE FOUR O'CLOCK when they returned to Blue Mansions, but seeing Darius's bicycle standing in the compound

Farida barely acknowledged Ratan's goodbye, slamming shut the door of his Plymouth, dashing up the stairs like Cinderella in reverse, bursting into the sitting-room to find Darius on the sofa. "Sorry, I'm late."

He got up. "You're not late. I came early." The clock chimed four in corroboration, but neither noticed. "Did you run up the stairs?"

Her face remained anxious. "Yes, but that's not why I'm out of breath. Silly of me to think a minute would make a difference, but I saw your bicycle downstairs and didn't want to keep you waiting."

He shook his head. "No place I would rather wait."

His voice had developed a vibrato through which you could shove a cello. She saw nothing but her lover standing in a void. Sofa, floor, ceiling, walls, all disappeared. There is a way people move when in love, they glide with preordained grace, floating through obstacles, becoming the other's compass, rudder, wind, and star. It is a state of grace and they had joined the select club, could have danced all night and still have begged for more. "Have you been waiting long?"

He shook his head again. "Just got here." The sitting-room was a goldfish bowl, Kaki and Sashi and other servants in dangerous proximity. He pointed to the studio door. "Shall we get started?"

She had issued orders they were not to be disturbed at their lesson. "Of course." Behind closed doors again they coalesced into a single egg, a single beating heart. Minutes later they remained entwined. Farida whispered. "My darling, how are you? How have you been?"

Darius shook his head. "I can't believe the difference a few minutes can make. I *feel* better—not just better, but like Superman—stop a speeding locomotive with my bare hands, that kind of better." He looked at his watch, grinning. "You know, it has been forty-five hours and forty-five minutes."

She knew what he meant, since they had last parted the day before yesterday. "I can bear it only because I know when I will be seeing you again. I know what it means now to be in a living hell."

He planted a series of soft slow kisses on her face. "Also a living heaven."

"Yes, yes, yes, yes." She kissed him back.

There was a knock on the door. "Bai. Tea."

It was the only interruption she allowed. They separated and Farida let Sashi in with a tea tray including a plate of assorted biscuits while Darius set the easel, smiling at Sashi. "Thank you, Sashi."

Sashi smiled—not unembarrassed, but pleased. Ratan never acknowledged her presence (any servant's presence) except when he wanted something. "Yes, thank you, Sashi—but remember, we are not to be disturbed now. If someone calls on the telephone, take a message."

"Yes, bai."

Farida locked the door behind Sashi. She had arranged red roses on a blue tablecloth. Darius squeezed pigments from tiny tubes into a palette, filled a small cup with water from a basin in the corner of the room. "I'm beginning to feel more confident about my nature drawing already. I'm never going to be a great painter, but all the little tricks help."

"Tricks? What tricks?"

"You know, what you said, adding white to make colors more solid, water to make them more fluid. It gives me so much more control."

"Those aren't tricks. This isn't a card game. This is painting. This is art. What you are doing is developing technique."

He grinned. "Sorry. That's what I meant. I'm developing technique."

During their first days, before the poker prod of her conscience, they had done no drawing, no painting, but rushed straight to bed. It wasn't until the middle of the second week, at Farida's insistence, that they had become more disciplined. He didn't care about the examination, what she gave him was so much more, but what she gave him was no more than what he gave her and she had no wish to burden their days with guilt, no wish either to cheat him of what he might otherwise attain, nor to bite the hand of the mechanism that fed them. They had developed a routine: the tea tray; the art lesson; the love lesson though the roles of teacher and student became increasingly confused in the bedroom and the love lesson often preceded the art. The most difficult part of the evening was always the leavetaking.

Farida had decided against other students, wishing if anything more time with Darius, but their evenings were restricted, parenthesized by the end of his schoolday at three-thirty and dinner at the Katrak household at eight. On Mondays, Wednesdays, and Fridays he arrived on his bicycle at four, scheduled for an hour which slipped easily into two, sometimes three. He had dined twice at Blue Mansions, but it would have been impossible to maintain their charade before Kaki, whose suspicions might already have been aroused though she had said nothing. If Darius's parents suspected they too had said nothing, but spoke so often to their friends of their Cooper connection, and with such pride, that it seemed they might have welcomed grounds for suspicion, and for once Farida was thankful for the magic of her name. "I wish, just once, that I could wake up next to you. It's as if hours turn into seconds when you're here, and into days when you're not, and I'm tired of living in this … this accordion of time. I want a grand piano. I want our love to be like a Steinway."

She was grinning at the fanciful language and so was he, but he wanted the Steinway no less than she, no less tired of subterfuge than she, their muffled muzzled lovemaking. "I know. I feel the same way. I have given it some thought and I have an idea."

They were in her bed, lying on their backs, damp and spent and reviving, clothes piled on the floor. "Really? What?"

"You remember my friend, Cisco?"

"Yes, your best friend."

"Right. He lives one floor downstairs from us. I don't actually know all the details, but here's the situation. His parents came to Bombay from Kerala when he was three or four years old. They were well educated, but his dad was promised a job which went to someone else and they couldn't find any other work. It went from bad to worse. His dad got caught stealing something and got sent to jail. His mum jumped out of a window, out of shame, depression, desperation—who knows what."

Farida turned on her side, raising herself on one elbow. "Oh, I say, the poor fellow."

"We don't talk about it, of course."

"Of *course* not!"

"What happened was Cisco got put in an orphanage and adopted by a psychologist, a Welsh fellow, Dr. Gregory Jones. He has patients in Breach Candy—mostly Americans, as you can imagine. He lost his wife in a drowning incident in England and his daughter to leukemia. Why he came to Bombay, I don't know—maybe just to forget—you know, start again, new life and all that—but it was a perfect fit, him and Cisco."

Farida shook her head in wonder. "I would never have guessed. He seemed so well adjusted when we met, maybe the best adjusted of everyone at the party—except, of course, you."

Darius remained on his back, grinning at the ceiling. "Of course—but you are also right about Cisco. He's a terrific fellow! The thing is, my folks own the flat downstairs from us. At the time my grandmother was living there by herself, but after she died they put an ad in the paper for a new tenant and Dr. Jones answered. Such a sad story, they thought, and what a philanthropic fellow and all that. Of course, it didn't hurt that he was Welsh."

Farida rolled her eyes in deference to the Parsi infatuation with all things western.

"They moved in downstairs from us and they have been there now for years—but here's my point. Dr. Jones is going to London for a month and he will be taking Cisco with him. The last two times they went I took care of their fish and they let me stay in the flat. I think, while they are gone, there is a good chance I might be able to use the flat—*we* might be able to use the flat."

Farida sat up straight. "I say! Really, Darius! You knew—and you didn't tell me right away!"

Darius laced his fingers behind his head, still staring at the ceiling, pleased with himself. "You were late. There was no time."

She slapped his shoulder. "I was not late. You were early."

He continued to grin at the ceiling. "Anyway, there are other problems—but if you are willing we can work everything out."

"Of course, I'm willing. What a question! What are the problems?"

"Well, I mean, you will have to make excuses to Kaki, I will have to make excuses to my family. You won't be able to go in and out of the house too easily. The chowkidar would certainly see you and he might tell somebody. That kind of thing—but if we are careful I think we can manage it."

She had known he was enterprising, but the evidence was welcome, proof that he wanted what she wanted, that he was willing to exert himself in their behalf, that he had been thinking about them. She caressed his shoulder where she had slapped him. "I hate to lie to Kaki, but we really don't have a choice, do we? I could tell her I'm staying with a friend—maybe Shobha. I will have to think about it—but, yes, I think you're right. I think we might just manage it— well worth a try, in any case. I'll never forgive us if we don't take the chance."

"Good. I was hoping you would agree."

She leaned forward on her knees, nibbling his nipples, leaving a sleek trail, kisses along his breastbone, lapping his bellybutton, teasing the delta of pubic hair with her fingers, raising his penis like a phoenix despite muscular intercourse barely minutes before, reveling in the power of the seventeen-year-old, no difference between his first lovemaking and his second, reveling no less in her own power, following the manipulation of her fingers with lips and tongue.

He reached down to cup a breast, loving the fleshy weight in his hand, marveling at the thrust of her round brown satin rump in the air, the slick piston of her mouth, her bobbing head. His sigh was long and deep, loosening air it seemed from the pit of his belly, releasing it in gentle tremors. "Ah, your kisses are like tiny hot water bottles."

She looked up, smiling from her ministrations. "I have made a poet of you. I'm so glad."

"Not a poet. That is *exactly* how it feels."

"Maybe, but you expressed yourself like a poet."

II

The Bharuchas lived on Women's Graduate Union Road in Colaba on the ground floor of Sea View, a large Victorian mansion of stone and timber, sharing the space at first with Jhangu's grandmother who owned the residence, and on her death inheriting the meandering multiroomed flat. A servant conducted Farida and Ratan through a dark winding passage to the sitting-room where they were the last of the guests to arrive. The floor was mosaic, the room of indeterminate shape, large enough to appear cavernous in a dim light—huge as the entire flat seemed huge for its apparent lack of design. The furniture was large, luxurious, solid. Bucky rose to greet them, dressed like Farida in blouse and slacks, but unlike Farida filling hers like a balloon. Jhangu hollered halloos from an adjacent room where he was assembling a slide show of their visit to the lowlands, the centerpiece of the evening. They knew the other two couples: Zubin and Vera Vazifdar, he a civil engineer, she known for her Mozart and Chopin piano recitals; and Minoo and Rose Dastur, he a doctor, she an Englishwoman, once a shopgirl on Oxford Street where she had bonded with her husband over a deerstalker he had purchased. Hands were shaken, men rising, women remaining seated. Bucky served a punch (Vera warned the fruitiness disguised the liquor), followed by samosas and patrel (Rose warned her husband, inclining to fat, to save room for dinner, but Minoo laughed, helping himself to another samosa). Ratan occupied a maroon club chair, punch in hand, plate of patrel beside him on a side table. "Such a nice spacious flat you have got, Bucky, just lovely."

"Thanks, but that is part of the problem. It is big, I will grant you—but also old and drafty."

Jhangu entered smiling, voice booming, a short solid barrel of a man, dressed as were all the men in a bush shirt and baggy pants. "So are we all—we are all getting old and drafty, most of all my wife."

"But it *is*—it *is* old and drafty. In the hot months it is too hot, in the cold months it is too cold—and nothing to be done, but to grin and bear it. Just look at the floor, no? If you put a marble at one end it will roll to the middle—like in an operating theater or something."

Jhangu kept his smile. "If you give her a diamond it isn't bright enough. If you take her to Netherlands she wants to go to America. If you take her to America she wants to go to the moon." He shrugged, laughing. "What to do?"

Vera wore a pleated skirt and lacy blouse, a pretty woman with slim wrists and ankles and thickening waist and chin. She leaned forward, laughing. "Arré, Jhangu. Give your wife some credit."

"Credit? If I give her some credit she will want more credit. If I give her a hundred rupees she will want a thousand. If I tell her she is pretty, she will want to be told she is beautiful."

Zubin grinned. "Then tell her she is the most beautiful girl in the world and be done with it. I tell Vera that all the time. If she plays piano she is the best pianist. If she cooks dhansak she is the best cook. You don't have to mean it, just say it."

His wife blushed. "What nonsense. He never tells me any such thing—and if he did, he had darn well better mean it. That's all I can say."

Jhangu looked from Vera back to Zubin. "If I say she is the most beautiful girl, she will want to be Elizabeth Taylor."

Bucky grinned suddenly, looking at Farida. "What did I tell you? Talks as if he has been struck by a windmill."

Jhangu grinned at Farida. "A little jargon she picked up in the Netherlands—meaning she thinks I am cracked. Who knows? Maybe she is right."

"No maybe about it. He thinks being president of the bank makes him president of the world."

Rose, sitting with the bearing of a model, the slimmest person in the room, the straightest back and shoulders, wearing a salmon miniskirt to match her auburn hair, stared at her husband's pudgy hand squeezing a wedge of lime over a slice of patrel. "Really, Minoo, don't you think you've had enough?"

Again Minoo said nothing, but Jhangu intercepted. "Arré, Rose, let the poor fellow eat if he wants. Pleasures get fewer as we get older."

Rose pursed her lip. "He's a doctor. He should know better."

Jhangu got up. "All right, chalo, everyone, enough small talk. Might as well bring your things to the screening room. We can eat while we are viewing the slides."

A PORTABLE SCREEN HAD BEEN RAISED against the wall in the screening room. Side tables were brought from the sitting-room by servants for the glasses of punch and plates of food. Jhangu sat in the back by the slide projector. "Sorry, Farida, not as advanced as your dad's projects—no music, no commentary, except what we remember as we view the slides, not even a silent movie—but what to do?"

"Don't be silly, Jhangu. Never apologize for bringing pleasure to others. I'm sure it will awaken many memories of my own."

"Right, right, Bucky was telling me you had gone. I didn't know—but, of course, you Coopers have been everywhere."

Minoo spoke, mouth full of patrel. "I also remember your dad's movies, Farida. Too good, they were—also your Horace's movies. I saw one at the Cine Society, about France I think it was. You did the commentary. Too good, his also. What a talent. Too bad about you and him. Condolences."

"Thanks, Minoo, but no need. The correct term is actually congratulations. The way I see it now, the condolences should all have been for the marriage."

Everyone laughed, but not comfortably. Jhangu frowned. "I say, Farida, you may have something there, you know. I mean, you have always been a pretty girl—I don't think anyone will argue—but I swear divorce seems to have made you positively radiant."

Farida beamed. "Maybe there's a lesson in it."

Vera stared at the floor, apparently unable to understand. The others stared at one another until Zubin spoke. "Hard to know what to say these days. Women's liberation is giving everyone a different perspective, no? Absolutely right, I say: better a divorce than a bad marriage anyday. The trouble is we are not used to seeing things that way in Bombay still."

Jhangu's voice boomed again. "I agree one hundred percent. Here, once we are married, it is for keeps, for better or worse, usually for worse, but what to do? I swallowed the bait—hook, line, and sinker. A pretty face, a nice body—and now I am paying the price."

Farida's voice sharpened, seeing her friend stiffen. "Yes, yes, Jhangu. Very difficult it must be to be president of the bank, and to holiday in the Netherlands, and to have a nice big flat—not to mention a good wife and two lovely children. Very difficult, indeed. I feel very sorry for you."

"Arré, Farida, I am telling you, I swallowed the bait. We could have done better on a double income—but the day we came back from our honeymoon, the same day, she quit, just like that. Good job she had at TELCO, might have become a manager, maybe a vice-president, maybe more. Instead, what? Gave it up. Supposing I just gave up my job, then what? But she is the wife, she can do what she wants. Tricked, kicked, and licked—that's how I felt, I can tell you. Tricked, kicked, and licked."

Rose was no less sharp than Farida. "What rot you're talking, Jhangu. Who would mind the kids if Bucky went to work? Not you."

"Kids? What kids? We didn't have kids then—and who minds the kids now? Not her. Gets up at God knows what ungodly hour, lies around all day reading magazines and eating chocolates—like Cleopatra or somebody. Thank God for servants. If it is a question of looking after the kids I would have been better off marrying one of the servants—less expensive."

Bucky grinned, face crimsoning. "What rubbish! There were no chocolates in Cleopatra's time."

"Arré, figs, apricots, asps, Nile juice—whatever it was, what does it matter?"

Vera spoke quickly. "He's really talking nonsense now—but speaking about magazines, Farida, didn't you used to write for magazines? You published some stories or something, no, in America?"

"Yes, mainly women's magazines—sentimental rubbish." She had imagined she had modeled her stories on her own marriage, but couldn't have been more wrong. "I've given it up."

"At least, she was doing something—not staying home all day eating chocolates."

Bucky glared at Jhangu, unblinking as a snake. "I do *not* eat chocolates all day."

Farida stared at the patterns in the Persian carpet at her feet. What had Bucky said? *I only got the degree to get married. Otherwise, he would not have married me. What is he going to do? Divorce me? He has to take care of me*—but Jhangu had only himself to blame, unable to see beyond *a pretty face, a nice body.* People made their beds, she as much as Bucky and Jhangu, marrying Horace because she had flattered herself he needed her, that she was his equal in maturity despite the difference in their ages, when more than anything he had offered a continuation of the life to which she was accustomed in Bombay, when perhaps Benjie, whom she had treated so cavalierly, might have treated her with more respect—but these were past and distant tribulations. Darius provided entrée to a new world and century.

The lights went off, the first slide flashed on the screen, Bucky waving from the passenger seat of a red convertible before a windmill. Sitting across from Farida in the first row she spoke at large to her guests. "Our car—it was a Fiat. We drove and drove and drove—terrific roads they have, you know."

"Actually, I drove and drove and drove. She rode and rode and rode, couldn't even read the map. We had to stop everytime we weren't sure of our direction."

Bucky's jaw dropped in silent reproach, eyes still glassy, face turning scaly—but Jhangu ignored her easily switching the slide.

THE ROOMS IN THE BHARUCHA FLAT ran like compartments in a train. A door linked the screening room to the dining-room where a long table had been set for eight, covered with a red tablecloth, laden with covered dishes revealed in turn to be eggs fried with potatoes, chicken in a teriyaki sauce, and a sweet prawn curry with cashews and raisins served with white rice, bowls of sweet corn soup steaming at each setting. Bucky's composure returned amid congratulations on her table and all animosity appeared to dissipate as the meal progressed. Jhangu, at the head, barely glanced at his wife, but spoke cordially. "Bucky, what was that old Dutch saying? You know the one I mean."

Bucky smiled from her end of the table, avoiding her husband's glance, speaking as if she were elocuting onstage again at her high school. "God created heaven and earth, but Holland is the work of man. They say half of the country has been reclaimed from the sea, and I swear, everywhere you go—dykes, canals, tidal barriers."

Rose spoke no less cordially though her eyes remained on her husband's plate. "I love the legend of the boy with his finger in the dyke."

Zubin nodded. "Arré, yes, but that is the same as Bombay. We were the same, islands in the sea, now reclaimed and joined at the hip to the mainland."

Bucky shook her head. "Yes, of course, Zubin, you are right—but what a difference in the countries. The Netherlands is like a country that has been washed by the sea—we seem to have got what was left behind. The Dutch take such pride in their country, so hardworking—we just cannot compare."

The talk turned to their children who were attending the Rayman Circus with friends, and Farida felt the sac of her stomach harden like clay. Minoo and Rose had a son and daughter, Vera and Zubin had three sons, but she had extinguished the thickening in her own body in a flight of rage and pathos despite her multiple miscarriages. Again, she was grateful for Darius, the mere thought of him dispelling her gloom like the sun.

Minoo became jollier through the meal and sat back after a second helping of chicoo ice cream. "So, I say, what about you two? Wedding bells in the air or what?"

Farida was startled from her brown study as much by the question as its suddenness. Rose was shaking her head. "I have to apologize for my husband. He seems to have forgotten you are still getting a divorce. He would forget his head if it weren't fixed to his shoulders."

Minoo waved the apology away. "What rot, what rot. I have forgotten nothing. Did she not tell us this very evening only, congratulations on the divorce and condolences on the marriage? Did she or did she not? You tell me."

Farida recovered her equanimity with a smile. "He's absolutely right, Rose. No need to apologize. The trouble is if Ratan and I choose to tie the knot it would be the end of the best friendship a girl could have. He is like a gay friend. I can count on him not to have any ulterior motives. I would gain a husband only to lose a friend."

Only Jhangu laughed out loud. Of the rest, some looked expectantly, others guardedly, at Ratan. Ratan himself leaned back in his chair, raising his eyebrows, staring at his plate. "I say, Farida, I don't know if I would go that far—a bit much, wouldn't you say, to think of me as a gay friend?"

Vera dabbed her lips with the serviette. "I don't know why you would think so. I think a gay friend would make the best of all possible husbands—much better than a glum friend."

Her husband smiled, almost to himself. "I think Vera might need a little explanation." He looked at his wife, who looked from him to the others, who looked back at her husband who finally spoke again. "Gay means homosexual—a gay man is the best friend for a girl because he is not ... interested—if you get my meaning."

Vera blushed again. "I *do* get your meaning—but I must say I don't know if I want to."

Farida spoke gently. "Sorry, Vera. Thoughtless of me. Let's just blame it on my bad Chicago manners, shall we?"

Vera seemed unaware that Farida had apologized only to her, not to Ratan. "No, no, not at all—I suppose, when you look at it like that, it *does* make a lot of sense. I just didn't know."

III

Darius slid both latticed metal doors of the lift quietly back on their rollers when they reached the third floor of Edgewater House. Farida stepped smiling from the iron cage onto the landing, almost giggling, a suitcase in one hand she insisted on carrying herself. The floor was tiled, wooden stairs winding around the lift shaft, two flats to a floor, front doors facing each other, bearing brass plaques. The door on their left bore the name Jagdish Kapur; the door on their right, Dr. Gregory Jones. Darius put a finger to his lips, whispering. "Very nosy neighbors."

"They must lead very dull lives."

"That's what makes them nosy."

"Such a bright boy, you are."

Darius grinned, finding the right key in his chain, pushing open the door, but Farida put down the suitcase and stood her ground. Darius's eyebrows rose. "What's the matter?"

"Aren't you going to carry me across the threshold?"

"Of course!" Suitcase in hand, Farida in his arms, he entered the flat shutting the door behind them with an expert backward kick.

Bending at the knees, he deposited the suitcase in a chair, all the while returning Farida's kisses.

"So strong, my darling is—my darling is so strong."

"Only for you." He was surprised by his own strength and grace—peripheral attributes, he recognized, of his desire.

She not only heard but felt what he said—felt not only that she could do no wrong, but that everything she did in his presence was exalted. "My darling, I can hardly believe it. Are we really alone in our own little pied-a-terre?"

"Yes, but we don't have much time, almost eight o'clock already. Let me just show you the place before we go upstairs."

She grinned. "Can't we say we were … delayed?"

The Katraks had invited Farida to dinner on a Friday evening, insisting it was the least they could do. Dr. Jones had left for London with Francis the day before, leaving Darius the key, mainly to feed the fish, giving him the run of the flat. Darius had moved books, records, comics, and clothes downstairs, returning to his family only for meals and laundry. During Dr. Jones's previous visit to London, Darius had invited friends for card games, chess, monopoly, or to sleep overnight chatting over Cokes and wafers into the small hours of morning. The one time Yasmin had called her friends for a sleepover, the Jagdish Kapurs across the landing had complained about a pillow fight that had raged past midnight. Occupancy privileges had reverted irrevocably to Darius. Yasmin's alternate suggestion, a mixed sleepover for both sets of friends, boys and girls, separate bedrooms, separate bathrooms, had further ruined her chances. Darius kissed her again. "We have just been delayed. Less than an hour ago we were delayed. We can be delayed again as much as you want tomorrow—and the day after, and after that."

Darius had gone directly from school to Blue Mansions for their routine before they had both returned to Edgewater House. "You're right. I'm being greedy. Sorry. The girl can't help it. Just show me the flat and let's go upstairs. The sooner we go upstairs, the sooner we can come downstairs again—and be delayed again."

He spread his arms encompassing the room. "Well, now, here we have the sitting-room." It was a long room, three light fixtures alternating with two fans along the length of the ceiling, divans lining the walls, carpets on the floor, a coffee table at each end, a long green bubbling fish tank at the far end, an air conditioner affixed among the windows in the far wall.

Farida dashed to the windows. Edgewater House, the farthest building in the row from the road, almost jutting into the sea, might have been a lighthouse, particularly for the view after sunset. "I had forgotten how savage the sea can seem, how desolate by night. I love it here already. I can't wait to get started—painting by day, Darius by night. Who could ask for anything more?" She planned to paint during the days while Darius was at school. "I couldn't love it more if we had just this one room, but we have the whole flat—and with you it's better than Buckingham Palace."

"Let me show you the rest of the place—I mean, the palace."

A hallway provided the spine of the flat, leading from the middle of the sitting-room through its length to the master bedroom. One side held two more bedrooms, each with adjoining bathrooms; the other side held kitchen, dining-room, and godown. Farida hardly paid attention, clinging to his arm during the tour. "Just think. I'm to be your kept woman. Do you want a kept woman? an *ol*der kept woman?"

He couldn't stop grinning. "More than anything."

"Good, then it's settled. You can tie me up, chain me to the bed, do whatever you want. Then I will be your prisoner completely. Will you like that?"

He surprised himself, uttering with ease what would have been unthinkable a month ago. "Yes, but we have to go upstairs now—and if you don't do as I say I will spank you."

She gave him a languorous look. "Is that a threat or a promise?"

"From the way you look I don't think you really care."

She swayed to an inaudible melody, hands clasped behind, arched shoulders deepening her cleavage. "I think you're right. Shall we find out?"

"Later. We have to go upstairs. Everything else later."

She screwed her nose. "Spoilsport—but I shall hold you to it. You owe me a spanking."

"My pleasure."

"Wrong. The pleasure will be mine."

THEY WENT UP THE STAIRS CHOKING BACK GIGGLES, but once Darius had let them in with his key they were on their best behavior, like children before the high school principal. The flat had the same layout as the one below, even the furniture was similar. The main difference Farida noted as she waited while Darius left to inform the others of their arrival was the lack of a fish tank.

Mrs. Katrak emerged first, conspicuous most for her smile, almost an entity itself. Her hair was fastened again in a bun, her spectacles enlarging her grey eyes. "There you are, Farida. So good to see you in our humble home. Welcome." She embraced her as if they had known each other all their lives.

Farida returned the embrace politely. "Thanks for having me."

Yasmin entered next in a bright yellow miniskirt, long black hair brushed in a barrette behind, also smiling but hardly as aggressively as her mother. "Hullo, Farida."

Farida understood Yasmin had dressed to impress her and smiled. "Hullo, Yasmin. Good to see you again. What a lovely dress!"

Yasmin's smile gained confidence. "Thanks."

Mr. Katrak appeared much as he had at The Darjeeling in a bush shirt and baggy pants, thinning hair brushed back, eyes narrowing as he grinned, offering a handshake. "Looking sharp as ever, Farida. Welcome to our humble home."

Farida had dressed informally, blue jeans, pink blouse, a single pearl necklace her sole nod to the event. Her smile brightened seeing Darius behind Mr. Katrak as she shook his father's hand. "Hullo, Mr. Katrak. Thanks. It's good of you to have me."

"Not at all, not at all. Don't be silly. What are friends for?"

Mrs. Katrak almost escorted Farida away from her husband. "Sit, sit, have a seat." Farida found herself in a sofa against the wall joined by her hostess, Darius in an adjacent sofa with Yasmin, Mr. Katrak in a club chair opposite Darius and Yasmin. "What will you have to drink?"

"Whatever Darius is having."

Mr. Katrak shook his head. "He is just a boy, only soft drinks for him—but have a whiskey if you want. I'm having a whiskey." He indicated a table alongside the middle of the wall set with bottles of liquor, an ice bucket, tall tapered frosted glasses. "Whiskey, vodka, rum—whatever you want. We also have some sherry, I think—or some wine if you want."

Farida smiled, accustomed to Parsi attempts to impress foreigners (as she was occasionally perceived for her years in Chicago) with openmindedness about liquor, accounting no less for their preference of Bach, Beethoven, and Brahms over Ravi Shankar. She realized the Dhuns were in sway no less than others to her Cooperness. "Thanks, but I think I'd rather have just a soft drink for now."

"Of course, of course, no pressure, whatever you want. Have what you want."

Farida looked at Darius, who asked for a Coke. Yasmin bounced in her seat, "I'll have a whiskey, please," but was ignored. Mrs. Katrak called Shakuntala, the servant, sending for four Cokes, turning her ponderous smile again on Farida. "We Parsis are sophisticated enough to drink or not drink as we please. We recognize the recreational attributes of drinking. Hindus recognize only the sinful."

Yasmin spoke, not without pique. "What nonsense, Mummy. Hindus drink just like Parsis—maybe even more. You should see Arun's family sometime—and they are supposed to be Brahmins."

Mrs. Katrak shrugged, giving Farida a sidelong martyred glance. "Arun Sarkar is this Hindu boy she runs around with—very bad influence."

Farida shook her head. "Maybe not. I met him that night at the party. He seemed a nice fellow, actually—very witty."

Mrs. Katrak turned her head away, smile frozen, eyes glazed. "Yes, he can be very funny—just like Bugs Bunny."

Darius grinned. "I think sometimes Hindus and Parsis are in a competition or something to show who is more sophisticated. Both drink like fish and brag about how sophisticated they are—but that is like bragging about who is the better alcoholic, no?"

Mr. Katrak laughed, fixing himself a drink from the table. "Actually, sophistication be damned. I am a sinner from way back and not ashamed to admit it. Recreation is good, but sin is better. Ogden Nash said it best: *Candy is dandy, but liquor is quicker.*" He winked at Farida. "Even during prohibition we had our ways, if you know what I mean."

Farida ignored the wink. "I suppose truly sophisticated people don't talk about it at all. They just drink what they want, when they want, without worrying about what it means."

Mrs. Katrak nodded. "Of course, of course, but in a backward country like our India what can you expect? They want to show they are as good as everybody else, and they have to talk about it because otherwise they are afraid nobody will notice." Her expression turned coy as she turned her eyes again to Farida. "Do you know, Farida, that we are actually related?"

Farida's eyebrows rose. "No, I didn't know, but I'm not surprised—I mean, as Parsis, being such a small community, we are practically all related, aren't we?"

"Yes, of course, but I mean I have traced the actual relation. You see, I am descended from Wadias, and my great grandmother and your great grandfather were second cousins. I knew there was a relation there. I just had to track it down. I thought it might interest you."

Farida laughed. "Always nice to find new relations—but as I said I am not surprised."

"Wadias were shipbuilders, as you must be knowing. They built frigates that were used in the Battle of Trafalgar, teak frigates—first time the English used frigates not built in England—for their quality, of course. One of my ancestors, Jamshetji Bomanji Wadia, was the shipwright of the *Marquess of Cornwallis*—and just for a joke he carved on the bottom of the hull: 'The ship was built by a d----d Black Fellow AD 1800.'" She laughed. "You can, of course, fill in the blanks." Her practiced smile reappeared. "You know, if my Dhun hadn't swept me off my feet I would probably have married a Wadia myself. I would have been a proper Wadia today."

Mr. Katrak grinned. "Quite a job it was too, let me tell you, sweeping away such a heavy family tree. You can see I am still bent over from the weight."

Farida laughed again. "Rubbish! I don't find you at all bent."

Mrs. Katrak shook her head, smile in place. "He is always making the same joke. He thinks it is so very funny."

Mr. Katrak shrugged. "Two sides to every story. If she said something different, I would make a different joke—but as it is ..." He shrugged again.

Shakuntala wheeled in a trolley bearing Cokes, bowls of peanuts and cashews, dishes of cheese straws and wafers. Despite Mrs. Katrak's iron grin Farida and Darius beamed easily and naturally, infecting the room with their spirits. The Dhuns seemed no less happy with Farida than Darius, Yasmin no less—even Shakuntala seemed unable not to smile. Mrs. Katrak patted Farida's knee. "Farida, we want to thank you for what you are doing for our Darius. Most teachers give tuitions for one hour, but you take him for two hours, three hours, and don't even charge—even gave him dinner, so very generous of you."

Farida scooped nuts into her plate, a handful of wafers, two cheese straws. "Not at all—the pleasure is mine. I couldn't ask for more. He is such a good student he has actually taught me a few things." She and Darius exchanged glances and smiles at the irony, directing their gazes immediately away, Farida back to Mrs. Katrak, Darius into space.

"That I cannot believe except as more evidence of your generosity."

"No, Mrs. Katrak, it is true. I find human nature acts out of selfishness—even when we perform good deeds, it is because in the end it is to our advantage. Darius is occupying my time in a way that fulfills me. Otherwise, what would be the point of the tuitions for me? I don't need money."

"Of course, when you put it like that—but Farida, really now, you *must* call me Dhun. With all that you are doing, I feel that we are almost family."

"Of course ... Dhun."

Mr. Katrak raised his glass. "And me, too, you must also call me Dhun."

Yasmin raised her voice, piping like a piccolo. "But not me, Farida. You must call me Yasmin only—and thank God. What a moniker, Dhun—sounds like a broken bell or something."

Farida laughed, struck again by the similarity between the twins, dimpled cheeks, clefted chins, and liked Yasmin better for the resemblance though in her deportment she seemed distinctly younger than her brother. "I agree, Yasmin is a better name—but your parents gave you the name in the first place. No Dhuns, no Yasmin, right?"

Yasmin laughed. "Yes, yes, of course, of course. I owe them everything: name, life, firstborn."

Mrs. Katrak turned her smile once more on Farida, shaking her head. "We never dared to talk to our parents like that, always with respect—my father's word was law. Of course, in our day we didn't have movies like they have now—delinquents are all heroes now. Elvis Presley is their model."

"Oh, Mummy! Elvis is *an*cient! He must be at least forty!"

Farida shook her head. "Actually, he just turned thirty-five. I should know. We were born on the same day, 8th of January, 1935. I'm actually a fan myself."

Yasmin's eyes widened. Adults of her acquaintance had nothing complimentary to say about Elvis. "Really? of Elvis? more than the Beatles?"

"I like both, but Elvis came first. Without him there would have been no Beatles. He paved the way for everyone else. Also, it's not a fair comparison. He is one man, the Beatles are four. His appeal is his voice and style, the Beatles' appeal is their songs. They are songwriters first, performers second, but not Elvis. He is a performer first and last, not a songwriter at all."

Yasmin shifted restlessly, black eyes glowing. "Cisco loves Elvis. He gets all his records when he goes abroad—you know, because we can't get his records in India. I bet he will come back with all the latest Elvis records. He is in London, you know."

Farida nodded. "Darius said something about that. He's taking care of their fish or something?"

"Yes, he gets to stay in their flat everytime they go abroad. I have to stay here. It's not fair—but who am I to complain? I owe everything to my parents. I have to do what they say."

She giggled, but Mr. Katrak's tone sharpened. "Enough now, Yasmin. Don't be a baby. Whose fault is it if you can't behave responsibly like your brother?"

Mrs. Katrak explained the situation to Farida who nodded saying she had heard the story from Darius. Mrs. Katrak's smile never wavered. "You two must talk about a lot of things."

Farida nodded. "Yes, we are getting to know each other quite well."

The smile seemed to tighten a notch. "Farida, what you said earlier, about all good deeds being basically selfish—I think you might be right. One reason I was thanking you earlier was I wanted to ask you a favor."

Farida bit into a cheese straw, holding the plate close to catch the crumbs, eyes on her plate. "Really? What?"

"Well, actually, it is for Darius's cousin, Zarir. He is also appearing for the same exam as our Darius and his mother was asking if you could also give him tuitions. I wouldn't normally ask, but she is family, my husband's sister—so I said I would at least ask."

Farida never doubted the innocence of the question, but it might have been a death sentence for the ash spreading across her face. She chewed her cheese straw slowly, nodding as if she were considering Mrs. Katrak's request, asking for patience until she was done chewing. When she spoke she kept her eyes on her plate. "I'm very sorry, Dhun, but I don't think that will be possible. You see, I hadn't realized I would be taking so much time with just one pupil. Two is out of the question."

If Mrs. Katrak noticed she gave no indication. "But they could take tuition together, no? I mean, at the same time. They are cousins, after all. That way it won't take any more of your time."

Farida hesitated and Darius stepped into the breach. "Mummy, no, that is impossible. I will never learn anything if Zarir is there. He is a complete duffer."

Mrs. Katrak's head seemed to bounce on her neck. "Arré, Darius, what a thing to say. This is drawing, after all—painting, not science, it doesn't take brains—and I thought you and Zarir were good pals. I thought you would *like* the idea."

"Mummy, you don't know everything. It just wouldn't work, I tell you."

"Well, I must say, I think that is up to Farida, not you." She turned to Farida. "What do you think, Farida? two birds with one stone? as a favor to my sister-in-law?"

Farida looked at Darius who looked at the floor. "I don't know, Dhun. I must say it doesn't seem like a good idea."

Darius responded immediately. "I would hate it. Zarir is a complete idiot."

Mr. Katrak laughed. "I know what it is. The boy is jealous. He doesn't want to share his teacher. He is being a dog in the manger and I can't say I blame him." He winked again at Farida. "Boys will be boys, not so?"

Farida ignored the wink again and Darius held his father's eyes. "Dad, that is nonsense. I'm telling you, it just wouldn't work."

Mrs. Katrak's head continued to bob as she looked at her son. "Arré, Darius, what do you mean it wouldn't work? What kind of answer is that? What am I going to tell your Gooloo Aunty?"

"You can tell her what you want. I'm telling you it will not work."

Farida spoke softly, but firmly. "Dhun, I think you might just tell her that *I* said it would be too much for me. I told you about the art gallery I want to open. That is going to take up so much time once I get started. I wonder if I will have time enough then even for just Darius—not fair to take on more pupils than I can manage. I am sure she will understand if you put it like that."

Mrs. Katrak seemed not to understand at all, looking from Darius to Farida and back, but didn't insist. "Well, if that is how you feel, of course I will tell her—but I really don't understand you, Darius, not at all. I really thought you liked Zarir."

"I like him, yes, Mummy—but he can also be a real pain."

"How is he a pain?"

"You don't have to know everything."

Mrs. Katrak shrugged, looking again at Farida as if to say: *See what I mean. Even my Darius. Can't tell them anything.*

Farida nodded, smiling commiseration, but Mrs. Katrak shook her head, her smile seeming momentarily to lose weight.

Mr. Katrak still grinned. "Who can blame the boy? Like father, like son—bred in the genes, you know." He winked again. "Pun intended."

Mrs. Katrak lost her smile. "Dhun, what a thing to say! No wonder people talk about you."

"Talk? Who talks?"

"Everybody, but what do you care?"

"I DON'T THINK YOUR MOTHER LIKES ME VERY MUCH."

They were downstairs again, though Darius had supposedly driven Farida home and returned to the Jones flat alone. "It's not you. She doesn't like anybody she thinks is better than her."

The dinner had passed without further incident. Farida had enjoyed the meal (egg lemon soup, sweet and sour chicken, mutton pulao, concluding with baked Alaska), but the evening had hatched unexpected doubts, like a lizard from a duck's egg. "That's worse—even scary—if she doesn't see me for who I am, only for what I represent."

Darius had sensed her doubt balloon through the evening, a mist of Cassandra in the air, the difference the dinner had made to her spirits—and grinned, wishing to set her again at ease. "But my father made up for it, don't you think? I think he likes you very much."

Farida laughed. "Oh, yes—but I'm not sure that's any better." She had chosen Francis's room for the walls splashed with pictures of the Beatles, the Shadows, Jack and Jackie, Elvis and Priscilla, Dylan and Baez, Gandhi and Nehru, Martin Luther King, Muhammad Ali, Raquel Welch, Jimi Hendrix, and Laika the dog among others. The doctor's room held photographs of his dead family (pretty wife, charming child), but also framed likenesses of Freud and Jung among other forbidding faces, not to mention diagrams of sections of the brain. "I don't think I was very convincing turning your mother down about your cousin. Your father may have been joking, but I *am* a dog in the manger about you. I want you all to myself, all the time, without interference, without interruption."

"Actually, he said *I* was the dog in the manger and he is right. It would have been impossible, of course, with Zarir—but he isn't actually a bad fellow. I just didn't know what else to say. I think even Yasmin was surprised." Darius was turning down the bed. "Less said about it the better, I suppose."

Farida's suitcase lay open on the floor beside the nightstand. She had brought three pairs of jeans, five blouses, a pair of slippers, toiletries, and enough undergarments for a week. Kaki understood only that she was staying with her friend Shobha Shirodhkar, who had instructions to relay all calls to the Jones flat. They had established a code: Shobha would hang up after a single ring, cueing Farida to call her back. "Yes, I suppose."

Her voice had descended an octave. She was kneeling before the suitcase, staring at its contents, unmoving. "I say, Farida, are you all right?"

She shook her head, before nodding, but kept her eyes turned away. "I'm fine. It's just that I hate all this secrecy, I hate lying to Kaki. It goes against everything I believe—except I don't know what else to do. It's so … sexist, you know. If our positions were reversed, if I were the man and you the woman nobody would complain, not even about the difference in age. They would say he will take good care of her, he will make her a good husband—but they will not let me be a good husband to you, they will not let me take good care of you, no matter what my means."

"We will take good care of each other. Don't you think this is right, what we are doing? Do you have any doubts about us?"

If they were caught she would be perceived as the aggressor, the seducer, the temptress—he, a boy, only to have succumbed, robbed of innocence—and she was afraid they were right, but the answer to Darius's question was never in doubt. How could anything so glorious be wrong? "No, my darling, no doubts. What we are doing *has* to be right. Otherwise … otherwise, there is no God. That is how sure I am." She stared at him, more frantic than firm, challenging him to disagree.

"Then, if it is right, why should we care what anyone thinks?"

"It's not that I care what they think, but that I am afraid of what they might do. This is all too good to be true. It cannot last. Even now, after all these weeks, it still feels like a dream. If they find out they will drag us into the gutter, they will make something beautiful seem dirty and vulgar, they will try to make us as unhappy as they are— not because we are wrong, but because they are so sick of their own lives they can't stand anyone else to be happy. *They* are the dogs in the manger." It was how she recalled her mother's unhappiness with Horace: if you were unhappy, you resented happiness in others.

"Farida, why these negative thoughts? They are so unnecessary. You are looking at the glass half empty. Look instead how far we have come. I just count my blessings. Even if it doesn't last—and there is no reason to think it won't—look what we have gained already: happiness enough to fill the Queen Mary!"

He laughed and so did she. "Sorry to be such a nervous Nellie. It's a disease of age—pessimism. You are right. We should count our blessings. We have so much."

"If worse comes to worst I shall leave them, but no reason to think that will be necessary."

"Would you really? Would you leave your family for me?"

"Is this a serious question?"

"Where would we go?"

"What does it matter as long as we are together?"

She sighed. "That is one of the blessings of money. We can go anywhere we want."

If either of them wondered about laws governing minors, neither said a word. Darius took her hand. "Good. I'm glad you're feeling better. You know, this is after all our honeymoon."

She smiled. "Yes, it is, isn't it?"

He got up. "Come, I want to show you something." She rose, returning the pressure of his hand, following him to the sitting-room, the room closest to the sea, leaving the lights off, until they stood by the window, silent and in darkness but for the hum and bubble, the dim green glow, of the fish tank. He held her from behind, locking fingers under her belly; she crossed her arms, holding his elbows.

Looking down they could see the driveway around Edgewater House, parked cars to one side, a narrow guard rail protecting the boundary, beyond the rail a steep decline culminating in dark rocks rising like black knuckles from the water. Surf foamed around the rocks, breakers flashing like giant fingers in the night with the crash of the tide. The breast of the sea lay black and still and oily and grand. Closer to the horizon a crescent moon appeared like a frown in the water, a smile in the sky. To the far left loomed the mass of Malabar Hill, to the right flashed the streetlamps of Scandal Point. Darius held her close. "This is what I wanted you to see—my favorite vista. Isn't it magnificent?"

She was happy, not just for the view which could not have been more magnificent, but his tact in her moment of weakness, the command with which he had squelched her doubt. Her fear was in her head: her own paranoia would cripple her before anything in the power of the world. "Yes, yes, darling, it is—and even more so because of you." They had ignited their love at a party, but ironically since they had become lovers they had done nothing so very social again, afraid to call attention to themselves. Perhaps the key was simply to relax and enjoy themselves, act like a regular couple, go to a movie, a restaurant. Despite all deceptions their consciences were clean.

"The best thing is that the view is from my own home. I don't even have to go anywhere."

"It is really magnificent. I think I would like to paint it."

"You will have plenty of time when I am in school."

"It must be even better from upstairs, but I suppose I better stay down here."

"Actually, yes, but not that much better. You can see more of the rocks, but looking farther out it is about the same."

"I think the rocks are the best part. I can just imagine Andromeda chained and the monster rising from the sea, can't you?"

"What about Perseus? Don't you see Perseus? Andromeda is hopeless without Perseus."

"Yes, yes, of course, I can see Perseus, swooping down in the nick of time. If I were Andromeda I would want you to be Perseus."

He laughed. "I don't know if I want to be Perseus. I think today I would rather be Superman or Spiderman or Green Lantern, or someone like that."

"Who is Green Lantern? I never heard of him."

"He is a superhero like the others. He wears a ring which runs on willpower. He can will himself to fly, bullets to be deflected, objects to materialize—anything he wants just by willing it to happen."

"My goodness, he seems more powerful even than Superman."

"Actually, Green Lantern is my favorite comic. They are getting into social consciousness now in the Green Lantern comics—very unusual."

"Social consciousness? How?"

"Well, in one of the recent issues, a negro fellow comes up to him and says, 'I've been reading about you, Mr. Green Lantern, how you helped the blue skins and the green skins and the purple skins on all those other planets—but what I want to know is how come you never helped the black skins right here on earth. Answer me that, Mr. Green Lantern, if you can'—and Green Lantern just bows his head and says, 'I can't.' Sounds a bit flat when I put it like that, but it's really quite powerful, and Green Lantern comes to the realization that evil doesn't exist only in the form of bugeyed monsters and mad scientists."

"And you would rather be this Green Lantern than Perseus?"

"Oh, yes, one hundred percent—and I think you of all people would be most impressed by the artwork. You can't call the artists cartoonists anymore. It's a new art form, really. I'll show you if you want. I can get it in a sec. Cisco also has the comic in his collection."

He loosened his crossed fingers, but she held him more tightly. "No, not now, it would spoil the moment if we turned on the light. Maybe tomorrow."

He tightened his hold again, leaning his face forward to kiss her ear, her cheek. "Right—tell you what. Wait for me here. I will be right back. I'm going to turn out the lights in the bedroom. That way we can save the moment."

"All right, my darling. Hurry back. I love you."

When he returned she was lying on the divan, adorned by just the pearl necklace, bathed in the green glow of the fish tank, her clothes in a heap on the floor. "My God, Farida, you are going to get so tired of hearing me say the same thing over and over again."

"Saying what?"

"I love you, I love you, I love you, I love you."

"Never, not unless you get tired of saying it first. Every time is a little different, a little more reassuring, and no less wonderful."

"You have changed my life. I never knew—I never dreamed how it could be."

She held out her arms. "My darling—my lovely Green Lantern. Come."

Standing before the fish tank he was outlined in green, as was she. He lifted her from the divan and their auras mingled in bursts of stardust invisible to objective eyes, but the eyes of lovers have heightened sensibilities: at every point of contact appeared bright miniature explosions of soft green satin.

IV

The following Friday Farida faced the sitting-room window in the Jones flat. Two easels stood before her bearing identical sketches, a wide panorama of the Arabian Sea, the horizon bookended by Malabar Hill and Scandal Point. She had engaged two paintings at once, one by day, the other by night, one a negative print of the other. She hadn't left the flat since they had arrived following dinner at the Katraks, but Darius had stocked the kitchen before their arrival and brought whatever else she needed as she requested it. Her culinary repertoire was hardly extensive, a mix of what she had learned from Rohini and women's magazines while married to Horace, but they could have survived on eggs for the duration if necessary. Cooking with Darius was part of the fun regardless of the result. He had run upstairs just once to say they were not to expect him, not even for meals; he planned to manage on his own.

They had spent every second of the weekend together, mostly in bed, surfacing for baths, meals, and drawing lessons, delirious with every activity. She was particularly happy with a portrait of Darius in the stance of Michelangelo's *David* for which he had posed as unselfconsciously as a professional model, casting two excellences in one, his body not unlike David's, but his head was immeasurably finer. She cast a fond glance at her drawing. Pen-and-ink was no match for flesh-and-blood, but provided welcome inspiration as she painted the panorama of rocks and road and sea and sky of the landscape below.

Surprisingly, her conception had been helped by the comics he had shown her, *Green Lantern, The Flash, Hawkman,* and *Aquaman* among others, displaying the art of Neal Adams, Carmine Infantino, Joe Kubert, and Jim Aparo, spectacularly kinetic renderings of the human form in highly imaginative positions, whether flying, swimming, running, or standing still, backdrops no less spectacular for their perspectives. Best of all her anxiety had been laid to rest. There would be time enough for it later perhaps, but for the present she focused as he had enjoined on the full half of the glass. She was grateful to everyone for everything, even the fish in the tank providing rationale for Darius's sojourn in the flat.

The horizon cast a fine wide arc across each page balancing the bustle of Scandal Point on the right with the bulk of Malabar Hill on the left. The panorama by day held a plethora of people, ambulatory and bicycling along Scandal Point, bordered by a stream of cars on Warden Road, buildings beyond. The night was brilliant instead with clusters of light along the road, a crescent moon peering at itself in the sea. Farida imagined a full moon like a Japanese lantern, the clear original hovering over its trembling reflection, and contemplated what art and imagination might allow, but in the next moment she froze. Someone had fitted a key to the front door, turning it in the sudden silence like a clanking chain.

It was ten o'clock in the morning; Darius had left at eight; she did not expect him until four in the afternoon when he would arrive gleaming with sweat having bicycled home, when she would draw his bath and put on the kettle before starting their lesson. There was no time to hide, certainly not to hide paints and palette. Her mind raced like a hamster in its wheel, but she arrested her panic, shaking her head, making fists of her hands, slowing and deepening her breath. Mrs. Katrak stood in the doorway, perplexed no less than Farida, dropping her jaw the length of her face. "Farida? You are here?"

"Dhun! Hullo! I suppose I owe you an explanation."

Mrs. Katrak shut the door behind her, never taking her eyes off Farida, smiling the moment she had retracted her jaw, advancing slowly. "I am sure there is a very good reason."

"Very simple, actually. Darius showed me the flat after dinner the other night—and once I saw it I had to paint the view. He said I could use the flat if I wanted while he was gone. Simple as that."

"He never said anything to me."

"I asked him not to. I didn't want to be a bother."

"Arré, no bother. Our pleasure. You should know that by now. I could have sent lunch." Her smile seemed momentarily to waver, her eye on the portrait of Darius.

Farida immediately turned it over. "Sorry. I don't like showing unfinished work."

"Looked like Darius."

"It's Michelangelo's *David*, actually—but I gave it Darius's face, just for fun, since he was here."

"May I see?"

"I will let you see it when I am happy with it."

"Arré, Farida, what does it matter? We are friends, are we not? No secrets between friends."

"No, Dhun. You must not be offended if I do not show it to you. I would not show it to anyone, not even to family, if I didn't think it was finished."

Mrs. Katrak's smile flooded her face again. "Arré, of course, no offence taken. It shall be as you please. You are the artist. I am just happy that the flat is serving a good purpose. Stay as long as you like. I just wanted to see everything was all right. Usually, the last two times, when Darius stayed, he was always coming upstairs for food, with his friends, all kinds of things. This time, no food, no friends, needs nothing, so independent he has become. Came up one or two times to get books for his homework, but didn't even say hullo. I just wanted to be sure he was all right. You know, mothers worry. That is all."

"I am afraid I am partly to blame, Dhun. I asked him not to tell anybody I was here because I didn't want to bother anybody, but I seem only to have heightened your anxiety. Sorry."

"Arré, don't be silly. Nothing to be sorry for. Just needed to find out. That is all. I'm not worried—now that I know the reason. What are you painting now?"

Farida raised her head toward the window. "Just the view. When I first saw it by night the sea was just magnificent—but I thought immediately about a dual project. I wanted to do it by day *and* by night, maybe also at other times of the day—like Monet did with Rouen Cathedral, many different studies of the same subject."

"Oh, yes, Monet—lovely water lilies he did, no?"

Farida felt safer talking about Monet. "Yes, but of the lilies he did different views. Of the cathedral he did the same view, the exact same view, eighteen times. He set up eighteen canvases at a shop in front of the cathedral and as the light changed he went from one canvas to the next."

Mrs. Katrak shook her head in apparent wonder. "Eighteen times, really? I did not know that. Such a genius! Sheer genius!"

"I think I mentioned to you that I knew the Engineers on the first floor here when I was a girl?"

"Oh, yes, Zarine—Jimmy and Mithu Engineer's little girl. All now gone to Canada—Toronto, I think."

"Yes, but I still remember how the rain came down during one of her birthday parties—I must have been five or six then—but they had the inside flat, could hardly even see the view from there. How the monsoon must look from here I can only imagine."

Farida wished to keep Mrs. Katrak too distracted to enter the body of the flat, afraid she would be unable to explain her clothing in Francis's bedroom, but to her chagrin she seemed to succeed too well. Mrs. Katrak settled in one of the divans. "Actually, quite good, but you have to remember to close the windows. Actually, I am now quite tired of it—but, of course, for someone who has never seen it …"

Farida forced a smile so wide her cheeks hurt. "Dhun, I'm afraid as a hostess you will find me a complete washout, but I need to be alone when I'm working. I hope you are not offended."

To her surprise Mrs. Katrak got up, her own smile less certain than Farida's. "No, no, of course not, I will not keep you—but, Farida, you are staying here now?"

Farida maintained the smile. "Darius was kind enough to give me a key. He said I could come and go as I pleased."

Mrs. Katrak nodded, but lost her smile, for a moment apparently unaware even of Farida's presence, before flashing her smile again. "Well, I suppose I should be going. I just wanted to be sure everything was all right. If you want anything, come upstairs. You just have to ask, you know."

"Yes, I do know. Thank you very much, Dhun."

"In fact, why not join us for dinner tonight also, no? Bring that son of mine also—or just send him packing if he gets in your way."

"Actually, he's been very good. We've been keeping up with the lessons, of course, but he stays in the bedroom when I'm painting. I'm very sorry, Dhun, but I wouldn't want to commit myself to dinner until I knew how the drawing was coming along—but maybe after I am finished?"

Mrs. Katrak's smile widened again. "Yes, yes, of course, sure. The muse cannot be programmed. I understand. Maybe tomorrow?"

"Maybe. Thank you very much for understanding, Dhun. I will let you know, then, okay?"

"If Darius gets in your way just send him upstairs."

"I will, of course. Thank you."

"Don't be shy now."

"I won't."

Farida smiled her broadest and Mrs. Katrak's smile broadened in response. "Good. You will come to dinner, then, sometime?"

"I will definitely come to dinner again sometime."

"Capital. Dhunji will also be very happy. Anything special you would like us to prepare, just you have to ask. Our Shakuntala can cook anything you want. I taught her myself."

The walk across the sitting-room to the front door was among the longest Farida could remember, Mrs. Katrak in all the hurry of a child leaving a picnic. When she finally left, Farida double-locked the door so she couldn't reenter, not even with a key. Her smile, as leaden now as Mrs. Katrak's, dropped like a hammer. Before she knew it she was stooped and weeping, making her way to the closest divan. The brief interview had tired her more than the week of revels with Darius. She didn't understand the tears following her elation barely thirty minutes earlier, but within seconds understanding spread like a shroud: the honeymoon was over.

She didn't wish to dampen Darius's optimism and set about wiping her tears, washing her face, hiding her things under Francis's bed, laying out ingredients for the dinner she would be cooking through the afternoon, a mutton stew with brinjals and tomatoes, but returning to her painting, struck by a fresh onslaught, bent and trembling again, she was assailed anew by doubt. What had possessed her to seize this mad chance? to consider so little her responsibility to herself, her family, her friends, most of all to Darius? to lie to Kaki, the Katraks, not to mention anyone who might interfere with her desire? Had the loss of her marriage left her so very bereft? the loss of her little Cyrus, her Ruby, the details of which she had related to no one in Bombay, not Kaki, not even Darius? What did it mean to hold secrets from those you loved if the secrets only isolated you? What did it say about her love except that it was selfish?

Darius was her darling boy and with time would only grow more suitable—but they would say only that he was a boy, nothing about their suitability, neither for the present nor the future. They would have said the same in Chicago, but in Bombay the words would be salted with a rage for which she had no stomach. She couldn't imagine life without Darius, but wondered whether she had made a convenience of love, been selfish in the name of love.

Genuine love was for the few, for the strong and the courageous, evidenced by the number of divorces, the number of bad marriages even perhaps outnumbering the number of divorces, couples locked through inertia and interdependence, or making the best of it for the sake of children who only grew to resent them for the obligation thrust upon them. People who needed people were simply the neediest people in the world. It had less to do with flowers and boxes of chocolates and even saying I Love You than with simply being in a state of love from which flowed all other rewards, making of love neither weapon nor cushion but a way of life. This she believed, and this was the reason for her doubt, her weakness in the face of adversity, the sudden floods, the irrefutable evidence of unstoppable tears. If her love for Darius incurred deception, whether of Kaki or the Katraks or even the servants, if it excluded her friends, it was a love founded on shame or fear, at best on expedience—a euphemism, again, for selfishness.

She wished to emerge from the cave into which she had pulled Darius, find a place on the open plain where they could be at home and at ease with themselves and everyone else. How she managed would be the test of her love. The order of business, then, was to explain herself to Darius, finish her panoramas, and return to Blue Mansions. They would face the problem of his minority when it rose, but in the meantime it was important to open their lives to freedoms enjoyed by other couples, to be seen in public without fear of reprisal, perhaps even to make a point of being seen in public. She didn't wish to hide their love like a dirty secret: what they did behind closed doors would remain, as with other couples, no one's business but their own; but she wanted no less for them to have a life in the light of day.

FARIDA COOPER, PARTY GIRL

The ground floor of Blue Mansions differed from the first mainly for the patio, accessible from the sitting-room through a series of French windows. Servants opened the ten central windows every morning, allowing light and air to circulate, shut them every night. An awning was raised every monsoon season to shelter the patio from rain, not to mention the piano, however far it stood within the doors, however much it was insulated, darkening the sitting-room even on rainless days (countable on the fingers of one hand)—but even then the glass panels allowed for more light.

The sitting-room formed the base of a U, the arms of which enclosed the patio. The patio spread in a widening arc into a garden, flagstones leading to a fountain spouting from a fairy's wand. The garden surrounded the house like a compound adjoining the driveway in front. Barely yards beyond the garden lay the beach, marked from the Cooper property by a picket fence which had long lost its color. Efforts were made to maintain the white of the fence, not to mention the blue of the house, mostly in vain, against mildew fostered by the annual deluge, the Bombay monsoon, not to mention the constant scratch and tickle of the salt sea air.

The sea was close enough to be heard clearly by night, the ebb and flow of waves rocking Farida to sleep, and sometimes even by day, but she liked best the nights her parents gave parties, the patio lit by fairy lights, cleared for dancing, gramophone playing Strauss waltzes and popular songs, the patter of the party highlighting the music like tambourines adding the final sparkle to an orchestra, guests (as many English as Indian) dressed in satin gowns, painted saris, pinstripe suits, and clinking uniforms.

The party started in the sitting-room, but guests moved to the patio to dance, and into the garden for walks and more intimate conversation, returning to sit out a dance or refresh their drinks. The grownups, foxtrotting in their finery to "Die Fledermaus" under fairy lights against the silhouette of coconut palms on the beach, the backdrop of sea and darkening sky, appeared to Farida, watching from the sitting-room, like magical creatures, exotic birds dripping plumage, the women flamingos, the men emperor penguins, their spirits dampened no more by the war than by the mildew.

Farida was too young to understand the war, but it seemed to blanket the world in endless night. There was no other conversation: if it wasn't mentioned, it was consciously left unmentioned; it was present in its absence as much as in its presence; it was in the air and even she, her sixth birthday less than a fortnight away, knew the names: Hitler, Mussolini, Stalin, Churchill, Roosevelt—but Kaki said there was nothing to worry about. They were all far away, all the bad people were far away. Kaki came to the parties only sometimes though she lived on the upper floor of the same house and could see the guests from her sitting-room as easily as from downstairs, but even on those occasions left early, offering apologies with a smile, joking it was past her bedtime.

Farida was a glum, plump, and pretty child, fluffy hair in a fat plait except on special occasions when it was freed and followed her in a train. She liked best the pull of her hair when she ran against the wind. She loved and hated the parties, loved being the only child, one with the grownups, hated leaving early for bed, taking Kaki's departure as her cue, before the others were called to the long table in the dining-room. She loved the fuss, drawing attention like a point of light, dressing in her favorite frock of the moment, usually a variation on pink taffeta, pink pumps over pink socks on her feet, pink band around her head keeping her hair from her face, but hated showing herself on cue, proud possession of her parents, ignored alike by both parents the morning after—and since the war the attention had become less focused, guests listening with just half an ear. "Farida, why the long face? Aren't you having fun?"

Jane Christie set her plate on a table across from Farida. Farida remembered her best in later years for her wide white bare shoulders. "It's because of the war, Jane Aunty, but thank you for asking."

"Oh, but my dear, the war has nothing to do with you. It's nothing for you to worry about. Don't you have a plate?"

"Yes, Jane Aunty, I do." She pointed to her plate of wafers and samosas and tomato sauce, her glass of cold fizzing Coke, and dipped a wafer in the sauce to be polite.

Colin Maclean sat beside her, putting an arm around her shoulders, kissing the top of her head. "Jane's right. The war's not for my little poppet to worry about. Is that a new dress?"

"Yes, Colin Uncle. Do you like it?" Farida smiled, leaning into Colin Maclean for a moment, glad of the attention of a large handsome blue-eyed man. She stuck out her feet. "I got the frock to match my socks and shoes. See?"

Vimla Vasudev smiled, her slender brown torso on display between the rim of her choli and the waist of her sari. "I would have thought you would have got socks and shoes to match your frock rather than the other way around."

Farida almost squealed, imagining Vimla Vasudev didn't believe her. "But I didn't, Vimla Aunty! I already had the socks and shoes first! I went with Kaki. It was a present from Kaki."

Persis Cooper spoke to the group though her gaze was directed toward the garden at her husband with Flora Diver beyond the fountain. He appeared to be fixing a sprig of bougainvillea behind her ear. "She's right. It was all Kaki's idea. She spoils the girl rotten, but I'm the one who pays the price."

"But, Mummy, Kaki paid! I saw her!"

Colin Maclean laughed, kissing the top of her head again. "If you saw her you must be right. Kaki must have paid—and we're all grateful. You look very pretty in pink."

Persis shook her head, still staring into the garden. "Colin, you're just as bad as Kaki. Pink isn't even her color. She's much too dark—better a yellow or a brown. It would suit her complexion better."

Farida's voice grew shrill. Her mother always drew attention to the fact that she and her father had fairer complexions. "I *hate* brown. Brown does *not* suit me. I will *never* ever wear *any*thing brown—not *ev*er. It's a dirty color."

Persis shrugged, looking finally at the group, smiling as if to say *see what I mean?* "Brown is a lovely color. It's the color of her hair—a very dark brown—but she won't admit it."

"It's *not!* My hair is black. It's as black as the piano. See?" She jumped from the sofa, dashed to the Steinway, laid her head against the top, and spread her hair. "See?"

The guests followed Farida with their eyes, but her mother didn't bother to look. "Don't be silly, Farida. It's much too dark to tell." Persis held her smile for the group. "We can't figure it out. Nariman likes to joke that she's adopted. I mean, she is so very much darker, isn't she?"

Faisal Basrai, a tiny brown man, pulled at the high collar of his brown sherwani with his finger. "Don't listen to what anyone says, Farida. It does not matter what color you wear. Anything that makes you smile becomes your color."

Farida smiled, but her mother remained unsympathetic. Nariman Cooper and Flora Diver were cutting through the dancers on the patio approaching the sitting-room, his arm around her waist. "Yes, but she hardly ever smiles. When I was her age I had to make my own dolls out of cloth and clay. Farida gets everything she wants and still she doesn't smile—books, toys, dolls, games, clothes, you should just see her bedroom. I really don't know what's wrong with the girl."

Farida lost her smile again, but Colin Maclean whispered in her ear. "It's the war, isn't it? I understand perfectly."

Farida nodded solemnly. "Yes, the war. It's the war."

Her father entered the sitting-room with Flora Diver, his arm still around her waist, both sporting broad smiles. He wore a tuxedo; hair, parted down the center, gleaming as much as his wingtips; Farida had said once she had the "shiningest" father in the world. He went to the bar for a martini. "The war? What bloody war? The war's bloody well over. We've won the Battle of Britain, we've licked the Italian navy, and it's just a matter of time before we bring the bloody Germans to their knees. All that's left is to hand out the decorations and bring out the champagne."

He spoke as if the British victories were his own. Faisal Basrai, the token nationalist, laughed. "Arré, Nariman, come on now. It is very far from being a sure thing still, and of course there is always the next thing. No offence to anyone present here, but the war is important to Indians mainly because of what must come next. Independence. Swaraj!"

Jane Christie nodded. "Well, I don't think anyone would argue that it's no longer a question of *If* as much as *How* and *When*. Our departure is a foregone conclusion."

Faisal Basrai nodded in sympathy. "Jane is right. That is what they said after the last war, but this time we will not take 'No' for an answer."

Nariman shook his head, no longer smiling. The twenty years between him and his wife were obliterated by his full head of hair and tennis regimen, not to mention the jolly dog of his presence, but in the presence of his wife he lost the jolly dog, gaining back the years and more. "If you ask me, that will be the end of India. If the British go, India goes with them. What do they know about running a country? They have never done it before."

He spoke as if he were not Indian himself, as if the British departure would be his own, as if an India without the British were no longer his country. Faisal Basrai spoke politely, but firmly. "They say when the British leave, they will leave behind many brown-skinned Englishmen. I think they might know something about running a country."

Nariman grimaced, showing impatience with the argument. "Well, then, if we are going to have brown-skinned Englishmen, all I can say is why not have the real thing? Why accept substitutes?"

Jane Christie spoke calmly. "Because in India the brown-skinned Englishman is the real thing. He is not a substitute. It is the white-skinned Englishman who has always been out of place."

Flora Diver spoke no less calmly, touching the sprig of bougainvillea behind her ear. "That is true, Jane, precisely because there have always been English who believe as you do that England never had a place in India—not pukka at all, I'm afraid."

Jane Christie drew a deep breath. "You may not call them pukka, Flora, but they will have their say—and they will have their way."

Faisal Basrai grinned. "And they will have their day."

Persis nodded grimly. "They will, indeed—but what will it matter? I mean, just look at us, fiddling while Rome is burning." She stared directly at her husband. "What do we really care about anyone else as long as we've got what we want?"

If Persis meant to get under her husband's skin, she succeeded. He turned his gaze from his wife. "You call it fiddling, but we have to show the Germans and all the rest of them that they cannot dictate the way we live. That is our civic responsibility. If we change on their account, they've already won."

Persis smiled. "Yes, right, maybe we should send them some snaps of our dinner—just to show them it makes no difference to us what they do."

Farida gripped her father's hand, looking up into his face. "Daddy, am I adopted?"

Nariman's eyebrows rose as he looked down at his daughter. "Now where on earth did you get such a notion?"

"Mummy says you said I was adopted because I'm not as white as you and her."

Nariman laughed. "What rot! Not what I said at all. I said you could well be another man's daughter, being so much darker and all that." He winked at the group. "That doesn't mean she's not Persis's daughter." He looked down again at Farida, clinging to his hand. "I don't think there's any doubt, my little golliwog, that you are at least your mother's daughter."

Mehernosh Lentin played "Roses from the South" on the gramophone and Nariman tore his hand from his daughter's to sweep Flora Diver onto the patio to dance. Faisal Basrai turned to Farida, her face trapped between a smile and frown. "Tell us, Farida. What do you want to be when you grow up?"

Farida smiled though she understood Faisal Basrai had posed the question as a diversion. "I want to be Cinderella."

Her mother's laugh swept like a shriek over the company, silencing everyone. "Fancy that! She is already a princess—and she wants to be Cinderella!"

Farida pondered what her mother said, but it was years before she thought of the perfect reply: *I might be a princess, but I also have a wicked stepmother.*

LESS THAN A MONTH LATER, days past her sixth birthday, Farida was called one morning by her mother from the garden beyond the patio where she had been playing with Bucky Bharucha and Roshan Tata. Her friends were driven to their homes in the car by the driver. Farida walked slowly, reluctantly, to her mother at a game of patience at the dining table. "What is it, Mummy?"

Persis sat at the head of the table; Farida stood almost at attention beside her. Persis kept her eyes on the cards as she spoke. "Farida, how many times have I told you not to play in the sun? Do you want to grow up black like the servants?"

"Mummy, we were in the shade! We stayed in the shade as much as we could." To her surprise her mother said nothing, still staring at her cards, apparently struggling for words. "I won't do it again, Mummy, I promise. We stayed out of the sun as much as we could— really, we did—and my skin turns violet in the sun, not black."

Her mother seemed not to hear. "Farida, don't jabber. Listen to me. This is important. You will know about it sooner or later, so I might as well tell you about it now. Your daddy wants a divorce, but I am not going to give it to him. I have told him he can do what he wants as long as he doesn't involve me, and we have decided that the best way would be for me to move into your part of the house."

Farida knew what a divorce was because the subject had come up before, but the fact of a divorce seemed easier to bear than the possibility; she had imagined either her mother or father leaving, finding herself alone with one or the other, and was relieved she would still be alone with both. The house was large enough for them to lead independent lives never seeing the others if they so wished. She was bewildered most by her mother's struggle to tell her, imagining she might consider the move an imposition on herself. "That's all right, Mummy. I have plenty of room."

"No, you don't. There's barely enough for one. You will be moving upstairs with Kaki. You will have the same space, but upstairs. That's all I wanted to say. Now go and wash up. It's almost lunchtime." Dismissing her with a glance, her mother resumed her game of patience as if she were already alone.

Farida remained rooted to the floor, unable to speak, barely able to move, turning finally so suddenly it seemed involuntary, as if invisible hands had spun her by the shoulders to wash for lunch. Her head seemed to buzz, helmeted with flies; her skin to thicken, turning to leather, impervious to needles and touch; her feet to lose solidity, turning to air though the room itself seemed to be losing air; and the floor to rise, but she was unconscious before she was aware of its solidity.

During the following days she heard the words of her malady for the first time, and repeatedly for a while: arrhythmia, same as her father, nothing serious, exacerbated by stress, any kind of stress, her mother's voice threading the confusion: *What about me? What about my stress? Do you think I'm on holiday or something?*

II

Farida's party guests, as many English as Indian, as many girls as boys, ranging all ages to fifteen, ayahs in tow, crowded the bookshelves in her playroom selecting books to borrow: *Swiss Family Robinson, Coral Island, Black Beauty, Little Women, Alice in Wonderland, Tom Brown's Schooldays, Girl's Own* Annuals, *Rupert* Annuals, *Eve* magazines, Grimm's Fairy Tales, and the series of almost twenty William books among others. She was generous, even nonchalant, with her possessions: those who had more than others were honor-bound to share what they had, so Kaki had said, and so Farida believed, having more than most, more even than most of her friends. Her cousin Ratan, older by two years, dashed from her bedroom with a large book in his hand. "I say, Farida, would it be all right if I borrowed this?"

It was a collection of Uncle Remus's Br'er Rabbit stories. She had kept the book in her bedroom for the cover, Br'er Rabbit looking over his shoulder inviting the reader into the book with a grin. She liked the stories, but liked even better what the artist had done with the night sky—not quite navy blue, not quite black, but shimmering and glittering with brushstrokes reminiscent of night skies shown her by Kaki painted by Vincent van Gogh. She had bought the book because she had wanted to reproduce the majesty of the sky in paintings of her own. She had accomplished her goal, learning how to add black to her blues, or white, or other colors, or just plain water, to get the desired effect, and kept the book in her bedroom for inspiration, but loaned it readily to Ratan. "Of course, but aren't you a little old for Br'er Rabbit?"

Ratan grinned. "It has comics—never too old for comics."

Farida laughed. "Of course not—but bring it back. I keep it by my bedside because it's special."

"Why? For the comics?"

Farida laughed again. "Yes, for the comics." It was easier than explaining anything to Ratan who never listened to anyone younger, especially not a girl.

She was eleven; the war had been over for almost six months, but hadn't affected the Coopers except to curtail travel outside India. Kaki meant to make up for it that summer, taking her on an extended tour of Europe, visiting in particular the tinier countries about which she knew less—Belgium, Luxembourg, the Netherlands, Switzerland, among others. She had educated her in the meantime with photographs and books and her own reminiscences.

As much as Farida loved Kaki, she could not have guessed how well they would get along when she had moved upstairs over five years ago. The parties had begun immediately, set for the third Friday of every month, to which all her friends were invited, her entire class at school, relatives, and neighbors—neighbors sometimes bringing their own friends. Kaki always prepared for twice as many as were invited—and after the party leftovers were packaged for the beggar children who gathered by the backdoor every third Friday. Kaki also organized games for the parties and guests borrowed books before they left to be returned at the next party. There had also been piano lessons and painting lessons once she had shown an interest, all of which had distracted Farida from the darker aspects of her young life.

Kaki had lived alone upstairs in the rooms corresponding to those of Farida's parents downstairs. The rooms corresponding to Farida's had served as guest-rooms. Kaki had suggested they move Farida's furniture just as it was to the upstairs suite to provide a modicum of continuity, and move the upstairs furniture downstairs—if Farida's mother (since she would be occupying Farida's old rooms) had no objection. Her mother had made some changes to suit herself, keeping some of Kaki's furniture, keeping some of her own, buying some new, putting the rest in storage.

"I say, Farida, thanks again for a wizard party!"

"Yes, really, Farida! It was great—as always!"

Maud Mayhew and Sunita Patel grinned into the playroom. Farida grinned back. "Glad you came. Hope you will come again."

"Of course." Maud Mayhew whispered conspiratorially. "I say, Farida, can we count on you?"

"Count on her for what? What's the big secret, I say, Maudie?"

Ratan grinned over the Br'er Rabbit book clutched tightly under his chin, but Maud Mayhew turned away. "Ratan, if I've told you once I've told you a hundred times not to call me Maudie!"

"Oh, I say, everyone calls you Maudie!"

"Only my friends—and you are not my friend, Mr. Nosy Parker Ratan Cooper! I'll thank you to keep your nose where it belongs!"

Sunita Patel laughed. "Yes, Mr. Nosy Parker Ratan Cooper, we will thank you to keep your nose out of our business!"

Farida knew Ratan fancied Maud Mayhew and was probably glad of Sunita Patel's retort which allowed him a sally he wouldn't have dared with Maud Mayhew. "Who asked you any way, Miss Know-It-All Sunita Patel?"

Sunita Patel giggled. "Shut up, Ratan. You're not invited."

"Invited to what?"

Maud Mayhew glared at Sunita Patel who giggled again, keeping her eyes on Ratan. "Mind your own business, Ratan Cooper."

Farida appreciated Maud Mayhew's veiled question. The invitation was to a slumber party, but not everyone present had been invited, and she didn't want to flaunt the invitation in their faces. "Maudie, I still haven't had the chance to ask Kaki, but she just took a plate downstairs to Mummy. If you can wait a minute I'll let you know."

"Of course."

Farida dashed down the stairs to find the front door open. She was about to dash into the flat when she heard her mother's voice enunciating slowly and clearly. "She has always had everything she needed. The very least she can do is to leave me alone. How ungrateful can the child be? She's her father's daughter to the bone. I really wonder sometimes if she's my child at all. We're so very different that I wouldn't be the least surprised if she were someone else's daughter. I don't feel like her mother at all—and I've had the feeling ever since she was born."

"What perfect nonsense, Persis! You know perfectly well you're her mother!"

"Well, maybe, maybe not. Babies do get switched, you know. One's always reading about such things happening in nursing homes. You just never know."

Kaki's voice was persuasive, polite. "You can have your little joke if you want, Persis, but it would mean so very much to her if you came upstairs for just a minute—you know it would. I assure you she's not the least bit ungrateful. She appreciates everything you do more than you realize."

"Nergesh, I don't know why you always take her side in everything. You are spoiling her rotten. Fancy having a party every month for a *child!* Who ever heard of such a thing? She's not the Princess Elizabeth, you know."

Farida didn't wait for Kaki's response, but her ascent up the stairs was as slow as her descent had been swift. She made an excuse to Maud Mayhew, promising to ring her the next day with an answer.

After the guests had left and leftovers had been doled from the backdoor, Farida approached Kaki for permission to attend the slumber party, readily granted as she had expected, but the permission was no longer foremost on her agenda. "Kaki, why doesn't Mummy like me?"

Tired from the preparations for the party, still in the dining-room supervising the cleanup, Kaki didn't look at Farida as her eyebrows rose. "Now why would you think a thing like that, my dear?"

"Because it's true, Kaki! I heard what she said to you. She wants me to leave her alone. She thinks I'm ungrateful … just because I want to see her."

Kaki took a deep breath, gave the servants their last orders for the day, took Farida tenderly by her hand. "Come, my dear, I think we need to talk."

Farida was passive, allowing herself to be led to her bedroom, but spoke defiantly when Kaki sat on the bed, seating Farida beside her. "Don't tell me she likes me, Kaki! She doesn't!"

Kaki smiled, squeezing her hand. "I won't say that, my dear, if you would rather I didn't—but I *shall* say that things are not always as they seem. If you want something badly enough, sometimes you have to be very patient. You see, your mummy feels very hurt—just like you. She thinks people don't like her, but they *do*. She just can't see it, and because she can't see it she can't show her own true feelings—but I believe very firmly that she loves you very much. She just doesn't know how to show it. Maybe she doesn't even know it herself."

"But *why*, Kaki? *Why* does she think people don't like her?"

"I don't exactly know, my dear. I can hardly understand it myself, much less explain it to you—but I do not doubt that her feelings for you are very strong indeed, and that if you are patient you will see it yourself."

"*How* patient, Kaki? *How* much longer?"

"Impossible to tell, my dear—but your mummy is right, isn't she, when she says you have everything you need?"

Farida cast her eyes to Kaki's hand squeezing her own, her voice flat. "Yes, Kaki."

"Then shouldn't you be grateful for what you have?"

Farida flared suddenly. "Yes, Kaki—and I *am!*"

"I know you are, my dear, I know you are. You're a good girl."

"I just wish sometimes … I just wish …" She sighed deeply.

"I know, my dear—so do we all. Did you have fun at your party?"

Her voice flattened again, as if her best friend had died. "Yes, Kaki!"

Whatever Farida said, Kaki could see her attention had drifted. She was growing up, needed more than parties for distraction, needed perhaps to be treated as less of a child. "Farida, I can see I haven't been of much help. You know, I really think sometimes a divorce might have been better for everyone concerned—better than staying in the same flat, I mean. It might then have been easier perhaps for your mummy to get on with her own life, but she didn't want a divorce—and no one had the right to tell her what to do." She pursed her lips. "My dear, I wish I could be of more help."

Farida was staring at her hands in her lap, but a break in Kaki's voice made her look up, a quality she had not heard before, a helplessness needing consolation no less than herself. She never saw the jughead, the lantern jaw, the spaniel ears, the black spectacles which framed eyes made tiny by thick lenses. She saw only Kaki and put her arms around her. "Oh, but you *are*, Kaki! You *are!* What would I ever do without my Kaki!"

HORACE FISCH AND
THE FEMININE MYSTIQUE

There is much to be said for the first years of marriage that might be wished for the last. It takes more than a wedding to lead naïve newlyweds and happy honeymooners into a mature marriage. Horace seemed to understand the principle (large wedding, small marriage), having traveled the road before, and Farida bowed to his wishes—getting him in turn to bow to an Indian honeymoon though he had visited India just the year before. She was pleased with the ease of their negotiation, the most major of their early life—small wedding for a large reception in Bombay to introduce him to her friends.

Suddenly swept into a world of two, a world of adults, a world of socially sanctioned sexuality, enlarged by a ceremony, a piece of paper, from girl to woman to wife, defined by her husband as much as by herself, Farida shone like a bulb of significant wattage, the mere fact of the wedding a shimmer and pop and crackle in her head, drenching her Chicago in starlight. She was no longer just Farida, girl student, English graduate, but wife of Horace, Professor of Humanities, man of Joyce, mature American—and he was no longer humdrum Horace, humanities drudge, failed husband, but husband of Farida, nubile knockout, daughter of India, heiress to the House of Cooper.

Farida recognized their mutual bask in the reflected glory of the other, not unlike Horace's bask in the reflected glory of Joyce, not unlike the bask of other such humdrums toiling in the vineyards of genius, scholars manufactured from the assembly lines of universities parroting dogma in the name of freedom of thought—experts certified by degrees rather than the lash of life, bottling in books the lives of the great in the quest to be bottled themselves, particularly in the humanities where the fashionable theories of the day provide grist for the mill of tomorrow. Her mature life had been propelled by three major thrusts: her arrival in America cutting physical ties with the past; her marriage providing an identity further removed from her family; her job providing an identity separate even from her husband. The job allowed her to be her own woman, independent of her husband, independent even of Coopers if she wished—but she had found herself a victim instead of the curse of the Batlivalas. Her mother had miscarried once before Farida's birth, three times after, before the doctors had deemed it unwise to try again. Farida miscarried twice in the first four years of marriage and was pregnant again in the sixth, but the glitter of the first years had been eroded. Sitting to lunch at the Gupta kitchen table, watching Rohini feed two-year-old Sangita in her baby chair, hearing the television in the living-room keeping four-year-old Sunil quiet and compliant, she couldn't help comparing her trajectory to that of her friend.

Rohini Mehta had become Rohini Gupta a year after Farida had married Horace. She and Rohini had twice become pregnant together, but the year of Farida's first miscarriage Rohini had given birth to Sunil, the year of her second to Sangita, and Farida's third pregnancy was lonelier because Rohini wanted no more children. Even the Cassidys, Ginger and Raymond, had two girls, Elizabeth and Anastasia. Rohini dipped her finger in her curry, letting Sangita slurp it clean. "She eats everything I give her—in fact, she just loves curry, but I don't want to give her too much too soon. Sunil was so sick once because I let him eat as much as he wanted—but he is actually the pickier eater of the two."

Farida said nothing, packing a morsel of chicken with the chapati, shoveling it into her mouth with her thumb. She ate with her hands whenever she visited Rohini, a habit she had developed from the time they had shared the apartment on Dearborn and Division when Rohini had cooked for them. Rohini had always eaten with her hands and Farida had joined her.

Rohini looked up from Sangita. "What's the matter, Farida? Why the hangdog look?"

Farida gave her friend a pasty smile. "Sorry. I will make it my business to be cheerful. I was just thinking about us, you know."

"Thinking about us gives you a hangdog look?"

"Not us, I suppose, so much as me. We are like the hare and the tortoise. I mean, just think, I was the hare, just haring ahead, getting married in a jiffy while you and Rohit waited so patiently for his degree and his job and all the rest of it—and then you started having babies, everything on time, everything in its place—and I'm just … sitting here, eating your dust, the dust of the tortoise."

Rohini laughed. "What a thing to say! Eating my dust—is that what you think of my chicken?"

"You know what I mean."

"Farida, it's not a competition, you know. I've told you before."

Horace was in Minnesota attending a seminar on "The Pertinacity of Porcine Imagery in Joyceland." Rohit was an internist, working long hours at St. Joseph Hospital. Rohini had worked at Belmont Pharmaceuticals until her pregnancy with Sunil, and planned to work again when Sangita started school. Farida still worked at Goldinger & Co., but had pled ill to spend time with Rohini, a benefit easily availed a pregnant woman with two miscarriages in her past. "I know— but I can't help thinking about it. I mean, just look at you, such a mother you've become—all healthy and vibrant and shining and … blooming with … with milk, I suppose. What a gift, to be able to bring forth children."

Rohini smiled. "Don't fret. They say the third time is the charm."

"Not for you. For you one time was enough. Rohit just looks at you and you swell up like a whale."

Rohini laughed. "Actually, no. Two children in five years is not that much."

"It is infinitely more than I have achieved."

"Farida, really now. Do buck up. You are pregnant. You have never come so far before in a pregnancy. What is it, six months now? Don't you think you should be at least just a little bit pleased?"

"No, I want to be like you, with a Sunil and Sangita of my own, fat with happiness—not with a foetus. Just look at you. You used to be such a skinny-minnie. Now you weigh as much as I do."

"Hardly! You're pregnant!"

"I mean, when I'm not pregnant. I want to be in bloom just like you."

Rohini laughed again. "You were always a ... blooming something."

"Don't get fresh, Rohini! You know what I mean."

Rohini still laughed. "Sorry—but just listen to yourself, sitting there feeling sorry for yourself."

"Mummy, I'm cold." Sunil stood in the doorway clutching his elbows, a skinny boy in baggy blue jeans and a baggy blue long-sleeved shirt.

Rohini had just fed Sangita another finger of curry followed by a sliver of chicken. Her own lunch lay cooling before her while Farida had almost finished. Sunil had gulped his meal to get back to watching television. Farida licked her fingers. "Sunil, you let your mummy and your sister finish their lunch and we will go into the bedroom and find a good warm sweater for you. Okay?"

Sunil nodded, smiling. "Okay, Farida Aunty."

Farida looked at her friend. "He sounds so American already, doesn't he?"

Rohini shrugged. "If you grow up among foreigners you become a foreigner."

Farida smiled, recalling the first thing Rohini had said when they had met in the cafeteria: *What a country this is! Everyone is a foreigner!*

Rohini smiled, perhaps recalling the same moment—it had been a relief to meet another Indian—but she spoke instead to Sunil. "You like your Farida Aunty, no, Sunil?"

Sunil nodded more vigorously, smiling more broadly. "Yes, Mummy. I love Farida Aunty."

Farida pursed her lips in a loud kiss. "Sunil, you are my own little darling." She finished eating, washed her hands at the sink, dried them on her jeans. "Come, sweetheart. Let's go."

Sunil held out his hand and she recalled when she had first held him, squealing herself at the tininess of his babyness—wriggly fingers, sculpted toes, rubbery limbs, bump of his nose, bow of his lips, all contrasted with big black eyes, a bawling baby, all dimples and fat, oblivious of the trouble he caused. She didn't take his hand, but picked him up instead, broadening his smile yet again. Rohini gave Sangita another slurp of her curried finger. "Thanks, Farida. His sweaters are in the second drawer."

Farida found a sweater for Sunil, helped him with the armholes, brought him back to the kitchen, and released him into the living-room. Rohini had finished lunch, placed the dirty dishes in the sink.

"Farida, is everything all right aside from the pregnancy? Ginger and Raymond all right?"

Rohini had not mentioned Horace, but Farida understood her concern. The first Cassidy baby, Elizabeth, had so distracted Ginger that Raymond had distracted himself with one of his students, Rhonda Lake. Discovery of the affair had precipitated Ginger frequently in tears into the Fisch household, leaving baby Elizabeth to the care of her nanny Ursula, seeking solace mainly from Horace though Farida too had been sympathetic. The matter had resolved itself when Raymond, returning from a party with Rhonda, a little too happy for his own good, had run the roadster into the back of a Greyhound, no more than skinning his shins but killing Rhonda, remorse precipitating his return to the fold. It had been a matter of barely a month during which Ginger had found herself pregnant with her second baby. Farida had resented Ginger's monopoly of Horace, but only Rohini knew of her resentment, her guilt at her resentment, and Farida shook her head. "Ginger and Raymond are fine. We're going to Anastasia's second birthday party next week."

"Then what is it?"

Farida sat at the table again, her voice falling another notch. "Oh, I don't know. I think sometimes I just need to sit still, do absolutely nothing, just think about what I really want to do. I don't know why I feel so unsure about everything. Things are not what I thought—but don't ask what I thought. I'm not exactly sure myself what I mean. I have to clear things up in my own head first."

"Do you mean something to do with Horace?"

"No, not with Horace. Horace is all right. He's been very understanding about … everything."

Rohini nodded. Horace had taken time off from his schedule at the university to spend time with her during the worst days. "At work, then? Is something going on at Goldinger's?"

Farida hesitated momentarily. "That might be a part of it. I don't know."

"Tell me."

"I told you about that fellow, Jim Currie?"

"Oh, yes! How could I forget Curry-Rice? You mean the idiot, don't you?"

Farida nodded. Jim Currie had married Trudy Rice, a joke that always went over better with Indians than Americans. "That's the fellow—nice guy, but not very bright, as I said, not by any measure—but just last week they promoted him to manager. I'm sure he will muddle through somehow, but there are at least two others I can name, excluding myself, who are better qualified. Doesn't seem right."

"Both women?"

That was always the rationale. A man had to support a family, a woman got married, or had babies and quit. "Yes, but still, they would do a better job. *I* would do a better job, they *know* I would do a better job—but I'm still the Research Assistant because, of course, I've had two miscarriages, and I'm pregnant again. Sooner or later, they assume I'll be leaving—but supposing I wanted to stay, supposing I wanted a career with the company, supposing I wanted to come back after the baby? Then what?"

"Then they will take you back, no? or you can go somewhere else, no?"

"Yes, maybe—but what about in the meantime? They just assume I'm going to quit and promote idiots like Jim Currie instead. They don't have the right to make such assumptions—surely not?"

"It's a man's world, Farida—just think how it is in India. At least, here, in Chicago, you have been able to make some contribution, however small."

"Maybe—but you know what really burns me up is that it wasn't always like this. I've been reading Betty Friedan's book, *The Feminine Mystique*—and she makes a good point. During the war it was women who managed the home front. They did the work just as well as the men, if not better—but when the men came home there weren't enough jobs for everyone, so of course they gave up their jobs to the men. *That's* what burns me up. She makes many good points: forty-seven percent of college graduates in 1920 were women, but by 1958 the percentage was down to thirty-five; in the nineteenth century women fought to get a college education, but in the twentieth century they go to college to get a husband. They drop out of college to get married because they are afraid if they get too educated no man will marry them. We're going backward, not forward. *That's* what burns me up. Look at me! I'm a good example! I got married and never even thought about a Master's degree, as if once I was married there was no need."

"Are you saying you want to go back?"

"I don't know! I don't know what I want!"

"But that is not a question anyone else can answer."

"I know."

"You must also face the other side of the coin. If the women get the same jobs as the men, will they also be willing to support families? Will they be willing to support men as men have supported women all this time? Would you want a man who stayed home and took care of the children instead of working? Most people would call him a freeloader—or a bum."

Farida was hardly listening. She was thinking instead of other points Friedan had made, but didn't feel like prolonging the discussion. "Oh, Rohini, I don't know. I'm all mixed up. That's all I'm saying. I used to think I knew everything. Now I don't know what's what anymore."

"So? Wasn't that your mantra? the beginning of real wisdom? Socrates and all that?"

"Very clever, Rohini. Hoisted by my own petard, you might say."

"What?"

"Forget it."

Rohini smiled, but her smile turned to concern when Farida gasped, momentarily shutting her eyes. "Farida, are you all right?"

Farida nodded, opening her eyes again, tenderly holding her belly, smiling more widely than she had all day. "Just someone saying Hullo."

II

"Farida?"

Bunny Wilkinson, Jim Currie's secretary, stood by Farida's desk, open-mouthed, a plain girl barely a year out of high school. Farida seemed not to hear, apparently lost in a sepia print of the original Goldinger store, west of Broadway on Lawrence, adorning the wall by her desk at the headquarters near Monroe and Wells. August Goldinger had opened for business during the first decade of the century, pulling the rug out from under his competition with retailing practices innovative for the time: newspaper advertising, competitive pricing, better service, liberal credit. The area, known then as the Wilson Avenue District, was shortly dubbed Uptown, adding jazz, pizazz, and razzmatazz to the neighborhoods. Money chased itself in a spiral, rapid development of residential and office buildings depressing rents, spurring the advent of legions of young and single inhabitants, spurring the development of theaters, ballrooms, and other pleasure palaces, spurring yet more rapid real estate development. Streetcar lines and el tracks expanded to draw downtown shoppers wishing to escape the downtown crunch and cost. By the time Farida joined Goldinger's in 1957, the company had long secured its own downtown location, not to mention ten others in the Chicago area, competing with Sears, Goldblatt's, Woolworth's, Marshall Field's, and Montgomery Ward's among others on State Street in the Loop.

Bunny rapped the desk timidly. "Farida, Mr. Currie would like to see you in his office."

Farida shook her head back to the present. "Oh, sorry, Bunny. I was daydreaming, wasn't I?"

Bunny's smile was wide, a concession to Farida's pregnancy. "It's all right."

Farida returned her smile. "Thanks. Did he say what he wanted?"

Bunny shook her head. "Your guess is as good as mine."

Farida nodded, guessing Jim very likely had little to say. He was older than her by almost ten years, but she had worked at Goldinger's longer by almost four, both at desks as research assistants, and he might easily have asked to talk with her himself passing her desk that morning, but since he had moved into his new office he used Bunny for the smallest tasks, as if a secretary and intercom extended his reach and voice and he meant everyone to know the difference, especially those who had known him longest who might not otherwise recognize the difference. Farida had long taken his measure, a bland handsome man, hair almost white making him seem older than his thirty-nine years. He compensated for his coloring with dark grey suits. Walking to his office, she popped her head in the door. "Jim, Bunny said you wanted to see me?"

Jim looked up from his *Wall Street Journal*, catching her eye briefly before closing and folding the paper. "Yes, I did. Please take a seat."

"Okay, Jim." She used his name intentionally, knowing he preferred subordinates to call him Mr. Currie. He tapped the *Journal* slowly, gazing into the distance as if he were still alone, deep in meditation, but Farida understood it was his way of enlarging himself at her expense, showing who had the upper hand. "Well, what is it, Jim? I have work to do."

His eyes bulged momentarily; he found her presumptuous for a woman and a foreigner who should have been grateful for any job, certainly one as professional as research assistant for market analysis, presumptuous also for wearing saris to work though not that day; but a smile immediately rounded his jaw. "Of course, of course."

Farida smiled, recognizing his pique, glad to have piqued him. Behind him, on a credenza, stood two photographs: one of himself with wife Trudi, bland as himself, pretty and smiling—a whiz, Jim liked to say, with a vacuum and chicken croquettes; the other of his three girls (Clara, Lucy, and Maggie), as bland and pretty and smiling as the parents—and, Farida liked to say, as doomed. The family photographs accounted for his managership, recalling Rohini's question: Would she have been content exchanging places with Horace, she the Joycean, he the graduate student in English working as a research assistant? Would Horace then have seemed no more than a bum? If so, what did that say about herself? But a woman's options were limited: either she surrendered to the bounty of a man or to a lifetime of gender discrimination, one path smacked of prostitution, the other of martyrdom. "Jim, what is this all about?"

Jim put his elbows on the desk, steepling his fingers, clearing his throat. "To put it in a nutshell this is all about the Image survey."

"What about it?" Farida was intentionally brusque. The Image survey reached beyond the consumer's thoughts about products to feelings about the store itself, shifting the focus from improving the product to improving attitudes about the store. Not only was she less happy manipulating customers rather than products, but less sure it was even ethical.

"I understood from Janis that you had told the interviewers to ask the questions however they saw fit rather than as they had been written into the survey. Is this true?"

Janis Palomo was the analyst who had developed the Image survey. "Yes, Jim, it's true—but only for one question, and I said so only to Colleen Rafferty, no one else."

"Well, it seems she passed the word on—and in any case we can't have even *one* interviewer ask the questions differently, not even just *one* question. If we're not consistent we sabotage the survey."

Farida almost laughed; surveys were routinely sabotaged to constraints of time and convenience, conjectures and ineligible respondents accepted to fill quotas though the matter was never acknowledged; but she resisted the impulse to tell him what he already knew and spoke without irony. "Jim, Colleen is a very sensitive girl, more so than the rest—and just that one question in the survey bothered her because it required her to lie. She was uncomfortable and

Janis wasn't around, so I told her to follow her conscience. It wasn't a big deal."

Jim pursed his lips, sighed, spoke slowly. "You may not have thought so, Farida, and I don't blame you. It *is* a very subtle point, but Janis was upset. The integrity of her survey had been damaged."

"Jim, do you even know what the question was?"

"No, but it doesn't matter. In this business we *have* to be consistent."

"Jim, listen to me. Whenever we do product surveys we always identify ourselves as the consumer research branch of Goldinger's, but for this Image survey the interviewers were told to identify themselves only as the Consumer Research Center. As you know, there is no such entity. If the respondents got more curious the interviewers were told to identify themselves as an *inde*pendent research group commissioned by Goldinger's. That is simply not true, and when Colleen felt uncomfortable misidentifying herself I told her to follow her conscience. That's what happened. I really don't see that it makes a difference to the survey—in fact, I don't understand why we don't simply identify ourselves correctly from the beginning. It's the falsification that undermines the integrity of the survey more than anything I might have told Colleen."

Jim shook his head slowly, speaking as father to truant daughter. "No, Farida, you see, if the respondent thinks Goldinger's is conducting the survey for itself they might respond differently than if they thought an *inde*pendent research group was conducting the survey. That's where integrity comes in: it's the purity of the response that matters, not the purity of the interviewer."

Farida was surprised by the subtlety of his distinction, but realized he had been coached by Janis Palomo. "Jim, don't you find that just a little bit specious? If integrity is the concern, surely we should have hired another organization to conduct the survey. Integrity should surely include both sides of the equation, not just one or the other."

"But it *does* include both sides. The interviewing staff are all temp workers—part-timers. They don't count as full-time employees. They don't get benefits due full-time employees—no pension, no profit sharing, no medical. It would not be the least bit specious for them to say they didn't work for Goldinger's—in fact, it would be the only thing they could say. They're just picking up extra money while they put themselves through school—or whatever crisis they may have got themselves into."

Farida sighed. "Jim, I don't know what to say except that I disagree with you one hundred percent—but it doesn't matter. It's not my business, it's not my survey, and maybe I should simply have referred Colleen to Janis instead of advising her as I did—but she wasn't there at the time and it's all over now. What more is there to be said or done?"

"Well, for one thing, Janis wanted to throw away the tainted interviews, but of course she didn't."

Farida allowed herself an ironic smile. "Of course she didn't."

Jim focused on his fingers, spread on his desk, palms raised making tiny tents of his hands, pretending to miss her smile. "Too much money had already gone into them and for the most part they were still useful. She wanted to tell you herself, but I thought you might take it better coming from me—I mean because of our long association. I explained to her that you probably just didn't know any better—I mean, what with your pregnancy, not to mention your history. I know how you must feel. We've worked together long enough, you and I, not to pull any punches. So, what do you say? Can we call an end to the matter? Can we count on you to keep this in mind in the future?"

Farida sat up straight. "Jim, I would like you to keep one thing clear—and I say this to you because, as you say, we have worked together long enough not to pull any punches. My history, as you put it, has nothing to do with it, and I will thank you not to refer to it in the future. That is personal, and it is presumptuous of you to say you know how I feel. You *don't* know how I feel. You are not a woman—and even if you were, you would first have to walk a mile in my shoes. About the survey, I don't think I did anything wrong, and you can count on me in the future only to follow my conscience."

Jim smiled, not unembarrassed, afraid the tone of the conversation if not the actual words might leak out of his office to Bunny. "All I meant, Farida, is that my wife has had three children. I know what she was going through at the time. That's all I meant."

Farida got up. "It is not the same thing at all. Your wife's experience is not your own and neither is it mine, but I have said all I am going to about this matter. Also, in the future, if you want to talk to me, I would like you to ask me yourself. Don't send Bunny after me."

She was breathing quickly, keeping her eyes on his face, but he kept his gaze on his tented hands on the desk, almost whispering. "Farida, take it easy. I do think you are overreacting. I do think it is because of your condition."

She slapped the desk, speaking firmly but not raising her voice. "Jim, this is the last time I will ask you. Do not ever mention my condition to me again. It is something about which you know nothing—and neither does your wife."

Jim didn't look up as she left the office.

III

Farida was accustomed to spacious living, but had a special affection for the Cassidy household, a penthouse in Lincoln Park overlooking the lagoon and beyond that Lake Michigan.

Raymond had bragged, when giving her the tour, that the apartment was to be measured in acres, not square feet. It had taken him a year to get the measure of the place, a new room appearing every month or so like a planet swimming into a constellation. Farida had laughed, but appreciated the sentiment. The elevator led into a foyer, and the foyer into a living-room so vast it was difficult at first to perceive its boundaries. A cathedral ceiling gave it the appearance of an amphitheater. Innumerable doorways led to an apparent maze of rooms beyond, two spiral stairways to a mezzanine and more rooms above. Raymond took great delight in drawing her attention to various tapestries, paintings, vases, objets d'art, not to mention fixtures of gold in the bathroom, but Ginger only smiled at his enthusiasm.

It was so very luxurious an apartment that it shed a brighter light even on Horace's friendship with Ginger despite her betrayal. If living well were the best revenge, Raymond and Ginger's lifestyle would have satisfied the Count of Monte Cristo. It was easier to forgive betrayal when compensated with luxury, but Farida's feelings remained mixed. Ginger's betrayal was no less monstrous for the compensation, and she had never understood Horace's benign response. He had to be either a saint or spineless, and even at her most benighted Farida had never mistaken him for a saint, but she had come to like Ginger better, consoling her through Raymond's affair though she saw no more of her than necessary.

Horace had argued, not without merit, that if not for the betrayal he and Farida would never have married, but Farida had become more forgiving only after Raymond's detour with Rhonda Lake, paying Ginger back it seemed in kind. She had witnessed Ginger's anger and desolation firsthand during what had seemed her permanent residence in their guest-room, and she had transferred her disapproval to Raymond. When the prodigal husband had returned, overflowing with repentance, Ginger had received him with open arms, open heart, not even a perfunctory reproval, as if there were nothing to forgive. She would have said Rhonda's blood on his head was punishment enough, but Farida had imagined her at first no less spineless than Horace, understanding better only when she learned Ginger was pregnant with her second child. Her emotions ran then from disapproval to forgiveness to envy. During the year of Ginger's second pregnancy, also Rohini's second, she had endured her second miscarriage.

"There you are, honey. I should have guessed. I wondered what had happened to you."

Farida had gravitated to her favorite spot in the Cassidy living-room, a recessed window-seat the size of a bed. She had removed her shoes and made herself comfortable against a wall among the cushions, gazing at the glass palace of the Lincoln Park Conservatory below, the Zoo to the right, the rookery beyond, all bound by the broad blue convex bow of the lake. "Sorry, Ginger. I was tired—had to get some peace and quiet. Hope you don't mind."

"Perish the thought. I know how you feel. Kiddie parties are killers—and you're pregnant." She kicked off her shoes, joining Farida in the window-seat with a sigh, leaning against the opposite wall. "I'm tired myself, and *so* relieved it's all over—until the next one, of course. Elizabeth will be three in June."

"She's so big she could be four—no surprise, I suppose, considering her father's practically a lumberjack."

Ginger laughed. "Raymond's big all right. I sometimes think that's what I like best about him."

"But Anastasia is tiny—such a big name for such a tiny thing. If she wasn't walking already I would have said she was barely a year."

"Well, just look at me. You might say, I suppose, that Anastasia is my girl and Elizabeth is Raymond's. I wonder who your baby will favor, you or Horace."

"Both, I suppose, in different ways—but Anastasia is so pale you can hardly see her against the sheets. She has Horace's color, don't you think, and the same kind of spindliness?"

Ginger stared momentarily at the wall beside Farida's head, apparently lost in thought, but laughing again in the same instant. "You know, I've thought the same thing myself. I think sometimes a great love leaves a residue—and he's always been such a dear to me, first when I left him for Raymond, and then when Raymond left …" She pursed her lips momentarily, but brightened her eyes again in the same instant. "I like to think sometimes that Anastasia might be a prototype for your own baby."

Ginger expected at least a smile in response, but Farida only sighed, casting her gaze at the earth below, bright now with streetlamps and traffic. "Lucky Horace, he has at least a surrogate daughter."

"Oh, honey, what a thing to say! If she is Horace's surrogate daughter she is most certainly also yours. You must pull yourself together. In another three months—even less—you're going to look back at this conversation and laugh yourself stupid. You'll have given him the real thing."

Farida sighed again, still looking below. "Maybe."

"Of course, you will—third time's the charm."

Farida looked again at Ginger, fainter now in the dimming light of day. The other end of the room was already lit by chandeliers. "That's what everyone says—but for most people the first time is enough. Just look at you." Ginger turned her head, saying nothing, and Farida finally smiled. "Sorry, just feeling sorry for myself.

Nothing to do but soldier on and hope for the best. From now on I'm going to put on the glow of the mother-to-be, no matter how I feel. I'm ready to join the others if you want."

"No hurry. The party's pretty much over. Just about everyone's gone home. I just saw the girls to bed. Why don't we take advantage of the time, leave the lights off? We hardly talk anymore. Let them come looking for us if they want."

Farida grinned. "All right. I'd like that."

There was a brief silence before Ginger spoke again. "So, back to Goldinger's tomorrow?"

Farida sighed. "Yes, I guess."

"I must say I don't understand why you don't just quit—especially now, with the pregnancy—and considering what's happened before."

"Actually, I have been thinking about quitting."

"Really? That *is* good news—and about time. When?"

"I haven't figured that out yet. I want to be more sure of what I want to do."

Ginger smiled. "The baby will answer all those questions, but I'm glad to hear you're quitting. You've proved your point. You've proved a woman can do a man's job—and now you've got a woman's job to do."

Farida grinned. "You may be right, but that's not why I'm quitting. I've just got so many things to think about."

"What, for instance?"

"Well, have you read *The Feminine Mystique*?"

"Oh, honey! Spoken like someone who has never been a mother. Who has time to read?"

Farida smiled. Elizabeth and Anastasia flourished mostly in the care of their nannies, Ursula and Kirsten. Ginger spent much of her time with women not unlike herself, lunching, shopping, traveling, attending events, charities, matinees, not unlike Farida's mother, Persis, the Bombay socialite. Ginger was too comfortable in her life to imagine it anything but selfless and brilliant, even useful. *Some*one had to show the less fortunate how to live, she would have said, with no sense of irony. Farida had little hope of converting Ginger, but told her what she had told Rohini about the drop in the percentage of women graduates—from forty-seven percent in 1920 to thirty-five in 1958. "We seem to be moving backward, but what interested me more than anything else was what Friedan said about the stories in the women's magazines. She went through back issues of *McCall's*, *Redbook*, and *Ladies' Home Journal* and found that during the Thirties and Forties the stories were about career-women, about women who gave up men for their careers only to find men who respected them for their careers—but the stories of the Fifties went the other way, women giving up careers for men. The first casualty of the stories was the career-woman: toward the end of the Fifties there was no such creature in the stories. Next to go was the housewife with any interest in community affairs, next the housewife with a mind of her own, leaving only the helpless housewife dependent on her husband for everything, appealing constantly to his ego. The stories are all about dropouts and clinging vines snatching men from women with degrees and women who can fend for themselves, women who win their men by losing to them in games of tennis."

"Oh, but honey, that's how things are sup*posed* to be!"

"What nonsense, Ginger! You are just proving my point! Why should a woman diminish herself to get what she wants?"

"Because it *works*, honey! Women get what they want by letting men think they're the boss. We cook and clean and give them babies— and they buy us clothes and jewelry and take us to the Bahamas. What could be fairer? It's foolproof."

Farida smiled again to think of Ginger cooking and cleaning. She was a fine cook, but her culinary expertise was a matter of vanity, not necessity. "Well, actually, that was what I thought at first too. I mean, just look at the stories I wrote—"

"And *pub*lished!"

"Yes, but just think of some of my titles—'Haute Housewife,' 'Bombay Bombshell,' 'Sitar Symphony,' 'The Dream from the East.'" Her stories had been variations on a single theme, an exotic Indian wife adjusting to the lifestyle of her modern American husband, grateful for his bounty despite bounty of her own, recognizing his wisdom in the conventions of the time, moving smoothly from a world of servants and money to one of appliances and convenience. "The stories of the

Thirties and Forties were written by women, but after the war, when men controlled the purse-strings again, they changed the mold to suit themselves. Not only did the stories become about women catering to men, but women ful*filled* by catering to men. It was supposed to be their sole reason for existence, but it left many of them *un*fulfilled— and apologetic for being just housewives. The stories idealized the male fantasy, not the female, because the formula was written by men—but they were passed off as women's fantasies."

"Honey, I know what you're saying, I've heard all the arguments— but being *just* a housewife means being a cook, a nurse, a chauffeur, a teacher, a tailor, an accountant, and God alone knows what else. It's a matter of perspective."

Farida smiled yet again to think of Ginger in any of the occupations she had mentioned. "Yes, yes, it sounds very good—but that is precisely the man's argument. If women need such arguments to remind themselves of their worth, that's a problem in itself, don't you think? If they have to be told how to feel then how can they trust their feelings?"

"Well, then, what do you suggest?"

"I don't know exactly—but I know I want to do things differently."

IV

"When the British followed the custom of the Mughals in making Kashmir their summer retreat from the furnace that was India, the ruling Maharajah, unhappy with the seasonal invasion of stoic palefaced men in uniform, their imperious palefaced women in crinolines, their solemn palefaced children, and their armies of nannies and servants, prohibited the ownership and construction of houses on his land. The logical Briton took the initiative of constructing houseboats, floating bungalows meant for mooring more than cruising though they were sometimes taxied between the lakes Dal and Nagin. The process was begun in 1888 and as of today it is estimated that there are more than a thousand houseboats on the lakes bearing all the comforts of a middle-class Victorian household, from wood-burning stoves to plush armchairs and warm carpets." Horace looked up from the guidebook in his lap with a grin. "Probably safe to say that was written by someone who didn't care for palefaces."

He and Farida lounged on a mattress, raised at one end like a hospital bed, under the canopy of a shikara paddled from behind by two oarsmen on Nagin Lake. The canopy could be made as private as they wished, curtains allowing them to regulate sunlight, communicate with the oarsmen behind, or haggle with traders paddling alongside hawking wares ranging from suits and coats to papier-mache, carpets, silks, furs, shawls, brassware, mirrorwork, jewelry, and woodcarvings among other things. Farida had bought twenty shawls of swirling floral motifs, impressed with the salesman's pitch. He had slipped a ring off his finger and drawn one of the shawls through its narrow aperture. The shawl was lighter than air, woven with the fur from the underbelly of the Tibetan gazelle. Horace might have remonstrated against the cost though she spent her own money, on herself as much as on him. "Don't be so paranoid, Horace. You are only saying that because you are such a paleface yourself."

His grin remained. The holiday was the tonic for the miscarriage though the initial reunion with her parents in Bombay had been stickier than he might have wished, Nariman apparently oblivious to his daughter's distress, Persis apparently pleased to have bested her daughter in the baby sweepstakes, triumphant with her second pregnancy to Farida's three miscarriages. She had followed with three miscarriages of her own, but the one success had vaulted her so far ahead that even her sympathy carried a sting. "Did you know all that, about the history of the houseboat?"

"Most of it—maybe all of it at one time, but I don't remember. Kaki was always insistent that I learn about every place we visited. She would read from the guidebooks, just like you." She wiggled herself next to him, tucking herself under his arm. "My lovely Horace, what would I do without you?"

Horace gathered her to himself, adjusting his arm around her shoulders. They had chosen Nagin Lake that morning, more secluded than Dal, both lakes ringed by snowcapped mountains, the valley lush with greenery, orchards of apple, cherry, walnut, and almond trees, avenues of poplars and chenars, fields of rice—and the still water, pinked with lotus blossoms, provided a perfect reflection of the panorama. Closer at hand the clear water revealed darting fish and streaming vines. "It *is* beautiful, isn't it? Reminds me of Switzerland."

Few would have questioned the preeminence of the Kashmir Valley as the most sightly panorama in India. "Mmmm. Horace?"

"Mmmm?"

"I want to make a change when we get back to Chicago. I'm not going back to Goldinger's."

"Of course."

"I want to give piano lessons, art lessons, nothing strenuous, just something to fill the time as comfortably as I can—until we have our baby."

Horace sighed. The doctor had blamed Farida's miscarriages on an Rh discrepancy and discouraged more attempts. "It's okay, Farida. I don't care if we never have a baby. It's not important."

"But it *is*, and we *will*. This time I'm going to do it differently. You are going to have the most lazy and languid wife anyone ever had. My focus is going to be one hundred percent on getting pregnant and carrying the baby to term. Wait and see. We will have our baby yet."

Horace sighed again, but said nothing.

"I know what you're thinking—and you're wrong. It has nothing to do with my mother. I'm doing this for us. I want the baby for us, not to prove anything to her."

Again Horace said nothing.

"What are we having for dinner tonight? I feel better already."

"Kababs, I think—and that creamy goat curry you liked the other day, with cashews and raisins."

The service on *Sunrise*, their houseboat, couldn't have been better, the cook proficient in Indian, western, and Kashmiri cuisines. "Oh, good. I can't wait." When Horace remained quiet she turned her head toward him. "Vare chhu, my darling?"

It was the only Kashmiri she knew, How are you? and the response, I'm fine, with which Horace obliged. "Khare chhu, my lovely."

PERCY FABER AND *THE LONG SUNSET*

T he pills had proven too weak a shield against the attacks launched on Alma's heart. What kept her going was the strength of her muscle; a weaker heart would long have capitulated; but the attacks became more savage, more frequent, and lasted longer, five in the past fortnight, once pounding her for three hours at a stretch. After an attack Alma was exhausted enough for a more profound sleep than when she had been well, and in between attacks she went about her daily business so refreshed, her smile so bright, no one would have been the wiser—as brave as any character played by Katharine Hepburn, but Farida no longer called her the Katharine Hepburn of Briar Place, unwilling to risk upsetting her even with a joke.

She saw Alma every day, staying when she brought her mail. There was nothing anyone could do but lessen the pain, and Farida had measured 0.5 ml of morphine into syringes and stoppered them for use in her absence. Thursday was television night from seven to nine. They watched in succession *The Cosby Show*, *Family Ties*, *Cheers*, and *Night Court*. It was 8:20, Sam and Diane about to be caught out on their weekly deceptions, when Alma turned to Farida, alarm etched like a claw in her face. "Hon, I think I'm in trouble again."

Farida was shocked by the suddenness of the attack; Alma had been laughing at Sam's clumsiness barely a minute ago; but took her cue from her friend. "Shall I get the morphine?"

Alma nodded.

The mess of syringes with their pale pink liquids looked like flowers of glass in the bowl on the dining table. Farida fetched one, unstoppered it, and gave it to Alma. She would have administered it, but her friend wished to maintain what autonomy she could. Alma placed the tip of the syringe in her mouth and depressed the plunger, returning the syringe to Farida who placed it with the other empties by the kitchen sink.

When she returned Alma looked up, mouth shrunk to a dot, voice barely audible over the television. "You don't have to stay, hon. There's nothing … you can do."

Farida switched off the television, shaking her head. "I can't leave you like this."

Alma sighed. "Oh, hon, whatever … happens … I'm going to be all right. This is what has to happen. I have—" A sudden intake of breath cut her off, shutting her eyes, followed by exhalations issued like the hiss of air escaping a tire, and she pressed down on her heart as if to still the tremor.

Farida's breath quickened in sympathy and she sat beside her friend. "I'm not leaving." She put an arm around Alma, conscious of rolling drumbeats threatening to burst their walls, shoulders jerking to the whip of her heart. They sat for fifteen minutes without a word, Alma getting clammy with sweat, Farida getting a towel from the closet to wipe her friend's face and neck, but Alma reached for the towel and Farida surrendered. She dried herself thoroughly and silently, put the towel in her lap, and bent her head to her knees. Farida sat beside her again, caressing the hard ridge of bone down her back with the palm of her hand.

At 8:50 Alma asked for another syringe. She was not to have more than one every hour, but the nurse had told Farida these were minor dosages and she gave her the second syringe without demur— and when asked at 9:20 for a third she gave her a third. Alma sighed, giving up the third empty, and leaned back in the sofa, arms outspread in a facsimile of crucifixion. Her heart was silent, but its jackhammer rhythm was visible in the throb of her jugular and the relentless tremble of her shoulders. She requested a fresh towel—and, after she had dried herself again, eased herself onto her back on the sofa, making a pillow of a cushion, raising her legs, clutching the towel.

When Farida offered her a pillow to clutch Alma shook her head, never opening her eyes. There was no space on the sofa for Farida. She sat instead by Alma's feet in an adjacent armchair.

Alma might have run a marathon for the ebb and flow of her breath, rasping like a rattle. Her face twisted in a rictus of pain, disappearing behind a sea of wrinkles. Hands clasped, fingers laced, she alternated between pressing down on her heart and raising her arms in a wreath. Sweat streamed continually, but she uttered not a syllable through her mime except once, a breathless whispered "Stop! Please stop!" hands raised toward the ceiling in an attitude of prayer, a gesture so private Farida felt at once prurient and privileged, recognizing the profundity of her experience. She wanted to let Alma know she was there, but not to intrude, and remained in the armchair caressing Alma's ankles and feet.

At 9:40, Alma shook her head, eyes still shut in a vise, and let another breathless whisper escape. "It's like someone is standing on my chest." She asked for another syringe and Farida honored her request, but that meant four syringes in the space of an hour and twenty minutes, and instructions had been for no more than one every hour. The dosages may have been small, but she wondered how many more she could administer with impunity, and called the hospice to reassure herself. The nurse who answered warned against more syringes within the next hour.

Farida settled again in the armchair wondering what she would say if Alma asked for another before the hour. Alma remained on her back on the sofa, wiping herself of sweat, stomach rumbling, but didn't ask for another syringe. Around midnight her feet slid to the floor and she leaned against an armrest, so still she might have ceased breathing, a scarecrow for the way her clothes clung to her frame, pants flopping, blouse sagging, hair a mop of straw. Farida said nothing, afraid to disturb her sleep, but a minute later she slumped further down and Farida sat beside her, arm again around her shoulders, barely breathing herself, desperately seeking signs of life in her friend. Gradually, Alma's breath returned and so did Farida's. Alma smiled, but her voice was a croak. "It's all right ... hon. It's over."

Farida stroked her friend's hand. "Thank God."

Alma leaned her head against her friend. "I love you, hon."

Farida nodded, speaking softly. "I love you, too."

Alma smiled. "I know."

Farida said nothing. She was crying.

They sat in silence for a while before Alma spoke again. "You know, hon … there are times when I feel that I'm not alone. I was reading the paper yesterday … and I could have sworn there were children playing by my side … just minding their own business, playing, as if I wasn't there … but when I looked, they were gone … but it was a good feeling. It was all … good. Candice says I'm hallucinating, morphine will do that to you, and I'm sure she's right, but it's still a good feeling."

Candice was the nurse from the hospice. "You seem to be living in two worlds."

Alma smiled again. "Yes … but you have no idea, hon … how tired I am. Thank you for staying. I'll be all right now. You must have better things to do."

Farida's sigh rose from the pit of her stomach. "What could I do better than what I'm doing now?"

Alma still smiled. "I mean sleep. It's way past midnight."

Farida laughed to cover her nervousness. "Yes, of course."

II

Two bright streaks highlighted Percy's head in the fluorescent lighting of his office as he poured over his *Wall Street Journal*. Farida was so silent sliding into one of the chairs across his desk, moving with all the heft of a hologram, that he didn't notice her until she spoke. "Percy?"

She had whispered, and when he looked up she seemed surprised she had spoken herself. Her mouth remained open, jaw dropped like an anchor, eyes wide and glazed, one slim hand combing thick greying hair with her fingers, the other holding a desk calendar in her lap. "Farida, are you all right?"

She nodded, retracting her jaw, removing the hand from her hair, the specter of a smile hovering on her lips. "Would you please just read what I've written here?"

She held up the calendar which he took. She had scribbled a figure on the page for the day, Friday, August 28, 1987: $10,000.00!!!! underlining it twice. Percy adjusted his spectacles and looked up from the calendar. "Ten thousand dollars?"

Farida joined her hands in an attitude of prayer, her smile broadening as she spoke. "I just received a call from Cedric Darnley, Esquire, Chairman of Butterworth & Blanding, offering me an advance of ten thousand dollars!"

Percy's smile lagged only because he had difficulty grasping what she said no less than herself, but soon caught up with her own. He had imagined at first something might be wrong: it had been almost a year since he had suggested she approach English publishers with the manuscript of *The Long Sunset*. "Congratulations! Well-deserved and well done—well done, indeed!" He set down the calendar and extended his hand across the desk.

"Thank you." Farida shook his hand, smiling more widely yet. She had mailed, months ago, the Prologue of *The Long Sunset*, forty pages, to four London publishers, of which three had declined to read more. Imogen Harley, an editor at Butterworth & Blanding, had requested the rest of the manuscript, said she had enjoyed it, that it was receiving a second reading, and written finally to say Butterworth & Blanding wanted to publish *The Long Sunset*, and Farida would soon be hearing from their chairman, Cedric Darnley. "I thought he would be calling with a timeline—you know, for galleys, the cover, that sort of thing—but instead he said …" (she affected an English accent, deepening her voice): "'Miss Cooper, we think very highly of your novel, *The Long Sunset*, and would like very much to publish it. We would like to make you an offer of an advance of ten thousand American dollars. Would that be sufficient?'"

Farida laughed, combing fingers through her hair again. "I was so nervous I didn't trust myself to speak—and so astounded I had to write the amount on my calendar in case I didn't believe it later!" She laughed again. "I was silent for so long that he finally said …" (she affected the English accent again): "'Is that not enough?' I was so ashamed to have kept him waiting I almost jumped into the mouthpiece. 'Yes, oh yes—more than enough! I'm very happy! I wasn't expecting it at all! Thank you so much.' And he said: 'No, thank *you* very much. We'll be sending you our standard contract, then, if it's all right with you?'— and, of course, I said it was all right with me, and thank you very much again. In fact, I couldn't think of anything to say except Thank You Very Much over and over again—and he kept saying No! Thank <u>You</u> Very Much. He was *such* a gentleman. There's really nothing quite like an English gentleman, is there? I think I might have made a bit of a fool of myself—but I don't care!"

Her excitement had rendered Percy speechless, but his smile slowly encircled his face like an equator. He could not have been more glad. He had become her support at Mandalay, but was due to retire the following month. He had wondered how she would manage without him, but she seemed now to have found a soft place to fall should she need one. He couldn't recall when he had seen her more radiant. "Percy, are you busy tomorrow night?"

His eyebrows rose, scraggly over the rim of his spectacles, contemplating his calendar. "No."

"Good. I'm taking you to dinner and I won't accept any excuses. I owe it all to you, you know."

Percy shook his head. "Nonsense. You owe me nothing."

"But I *am* taking you to dinner, so get used to the idea."

Percy smiled again. "Thank you. I think I would like that."

Farida couldn't stop grinning. "I don't mean just for the publication either. Even the university correspondence has taken a positive turn since I took your advice. I want to show you a couple of letters in particular—but, in the meantime, do we have a date for tomorrow?"

"We do—indeed, yes, we do."

"Good. I shall be at your place at seven-thirty. I shall have reservations at La Creperie for eight."

Percy had not been happier for her in all the time they had worked together. "Why don't I pick you up? After all, I do have a car and it needs a workout."

"No, you're always doing things for me. Here's what we'll do. We'll take your car, but I'll come to your place on my own—and if you don't mind I'll do the driving. It will be your responsibility only to enjoy yourself."

Percy smiled. "I can't think when I last received so irresistible an invitation."

III

Farida had written to Greta Frumpkin that she would appeal to someone whose hands appeared less tied, and that was what she had done, writing to David Constable, Head of English, copying the entire correspondence to date for his benefit, flagging the pertinent letters. David Constable responded the same week saying he would be in touch with her again after he had talked with Greta and she heard from him again the following week.

[David Constable to Farida Cooper]
April 4, 1986
Dear Ms. Cooper,

I have had a chance to review your case and talk with Professor Frumpkin. She and I have devised a possible solution. As you know, it is her judgment that some evidence is needed of your current understanding of the four courses from 1974-75. With the agreement of the faculty who taught those courses (Professors Bennett, Brownlow, Handy, and Hale), Ms. Frumpkin has proposed that you consult with them to devise exercises to demonstrate the currency of your understanding of the subject matter. The nature of the exercises will be up to the faculty, but not as extensive as your proposal of a 200-page paper or a review of recent critical developments. If the results are satisfactory, as I have reason to anticipate they will be, you may proceed to the degree.

Professor Frumpkin will then need to forward a petition to the Graduate College with a positive recommendation that they allow these credits from twelve years ago to count toward your current degree program. *Of course, the final decision rests with the Graduate College. I trust I will hear from Professor Frumpkin about what you have decided to do.*

Sincerely,
David Constable
Professor and Head
cc: *Professor Frumpkin*

[Farida Cooper to Greta Frumpkin]
April 27, 1986
Dear Ms. Frumpkin,

As you know, I have been in touch with David Constable since we last corresponded, and with Professors Hale, Handy, Bennett, and Brownlow since I heard from him. Each of the professors has graciously agreed to an exercise whereby I might demonstrate the currency of my understanding of the subject matter, a process I find far more salubrious than the examinations you had suggested.

I look forward to hearing from you soon. Thanks.
Farida Cooper
cc: *Professor David Constable*

[Greta Frumpkin to Farida Cooper]
2 May, 1986
Dear Ms. Cooper:

I have just received your letter of April 27. Questions will be raised by the Graduate College about your priorities when the writing of novels has repeatedly prevented your finishing the work for the degree. I shall nevertheless forward a petition to the Graduate College recommending we accept your coursework from 1976 onward, and that we accept the recommendation of the professors in the earlier courses once you have completed the exercises.

If you have any questions, please get in touch with me.
Sincerely,
Greta Frumpkin
Director of Graduate Studies
cc: *Professor David Constable*

[Farida Cooper to Greta Frumpkin]
May 24, 1986
Dear Ms. Frumpkin,
 Thank you for your letter. You may be right to say questions will be raised regarding my priorities when the writing of novels continually prevented me from finishing the coursework, but I think we may more pertinently question the rationale of students who fulfill all the requirements of Graduate Writing Programs and never actually write a novel. Let me say in my behalf that I returned to the program at every opportunity and that should count for something.
 I would like to thank you nevertheless for forwarding the petition to the Graduate College.
 Sincerely,
 Farida Cooper
cc: *Professor David Constable*

IV

Farida found a parking space almost at the entrance of La Creperie, a tiny restaurant visible behind French doors from Clark Street, wooden tables holding candles, travel posters on the wall, a narrow bar to one side, a tiny courtyard behind. Percy had been quieter in the car than usual, and she had supposed he felt awkward on the first date of a working relationship of almost two years. Determined to fill all gaps in the conversation she had brought him up to date with her university correspondence along the way and continued her story over a warm breadbasket and glasses of champagne after they had ordered (appetizers of pate and escargot, chicken and mushroom crepes for her, beef bourguignon for him). Her enthusiasm bordered on a rich creamy gloat, but Percy smiled. Considering the gauntlet she had run she was entitled. He had been about to propose a toast when she had interrupted, and he had nodded, slowly rotating his glass by its stem, ready for any opening to raise the glass again, but her words fell like weights on his wrist, and his smile turned gradually pasty.

Despite her preoccupation, his thickening smile, stiffening back, and wrinkling brow weren't lost on her, and she wondered if she were talking too much. "I feel just as strongly about those dilettantes who get degree after degree and never actually do any work that matters. Imagine getting a doctorate in Creative Writing and never publishing a novel—never even *writing* a novel. All they're qualified to do is teach what they've never practiced themselves. How phony is that!"

The pasty smile gave way to pursed lips. "Well, now, some might consider that a handicap."

Farida stared, dropping her smile, his reserve beginning to erode her confidence. "What do you mean? What handicap?"

Percy stared into his champagne. "I mean, if they are offered positions with benefits and comfortable compensations and promises of pensions and tenure and all the rest of it, it would be somewhat difficult to abandon the security in search of the holy grail of a novel, wouldn't you say, especially if they had families to feed?"

Farida looked away, sensing a rebuke. His argument was not without merit (society handicapped men and women in different ways: men reduced to servitude in their role as providers, women to ennui as housewives), but the rebuke determined her instead to challenge him. "Maybe—but Edmund Wilson said that a person serious about being an artist has no business getting tied up with responsibilities to a family, or maintaining a standard of living, or worrying about security and all the rest of it. Wouldn't *you* agree?"

He nodded slowly, still staring into his glass, speaking through stiff lips. "Even artists have to live—otherwise, it harms their art. If they get too cynical it harms their art. The point is to understand *all* points of view, to present them *all* clearly, not just that of the artist—at least, that's how it is with the greatest artists. They spread more light than heat."

Farida laughed. "Right, and I suppose you'll be telling me next that everything is beautiful in its own way." Percy remained silent, and she laughed again, a harsher laugh than before. "Oh, my God! That *is* what you are saying, isn't it?"

Percy shook his head. "No, nothing so facile. What I am saying is that a little tolerance is not such a bad thing. We all have to make choices, and we all have to live with the consequences of our choices. If you want to be a writer you accept the possibility of living alone without fretting and fuming—and if you want to have a family you accept the possibility of never being a writer."

She sensed again rebuke. "But some *do* manage to do both."

"Some do, but we don't know what sacrifices they have made. At the risk of sounding like a blithering idiot, I must say I think the key is to be satisfied with what you have. I don't say you shouldn't reach for the moon—in fact, I would even say that you *should*, it's important to test your limits—but if it drives you crazy, be satisfied with the earth."

He had surprised her, not so much with his words but the disapproval in his tone. She wondered how she might have provoked him when she had wanted only his comfort. She took another deep breath, releasing him from her stare, caressing his hand still holding the champagne glass by its stem. "Percy, what a thing to say. You're no blithering idiot. That's the last thing that you are. I never want to hear you say it again and I'm sorry if I made you feel that way."

Percy caught her eye and smiled again. "It's just my way of speaking, old fogey that I am. If anything, you make me feel less blithering."

She shook her head, understanding only that she made him feel old. "No, neither blithering nor an old fogey—not even a young fogey. Now stop it, Percy, really, before you turn into a real fogey before my eyes." He laughed, but said nothing, and she smiled, still caressing his hand. "I'm sorry. I guess I've been talking too much, haven't I?" He opened his mouth to protest, but she squeezed his hand hard and he remained silent though still smiling: the irony appeared to have escaped her, first confessing to talking too much, then insisting on talking more. "It's just that sometimes I feel as if I've been living all these years in a tunnel, and now that I've come into the light I feel I have to somehow justify all those years in the tunnel—all those years while others were busy being model citizens, getting ahead, raising children."

Her voice dropped at the mention of children and Percy understood better. His discomfort diminished: her regret about children balanced his own regrettable inexperience with women, regrettable only because a greater experience might now have stood him in good stead. He spoke more kindly. "I would say that's just part of the deal. Artists need time in the wilderness, much like prophets or mystics, just finding their own voice, their style, their subject, learning what sets them apart from those who have gone before. That's why they tend to be loners. What they do is so much more difficult—to go consciously against the grain of society to accomplish what they know is most important for them to accomplish—and to do much of it alone. That artist has almost no place in society today—writers bonding around picnic tables to discuss one another's work, paying good money to attend retreats and obtain degrees. What would Tolstoy and Hugo and Dickens have said about writing workshops and MLA conventions and academic qualifications in the arts? Those are for networking more than writing, but writers aren't made for networking, and many who are tend to be lesser writers, cutting their cloth to suit the conventions instead of finding their own voices. A degree qualifies you to teach, but not necessarily to become a better writer. You can be a writer who teaches or a teacher who writes. The choice is yours." It was the most he had said all evening and, catching her eyes, finally seized his moment, raising his glass. "To *The Long Sunset*."

She clinked her glass against his, smiling again. "And to the person who gave it a much-needed kick in the ..." (she smiled, rephrasing words in her head, mindful of his sensibilities) "right direction."

Percy grinned, aware of her delicacy in his behalf, recognizing the difference in their ages and personalities, a difference that shone a bright beam on the dark narrow comfort in which he had cocooned himself since Erica's death, a bright beam broadening his panorama of possibilities. "Hardly. Maybe just a very small push."

"Yes, yes—just a little push across the Atlantic." Percy smiled, hoping their amity was reaching critical mass, but her next comment dashed his hope. "That was a complete rout for the Frumpkin, you know—to go from requiring four examinations in almost forty texts to four exercises of *my* choosing to be negotiated with each of the professors."

He had underestimated her obsession, but nodded, buttering bread while she talked it out, spreading pate when the appetizers arrived, drawing escargots from the shells, refilling their champagne glasses. She had lived too long embattled in the cave of her apartment. He had heard the story before, but she needed to savor her triumph anew and he let her run on of her own accord before she stopped herself, laughing. "Sorry. I went off on you again, didn't I?"

"It's all right." Percy smiled, speaking more freely as the evening progressed, mostly about his family, Farida listening more closely. They topped the meal with an apple and caramel crepe for Farida, banana and chocolate for Percy, both laced with Grand Marnier, followed by herbal teas. It was ten o'clock when they finished, past Percy's bedtime, but he welcomed Farida's suggestion of a drive, both feeling something else needed resolution. Farida drove, exiting from Lake Shore Drive on a whim, suggesting further a walk along Montrose Beach which Percy welcomed again without hesitation.

The night was warm, an invitation to walkers, among them couples arm in arm, but Farida and Percy were careful not to touch as they walked barely six inches apart. A half-moon beamed, cloudy in appearance, grained with silver. The air around seemed enchanted, thick and bright with the zigzag flight of fireflies. It would have been natural for Percy to put his arm around her, but he didn't, not even giving her his arm, his earlier fear returning, of what was expected, his inexperience with women against her experience with men. Between him and Erica there had been an attraction of equals, but with Farida he felt presumptuous. Even among women half her age she took centerstage despite greying hair and encroaching wrinkles she did nothing to hide. She was a Cooper though she lived like one of their servants, but he had never asked why, and she had never volunteered information. He had wondered how she would manage after he retired from Mandalay, but now wondered how he would manage without her.

Unaccustomed to reticence from men, Farida was puzzled and not a little frustrated by his apparent disinterest. It would have been no less natural for her to take his arm, but she had taken the initiative all evening and wanted some indication he wasn't merely following her lead, some indication he wished to be with her as much as she with him; it was enough that she had provided the opportunity. Their six inches of separation grew into a chasm, the walk got drearier as it got longer, the conversation larded with banalities about the wonder of fireflies until he suggested it might be time to go home. Walking to the parking lot he offered to drive.

She didn't look at him. "I don't care."

They slid silently into the Volvo, remaining silent during the drive to Briar Place. Farida stared blankly out of the window, leaning away from him into her door. Percy stared at the road ahead, but it was questionable how much he saw. He jumped a red light, setting another car screeching, but Farida gave him not even a glance. He wished she would say something, but realized she had long said more than necessary. He wished for something to say himself, but realized the time for talk was past. He had talked easily earlier about shedding more light than heat, but wished at that moment to generate more heat, wished he were more a man of action.

When they reached Briar Place he sprang out of the car to open her door. She smiled getting out of the car, but he couldn't be sure she wasn't mocking him, particularly with her remark. "Thank you, but that was quite unnecessary."

He had known before leaping from the car that it was not the action required, but having come so far he had to go further. "Let me walk you to the door."

Her voice was desultory. "Thank you. It's only a few steps. I can manage."

The formality of her words crowned his discouragement. They stood under a maple on the pavement. He leaned forward, but she turned her mouth away. He kissed her cheek, dutiful as a schoolboy, embarrassing them both. Still, he persevered. "Thank you for dinner. I enjoyed it im*mense*ly."

His emphasis rang false. She didn't look at him. "You're very welcome."

He stepped back, getting out of her way. "Goodnight, then."

She nodded, saying nothing, getting keys from her purse, smiling as if he were a child. He admired her silhouette walking away outlined in the light from the lobby, opening the outer door, unlocking the inner. He wished she would turn just once to wave, but she disappeared around a corner never looking back, and he imagined he had lost her good will forever. He knew she was angry with him with good reason, but hardly as angry as he with himself, hiding behind a shield of words and wisdom. He got slowly back in the car, drove slowly home, as gauche and ardorous closing on sixty-six as he had been at sixteen.

ENTERING HER APARTMENT, Farida sat disconsolate at her dining table, still in her coat. The evening had not gone as she had planned, not at all as she might have wished. She had wanted it to be Percy's evening, everything as he might have wished, but consumed with her dual triumphs she had focused like a laser on herself, allowing not even an opening. He was older than her by far, but no older than Horace. He was not the dashing man she had envisioned for herself, but she could be dashing enough for two. He was self-effacing, but he had been her rock. She couldn't have said how long she sat, but was wrenched from her reverie by the telephone. Cold fingers pinched the back of her neck. It was eleven o'clock. "Hello?"

A gruff male voice answered. "Is this Farida Cooper?"

"Yes. Who is this?"

"This is the police. There's been an accident, ma'am."

Her throat closed in on itself, malign as the hand of a strangler. She almost dropped the receiver.

"Ma'am, are you there? Are you all right?"

"I'm here. Is Percy all right? Where is he? How did you know to call me?"

"Take it easy, ma'am. He's going to be all right. The ambulance is here. They're taking him to Augustana Hospital. We found your card in his wallet."

Augustana was on Lincoln Avenue, between her place and his. "Thank you so much. I'm on my way. Thank you so much."

She dashed from the apartment, dashed back a moment later to her petty cash drawer. She would need money to pay the cabbie—but this could *not* be happening again. This was why she had run from Bombay. She had been so sure she had learned her lesson, but people were still paying a price for her carelessness.

V

It was nine o'clock in the evening, Farida debating whether to open the sofa bed for an early night, when the phone rang. "Hello. Is this Farida?"

"Yes. Who is this?"

"I'm Zelda. I'm a friend of Alma Hall."

Farida gripped the receiver more tightly. "Oh, yes. I know who you are."

"I'm very sorry to bother you so late, but I was just talking to Alma and … I don't know what to tell you, but she wasn't making any sense."

"What do you mean? What did she say?"

"She said the room was flooding. Everything was wet. The walls were wet, her clothes were wet, the carpet was wet. There was water everywhere. There were some women with her. They were all wet. I don't know what to make of it. She said she was all right, but I didn't want to leave it at that. Would you go upstairs, please—just to check?"

Farida took a deep breath. "Of course. I'm sure she's just hallucinating again. It's the morphine. It does that to her. I'm sure she's all right—but I'll check."

"Would you, please? Thank you."

"I'll call you later."

"Don't tell her I called. She'll be mad at me. She doesn't like to be a bother."

"I know."

FARIDA HAD SEEN ALMA EARLIER IN THE DAY, taking up her mail. They had talked about moving her to a nursing home—but, considering she preferred to maintain as independent an existence as she could for as long as she could, the hospice had assured her that wouldn't be necessary until the very end. She would know when the time came, Farida would need to call the hospice and they would know what to do. In the meantime, Farida had the key to the apartment, and in addition to the newspaper and mail she brought groceries, managed Alma's bank statements, and did her laundry. She was sure Alma was hallucinating, but she turned the lock warily.

She didn't know what to expect—a circle of women playing ring around the roses, water leaking down the walls, mildewing carpet squelching underfoot—and glanced around to reassure herself there was no cause for alarm. Alma sat on the sofa in the darkened room, hunched forward, head down, arms crossed, elbows on knees. She was naked. She looked up. She said nothing.

Farida was shocked but relieved she didn't appear to be in danger. "Alma, are you all right?"

Alma nodded, her smile crooked with the worm of shame as she crouched more tightly to cover her nakedness, turning her face toward her walker. "Over there. They were wet. I had to take them off."

The walker was hung with clothes by the bathroom. The clothes were damp to Farida's touch, so was the carpet. She went into Alma's closet and returned with a robe, bunching it into a concertina to put over her head. "What happened?"

Alma inserted her arms and head into the bottom of the robe without rising. "I wanted to go to the bathroom. There were women. They were in the way."

Farida nodded, sliding the robe down Alma's back, conscious of the horny ridge of her spine, upper arms slack as the sac of an IV. "Can you get up for a moment?" Alma rose with a struggle, Farida slid the robe under her, and zipped it from the front. "How many women?"

Alma shrugged. "Four or five."

Farida sat in the armchair again. "Alma, you know you were hallucinating, don't you?"

Alma nodded, embarrassment turning to contrition.

"It's all right. Tell me what happened next."

"We were all trying to go to the bathroom, and we fell—all of us, together, over there—and there was water everywhere."

She pointed to where the carpet was damp and Farida understood what had happened. Morphine eased pain, but created hallucinations, also constipation, for which Alma had been given a diarrhetic. In her hurry to get to the bathroom Alma had fallen and peed on herself.

"I had to take my clothes off. They were wet."

Farida caressed Alma's face. "How do you feel now?"

"Better."

"Not hurt?"

Alma shook her head.

"Will you go to bed?"

"I have to change."

"You don't have to change. You can sleep in the robe."

Alma nodded. Farida got her a sleeping pill, led her to the bedroom, tucked her in, and kissed her cheek. "Goodnight, sweetie. I'll be in the living-room if you need me."

"Thank you, hon." Her eyes shut and she was asleep almost at once. In the dim light the jowls on her pudding face looked plumped like a baby's. Age returned a person to the womb; without her walker she would have been crawling; letters were a blur to her eyes, music jagged to her ears, reducing her to eating, sleeping, and shitting. Farida called Zelda to set her at ease, did dishes she found in the sink, and sank into the armchair for the night. She didn't ask why an old woman had to be bullied by her health: the way to understand God's will was to accept it; she did what she could to change what seemed wrong, but beyond that she resorted to faith; to do otherwise was to question God, to put herself above God. Malcolm Muggeridge said it best: faith was like reinforced concrete, doubt the steel within; one was the dialectical partner of the other. She woke an hour later, cheeks wet: she had been crying in her sleep.

FARIDA COOPER'S TWO MOTHERS

Farida groaned, recognizing her mother's knock, loud and aggressive, not asking permission to enter but warning of an invasion. True to form, impatient of entry, she barged into the bedroom before Farida could say a word, wagging a letter in her hand. "Farida, what is this? Why has no one ever told me about this?"

It was four in the afternoon. Farida had returned from a luxurious lunch at the Willingdon Club with Threaty and Vera to nap before her piano teacher came for a lesson at five, to be followed by Lekha Kilachand's party later in the evening. She lay curled on her side in bed, in jeans and blouse, a flap of hair hiding her face, turned away from her mother. "Please, Mummy. Lay-Ter. I'm tired. We ate too much."

Her mother stood over the bed, hands in such furious motion she appeared multilimbed. "You will answer me *now!* I will not stand such cheek from my own daughter!"

Farida groaned again. For all her mother's fury she held no fear for her, but she realized her sleep was at an end. Her mother would not leave without an answer. She rolled onto her back, graceful as an invertebrate, stretching young limbs in arabesques, putting her feet to the floor, elbows to knees, forehead to the heels of her hands, never opening her eyes, speaking like a martyr. "What is it, Mummy?"

Her mother thrust the letter in her face between her hands, forcing her to open her eyes. "That is just what I want to know! What *is* this? *Why* is it here?"

Farida read the letter. It was from Chicago University, part of her correspondence with half a dozen universities seeking admission. She kept her eyes on the letter. "I have never seen this. How did you get it?"

"Don't be coy with me! Don't play dumb! Of course you haven't seen it. It was delivered to me by mistake. The postman, stupid fellow, doesn't seem to think it makes a difference if the letters go upstairs or downstairs. But you still haven't answered my question. Why are you getting letters from Chicago?"

Farida put the letter aside on the bed. "Oh, Mummy, it's just one letter—and why do you think? I'm applying for admission to the university. What is the big deal?"

"Why didn't you tell me? Why have you kept it a secret?"

Farida fell on her back again, feet still on the floor, rubbing her eyes with the backs of her hands. "It's not a secret, Mummy. When I got an admission I would have told you. Otherwise, there was nothing to tell—and, in any case, I didn't think you cared."

"Why not? My only daughter wants to go halfway around the world and I shouldn't care?"

"Oh, Mummy, no need to be so dramatic—really! You don't really care about anything I do—so why about this?"

"What nonsense! Of course, I care! As if the HSC isn't too much education as it is. What I don't understand is why you are doing this at all? What is the point of it? Why do you want to go?" Farida was to appear for her A levels later in the year. Persis sat on the bed beside her daughter and spoke more softly. "Is Kaki upsetting you? Is that what it is?"

Farida removed her hands from her eyes. "Don't be silly, Mummy! That is the silliest thing I have ever heard. If anything, Kaki is the best reason for me to stay—but she thinks it's a good idea."

Both mother and daughter understood the sting in Farida's reply, both ignored it. Persis sat straight in the bed, turning her face from Farida. "Oh, she does, does she?"

"Yes, she does."

"Well, you're not her daughter—so why should she care?"

"Oh, really, Mummy! Relax! It's not a big deal—really, it's not—not at all. Everybody I know is going—either to England or America or Canada."

"Who is going? I would like to know. Tell me who is going? Who is this everybody?"

Farida sat up again in bed, counting names off the fingers of one hand: "Sharookh Lala, Vijay Mittal, Auduth Timblo, Rohinton Hirjebehedin, Sohrab Banker." She started on the fingers of the other hand: "Saiprasad Chaudhuri, Noshir Toddyvalla, Zarire Screwvalla, Shiv Mathur, Faisal Ahmad." She looked at her feet, touching one toe after the other: "Arun Pinto, Leela Samson, Dolly Taraporevala, Rajiv Dua, Christopher Baptista—you want more?" She looked up, grinning at her mother.

"Don't get smart with me, Farida. The point, which you appear to have missed, is that they are all boys—all of them are boys, and for a good reason. They go abroad so they can make more money to support their families—but what is your need? Are there any girls who are also going?"

"Leela and Dolly are girls!"

"Two—only two out of so many boys!"

"Ruby Contractor is going, and Pamela Wright, and Edwina Keidan—and I think also Asha Nehrurkar."

"Four—out of which, one is going with her whole family, and two are anglos. You see what I am saying. The girls are going to college in Bombay, mostly Sophia College. A girl needs a good education, but not too much. Otherwise, no one will want her. It will be difficult enough to find a good boy for a Cooper, and bad enough you are appearing for the HSC—but with a foreign education you will be completely out of reach. You will find no boy good enough for you—as if you don't have a high enough opinion of yourself already." She got up again, raising her hands to her hips. "I shall have to put an end to this. You are not to go. There is to be no more foreign correspondence. You will go to Sophia College—or to another college in Bombay, if you wish—and that's that."

Farida got out of bed, drawing back curtains, realizing there would be no more sleep for the day. "Mummy, I'm sorry, but *that* is certainly *not … that*. I am seventeen years old, and I will do e*xact*ly what I want. You don't have the right, all of a sudden, to tell me what to do. If anyone has the right, it's Kaki—and she thinks it's a good idea."

Persis stared at Farida, momentarily lost for words, before picking up the letter. "Well, we'll just have to see about that." She strode from the bedroom calling Kaki's name. "Nergesh!"

Farida followed her out. "Mummy, there is no need to shout! She may be asleep, just like I was."

Her mother ignored her, striding across the apartment. "Nergesh! Are you there?"

Strains of Schumann's *Novelletten* reached them as they approached Kaki's rooms and Farida knew at least she had not been asleep. She had more likely been knitting to Schumann as she sometimes did in the afternoons, and sure enough she appeared in the doorway of her den clutching needles and a skein of yarn. "Persis, is something wrong?"

Persis wagged the letter. "What I want to know is if you know anything about this letter?"

Kaki spoke reassuringly. "What letter are you talking about?"

"This letter from Chicago University."

"No, actually, I don't know anything about it, but let's go inside and sit down, shall we? Then we can talk about it more comfortably."

The den itself (plush Victorian furniture, gently whirring ceiling fan, window overlooking the garden and sea, Monet prints on the wall alongside Farida's early watercolors) had a soothing effect. Kaki emptied her hands on the table, stopped the music on the gramophone, and invited Persis to join her on the sofa. Farida sat in an adjoining chair, shaking her head to indicate disapproval of her mother's tactics to Kaki. "Now, Persis, what is it? What is this letter about?"

Persis handed Kaki the letter. "Did you know that Farida was corresponding with a university in Chicago?"

Kaki took the letter, but barely glanced at it. "Yes, of course, I did—and others also, I believe. I think it's the best thing for her to do."

"I don't see how you can say that. The best thing for her would be to get married. You would, of course, have to be married to understand that, and I don't blame you—but, believe me, going to America would only hamper her chances of marriage."

Kaki might have taken offence though Farida doubted her mother even realized she had been offensive, but she shook her head instead, keeping her reassuring tone. "With all due respect, Persis, I have to disagree. I may not have married myself, but I have seen plenty of marriages in my time, and I know that things are very different from how they were when we were growing up. If she broadens her horizons it will only increase her options."

Persis shook her head. "She doesn't need to increase her options. She has too many options as it is. If she gets too many more she will only be confused—but you have only to look at me to see that I am right. I did all right, didn't I—and I didn't have to go abroad. I didn't even need a college education. I had what I needed right here—to marry a Cooper." She placed her hand over her heart.

And to lose him, Farida wanted to say, but didn't.

"Yes, yes, Persis, of course, but so does Farida—and what I am saying is just this. If she has the chance to be more, why not let her take it? What she makes of it is, of course, up to her—but we shall at least have given her the best chance."

"If she goes away she may never come back. Did you think about that? If, heaven forbid, she marries an American, God only knows what will happen. It would be a complete fiasco. Who will answer for her then? Will you?"

"Persis, I'm sorry, but I just can't agree with you. There are good marriages between Americans and Parsis. Look at Jal and Bobbie Bharucha. Look at Alice and Fali Pestonji—not to mention bad marriages among Parsis."

Look at yourself, Farida wanted to add. *People who live in glass houses....* Instead she shook her head. "Mummy, I'm not going to get married—not to anyone, not to a Parsi, not to an American. I'm only seventeen. I want to experience some life on my *own* be*fore* I get married. Afterward I will never have the chance again."

Persis stared at Farida as if she had forgotten she was there. "There is no reason for a woman to be on her own, Farida—unless she is too ugly to attract a husband. You may be too stupid to know what you are talking about, but at least you are not ugly. I'm not going to let you throw your life away." She raised her chin, turning back to Kaki. "In both those cases, Bharuchas and Pestonjis, the man was the Parsi, and he brought his wife back to Bombay to live. How do you think it would be if she married an American and *stayed* in America?"

Kaki smiled. "Come, now, Persis, we must have faith. If we have done our jobs right she will be all right—in Bombay or in America or wherever she wants to be, married or not. She can always come back if she wants, but she will never again have the chance to go to university in America. She will never be the same age again. If she is going to do it, this is the time. That is all I am saying. Let her take the chance and let her make her own decisions. She is old enough to do that now. We have to trust her."

"You can say that because you have never been a mother, but as a mother I find that a very bitter pill to swallow—and I shall not have it. She has everything she needs right here in Bombay. You would see it my way if you were her mother."

For the first time, Kaki's voice hardened. "Persis, there is more than one way for a woman to be a mother. I would hardly presume—"

Farida couldn't keep from interrupting, almost jumping out of her seat. "Yes, Mummy, that is just what I would say—and there is more than one way for a girl to be a daughter."

Persis gave her daughter a sharp look. She might have said something, but Kaki interrupted. "Persis, to get back to what I was saying, I would hardly presume to say this to you, but of course you know it already. Farida is as dear to me as any daughter. The only reason I say it is to make it clear that I too want what's best for her. Believe me, I would love to have her stay—but that would be so selfish, to keep her just for myself. I trust her, and I want to give her as many options as possible so she can make the best choice for herself. If she wants to come back, of course she can, but it should be *her* choice, not ours. I want her to have whatever she wants for herself— and I am sure you do too."

"Don't be too sure. I suppose I should have seen this coming a long time ago, that you would turn my own daughter against me.

I can see how you've been buttering her up all along, giving her parties, putting her little pictures on the wall, holidaying with her around the world, making her feel like a little princess, but it doesn't mean—"

"No, Persis, we are on the same side in this—really, we are. You will see. I know my brother did you a terrible wrong, and I am very sorry about that, but I was helpless to do anything myself—but, believe me, I shall *not* let *a*nyone do *a*ny wrong to Farida."

She had spoken reassuringly again, but Farida had never heard her speak more firmly. She could not have been more precise; it was clear she included Persis in her warning though she had named no one.

Persis raised her eyebrows, shaking her head, getting up. "You have something to say about everything, Nergesh, but you have not heard the last of this yet. I cannot imagine Nariman will allow it."

She looked at Farida again as if she had forgotten again that she was there, but left without another word. Farida grinned as her mother's footsteps receded, jumping from her seat, pulling Kaki to her feet and hugging her long and hard. "Kaki, you are my hero, my champion!"

Kaki returned her grin, no less pleased, both with her performance and Farida's response, but embarrassed by the fuss. "Take it easy, my dear. You are going to suffocate me." When Farida finally released her she continued helplessly to grin. "I really did it for all three of us, you know. Your mother has had a difficult life and it is understandable that she is afraid to lose you, especially now that you are becoming an adult and can talk to her as an equal, but what she doesn't understand is that if she clings to you she will lose you anyway. She can't stop you if you want to go; your father doesn't care what you do any more than she does; but you must make your departure as easy for her as you can. Give her her due, so she will give you yours."

"Of course, Kaki! Of course! I have no intention of getting married. She has absolutely nothing to worry about. I don't know where that worry comes from." The doorbell rang and she hugged Kaki again, a quick hug followed by a quick kiss. "That will be Mr. Nunes for my piano lesson."

She had originally been classically trained, but when she had complained about practicing scales and arpeggios and exercises Kaki had found Manuel Cajetan Nunes, who played in nightclubs, who taught her to syncopate chords in the left hand against melodies in the right and to accompany a singer with jazz riffs, which suited her better. She enjoyed the lessons as much for what she learned on the piano as for stories about the Nunes family: wife, Concepta, and daughters, Cecilia, Mathilda, and Juliet. She had never heard a man speak more happily about his family, filling her with no less a glow. She dashed off to ask Mr. Nunes if he would like some tea and biscuits before leading him to the music room.

II

The tour bus picked up Farida and her mother from their hotel with three others and rolled through busy Tokyo streets, stopping at other hotels along the way for more passengers before heading for the country. Farida sat by the aisle, her mother beside her gazing out of the window. A pretty Japanese woman stood smiling in front. "Hullo, everybody. I would like to welcome you all to the tour. My name is Narumi Ikezawa, meaning 'Bearing Fruit,' I am 48 years old, and I will be your guide today. My English is not so very good as to write a novel, but it is good enough to tell a joke, so I think you will enjoy yourself."

She waited for the titters to die before continuing though Persis and a few others still peered from their windows.

"I am married and I have four sons. My husband says I should stay home like other Japanese women and care for my family, but I tell him I am a modern woman. I do not care about my family."

She waited again for the hilarity to die. Persis turned to Farida, nodding knowingly. "Like you."

Her mother had argued that working women had no time for families, vehemently opposing Farida's decision to remain in Chicago, working at Goldinger's following graduation, but in vain. Farida smiled, agreeably returning her nod. "Yes, Mummy, but she also has a family—like you."

Her mother returned her smile. She appeared to have developed a sense of humor, however belatedly, and however lame. In Atami, the Japanese Riviera, known for its hot springs, when the guide had remarked that a single bath would strip ten years off anyone's age, she had turned to Farida. "With two baths I could look like you."

Farida had smiled, suspecting she was flattered when they were mistaken for sisters. "You already do." They had spent summers touring Europe together since her departure for Chicago: Germany, Austria, and Switzerland after her Freshman year; Scandinavia and the British Isles after her Sophomore; France, Italy, and Spain after her Junior—but her father had visited Hong Kong and Japan with his girlfriend during the Junior summer, accounting for their nod to the east following Farida's graduation.

They had spent a week in Hong Kong, staying with business friends of the Coopers, flying next to Tokyo which they had used as a hub, casting a loop first to Hiroshima, Kyoto, Nara, Kamakura, and Osaka in the west—then to Nikko in the north, before settling in Tokyo to explore the city and its environs. Kaki had made plans with her own friends for all the holidays, wishing Farida and her mother to get acquainted as adults. Farida appreciated her wisdom only later, realizing the continual proximity with her mother had been mitigated by the splendor of Europe, as Kaki had no doubt anticipated—but she appreciated as well the chance to bond with her mother as an adult. In Hiroshima, for instance, Persis had viewed the damage clinically. "I guess that will teach them to attack us as they did."

"*Us*, Mummy? *Us?* What do you mean, Us? We're not American."

"I mean the free world, of course. They were in Burma, you know—practically at the gates of India. It serves them right. It was the only way to teach them a lesson."

Farida had shaken her head in disbelief, imagining her apparent lack of compassion sprang from a guilt she was unable to acknowledge. It had been enlightening also to see her side with the free world (meaning America), and she suspected her mother envied the independence she had achieved in Chicago.

Narumi Ikezawa now had everyone's attention. "My sons are more like me, more modern than my husband, and my youngest son is the most modern of us all. He says it is a good thing I have this job because I like to talk and he doesn't like to listen to me all the time. Now, when I go home, I have got all the talk out of my system." She grinned, pleased with the appreciative response, before outlining their itinerary for the day.

The plan was to drive halfway up Mt. Fuji to the Fifth Station, lunch in a restaurant along the way, visit the Peace Pagoda attended by four Golden Buddhas on a nearby hill, drive through the mountainous area to Lake Ashi for a cruise, and ride an aerial cable up and down Mt. Komagatake. Narumi beamed. "You are so lucky. This is the first year we have constructed the aerial cable ride. You will see everything like from an aeroplane."

When they stopped at one point for those who wished to take photographs or visit restrooms or buy souvenirs or simply enjoy the view, Farida remarked to her mother staring at a range of hills. "I never understood what Hemingway meant by 'hills like white elephants,' but looking at those hills it becomes quite plain—though I would have said 'hills like woolly mammoths,' wouldn't you?"

The succession of hills resembled the hard round shoulders and knobby temples of a row of elephants—or, considering the vegetation, a row of woolly mammoths. Persis said nothing though she continued to stare at the hills, but a young woman behind Farida laughed. "I was just thinking the same thing—but I was thinking sheep."

Farida had smiled at the woman, sitting across the aisle on the bus, alongside an older woman who appeared to be her mother, and a father in the seat behind. "Sheep?"

"Merino sheep—we manage a sheep station near Wellington."

"In Australia?"

"No. New Zealand."

"Oh, sorry. My geography's not so good."

"It's all right. No one knows Wellington. We don't expect it— certainly not from Americans."

It surprised Farida that she had been mistaken for an American, but her accent was now perhaps more American than Indian. "I'm

Indian, actually, from Bombay—but Americans can be very nice people, you know, just as good as New Zealanders."

The woman winced. "Sorry, just my joke—but you do *sound* American."

Farida smiled. "I just got my Bachelor's degree from Chicago University." She held out her hand. "My name is Farida Cooper."

The woman shook her hand, also smiling. "Pleased to meet you. Jill Kraus—on holiday with my parents."

"Me too." Farida looked around to introduce Persis, but was surprised to find her down the mountain road, the farthest person among the group from the bus. She shook her head. "I better go see what my mother's up to."

Jill nodded. "See you on the bus."

Farida took quick long strides toward Persis. "Mummy, why did you run away? I was going to introduce you."

Her mother didn't look at her. "I don't want you talking to those people. I heard what she said. They are farmers—*sheep* farmers. Can you imagine?"

Farida wasn't surprised. She had learned from Kaki: scratch a snob, find a bigot. Her father's behavior greatly affected her mother's, but by imagining she was better than others she suppressed her fear that she was worse, that she deserved the punishment meted by her husband. Farida had promised Kaki to be patient with her mother. "Don't be silly, Mummy. They're perfectly good people."

"They *work* for a living. They are *not* our kind of people."

"Oh, Mummy! Just about everyone works for a living. Otherwise, how would anything ever get done? How do you suppose the Coopers got where they are?"

"Coopers don't work. Other people work for them. There are those who are meant to work and those who are not—and never the twain should meet. That's all I'm saying."

"Well, what about me? I'm going to be working next month. Does that mean I'm all of a sudden a different kind of person?"

"You are only doing it because of that Jewish boyfriend of yours. All they think about is money—and they don't care how they get it, not even if they have to make their women work for it."

"Oh, Mummy, really! First of all, I'm *not* Benjie's woman—and, yes, he suggested it, but I *want* to work. I *want* the experience of working. I *want* to do something meaningful."

"As opposed, I suppose, to what I do? Is this what America has done to you?"

"Now you're just twisting my words around. If you don't want to work that's your choice, and I respect it—but if *I* want to work that's *my* choice, and *you* should respect it."

Her mother sighed, looking away. "I don't know what to say to you anymore. I realize I can't *make* you do anything against your will. God knows, I've never been able, certainly not against Kaki's influence—but I just hate to think of you, of all people, *wor*king for a living—consorting with people who work with their hands. It's not right—these sheep farmers, for example. It's all right for *him*, I suppose—but what about his wife and his daughter? What kind of man makes his women work?"

Farida sighed. She was saddened by the kind of woman her mother had become, but she had learned well from Kaki. Her mother was complaining, but not about the kind of man who made a woman work. She was complaining about the kind who abandoned a wife. "Oh, Mummy! They seem like such lovely people, really they do— and so friendly. I do wish you would reconsider. We might have such a good time."

"Aren't you having a good time?"

"We could have a better time."

"I don't want you talking to them."

"But Mummy, I can't simply ignore them. That would be so rude."

"You do what you want, but don't introduce me. I shall not mind being rude enough for both of us."

Farida sighed, shaking her head. "Oh, okay, I won't, but you are really being very very stupid."

Persis stared as if she might say something, but remained silent, walking back toward the bus.

Farida was polite to the New Zealanders for the rest of the tour, answering questions though briefly, never initiating conversation though she still sat across the aisle from them, never introducing Persis, focusing instead on the landscape, in particular on Fujiyama, separated from the other peaks by height and distance, majestic in separation, white peak hovering over clouds like a presiding spirit, snowy sides sloping from the crater like the wings of a giant dove poised for flight.

HORACE FISCH PRACTICES DECONSTRUCTION

W hy don't we sit right here? Nice and shady under this oak."
Rohini put down the icebox she was carrying to look at her
friend. She wore a blue sari, Farida baggy blue slacks and
a white top resembling a housecoat. She put down the wicker picnic
basket she was carrying.

"Yes, this looks fine. Sunil, please—the chair."

Sunil, now eight years old, unfolded the folding chair he'd been
carrying for Farida. His friend, Robin, wore two catcher's mitts on one
hand into which he continually plopped a tennis ball. Both boys wore
baggy jeans, short-sleeved shirts, and baseball caps. Sangita, now six,
and her friend, Alice, carried a blanket apiece which they unfolded,
one atop the other on the ground. Hickories and honeylocusts loomed
like ships of state. The children's playground and tennis courts lay
ahead.

Farida sank into the chair. In the five years since their return from
Kashmir, she had stuck with her resolve to be the laziest wife, but
with sparse results: two pregnancies, the first of which had miscarried
during the sixth month, the second of which had now entered its
third. She joked that she was an expert on every aspect of pregnancy
except delivery. She had long quit her job at Goldinger's, but busied
herself with writing, painting, piano lessons, and volunteering at the
Children's Memorial Hospital. "Thanks so much for coming, Rohini,

and bringing everyone. I'm enjoying this so much already. I hardly get to see you anymore. You tell that husband of yours I am very angry that he has taken you so far away from me. It is a crime against friendship, doesn't he know?"

As Dr. Rohit Gupta's career had flourished, they had moved to Highland Park. The suburb was far enough away for Farida to stay the night or weekend when she visited, but since she was pregnant Rohini had insisted on driving to Hyde Park, bringing with her the gang of kids, Alice, their neighbor from the new suburb, and Robin from the house on Wellington and Waterloo, whom she had picked up on the way. Rohini shook her head as if Rohit were no less a mystery to her. "He has got it into his head that we must be examples to all Indians. If we are doing well, we must show that we are doing well. Otherwise, what is the point? We have to live the American Dream as well as any American: have the best house, the best car, live in the best neighborhood. You know how it is."

Robin tuned a bright red transistor radio to WLS, broadcasting "In the Year 2525." Rohini took paper plates, cups, and napkins out of the picnic basket. Sunil passed them around. Farida protested she was just two months pregnant, hardly handicapped, but Rohini had made it a condition for the picnic that she was to do nothing but gestate. Farida had agreed on the condition that she would bring the refreshments. She had baked brownies, brought chicken sandwiches and chips, and stuffed the icebox with Cokes, orange juice, and water.

Rohini continued to vent as they ate. "On top of all that he gets mad. He doesn't think I appreciate him enough. I don't dress in the latest fashion, I don't cut my hair like he wants—but he knew what he was getting when he married me. I'm not going to change my saris for miniskirts now for him."

Alice reached for her third chicken sandwich. "Mom thinks you look lovely in saris, Mrs. Gupta. She loves the sari you gave her, but she doesn't have the guts to wear it out herself."

Farida laughed. "I think your mom and Rohini should go out together sometime, she in her sari and Rohini in a miniskirt. I think they would look fabulous together."

Robin laughed loudest. "My mom loves to wear the sari you gave her, Mrs. Gupta, but she only wears it when my dad's not in the house. He says she doesn't look like the woman he married in a sari."

Robin's mother worked at Penneys. Farida sighed at the thought. Rohini nudged her friend. "What are you sighing about—like the west wind? You are the only person I know who can carry off a sari and a miniskirt."

"It's not that. Robin's mother works, doesn't she, Robin?"

"Yeah. She's a buyer."

Farida turned back to Rohini. "And I do nothing. I would give anything for a job again, even at Goldinger's, even working for Jimmyboy Curryman again. I hate being just Mrs. Horace Fisch—no, don't argue. Without him, I have no identity. I was saying to him just the other day, 'What are we going to do with Horace's wife?' He just looked at me as if I were crazy, but you see what I mean? I don't do anything anymore, nothing that matters."

"What about the children's hospital. That's not nothing."

She played games with the children, read them stories, played the piano, and loved what she did, but shook her head. "That is maybe the best thing I do—and don't get me wrong. I love the kids, but it's so little. Anyone could do it. I could be doing so much more—I *should* be doing so much more. I wish sometimes I had started graduate college. At least, then, I'd be doing more than just spinning my wheels."

"Arré, but you can still go if you want, you know."

"I don't know. I don't even know if that's what I want anymore. College doesn't teach you *how* to think as much as *what* to think. I mean, for example, Rousseau tells us that law is an invention of the strong to curb the weak, and Nietzsche tells us that morality is an invention of the weak to curb the strong. Both are right to some extent, but we quote one or the other depending on what suits our argument of the moment, kidding ourselves that we are wise because we know these things, but never asking why and what we think ourselves—more important to ask why Rousseau thought one way and Nietzsche another. After all, both were nutcases, one was certifiable and the other was certified." She laughed. "The biggest irony is that people who have the luxury to debate these issues remain untouched by their own arguments. It's all armchair philosophy. Nothing touches us."

Rohini shook her head. "Just wait till the baby gets here. You will know exactly what to do then. There is nothing like a baby to concentrate your mind."

"That's what everyone says every time I get pregnant—and it never happens. I'm always a bridesmaid, never a bride."

"Really, now, Farida! You're just feeling sorry for yourself. This is not like you."

Farida sat up straight. "Sorry, you're right. No more whining. Sunil, careful! You're going to drop your chips."

Sunil, sitting crosslegged on the blanket, was bobbing his knees to "Sugar, Sugar" on the radio, his plate at an awkward angle. He smiled, righting the plate. "Fat chance, Farida Aunty."

Farida grinned. "Is that a fat joke, Sunil?"

Sunil's mouth dropped. He had no more sense of humor than his father. "No, Farida Aunty! I swear it was not! Really, it was not!"

Robin laughed. "She gotcha, Sunil! She gotcha good!"

Farida turned unsmiling on Robin. "Robin, don't you think I could getcha if I wanted?"

"Fat chance, Mrs. Cooper!"

Farida laughed. "Look, Alice, there are your parrots. You didn't believe, did you?"

Alice looked to where Farida pointed and, sure enough, there were parrots in the sky. Stories proliferated regarding how parrots had come to Hyde Park, some saying they had been ordered from a Sears Catalog and escaped, others that they had escaped from the 1934 World's Fair and multiplied.

The children stared, eyes large and round. Rohini, too, looked up into the trees. "They look surreal, no? I mean, so high in the sky? You don't expect to see parrots so high—seagulls, maybe, and eagles, but not parrots. Parrots you expect in a cage."

Farida glanced at Robin, head in the sky as he slurped his Coke from a straw. "Or on the shoulder of some pirate."

Rohini laughed. "Yes, I know—something so funny also about the color—such a bright tropical green against our Chicago sky—like seeing a polar bear in a jungle or something."

Farida deadpanned. "Or a monkey in a cowboy suit."

Robin snorted, siphoning Coke through his nose.

Farida grinned, pointing at him. "Gotcha!"

No one laughed louder than Sunil, screaming suddenly. "Farida Aunty gotcha good! She really gotcha, man! She gotcha good!" Robin just grinned, mute and red in response.

After they had eaten the boys moved farther afield, wearing mitts, tossing the ball to each other, gradually widening the distance between them. The girls played with a jump rope and frisbee. Farida sighed, drawing Rohini's attention again. "There you go, sighing again. Now what's on your mind?"

"I was just thinking how people's perceptions can be so different. Rohit wants you to wear miniskirts and do your hair to look modern, but Horace would say that's just bourgeois. That's his favorite word for anything that doesn't correspond to his way of thinking. If he liked Dickens (whom he doesn't, by the way) and you liked Faulkner, you would be hopelessly bourgeois— but if *he* liked Faulkner and *you* liked Dickens you would still be hopelessly bourgeois. It's just a convenient label—the lazy man's way of saying he can't be bothered to argue." She shrugged. "I could never take him seriously—I mean, I listened because I wanted to understand, but I never converted to any of his causes, not to Joyce—and especially not to Derrida who seems to have become his guru since he heard him speak at the Johns Hopkins conference. He knows I don't take him seriously and he doesn't like it—but the funny thing is Ginger never cared about any of this, not a jot, but he thinks she's terrific because she stares at him like he's God whatever he says."

Rohini laughed. "It's an ego thing … but it's very strange, if you don't mind my saying so, this thing between him and Ginger."

Farida sighed again. "Oh, I know. Everyone thinks it's strange, but it's really quite harmless. She is his Rohini—no, I mean it. He doesn't have anyone like I have you, but that's all there is to it. After all, I knew about it before we got married, so if he takes me as I am then I should take him as he is, shouldn't I?" She shrugged again. "We're dining with them tonight. I actually like Ginger, but I never have much to say to Raymond. I suppose I submit myself to these occasions for Horace's sake. I know he likes them—and he does the same for me."

Rohini understood more than Farida realized. Horace had done the same for Farida on the occasions they had dined with the Guptas, increasingly infrequent since the birth of the little Guptas and only once since the move to Highland Park. The occasions had been cordial, but Horace and Rohit had little in common, both trumpeting their triumphs as much to impress themselves as the women, neither impressed with the other. "I know what you mean. Marriage is a compromise—has to be."

"In any case, I don't care what anyone says. Why should I? It's no one else's business."

Rohini spoke cautiously. "True, but sometimes … you know, where there's smoke …"

Farida laughed. "Rohini, really! What are you suggesting, you of all people?"

Rohini's voice rose in protest. "I'm not … I just … I mean, I *care* about you, Farida! That's *all* I'm saying. In any case, if anything happens, God forbid—at least, you know who your friends are."

Farida still laughed. "Really, Rohini, and you accuse me of being melodramatic—but rest easy. I must confess I sometimes envy her—I mean, she plays piano better than me, she's a better cook, and God knows the Burnhams are very likely richer than the Coopers. I used to think Horace sometimes saw in me just a variation of Ginger, and maybe he did—but, you know, she cheated on him with Raymond. That has a way of ripping apart the most tightly wound fabric. I think the fact that he remained a friend despite everything she did made her see him in a different light—maybe that's why she thinks he's so wonderful. She had to put him through hell, see how much he would take, before she made up her mind about him—but by then it was too late. She remarried and so did he. I mean, they were always close, even when I met Horace, but it wasn't until Raymond fancied himself the Lothario of Lincoln Park that she understood Horace. When Raymond gave her a taste of her own medicine, that was when, I suppose, she realized what she had done to Horace—but by then it was too late. Then Raymond, supposedly, came to his senses—and that's where we stand now."

Rohini sighed. "Americans lead such complicated lives, divorces and multiple marriages and God knows what else, trying to squeeze three lifetimes into one. Whatever my Rohit's faults, he's a good provider and an honest man and I'm grateful for that. The rest I can manage on my own."

Farida, gazing at the boys throw the ball to each other, spoke vaguely. "Good old Rohit!"

Rohini followed her gaze and they watched the boys for a while before she turned her attention again to Farida. "Farida, I know you've mentioned this fellow Derrida before, and I know he's all the rage in academic circles, but I have absolutely no idea what he's about. Can you tell me something, in your own words—very briefly, I mean?"

Johnny Cash was singing "A Boy Named Sue." Farida turned it off. "You should really ask Horace, but, well, let's see, basically what he's saying is that we are all prisoners of our points of view. For example, in a Christian society Christians form the center, and non-Christians are marginalized—all Hindus, Muslims, Jews, Buddhists, Zoroastrians are marginalized—and Derrida suggests we can broaden our understanding of Christianity by approaching it from the marginalized perspectives, from the outside, from the point of view of Islam or Hinduism or any non-Christian religion."

"Not a bad idea."

"Right, not at all, even noble. The point is to understand the matter as fully as possible."

"I suppose, then, my question becomes, how does this apply to literature? I mean, isn't that what it's supposed to do? to increase our understanding of the classics?"

"Technically, yes—but it applies to words more than to literature—in fact, to any subject you choose. It can be applied to history or psychology or philosophy or physics—even to a news headline or television commercial, anything that has words, what he calls Text, all words are Text—but, okay, let's take an example. Give me a line, something literary if you like, but not too long."

"'Call me Ishmael'?"

"Perfect! 'Call me Ishmael.' Now, what Derrida would recommend for the purpose of deconstruction, which is what he calls his analysis, is that we mine this Text for meanings that are not apparent at first—maybe not even to the author. The average reader might understand from 'Call me Ishmael' that Ishmael is the name of the narrator of *Moby Dick*, and carry on reading—but, just for starters, Derrida might say, if Ishmael is his name why doesn't he just say 'My name is Ishmael'? Why does he say 'Call me Ishmael'—*as if that might not be his name*? There is an implication here that the narrator is playing games with the reader. We might infer that it is Melville himself suggesting we call him Ishmael, in which case we might read *Moby Dick* as a fictionalized life of Melville. Still with me?"

Rohini nodded.

"Then, of course, there is the Biblical meaning. Ishmael means 'God hears,' Ishmael was the son of Abram, before God renamed him Abraham—and Abram was married to Sarai, before God renamed her Sarah, but since she couldn't conceive she suggested Abram take Hagar, their maid, an Egyptian girl, for a second wife—and so he did, and so Ishmael was born. God, you see, *heard*. Later, after Sarai became Sarah and God enabled her to conceive Isaac at the age of ninety, she insisted Abraham banish both Hagar and Ishmael, which he did. So Derrida might say Melville was suggesting his Ishmael was a banished man just like the original Ishmael. The meaning of all this is, of course, up to the reader. You get my drift?"

Rohini smiled. "Drift as direction and drift as *lack* of direction."

Farida laughed. "Yes! E*xact*ly! And *Ulysses* is the perfect Text for this kind of analysis. Every chapter represents not only a particular episode from the *Odyssey*, but a particular time of the day, *and* a particular part of the body. There are code words that need to be picked up from paragraph to paragraph, some of it can be read astronomically, some geologically. You are not supposed to ask what it means, only what *else* it might mean. It becomes a kind of game for intellectuals. Only a bourgeois would ask simply what it means. A Joycean would say meaning is irrelevant—but mea-*nings, plu*-ral, are not!"

Rohini's brow furrowed. "I get it. To take it a step further, then, Derrida might even make something of the fact that Melville doesn't say '*Please* call me Ishmael,' but just '*Call* me Ishmael,' like a command—maybe provoking some readers to say, 'And what if I don't?' implying that Melville wanted them to challenge the name. Make sense?" Rohini laughed as if she had made a frivolous suggestion.

Farida nodded without laughing. "Yes, yes, you can laugh, but you are right on the money. Most people find this ridiculous, so much mental masturbation over three words. They would say sometimes a cigar is just a cigar—but not to a deconstructionist, *ne*ver to a deconstructionist. He would say we have only just begun. The point is to be mad for meaning—any meaning and every meaning that we can possibly tease out of the phrase, whether the author means it or not. The trouble is by allowing *all* meanings equal value, they are *all* reduced to meaninglessness. The author himself is marginalized for his meaning, and the deconstructionist is centralized for his mea-*nings*— but the meaninglessness is never ascribed to the deconstructionist, only to what he deconstructs."

"So why has no one ever challenged this ... deconstruction?"

"Some have, but they are not strong enough. Maybe because it hails from Paris, and American academics fall all over themselves welcoming anything from Paris while knocking down everything American. Maybe because those who have reputations don't care enough to protest, and those who don't can't jump on the bandwagon fast enough. Maybe at first the detractors didn't take it seriously, and by the time they did it had too many adherents. You know how that goes. If you spend a lot of time on something, you defend it just to defend the time you've spent on it. Otherwise you look foolish for spending so much time on something so foolish."

"And they would rather look foolish than bourgeois?"

"Horace would, but he would say he looked erudite, not foolish—but there does appear to have been a mass capitulation as with a demagogue, everyone too afraid to tell the emperor he has no clothes—but that's the nature of academics, isn't it? Like sheep before they get tenure and like goats after?"

The friends stared at each other before dissolving into mirth, Rohini clutching Farida's arm. "You don't think tenure promotes freedom of thought?"

"No more than in architecture or plumbing or any other line of work—and if it's allowed to academics it should be allowed to everyone. If you feel strongly about your ideas you should stand up for them whether you have tenure or not. Instead professors toe the academic line *just* to get tenure. What kind of freedom is that?"

"Hmmm! What does Horace have to say about all this?"

Farida stretched her legs. "Who cares? I say, Rohini, I'm tired already. You got me all worked up. I'm going to catch forty winks. Wake me in ten minutes, will you, if I'm still dozing?"

"Go ahead. Get your beauty sleep. I came prepared." She brandished a book from her purse, Maugham's *Of Human Bondage*.

Farida grinned. "Now there's a title ripe for deconstruction."

Rohini laughed as Farida shut her eyes. "Don't even start."

FARIDA SOMETIMES AMUSED HERSELF watching the fastidiousness with which Horace dressed, shaving before showering to save himself the trouble of drying his face twice, arranging clothes so precisely on a chair before entering the shower he could have dressed himself blind, pants slung over the back, tie draped in two folds over the pants, shirt hung by the shoulders over tie and pants, white undershirt in the lap of the chair atop white silk boxers, shoes seated at the feet of the chair, socks across them like a clamp, watch and wallet seated beside his underthings in the lap of the chair.

She was neither as fastidious nor as meticulous, neither about her clothes nor her makeup, and took less time dressing as in all things, showering earlier so they wouldn't get in each other's way, particularly now that she was pregnant. She had returned from the picnic in plenty of time for dinner with the Cassidys, showered and lain in her robe in bed, falling asleep until Horace had emerged in his robe from the bathroom furiously toweling his head. He had a phobia about electrical appliances for personal care, electric shavers and hairdryers, which she found strangely endearing. She had heard him in the half-sleep of her afternoon nap, pad of his footsteps, spray of the shower, slide of the door, but remained in her dream-state until he had joined her again in the room, waking slowly as she watched him, eyelids still heavy and lazy with sleep. She tired so easily now that she was thinking of quitting even her volunteer work, useful though she felt among the children. Through the grating of her lashes his albinal form appeared like a large upright fish hanging his robe on the hook behind the bathroom door.

He returned toweling his back, neck to buttocks. Draping the towel around the back of another chair he began dressing, bringing her focus to the soft white tire of flesh around his waist, filigree of pale hair on his sunken chest, webs no less fine in his armpits, flabby upper arms white as clouds, as his head disappeared into the undershirt.

Next he stepped into his boxers, holding them open in a rectangle with thumbs and forefingers, stretching the elastic around as he pulled them up. Farida wondered how many men tucked undershirts into underpants. "Hi, honey!"

He was reaching for his blue silk shirt. "Oh, hello, darling. I thought you were asleep."

She yawned, stretching first one arm, then the other. "I was—but, you know, half in, half out. I've slept altogether too much today—probably won't get any sleep tonight."

"I thought you went on a picnic."

"We did, but I got a little shut-eye in the park as well. I told Rohini to wake me up in ten minutes and she let me have thirty."

"You must have needed it—or you'd have got up yourself."

"Maybe, but I've overslept now—by which I mean I've slept too much, not too long."

Horace gave her a fond smile. "Ha! My wife, the deconstructionist! It's not as if I've taught you nothing after all, is it, darling?"

Lying on her back in bed, Farida welcomed the banter. She always got the better of him, but he never gave up. "You have taught me not to accept anything at face value. It might interest you to know I gave Rohini a lecture on deconstruction today."

"Really? Whatever brought that on?"

"Oh, just idle chatter really. She's heard us talk about it so much she wanted to know more."

"And what did she say?"

"What do you think? She agrees with me. It's a scam. It's a fraud."

She was tweaking him and awaited his defense, but he buttoned his shirt, seeming reluctant to accept her challenge. His had always been a dreamy helpless personality; it had been, in part, his attraction, nourishing her maternal instinct; but of late he had seemed increasingly a caricature of the absentminded professor. "Shouldn't you be getting ready?"

She waved a lazy hand. "It will only take a minute. We're only going to Florian's."

It had been her turn to select the restaurant. Caffe Florian, frequented by a large student population, serving American cuisine, was much enjoyed by Horace though he didn't readily admit it; also by the Cassidys who would enjoy no less slumming it as Ginger would say. The menu was eclectic, mixing pasta and pizza and chili with burgers and steaks—but Farida's reasons had been entirely practical. The restaurant was downscale and nearby: she would need neither to dress up nor travel far. Horace stretched his watchband onto his wrist. "It's a quarter to six. They'll be here at six-thirty."

"Plenty of time—but you're changing the subject."

"What? Oh, still on that, are we?" He snapped out of his brown study. "If Rohini keeps an open mind, I dare say she will be receptive to my arguments."

Farida might have shaken her head had she felt less lazy. "I think not. She knows exactly what you will say. I already told her."

Horace picked the tie from the chair and wound it loosely around his neck. It was one she had bought when they had visited Disneyland, white with Mickey and Minnie waving from a pink heart. "What did you tell her?"

"Well, one, that I'm too bourgeois to know better. Two, that it's too complicated to explain. She also knows that these are evasions, not arguments."

"But they *are* arguments, darling, if they're true."

"Rubbish! Even *if* they were arguments—and I emphasize *if*—they are elitist arguments. They assume you need a high octane intellect to read a book, and that's just not true. If you don't know a word, you look it up in a dictionary. If you don't know the background, you look it up in a guide—or simply ask someone. That's how people have been reading for centuries, and doing quite well at it I might add."

"It's not that simple."

"It *is!* If it isn't, it's the writer who is at fault, not the reader—assuming, of course, a basic intelligence and education. When I read I ask myself what the author is trying to say, and then I ask myself how effectively he's said it. The more memorably he says what he wants to say, the better the book. Case closed!"

Her grin turned triumphant. He sat beside her on the bed, socks in hand. "I think not. It is true, you must have your comfort in all things, in reading as in life, and that is what makes you a bourgeois; but I have said that before, and I won't say it again. To tell you the truth—"

"Don't be sneaky, Horace! You *just* said it again! To tell *you* the truth, if you had the same faith in your intelligence as I have in mine, you wouldn't argue with me. You wouldn't need to pretend something is more complicated than it is just to make yourself feel intelligent."

Horace shook his head indulgently. "As I was saying, I won't say it again. After all this time, if nothing else, I suppose I need a different approach—I need to make a different appeal."

She raised her eyebrows. "It won't matter how different it is, if it still doesn't make sense. You can't just call everyone bourgeois who doesn't agree with you. I mean, just look how we live. Look at our house, our possessions, our lifestyle. We're as bourgeois as Babbitt. Our friends are mostly academics—armchair revolutionaries. Their revolutions are all without risk. How bourgeois is that?"

He frowned, pulling on a sock. "It has nothing to do with how we live, everything to do with how we think—but I wouldn't expect a bourgeois to understand."

Farida laughed. "I thought you just said you weren't going to call me that anymore."

"I wasn't. I'm making a different point altogether."

"But you just said I am a bourgeois because I don't understand—and now you are saying I don't understand because I am a bourgeois?"

"Yes, precisely."

"Black isn't white because white isn't black? Catch-22?"

"Yes, precisely, Catch-22—it's the nature of the universe."

She laughed again. "Oh, Horace, you know, all I can say is you should really get down on your knees and thank God for the bourgeoisie. Without them you would have no one to feel superior to."

He turned to her in the bed, one sock on one foot, the other in his hand. "I told you I wanted to try a different tack, and that's what I'm doing. Give me a chance."

She raised her eyebrows again. "Okay. Go on. I'm listening."

"You know, as with anything new, as with anything difficult, sometimes it is a matter of faith. You have to accept on faith that which you cannot understand. Then, once you have faith, everything falls into place. You will wonder why you ever resisted. It is resistance that is your problem, not your intellect. If you stop resisting, you will understand. All you have to do is come to the other side and you will see for yourself. Everything will be clear, all your doubts gone—obliterated."

Her eyes grew large and white like eggs. "My goodness, Horace, do you realize how evangelical you sound? I *do* have faith—but where it is required. I have faith in God, because God is hardly a rational concept. When I am confronted with things I do not understand—wars and earthquakes and suffering and the like—that is when I have faith that God knows what he is doing even if *I* don't understand—but ... faith in Jacques Derrida ..." (she started laughing again) "is really asking a bit much, don't you think?"

"No, I don't." He looked away, heaving a sigh that seemed to rise from subterranean depths, and Farida stopped laughing. His albinal face turned grey, drooping like wax. His voice, customarily thin as a flute, thickened, seeming to droop with his face. He might have been a different person—a gentle Mr. Hyde, but a Hyde no less. "You know, I wish I didn't have to be explicit. It's so vulgar. If you only had more faith—the kind I'm talking about—you would understand important aspects of your own life better, of which you are now so woefully ignorant."

Farida squirmed to a sitting position, suddenly fully awake, her back against the headboard. The temperature in the room had dropped. A knot rose in her gullet, shrinking her own voice box, raising her pitch. "Horace, you are scaring me. What the *hell* are you talking about?"

He leaned forward, elbows on knees, sock still in his hand, still avoiding her eyes, Mickey and Minnie waving from his dangling tie. "You really should have figured this out a long time ago, darling, but I suppose I should tell you. If you had the kind of faith I'm talking about you would know, and this would not be an issue. I've been wanting to tell you, but …"

"Tell me *what*, Horace? For God's sake, what the *hell* are you talking about? *Tell* me!"

He spoke slowly, deliberating each word. "Well, take the word 'marriage,' for instance."

Her voice went from a scream to a whisper. "What do you mean, 'take it'?"

"I mean, let's deconstruct the word. What does it mean to you?"

"Horace, please stop talking nonsense. What are you getting at?"

"Humor me. What does the word 'marriage' mean to you?"

"Love, honor, trust, respect, loyalty, fidelity …"

"Ah, yes, good, fidelity. What else?"

"What do you mean?"

Horace got up, standing beside the bed in boxers and socks, tie and shirttails hanging loose. "This is all one aspect of marriage. Think about what might have been marginalized in the process."

"Horace, really, I have no idea where this is bloody well leading. Just *tell* me whatever the hell it is you are trying to say."

"I'm trying to make a point. I'm trying to get a fuller understanding of marriage. I'm trying to widen the breadth of our marriage, expand our horizons. That's what I'm trying to do. Now, you mentioned 'fidelity.' If 'fidelity' becomes the center, what would you say becomes marginalized?"

Farida felt the throb of her heart in her stomach and womb. "Infidelity?"

"Yes, precisely! Isn't that also a part of marriage?"

"What are you saying? You have been unfaithful?"

"No, that is not what I am saying. What I am doing is expanding the meaning of 'fidelity.'"

"Oh, my God! With whom?"

He said nothing, shaking his head.

"Ginger? Oh, my God! Is it Ginger?"

Still he remained silent, head turned away.

"Oh, my God! I knew it! I knew it! I should have known!"

His voice was the lowest she had heard. "It was during that trouble with Raymond—when she needed help ... and then ..."

"And then? And then what? Is it over now? Is that what you are saying?"

"And then Anastasia was born." He turned finally to meet her eyes.

Farida's face turned blank, drained of blood as much as comprehension. Her gaze lost focus on the wall behind Horace.

Horace tightened the knot of his tie. Having said his piece his confidence seemed in inverse proportion to Farida's. "Please, let's not have a scene. There's no need. If you stop to think about it for just a minute you will see we're actually a step ahead. You were in the dark, now you are enlightened. We have brought our marriage into the light of day. That is how you should see it—it's the *only* way."

She swallowed. Her voice was again a whisper, comprehension slow to dawn. "Anastasia ..."

"Yes—and if you think about it, it is yet another extension of the meaning of marriage."

Farida blinked. When anything could be made to mean everything, nothing meant anything. Horace appeared benevolent, holding out a hand to help her up, but instead of taking his hand she grabbed his tie, jerking his head down to slap him with her free hand. He jerked his head back, but her strength surprised no one more than herself and she held him by his tie like a dog on a leash, slapping him again. He tugged at her hand on the tie, but she slapped him until she lost count before letting go. The sudden release sent him crashing to the floor, stumbling over his shoes. Farida got out of bed, standing over him. She didn't know what was worse: what he had done, or his justification. Her voice was a hiss. "You *bas*tard, Horace! At least, have the *guts* to admit you are wrong. How low can you get?"

Horace picked himself up from the floor, patting himself down, left cheek still showing the fire-engine red imprint of her fingers, speaking calmly enough for both. "If you will only think for a minute you will see that I have been true to my principles all along. If anyone is at fault it is you for not listening to what I have been saying."

"Horace! Shut up! This is the last time you will tell me what to do and what to think. If marriage means infidelity, it can also mean divorce—it can also mean murder!" Her voice rose again. "Just Shut Up! *Shut! Up!*"

Horace remained calm. "Farida, there is no need to be melodramatic. Get a hold of yourself."

"I just *told* you not to tell me what to do! What are you? Fucking stupid on top of being a bastard?" She moved as if she were no longer pregnant, extracting a bag from the closet, packing it with necessaries.

"Farida, where do you think you are going?"

"What do you care? What difference does it make to you if I go to Canada or Bombay or Timbuktu—or if I go to hell? It's all the same thing, isn't it? You can even prove it, can't you?"

"Darling—"

"Don't you *ever dare* call me darling again!"

Horace's voice reached again for its fluty pitch. "Farida, you are being irrational. You are not thinking about what you are saying. If we only talk this out I am sure we will see eye to eye."

"No, we won't—because we are a pair of eyes short. One of us is blind—and the other is only beginning to see."

TURNING ONTO LINDEN AVENUE IN HIGHLAND PARK with Sunil, Sangita, and Alice, Rohini gave silent thanks again for her life. An only daughter, one of four children of a businessman father and housewife mother, both Surat Gujaratis, she had been spoiled, but not like she was spoiled in America. The contrast was stark: the dust of Surat, narrow rutted roads, horses and buggies, cars like furnaces, phalanx of bicycles and pedestrians, bells and horns and hooters like an orchestra out of tune, flies and heat, shit in the street, jostled by beggars, crammed in close quarters like spoons; and the clarity of Chicago, in particular of a Chicago suburb, wide gleaming roads often cruised by no more than a single bicycle for an entire hour, lawns on Linden Avenue bright as slabs of emerald, sprinklers intersecting in sunlight like diamonds, homes large enough to house an entire Gujarati village. Even her friendship with a Cooper, a matter of pomp in Surat, could not have been more natural in Chicago. She stopped by the Peterson gate to let Alice out, happy with her day as she put the Ford again in gear, losing her smile approaching the Gupta house at Sunil's sudden shout beside her. "Look, Mummy, Farida Aunty's car!"

Sangita jumped in the backseat. "It *is*, Mummy! It *is* Farida Aunty's car, isn't it?"

Farida's red Chevette sat in the driveway. Rohini's face shrank into a frown of puzzlement. They had seen *Oliver!* at the Biograph after she had driven Farida home from the picnic, and driven Robin home next after the movie, giving Farida plenty of time to beat them back to Highland Park if she wished, but the very unexpectedness seemed ominous. "Yes, it is." She steered the Ford into the garage next to their Olds.

Sangita and Sunil dashed out of the car and into the house. "Farida Aunty! Farida Aunty!"

In the living-room they found only Rohit looking grim, but he always looked grim, a short man in a world of tall women, a stranger in a strange land no less than his wife and her friend but a man, and hence with greater responsibilities—which were taking their toll, rounding his belly, smoothing his head. The cabinets showcased a marble Taj, wooden Ganesh, bronze Kali, ivory elephants, peacock feathers; mirrored cushions brightened the furniture, Kashmiri rugs the floor; Krishna, Gandhi, and Nehru smiled from the walls alongside Presidents Lincoln, Kennedy, Johnson, and Nixon; slippers, shoes, and sandals crowded the front door (though the Guptas weren't religious about bare feet in the house); beaded curtains shielded doorways. Sunil and Sangita looked around as if Farida might be hiding. Rohini held Rohit's gaze, eyebrows rising in question. He nodded. "Go to her. She wants to see you. In the spare bedroom, she is. Sunil! Sangita! No! Stay here, or go to your rooms. Farida Aunty is not to be disturbed."

"Why, Daddy? What's the matter?"

"Why is Farida Aunty not to be disturbed?"

"Don't ask questions. Do what I say. Mind your business. Grownup matter—not for kids."

Rohini mounted the stairs to knock on the bedroom door. "Farida, it's me. May I come in?"

There was a brief silence before a muffled voice answered. "It's not locked."

Rohini pushed the door slowly into darkness. Curtains had been drawn, no lights lit. "Farida?"

Farida was in bed, under the covers, staring at the ceiling, hands crossed over her breast. As Rohini crossed the room Farida caught her friend's eye, her face glistening, smooth with tears. Her voice was apologetic. "Rohini, thank God you are here. Please shut the door behind you."

Rohini sat beside her friend on the bed. "Farida, what is the matter? Just in the afternoon everything was all right, no?"

Farida turned her head from her friend, staring at a picture on the wall, Hanuman ripping open his chest to reveal images of Rama and Sita scored within. "Oh, God, Rohini, I don't know where to begin."

Rohini wiped her friend's moist face with a Kleenex. "First of all, why are you here? I thought you were having dinner with Ginger and Raymond, no? Isn't that right?"

"I was, but that feels like a different life. I have been a complete four-twenty fool, Rohini. I have been an absolute asinine bewaquoof dummkopf village idiot."

"Really, Farida, no need to talk like that. Where is Horace?"

"I don't know. I don't care. I never want to see him again. I wish we had never met."

Rohini took a deep breath, squeezed her friend's hand. "Tell me what has happened. Tell me from the beginning. What happened after I dropped you off at home just now?"

Black isn't white because white isn't black? Catch-22? So she had said to Horace and he had agreed, but it seemed now that black *was* white and white black, a single conversation changed the world, an hour became a lifetime, truth became falsehood, lies became reality. Her voice remained drugged. "May I have some water?"

"Of course." She left the room, returning with a tray holding a carafe of water, a glass, and filled the glass. "There you go. Take your time."

Farida took the glass, sitting up to drink, grateful once more for her friend. In the world at large she was a cabinet with a hundred secret compartments, but in Rohini's presence the cabinet flattened into glass with nothing to hide, a transparency yielding a comfort, relief, and joy no one and nothing else could provide. Bit by bit, relating her story, responding to Rohini's sympathetic presence, her voice grew more animated, strongest toward the end. "All I could think was I wanted to be away from him, away from the house, away from Chicago. I just drove as fast as I could."

Rohini smiled. "You slapped him?"

Farida almost returned her smile, but looked instead at the wall. "I lost count of the number of times I slapped him—but, you know, now I can't help thinking maybe he was right all along. Maybe he wasn't deceiving me and I was just too stupid to see."

"What do you mean?"

"I mean, if he truly believes all that rubbish about deconstruction, as I think he does, then he's really not cheating." *You have taught me not to accept anything at face value.* So she had said, but she had been smug, fooling only herself, accepting him at face value whatever she had said. What, after all, had she done with her own life, having so much, giving so little, working when she felt like it, resting when she didn't, relying all the while on Horace to attend her needs, doing little more herself than pandering to her own comfort and whim?

A president of Bryn Mawr had once said *Our failures only marry.* That was her, a failure. She had lived her life like a dilettante. All she had done was marry. Even a prostitute earned her own living, but a wife, particularly a childless wife, was the most parasitical of drones, a prostitute of sorts herself to her husband, as Steinem had suggested—or a person with no identity of her own, just somebody's wife, somebody's mother, as Friedan had suggested. She couldn't blame it all on Horace. "I mean, in a perverse way he has been honest and I have been stupid—too proud for my own good. Maybe I deserve this after all—for being so stubborn."

She looked like a girl again, bright-eyed, damp-cheeked, seeking reassurance, deliverance from a nightmare. Rohini shook her head emphatically, speaking firmly. "That is complete nonsense, Farida! You must not even think like that. He deceived you and he deceived you intentionally. Maybe from his perspective he wasn't deceiving you, but from your perspective he was *cer*tainly deceiving you. In the eyes of the world he was *cer*tainly deceiving you. What is more, he knew it. There is no doubt in my mind that he knew it, he *knew* he was deceiving you. I only learned about all this theory today and maybe I haven't understood it properly, but this deconstruction sounds like a ... a kind of formalized deception."

Farida shook her head. "I wish I could be sure. I just don't know anymore."

"Don't be silly, Farida. You have always had a good head on your shoulders. I mean, just think about it. What about your baby? Is that also just a matter of perspective, whether it is born or not? Does nothing have any kind of concrete reality?"

Farida shook her head, mouth shrinking to a dot, eyes misting again, and flooding.

Rohini took Farida's hands in hers. "Farida, listen to me. The world is a mystery, we all know that, but just because we can't be one hundred percent sure of anything doesn't mean we sit on our hands wondering what to do. If we cannot have a ton of certainty we operate with a pound, and if not a pound then an ounce, but we have to go on. The point is that we all have to do what we have to do. We have to do the best we can within our limitations. That much at least is up to us. The rest is up to God. If that Derrida really believed what he said he would have done nothing, but instead of standing by his beliefs he chose to cast doubt on everyone else's."

Farida shook her head again. "Rohini, I don't want this baby."

Rohini's eyebrows rose, her grip slackened on Farida's hands.

The thought had haunted Farida during the wild drive to Highland Park, but she had been afraid to give it voice. "I mean it, Rohini. I don't want this baby."

"Farida, this is not the time to make such a decision. You are not in your best frame of mind. This is irreversible, what you are considering, not something to be decided in a moment."

"But so is this, what he has done, irreversible. I can get pregnant again, but he can't take this back. What about that?"

Rohini shook her head. "All I am saying is you should give it some thought. Give it some thought, no, why don't you? What have you got to lose? No need to make immediate decisions."

"But, Rohini, it isn't just this. If it were just an isolated adultery I might have forgiven him, but it is a long-running adultery—and with Anastasia in the mix it becomes a never-ending adultery. Sharing a child with him I will be bound to him—to *them*—forever—and I want nothing more to do with them—*any* of them—not *ever* again. They make my flesh crawl—literally—as if they were cockroaches or something. Surely, you can understand that, no?"

Rohini took a deep breath. She didn't always agree with Farida, but stood by her friend. Her own feet were too firmly fixed in the ground to understand a woman with her head in the sky, but Farida gave her buoyancy as much as she grounded her friend. Farida would never admit the Cooper family problems rendered her defensive, but if she were as unaffected as she liked to think she wouldn't need continually to prove it, if she were confident she wouldn't need to prove her confidence, sometimes doing the silliest things to show she didn't care what others thought. "All I am saying, Farida, is you should give it some thought. No need to make decisions right away. That is all I am saying. Just take some time, at least a week—even a month, I would say. Then see how you feel."

Farida shook her head. "Rohini, I don't want it. I don't, I don't, I don't. A month will be too much. A month may be too late. It may be battering my womb like a cage by then. I can't wait that long."

"Then what are you going to do?"

"Can't you help me, Rohini? Rohit is a doctor. He must know someone, no? Maybe he could even do something himself?"

Without moving, Rohini appeared to glide away from Farida through no volition of her own. "That is not up to me. I think you should wait at least a week. Otherwise, you may be sorry for the rest of your life. I really do wish you would think this thing through, Farida."

Farida seemed not to hear, rising to follow in Rohini's wake. "Rohini, maybe even you could do something? You are a pharmacist, no?" Rohini swayed further back on her axis and Farida backtracked, recognizing her importunity. "Sorry, sorry, I don't even know what I'm saying anymore."

Rohini got up from the bed. "Wait. For now, just wait. No rash decisions. Did you have dinner?"

Farida shook her head.

"Will you join us?"

"Rohini?"

"What?"

"Thank you for putting up with me—yet again."

Rohini shook her head. "Don't be silly. Some people just need more help than other people."

II

Rohit made Farida uncomfortable because he smiled too much. She wouldn't have minded, but much of the time the smiles were unnecessary, staged it seemed for her benefit. He was a practical person no less than his wife, but whereas his wife gladly accommodated persons different from herself he was less accommodating. He defined himself by his ability to blend, perhaps understandably considering the paucity of brown men in Highland Park, considering his own children spoke less idiomatically than he did, and considering his wife did too because she was a reader and spent much time with Farida, but it led him by the same token to shun differences others might have welcomed.

Farida aroused in him only conflict. On the one hand, she didn't resemble the Americans with whom he wished to identify; she was, as he had said to Rohini, an arts drone, living off her husband with pretensions of independence, but as Horace had said to Farida, Rohit was the perfect bourgeois, unable to distinguish good art from bad and intimidated by his inability. Farida had laughed, providing her own interpretation: he liked art, but not artists—the order in their work, not the disorder of their lives.

On the other hand, she was a Cooper, and Rohit never lost the chance to extol to his friends the grandeur and glamor of the Coopers in India, finding himself aggrandized and glamorized in the process— but her current predicament was anything but grand and glamorous, her plans for the future even less so, rendering his smiles even more fearsome. "This is a good show, no? I enjoy it very much—very American, only in America, no?"

They were watching *Here Come the Brides*, a television spinoff of *Seven Brides for Seven Brothers*, in the living-room. Sangita was with Alice in the neighboring Peterson household and Sunil at a Little League practice from which Rohini was picking him up. Farida had offered to join her for the ride, but Rohit had surprised her, suggesting she stay, the rest would be better for her, they never spent time together, just the two of them alone. It was his day off from the hospital and he wanted to take advantage. Rohini had been no less surprised, but gave no indication aside from a raised eyebrow and a shrug. Farida, too, had shrugged, not wishing to be rude to the husband of her best friend, but felt immediately his smile descend like a wet blanket, eyes focus like a spotlight. She detested the show, but smiled politely, knowing the fragility of his taste in all things cultural. "It's all right. I've seen worse."

"You can get, you know, what you want. Not a problem—if you have got money, if you know the right people, it is not a problem."

He had changed gears without warning, but his smile remained the same, and for a moment Farida remained in the dark. "Get what?"

"You know, what you want—illegal, but it is happening all of the time. It is even legal if you call it therapeutic abortion. If you have got money, if you know where to go, anything can be done."

"Oh, yes, of course. Thank God for small blessings."

"Illegal, but not immoral, you know. Early in the nineteenth century there were no laws. Everywhere people were having abortions, right here in the house they were having abortions—and not even by doctors. Midwives, friends, the women themselves were giving themselves abortions, everyone was giving abortions—but when doctors started to become medical professionals they of course wanted to take the business away from everyone else. So they started talking about morality thinking it would elevate their status, and then they started having laws, and then it became a question of morality and legality—and also professional skills."

Farida smiled, imagining he was attempting to comfort, even impress her. "Really? I did not know that."

Rohit laughed. "Oh, yes! Oh, yes! Very really! In those early days, actually, it was at least one guaranteed way to save lives—illegalizing abortions. In those days, doctors, they were pretty much quacks. Best thing was to do nothing." He laughed. "Like those monkeys, you know—see no evil, hear no evil, speak no evil. That is how doctors were doing."

Farida smiled again, nodding. "I'm afraid I don't know very much about it."

"Oh, yes! Oh, yes! That is how it was, and you have aborted before yourself—what is it? four times? five times? No big deal." He seemed unaware of her sensitivity, but noticed immediately when her attention was diverted by the sound of a car coming up the driveway and chucked his head in the direction of the door. "Must be Rohini."

"Already? But she just left."

"Must have got over faster than she thought." He got up to answer the doorbell. "Wait. I will just go and see who it is."

Farida frowned. Rohini had her own keys. She got up to head for the bedroom, but chose almost at once to stand her ground, realizing what must have happened. As she expected, Horace stepped smiling into the living-room from the hallway. "Hello, darling."

Less expected, Ginger followed, also smiling, in his wake. "Hi, honey."

Farida couldn't believe he had brought Ginger with him, but stood straight, ignoring Ginger, focusing on Horace, words like icicles. "How did you know where I was?"

Rohit followed behind Ginger, his smile more fearsome, eyes fluttering. "I thought it would be for the best."

Farida turned her head slowly toward Rohit, but Horace spoke first, more softly even than usual. "Don't be mad at him, darling. I had guessed, in any case, where you would be."

"Don't call me darling."

"I'm sorry. I was worried about you, that's all."

"Why were you worried—if you had guessed where I was?"

"I was worried about the baby. You haven't exactly been lucky with pregnancies."

She sat, closing her eyes, sighing. Horace could not have sounded nor appeared more sincere, voice close to cracking, eyes squinting with compassion, and she wished even then she might believe him, she had invested so much in the marriage, but she knew him better than he knew himself. He wanted her not for herself but for the baby, and he wanted the baby not for itself but because it was *his* baby, the only tie they now shared, a tie she would happily relinquish—but, apparently, not he. Worst of all, he had come with Ginger.

Horace and Ginger took a loveseat, his voice still a whisper, uttering words with apparent difficulty, releasing them one at a time. "I was afraid what you might do."

Farida opened her eyes to glance at Rohit, understanding he had informed on her more than she realized. He seemed more reprehensible in light of his remarks just minutes earlier, giving the lie to his intentions, but he stood his ground, smile more fearsome by the minute, eyes on one of the Kashmiri rugs, waggling his head in figures of eight. "I will make coffee for everyone—Nescafe."

He went to the kitchen. Horace and Ginger bore the benevolent smiles of a sensible couple, Farida the recalcitrant spine of an obstinate child. Horace leaned forward, elbows on knees. "I was afraid you hadn't understood what I said, darling—"

"It is *you* who do not understand. How many times do I have to tell you *not* to call me darling?"

"Sorry … Farida. Old habits die hard. I won't until you want me to again. I know I've done the wrong thing. I want to make it right. I want to earn your trust again. That's why I brought Ginger with me. She'll tell you there's nothing between us."

Ginger too leaned forward, hands clasped, and Farida saw how well the two looked together. Both had put on weight, but not unattractively. Both were pale, Ginger more freckled, but they could have passed for siblings. She recalled her first dinner with Horace, grilled mutton kidneys which she had never learned to cook to his satisfaction, and Hawaiian Chicken, prepared by Ginger for Horace and his new girlfriend, but how cozy Horace and his old girlfriend had seemed, despite their divorce, despite her remarriage. The writing had been on the wall even then, but she had opted for a rewrite—this hopeless revision. "Listen to him, honey. It's the truth. I would hate my best friends to break up over some silly misunderstanding. When we were having that trouble, Raymond and I, you were *both* such a comfort, and that's when it happened—but it's ancient history now. We should have told you—and we meant to—but it seemed a matter of throwing good money after bad."

Horace's smile could not have been more solicitous. "Why mend what's not broken. I can see now that we were wrong, but the point is … we didn't want to hurt you, and for the longest time we didn't—and that's the crux."

Ginger smiled, no less solicitous than Horace. "The *whole* crux."

They were patronizing her. Farida hadn't looked at Ginger yet and looked away now even from Horace. "I don't want to talk while she's here. I don't want her here."

"Farida, she's your friend. You should know that. She's been your friend for years."

Farida didn't move, still looking away, saying nothing, bringing Ginger to her feet. "It's all right, Horace. She's right. This should be between you and her as husband and wife. I've said my piece. I'll wait in the car—but don't hurry on my account." She addressed Farida though Farida ignored her. "Bye, honey. Please listen to Horace.

We're both sorry for what's happened. We want to make it right, honest."

Farida kept her eyes turned away. Ginger's situation was perhaps the most ironic of all, cheating on Horace with Raymond when she had been married to Horace, then cheating on Raymond with Horace when she had been married to Raymond—but Farida realized she herself had always been the outsider, more even than Raymond who, after all, had cheated with Ginger against Horace and then against Ginger with the unfortunate Rhonda Lake, dead now in consequence of the roadster accident.

Farida remained silent until the front door slammed, eyes on the wall when she spoke. Horace's presumption, appearing unannounced, coupled with Ginger, only drove higher the waves of anger welling within, the sheer unconcern for what she might want, surprising her so unfairly. Only Rohini knew how she cried in bed, hour after hour, nightfall to dawn, soaking her pillow with the evidence—but her voice remained icy. "I must say I am surprised to see you here, Horace. I don't understand your worry at all."

"I *am* worried … Farida … about the baby. I told you. I know how much it means to you. I want you to have a healthy baby—I want *us* to have a healthy baby."

She turned her eyes on him, narrowed and unblinking. "That is what I don't understand. If infidelity enlarges the meaning of fidelity, then surely miscarriage enlarges the meaning of birth. Isn't that so? Isn't it simply a matter of perspective?" When he remained silent she almost shouted. "Well, *isn't* it?"

Horace appeared as worried as he claimed. He did not want to lose his wife. In his own way he loved her, was even faithful to her, and she provided all the appearances he wished in a wife: elegance, intelligence, independence, status, wealth, youth, beauty—and (a bonus) exoticism. It had been easy to confuse the issue of fidelity with Ginger owing to their history, but they had confused the issue not even half a dozen times before Raymond had returned to the fold, and they had come to their senses. "Farida, two wrongs don't make a right."

"So, now it's a wrong? When did it become a wrong? When it was no longer convenient?"

Horace pursed his lips. They had imagined their troubles behind them, but Ginger had conceived. He had suggested an abortion since they couldn't be sure of the father, but Ginger had insisted mysteriously it could only be Raymond. He realized only later that she had wanted the baby regardless of the identity of the father. "That's not it, Farida. That's not it at all. I wasn't *wrong* as such. I simply didn't explain myself clearly."

"But why should that make a difference? If I'm free to choose any perspective I wish, then one explanation is as good as another—or as bad. What difference does it make?"

Whether he had confessed through hubris or guilt or selfishness he did not know, but the question of Anastasia had lain between him and Ginger like a sword, another man raising his daughter as his own. Raymond knew, others guessed, and however much Ginger attempted to find time for him with his daughter it wasn't enough. It wasn't time he wished, but acknowledgment of the truth, an end to the lie—but he had surprised himself with his timing, the prospect again of fatherhood ahead, expecting perhaps in an exuberance of hope and stupidity that Farida would coddle his folly as she had coddled so much else about him. "Farida, this is our baby we're talking about."

"Well, now, that, too, I don't understand. That, too, is open to debate, isn't it? Our baby could mean yours and mine, but it could also mean someone else's, or everyone's baby for that matter—and, oh, yes, of course, it could mean no baby at all, couldn't it? I mean, *could*n't it?"

"Strictly speaking, yes, it could."

"And you could *prove* it, couldn't you?"

"Yes, I could—but I don't want to talk shop. I want my wife back. I want my wife back home."

Rohit reentered with a tray bearing four steaming cups of black coffee, milk and sugar in silver canisters. "Where is Ginger?"

Horace looked up, apparently unable to account for his presence. "She's outside."

"Ah, yes, yes, I heard the door banging shut. I shall take her the coffee outside, shall I?"

Horace shook his head. "Ginger doesn't drink coffee—and neither do I."

Rohit raised his eyebrows. "Farida?"

"No."

"Aha, okay, then I will help myself." He seated himself, pouring milk into his coffee until it was almost white, adding three heaping teaspoons of sugar, swirling coffee with a noisy clinking of china, smiling again fearsomely, speaking as if he were at a party. "So, how is it going? All made up yet?"

Horace bowed his head in Rohit's direction, keeping his eyes on the steaming cup. "Would you please give us a moment?"

Rohit appeared to misunderstand. "Oh, yes, sorry, mum's the word, zip my lip. I will just shut up and keep the peace."

Horace didn't move. "I mean, would you please give us some privacy?"

Rohit's smile faltered at the dismissal from his own living-room, but he forced it back in place, rising with his cup. "Oh, yes. Of course, yes. Sorry, didn't understand." He faced them again momentarily from the bead curtain in the doorway, smile now screwed in place. "Farida, listen to your husband. Father knows best, after all, isn't it?"

Horace smiled, lowering his voice in case it carried to Rohit behind the rustle of beads. "At least, you know I don't believe that—father knows best, I mean."

Farida neither returned his smile nor acknowledged what he had said. She was beginning to realize she had married her father. Both made movies, both made wrecks of wives, both excused inexcusable behavior, Horace appealing to deconstruction, her father to his wife's inability to produce a male heir—or had that been just her mother's rationalization? She shuddered to think she might begin to bottle her emotions like her mother. Losing her stomach for the conversation she was glad for the sound of another car in the driveway finally announcing Rohini's return.

Horace continued his plea in the confidential tone. "Farida, please, listen to me. I would like very much for you to come home with me so we can start over. You have only to name your terms. Everything is negotiable. Everything is on the table. It was a mistake for me to tell you anything at all. It was all so very long ago I didn't see the harm, but I should have. It was selfish of me and I *am* sorry. Just tell me what I can do to make it up and I'll do it."

She wanted to believe what he said, but couldn't. He wanted the baby to tie them irrevocably; he wanted her back so he might return to his former life; his mistake had been the revelation of the deed, not the deed itself—but the revelation alone had been selfish, shattering her peace of mind to salve his own. "You were selfish, but I don't believe you are sorry. You're only sorry you told me about it. You're only sorry because you need someone to play the part of your wife, and now you're going to have to start the search all over again."

"Farida, I wish you wouldn't talk like that. I want us to have the baby. Don't you believe I want you to have my baby?"

Farida sighed. "It doesn't matter what I think now. What matters is what I will think tomorrow, and the day after that, and after that. I need time. That is what I need."

"Take all the time you need, but come home. Please come home."

"No!"

"Why not? You can take all the time you need at home to decide what you want to do."

"I need time alone. I don't need to be told what to think. I need to be away from you."

"I don't want to tell you, I want to show you—but I can't show you if you won't come home."

"You've had ten years to show me. I need to figure out first what you've already shown me."

Horace's eyes seemed to lose focus. "Don't you believe I'm sincere?"

"I don't know what to believe. That's what I need to find out."

Horace sighed. "What can I do to make you believe me?"

"For now, you can just go home—leave me alone."

"Farida, how can I persuade you to come home?"

"I don't know."

"Can I at least expect to hear from you?"

"I don't know."

"Won't you give me something to go on? Anything?"

"Have faith, Horace. Have faith. That's all I can say for now. Isn't that what you said to me?" She almost grinned, but the irony was too bitter.

Rohini entered and Sunil dashed toward Farida. "Hi, Farida Aunty."

Farida opened her arms. "Hello, my darling. How was your practice? Never mind, I can tell. My goodness, just look at you, sweating like a little piggy."

Sunil's blue t-shirt was damp with sweat, armpits black. "I caught two fly balls, Farida Aunty—not one, *two!* You should have seen."

Rohini put her keys in her bag. She had waved to Ginger at the wheel of her Jaguar and Ginger had returned her wave, barely. She had not stopped to talk: Ginger had turned her face following the wave. "Hi, Farida—Horace. I saw Ginger outside. What's going on?"

Farida pulled Sunil close, kissing his damp cheek. "Nothing much. Horace was just leaving, weren't you, Horace?"

Horace looked at Rohini. "Rohini, I want her to come home on whatever terms she wishes. Maybe you can talk some sense into her. You know how stubborn she can be."

Farida hugged Sunil. "Goodbye, Horace."

Horace got up. "I'll call you tomorrow." He caught Rohini's eyes again. "Anything she wants, on her own terms, I want her back. I've been stupid. I want to make it up. Please see what you can do. It would mean a lot. I'll be forever in your debt."

Rohini said nothing, but her eyes roamed between Horace who seemed to cage her with his gaze and Farida who attended only to Sunil, repeating all the while: "Goodbye, Horace."

Sunil enjoyed Farida's often lavish attention, but his eyes grew larger as she almost dragged him into her lap, kissing him madly, drenched t-shirt and dank head notwithstanding. He had asked what the matter was with his favorite aunt, but his father had simply told him to mind his own business, he would understand when he was older. He pulled himself away, discomforted by her for the first time, afraid she might burst into tears. He almost shouted. "Please, Farida Aunty, I have to shower! Let me go!"

Horace stopped midstep, momentarily paralyzed, as she let Sunil go. Rohini had been still a long while already. Rohit stood suddenly in the doorway, cup in hand. "Rohini, you want some coffee?"

Rohini remained too bewildered for speech, staring from Sunil running out of the room to her husband curtained in part by beads.

Farida couldn't explain, but started to laugh uncontrollably, nodding to Rohit. "I think I would like some coffee after all, please, Rohit. Coffee would be just the thing."

THE NIGHT FOLLOWING HORACE'S VISIT was no different from the others. Rohini mitigated Farida's fears by day, as did the hundred and one cares of daylight, from brushing her teeth to cooking and cleaning and showering among so much else, but under cover of night her tears ran like a river. Night was the realm of solitaries and ghosts, rippers and prowlers, mists bearing tooth and claw, when helping hands appeared like hammers of doom, and encouraging words like the growls of beasts, and not even Rohini could hold at bay the hound she had unleashed upon herself.

Her conflict lay between two worms: she wanted time to debate the wisdom of staying with Horace despite the worm of his betrayal; but time itself was a worm gnawing at her womb, threatening to manacle her to a man she might never again trust. The alternative, holding motherhood at bay, would give her time to rekindle trust, but considering her history she might well be spitting in the wind—but if she could have five pregnancies she could surely have a sixth, and under more salubrious circumstances.

She had wondered as well about Horace's timing, wondered if he hadn't meant in his own passive way to make a break with her whatever he might have said about wanting her back, but whatever he had meant his timing had been a blessing. Had he waited just a little longer he would have impossibly complicated her choice. For the present, she was more easily fatigued, prone to regurgitate, rush to the bathroom, but remained essentially an entity unto herself, bound to nothing and no one else—but she would soon embody a quickening, kicks and tickles and gurgles she could never call her own. She might never have such a chance again.

She had experienced miscarriages enough to consider herself mistress of the art. Her cervix, reliably unreliable, dilated too easily and early. It would be a simple matter to irritate her cervix into dilating itself. She had heard of women dilating themselves with knitting needles, crochet hooks, wire-hangers, catheters, scissors, hairpins— even chicken feathers. They suffered hemorrhages, some lost their lives, but considering again her history she imagined her cervix would need less manipulation than most, her life in less danger than most.

Ginger's betrayal was a matter apart, less heinous because she meant less than Horace, but more for her interference, her nose where it didn't belong. *You know,* she had remarked about the resemblance between Horace and Anastasia, *I think a great love leaves a residue.... Anastasia might be a prototype for your own baby.* The prevarications were the worst: conversations, apparently benign, recollected at leisure for their double entendres, providing a slap and sting from the safety of time and distance, leaving words and images hovering over her nightbed of horror, her eyes unlidded, reptilian.

Unable to sleep she slid her legs off the bed, sitting and staring into the dark. It was among the smaller bedrooms in the Gupta house, but large enough for comfort, even luxury. A wall clock with a round white face ticked the seconds like heartbeats making a womb of the room. Medical and pharmacological books and journals dating from the Fifties lined shelves on the wall, betraying the original intent of the room as a study. A small writing desk, complete with a gooseneck lamp, provided further evidence.

Farida lit the bedside lamp and got out of bed to examine, without curiosity, books on the shelf, but sat soon enough at the desk. A narrow white vase held sticks of incense, a trace of jasmine hung in the air. She took a deep breath, inhaling the wisps like oxygen. She was tired, but couldn't sleep, and foraged in the desk for something to do. The top drawer held a stapler, ruler, flashlight, batteries, highlighters, envelopes, tweezers, ballpoint pens, paper clips, Scotch tape, wooden backscratcher, aluminum letter opener. She almost fell asleep finally at the desk, but managed to slip back in bed, turning off the lamp.

The middle of the night found her once more awake, sitting in bed, feet to the floor, staring at the drooping moustache of twenty minutes to four on the white face of the wall clock, the sheets sticky, pillow clammy, a stench of sewage permeating the room. She lay again in the bed, curled on her side, herself a fetus, shutting her eyes, turning possibilities in her head, wondering if she had peed, or worse. Sweat congealed around her like a cocoon, packing her in the waxy fluids of her body, cushioning her in her grime. She was drowsy, unsure whether she was dreaming, and opening her eyes again imagined someone standing at the foot of the bed, more shadow than person, black against black, the elongated body and grinning head and extruded eyes of a giant mantis watching the black swamp of her sleep.

The next morning she called Rohini into the bedroom from the hallway. Rohini stepped in, fastening her green robe around her waist. Farida lay still in the fetal position, looking more pale and plain than she could remember. "What is the matter, Farida? Aren't you well?"

Farida's breath came in gasps, her voice barely a croak, her face damp with sweat, hair plastered to her head. "I think … Rohini. I need … hospital."

Rohini noticed the sheets were dark brown. "Oh, my God, Farida! What have you done?"

"Nothing … nothing … I swear."

"Does it hurt very much?"

"Yes…. Cramps."

Rohini's eyes fell on the letter opener, also stained brown. "Oh, my God, Farida! Oh, my God! Can you get up?"

"I think so."

"Wait, let me get Rohit. He will know what to do. I will be right back."

ROHIT DROVE THEM TO HIGHLAND PARK HOSPITAL, drove back to take Sunil and Sangita to school leaving Rohini with Farida for the day, and drove back to the hospital in the evening. From what he had seen Farida would be all right, but she had been lucky; she might have lacerated her cervix, she might have bled to death. He had taken her to the hospital mainly to ascertain that she was free from infection, but whatever face he might have adopted he resented the intrusion in his life, the demand on his time, the trouble for Rohini and his children.

He meant to lecture her on her responsibilities and adopted his sternest face approaching her bed, wagging a warning finger despite the warning in his wife's eyes. "You did a very stupid thing, Farida—a *ve*ry stupid thing!"

Farida smiled, pale from her ordeal, and gripped the offending finger in her fist like a child. "Dear Rohit, you must not be angry with Rohini—you absolutely must not be angry with Rohini—for my sake."

He tried to free his finger, but she held his hand to her cheek, apologizing for the trouble, thanking him for his goodness, and he found himself able only to repeat stupidly, shaking his head. "*Very* stupid thing you did! *Very* stupid!"

She had confessed nothing, but didn't argue. "Then call me a stupid girl, call me a naughty girl, punish me if you want—but don't take it out on Rohini. She is the very best thing in both of our lives."

Rohit tried again to loosen her hand, again in vain, but found himself relenting, flattered by her encomium to his wife—and however pale and weak she appeared, however stupid she may have been, she remained an attractive woman, *and* a Cooper, impossible to resist long, especially holding tight his hand—at least, for him. He waggled his head. "Rohini is … all right."

Farida squeezed his hand again. "Promise me you will not be angry with her."

"Why should I be angry with her? I am not angry with her. I am angry with you."

Whatever he might have said, however he might have hectored, his relent had turned to a smile, and Farida returned the smile, letting go his hand with another squeeze. "Thank you, Rohit. Then that is as it should be. You are more of a sweetheart than you let on—such an American you are turning out to be, hard outside, soft inside, all bluff and red—like a broiled lobster."

She wasn't surprised by his smile rendering his face round as the moon. Nothing pleased him better than to be called American.

SHE WAS COMFORTABLE WITH HER DECISION and confident enough soon to make another, no less momentous. She wanted nothing from Horace, but she had not wanted the father of Ginger's daughter to be the father of her child, nor had she wanted to be the wife of the father of Ginger's daughter. That had been her bottom line.

A month later came news of her father's death. She had already decided to return to Bombay for an extended stay, distance herself from her problems, give herself time to put some plans into action, do something useful, teach what she knew—and, in particular, open an art gallery.

DARIUS KATRAK, THE GRADUATE

Bach had been supplanted in Farida's affection by Chopin, the *Brandenburgs* by waltzes, nocturnes, and polonaises, in particular the *Heroic Polonaise*, now an erotic polonaise for the soundtrack it had provided one memorable evening, a memento to evoke not only the sight and sound of her lover, but his taste and smell, a phantom evocation that could bring a smile to her face in a crowded room deepening her own mystery.

She and Darius had expanded their prior routine to include dinner with Kaki on Monday and Wednesday—and on Friday, the night before, they had driven to the Eros to catch *Butch Cassidy and the Sundance Kid*, after which they had discussed the movie over steaks at Gourdon's. Not even Paul Newman could save the movie from its hateful conclusion for Farida, not even coupled with Robert Redford, but Darius had enjoyed it better, too young perhaps to appreciate the movie's final statement except as a token of heroism. Death evolved in meaning as it grew nearer and chronologically Farida was nearer death than Darius. It might have meant no more to him than a final chapter in a book, a last scene in a movie, but it was a reminder to her of how much she had yet to accomplish, the chasm between her goals and achievements.

She had begun organizing herself the same week, visiting Sea Mist, a residential building near Blue Mansions deeded to her on the death of her father. Four floors had long been rented, but the ground floor was empty. Her father had rented the space for the longest time to a Soviet company dealing in farm machinery, but after their contract had expired he had refused all subsequent offers. He didn't need money and the experience had soured him—not to the Soviets in particular, but to business in general. He was impatient with the thousand and one details that a new collaboration would entail and too mistrustful of others to delegate comfortably—not without reason. He had been cheated more than once, by the bureaucracy as much as by his managers, and preferred to make no money at all than be unfairly fleeced.

Farida had scouted the space for its possibilities as an art gallery, shaping and reshaping the layout continually in her head. This single step toward realizing her goal had put a spring in subsequent steps, restoring balance to her life, filling her days with meaning, keeping entropy once more at bay. Surprisingly, the first gorgeous bloodgorged days with Darius had served the same purpose—with more intensity, but also a major difference: one activity left her dependent on Darius, the other on herself, and whatever she felt for Darius she wished to maintain independence for both their sakes.

She bore the greater responsibility in their story, she had been the aggressor, she was the elder (twice the years, twice the responsibility), but she couldn't explain everything to him—or, perhaps, simply, wouldn't. She understood better the paternalistic husband of the Fifties doing the heavy lifting for his child wife, meeting his grave before his time, not unlike many Parsis of her day, including Mr. Katrak. She knew what Darius would say (equal partnership, equal responsibility), but rather than broach a bottomless argument she had chosen to remain silent about some things. Love meant both more and less than full disclosure: in providing less than full disclosure it accepted more responsibility.

Darius had not understood why she had cut short their honeymoon in Dr. Gregory Jones's flat, disagreeing that burning too brightly they would burn out sooner, agreeing finally only because he believed his mother's visit had spooked her and accepting it could no longer be a honeymoon if one of them no longer wished it, but he had been compensated by her suggestion to present a more public face to their friends, understanding that if they didn't move forward they would fall back, that by excluding the world they put themselves in a box no less claustrophobic than the one designed by the world.

It was ten o'clock. She had breakfasted with Kaki, telling her about *Butch Cassidy and the Sundance Kid*, wondering if she might show curiosity about Darius, but Kaki had remained her usual amiable self. Farida had retreated to her studio after breakfast, set a cassette to play the nocturnes, unfolded a floor plan at her desk of the space at Sea Mist, and speculated how best she might partition it for the gallery. Her reverie was interrupted by the doorbell and shortly by Sashi's knock on her studio door. "Farida-bai, Katrak-seth is here."

Farida's conscience was clear, secure in the direction she and Darius had chosen. She expected their new routine to raise comment and welcomed the chance to test herself before Mr. Katrak. Her breath came more quickly as she propelled herself into a higher gear. "Tell him to sit. I am just coming."

When she entered the sitting-room Mr. Katrak was standing with his back to her, much as Darius had been standing when he had brought his portfolio, admiring the print of Degas ballerinas. Even his stance was similar, hands in pockets, elbows sticking out, making a hexagon with shoulders and waist, but instead of jeans and shirt he wore loose slacks and a bright Hawaiian shirt. Darius was trim with the effortlessness only a teenager could manage, but Mr. Katrak had none of the rotundity that came with age, just a mild thickness under the bright shirt. His hair was thinner, whiter, but sleek and tidy, giving him the appearance of a man in his prime, not aged as much as well aged. Seeing him she stood with a straighter back herself, imagining he might some day be her father-in-law, wishing to put her best foot forward, expecting to be challenged on her kinship with Darius, echoing the smile on her face with a smile in her words. "Hullo, Dhun! What a surprise to see you!"

Mr. Katrak had heard the nocturne rise and fall with the opening and closing of the door as Farida entered, but remained apparently engrossed in the painting. He had seen her reflection in the glass of the Degas as had Darius before him and straightened himself knowing he was watched. At the sound of her voice he turned, grinning, holding out his hand. "Hullo, Farida. Not too bad a surprise, I hope?"

She smiled, returning his firm handshake. She saw him with new eyes, more handsome than before, and found herself tracing her Darius in his face. "No, of course not, but you'll have to excuse my dress. I wasn't expecting company."

She wore a blue robe reaching her ankles. "Not to worry, Farida. Looking fetching as always. I hope I am not interrupting you too much?"

"I was doing some work—but nothing that can't wait. Please, sit. Something to drink? Tea or coffee—or a cold drink?"

"Tea would be nice."

"Of course." She raised her voice for Sashi, ordered tea for two, and turned back to Mr. Katrak. "I think I told you about my art gallery project?"

"Oh, yes, I remember. When is it going to be?"

"Oh, probably not for a while yet, but I was just going over some plans for how to arrange the space—on the ground floor of Sea Mist. Maybe you know the building?"

"Right here, on Warden Road only—yes, of course, I know it. Actually, as you know, I am an architect. I could help you if you want, you know, designing the space."

Farida was momentarily nonplussed, but regained her composure without effort. "Thank you, Dhun. I shall keep it in mind if I need any help, but there are a hundred and one lafrans to take care of first. You know how it is in Bombay—falanu and dhiknu and all the rest of it."

Mr. Katrak smiled at the colloquialisms. "What sort of things do you mean?"

"Oh, you know, the usual—clearance from the municipality, applications for telephone, electricity, flooring, lighting, decorations, pedestals for statues, shelving for ceramics—and that's just for starters. I don't even have a name yet, but after that will come the usual office stationery, logos, advertising, all that and who knows what else— patrons, press agents, exhibitors. The thing is to get started and deal with the problems as they arise. Even a thousand mile journey ... you know how it goes."

Mr. Katrak nodded. "Begins with a single step—yes, I know. Very creditable, Farida, what you are doing—much more work than most people would think."

"But it's what I want to do. That's what makes it a pleasure. I expect the work to be quite grueling, but I know the rewards will make up for it—and artists need all the help they can get. You know how they are, most of them, no sense at all about how the world works."

Mr. Katrak laughed. "Tell me about it. We have a fellow in our family—that same Zarir, Darius's cousin, my stupid sister's son—wants to be an artist, like Gauguin or somebody, going off to Tahiti or somewhere—nice boy, but no sense at all. My sister's own fault, actually—spoils him rotten, encourages the fellow in his folly. Tells everybody he is the Indian Picasso. Then who can blame the boy?"

"Ah, but you see your Zarir is *exact*ly the kind of person I want to exhibit—assuming, of course, that his work is good. I don't expect an artist to be practical. If he were practical he would be a banker or an accountant or a solicitor or some other such dull rock of society. I'm not saying *all* artists are impractical, but I must say I find practical artists somewhat suspect. After all, it *is* an impractical choice—to be an artist, I mean—unless he's a commercial artist, of course, but that's not what I'm looking for. A pure artist is impractical almost by definition, wouldn't you say?"

"I suppose, yes, of course, there is something to what you say."

"No, really, just think about it. A pure artist is someone who loves what he does, a commercial artist loves the money he makes. They may be equally skilled in what they do, but one creates out of himself, the other gives the people what they want. For one it is a sacrament because he sacrifices so much to get his work done, sometimes his life, for the other it is a business. Nothing wrong with either approach, but the distinction should be made. The professional artist knows how to package himself better than the amateur, he knows how to cater to the fads and fashions of the times, how to say the right things—that is his business—and because he is interested in success more than in art he wins all the grants and prizes as well. I want to exhibit the *pure* artists, who don't have a clue how to manage themselves, who do their work whether or not they have a sponsor or a dealer or an audience or whatever."

Sashi brought the tea tray and Farida busied herself pouring while Mr. Katrak watched. "Well, I will not argue with you—but this much I can tell you. That idiot Zarir is no artist, pure or impure—just the idiot son of an idiot mother."

Farida smiled. "Maybe, but I would want to be the judge of that myself. Milk and sugar?"

"Yes, please, three lumps—just a dash of milk, thanks."

She did as he bid, passing him his tea, placing just one lump in her own tea with the tongs.

Mr. Katrak took a sip. "Perfect! Just right! I see you like your tea the American way—no milk."

Farida smiled again. "You know Darius said the same thing? Like father, like son, I suppose."

Mr. Katrak laughed again. "Maybe in more ways than one."

Farida kept her smile though she sensed the conversation darkening. She didn't understand the remark, but preferred not to ask for an explanation. "So, anyway, to what do I owe this pleasure? Why haven't you brought your wife with you also?"

Mr. Katrak took another sip of tea before putting down his cup, leaning back in the sofa. "Actually, she asked me to come—something she wanted to ask you, but didn't feel comfortable."

Farida's smile became rigid, her stomach turned to stone. She put down her cup as well, but leaned forward, elbows on knees. "Yes?"

Mr. Katrak peered through narrowed eyes. "Some picture she saw of Darius—naked?"

Farida drew a deep whistling breath. "Oh, that. I know what she's talking about." She shook her head. "That was a mistake. I explained it to her, but ..." She drew another deep breath.

"What did you tell her? What did you explain?"

"It wasn't Darius. It was *David*—Michelangelo's *David*—but I gave it Darius's head. It was just a joke between me and Darius—but maybe I made a mistake."

"May I see?"

She shook her head. A single clear look would reveal she had modeled Darius, not *David*. "No, I'm sorry. It's not complete—and I hate showing incomplete work."

"When will it be complete?"

She wondered how soon she might make a drawing of *David* with Darius's head. "I don't know. I couldn't say. I've got sidetracked now with designing the space for the gallery."

"Farida, I am sure everything is as you say—but just to pacify my wife, could you at least show me the room where you do the tuitions?"

Farida didn't understand how that would pacify his wife, but was glad for the opportunity to stand. Mr. Katrak's presence was affecting her like hemlock, petrifying muscles and joints as she sat. "Yes, of course. Right here."

Strains of a nocturne swelled from the cassette player as she opened the door again, Mr. Katrak following close behind. "Chopin, very nice."

Farida stopped in the middle of the room, eyes hardening when she noted he had shut the door behind them. "Well, this is it. Was there something in particular you wanted to see?"

"Not in particular. Where does that door go?"

"My library."

"Very nice—and that other door?"

"My bedroom."

He grinned. "Ah, so very convenient."

The conversation had darkened again; he was baiting her, but ignoring such bait would only call attention to her. "What do you mean?"

"Come on now, Farida. It is no secret. Jagdish Kapur told us what is going on."

"Who is Jagdish Kapur?"

"Arré, forgotten already? He and his family live across the landing from Dr. Jones."

Farida realized he had known all along, but kept his cards close to his vest until they had reached the privacy of the studio. "What did he tell you?"

"Saw you the very first day. Darius picked you up across the threshold—talking about honeymoons. Walls have ears, you know."

"You had him spy on us?"

Mr. Katrak adopted an injured tone, she might have accused him of cheating in a game of canasta, but his smile was sly as if he knew he had won. "Arré, spying? What a thing to say? No need to be melodramatic. I asked him to keep an eye on the flat—just to keep an eye on Darius, you understand? I mean, after all, when all is said and done, he is still just a boy, no?"

Farida said nothing, afraid to perjure herself further, suddenly on her guard. If he didn't know everything, he knew enough to cause trouble, perhaps worse.

"Arré, Farida, nothing to be concerned about. These are modern times. You did nothing wrong. Nothing to worry about with boys anyway. They are not going to get pregnant or anything."

Mr. Katrak laughed, waiting it seemed for her to join him, but she remained tightlipped. "You had him keep an eye on Darius—and an ear to the door?"

"Arré, Farida, that was not our plan. That was really stooping—I mean, literally, stooping—but by his own initiative. You know how people are, always minding other people's business—something he heard, he was saying, about Green Lantern?"

Farida realized the man had been snooping outside the flat at the oddest hours. "Green Lantern is a superhero in comics. Darius mentioned him for the illustrations. They are really quite excellent."

"Of course, of course. There are explanations for all of these things I am sure."

Farida said nothing again. It wasn't what he had said she found damning as much as what he had left unsaid, and his confidence convinced her he had left much unsaid that she would prefer left unsaid. What it meant for her and Darius she could only guess.

"Farida, really, no need to be alarmed. Darius is a good-looking boy, but still a boy. I can understand because of your die-vorce—and because of your father—you are not thinking too clearly, but what you need is a man, not a boy."

In the ensuing silence the nocturne sounded like a hundred pianos.

Mr. Katrak smiled, speaking reasonably. "Maybe the music is too loud, do you think?"

Farida hesitated only a moment before she recognized her chance, and crossing the room cut off the nocturne. "What are you saying?"

"What I am saying is this. In my day I would have wished for his luck—any redblooded boy would have wished—but for his mamma it is a different story, no? He is still her bachchu, her baby. For her sake, no other reason, we need to come to an understanding. You understand, I am sure. After all, you have lived in America—in Chicago things like this must be happening all the time, no?"

Farida's voice was a whisper. "Things like what?"

"Arré, premarital, extramarital, ultramarital—whatever you want to call it. I met Gloria Steinem once, you know. I know about women's liberation. I know it is all the rage in America, and I am all for it. I am a modern man."

"What exactly are you suggesting, Mr. Katrak? I must ask you to be frank. Please, spell it out."

"Arré, Mr. Katrak again? Call me Dhun. What I am suggesting is simply this. Why get mixed up with boys at all? Why not take the oak from which the acorn fell? Why take the sapling when you can have the trunk? We are all sophisticated now, we Parsis. We understand a man's needs, no? Also a woman's needs."

Farida wanted to say *better a sapling than a sap*, glad the silently spooling cassette allowed her to present an imperturbable front. "What about your wife? Is she also as sophisticated as you?"

"She is sophisticated enough not to worry about what she does not know. After all, who are we hurting? Nobody. Why make a fuss? Live and let live is what I say."

"And what about Darius?"

"You can do what you want, carry on like before. I will tell my wife I saw the picture, Michelangelo's *David*, she was mistaken. It was all a big joke. I will tell her. She will believe me."

Farida dropped her gaze, remaining silent.

Mr. Katrak squeezed her arm. "So, frank enough for you? What do you say?"

It took all her willpower not to flinch. "Not today, I am not prepared—but maybe we could go over the plans for the gallery sometime? I think I might need a little help."

His grin grew as if someone had blown his head like a balloon and he wrapped his arms around her. "Of course, of course—no pressure, no rush."

She kept her arms stiff by her side, but smiled, rubbing herself against him. "Just make sure your wife understands what we are doing—wouldn't want her to worry about you also."

"Don't worry about my wife. She will believe what I tell her." He held her more tightly, leaning forward, closing his eyes.

She kissed him quickly on the cheek. "Not now. I want to be prepared."

He lost his smile. His voice sharpened. "Just a taste—one for the road."

She realized it was no time for half measures. Closing her eyes she kissed him again quickly, flicking his lips with her tongue. She wore only a nightgown under her robe, but returned the kiss she had invited until his hands slid down her back to knead her buttocks. "Now, Dhun, really, enough. I will call you tomorrow or the day after. We can set a day then—but now you really must trust me."

He hesitated, but nodded finally, smiling, backing away. "I will be counting the seconds."

She debated whether to echo his remark; a man ready to puff was easily puffed; he would believe anything that flattered him; but she didn't want to risk the ground she had gained and smiled again. "I bet you say that to all the girls."

She had struck the right balance. He grinned as if they were old friends, giving her a mock salute. "Only to you—only you."

After he left she returned to the cassette player; she had lost a nocturne or two, but they were replaceable; he had given her a sword and if the need arose she meant to use it.

II

But for the developments of their meeting, Farida would have welcomed Mr. Katrak's offer to help plan the ground floor of Sea Mist for her gallery. Sooner or later she would need an architect, at least some kind of builder, to look at her draft. She had a number of rooms available, but wanted in particular a long space within which she could set dividers to change the dynamic from exhibit to exhibit, allowing each exhibit to tailor its own ideal space. To achieve her design she would need to demolish some of the walls, but needed assurance they were not loadbearing or otherwise necessary. She pored over the floor plan every morning, understanding bit by bit what she wanted, but not whether it was practical or even possible. About plumbing and electrical requirements she knew nothing.

It was two days after Mr. Katrak's visit, ten in the morning, she was poring over the plan yet again in the studio, Chopin's "Minute Waltz" spiraling out of the cassette player, a tray of toast and tea on the table, the tea cold despite the cozy, when Kaki knocked on her door, twice, but so feebly she seemed to be having second thoughts even as she knocked, her voice no less feeble. "Farida, may I come in?"

"Yes, of course, Kaki. The door's open."

Farida had attributed the feebleness to her good manners, not wishing to interrupt; Kaki's appearance in the doorway, like a puppet whose strings had just been cut, confirmed her judgment; but her first words proved her purpose was all too clear. "I hope I'm not intruding, my dear, but have you told me everything I should know about Darius?"

Farida realized it wasn't good manners that had made Kaki hesitate. She looked up from her plan, but couldn't face Kaki and bent her head again over the drawing. "What do you mean, Kaki?"

"I mean—and please don't misunderstand—he's a very nice boy—and I like him, you know I like him—but are you sure there is nothing you want to tell me about him?"

Farida winced. Kaki had called him a boy. For a moment she wondered if Kaki meant to annoy her, but the thought was immediately replaced by another more insidious: *Had she regressed so far herself she could no longer see the truth? Where did her doubts originate if everything were as conscionable as she imagined?* She kept her eyes on the plan. "Kaki, why do you ask?"

"I'm sorry, my dear. I am intruding. I have no right to ask these questions, but …"

Despite her elliptical thought, Kaki's voice had grown more confident, Farida's less, reduced to a murmur. "Then why do you ask? Has anything happened?"

Kaki stood up straight. "I think, my dear, we should talk. I think we should just sit down and thrash it out. I think it might do us both a world of good."

Farida nodded, leading the way to the adjoining library, hanging her head like a condemned woman, Kaki following, dragging her feet. The library, shelved with books and games from floor to ceiling alongside two walls, was fitted with two sofas, an end table, a coffee table, and two freestanding lamps, not unlike a sitting-room. When they were seated, Farida spoke again, eyes still on the floor, voice resigned and acquiescent. "All right, Kaki, tell me. Has anything happened?"

Kaki was gentle, but firm. "That is what I am asking you, my dear. As far as I know it is just a lot of talk—but I fear it might be worse."

"What do you mean by just a lot of talk?"

"Sashi told me—and you know she means well. There is apparently some kind of whispering campaign going on among the servants. I wondered if there might be any truth to it."

Farida wasn't surprised. Servants were often the first to know, spreading stories when they met in the parks squiring the miniature masters and misses of their households. Some so-called masters (Ratan, rich and spoiled, among them) imagined servants lacked the capacity for rational thought, unable to do anything unless ordered, a holdover in part from the days of the Raj. She herself had been guilty of no less, sauntering bag in hand past the chowkidar of Edgewater House, up the lift with the liftman, grinning and chuckling with Darius, as if chowkidar and liftman were invisible. Of course, she had been seen, and there had been the neighbor, Jagdish Kapur, nosier than the servants, panting after every revelation he could discover, eye to his peephole, ear to their keyhole.

"Farida, I don't want to be difficult. If you say there is nothing to it, there's an end to the matter as far as I am concerned, but do tell me. Should I place any credence in what Sashi says?"

Sashi had been witness to their assignations more than anyone else, bringing tea to the studio, warned not to interrupt, not for telephone calls, not for anything, but Farida knew she could rely on her discretion. The ill wind precipitating Sashi's concern to Kaki had been an invading wind, crashing the gates of Blue Mansions from the street, blowing most likely from the watch of Edgewater House. "Oh, Kaki, I cannot lie to you. I love him. I love him madly. I have never loved anyone so much—not even Horace, not even on our best days! I have never been so much in love!"

Kaki might have expected no less than just such a confession, but its intensity rendered her speechless. She screwed her eyes shut as if to will herself away. She had wondered sometimes whether she might not have spoiled Farida, indulging her with parties and gifts and just about anything she might want to compensate for the disaffection of her parents, only to bring her to the pass she now found herself.

The unexpected volley of words, not to mention Kaki's silence, not to mention the waltzes from the studio, spurred another volley. "I never meant to keep it a secret from you, Kaki—really, I didn't. I just didn't know what else to do. It just happened. Please don't be angry with me. I couldn't bear it if you were. I just love him so much. All that idiotic romantic poetry we learned in high school, all those silly love songs, all the stupidest love stories—they all suddenly make so much sense. Can you understand what I am saying?"

Kaki took a deep breath, suddenly dizzy, unable to hold her gaze, scorched by a confession so unexpectedly ardent, overwhelmed as much by the extravagance of her words as her manner, the pent rapture pouring in a flood so sweeping she wished only to get out of the way. Farida appeared strangely young again in her importunity, a teenager begging for an extension of curfew, a child learning there was no Father Christmas, and Kaki recognized her responsibility even as she wished to avoid it. Persis had been right: she had spoiled Farida, and in spoiling her had indulged herself as much as Farida, providing a sentimental love for which Farida was now paying the price—but she had been helpless herself, attempting to compensate for two unloving parents, no less for her own childlessness.

Farida grew restless in her seat, rising and falling as if preparing for flight. "I wish he had been born sooner, or I had been born later— or that I were a man and he a woman. Then none of this would matter." Her voice grew plaintive. "Kaki, please don't be angry with me. I can't help the way I feel. I just *can't!*" She went as suddenly from ardency to defiance. "What's more, I don't think I should have to! I don't think we have done anything wrong!"

Kaki took another deep breath, engaging Farida's gaze again, speaking as before, gentle but firm, grounding herself as Farida grew more airborne. "I don't say you have done anything wrong, my dear— but, oh, what a pity."

"Why a pity?"

"Because I daresay you have brought upon yourself a great deal of trouble."

Farida slipped as suddenly from defiance to insouciance, even grinning. "I daresay I could do that without even thinking."

Kaki blinked, pursing her lips, brow furrowed in a frown. "It is not a matter to joke about, Farida. It is precisely because you didn't think that this thing has happened."

Farida was defiant again, head wobbling stiffly as she spoke. "Kaki, I'm not sorry that this *thing* has happened. It is the best *thing* that has ever happened to me. The problem isn't this *thing*, but keeping it a secret. I hated keeping it from you, and I'm so much happier already just knowing that you know. We had actually planned to tell everyone—at least, planned *not* to keep it a secret any longer. We've been doing more things in public together. We *want* people to know. We just didn't know how to tell them. We thought the best way might be just to show them—show them how we feel when we are together."

"Is that why Mr. Katrak was here the other day? Does he know?"

Farida looked away, losing her defiance again. "He was here because he thought he might be able to help me with the space for the gallery. He's an architect, you know, and I had talked with him about what I was doing."

"And is he going to help you?"

"I might call on him once I get properly started. It's good to have options."

"And does he know about Darius? Have you told him about the two of you?"

Farida wished she might tell Kaki the truth about Mr. Katrak, but felt she had burdened her with enough truth for the moment. "No, not yet—but we will. Just waiting for the right moment. No hurry."

Kaki took yet another deep breath, leaning back in the sofa, gazing again into the air. "I must say, my dear, I find myself completely at sea. I find myself completely stymied. I wish I could understand better *why* this has happened."

"What is there to understand, Kaki? We are in love. It is a good thing. You should be happy for us."

Kaki spoke slowly, surer of herself. "My dear, I *would* be—but *you* don't seem very happy to me yourself. No, hear me out. You have seemed more excitable recently than anything else, and that is not the same thing. Excitability I worry about. It is a sudden eruption of feeling. Happiness is more stable, more steady and enduring, willing to take a backseat—but excitability wants to run the show. There is a root cause here I do not understand. There is a piece of the puzzle I do not have. There is something you have not told me, and I can't help thinking it has to do with Horace. I hope you will feel free to tell me about it sometime. I think it might make a difference."

Farida's backbone stiffened, her face froze. She spoke before she knew she was speaking. A nerve throbbed in her temple, her fingers fidgeted in her lap, Chopin seemed no longer appropriate, but her voice was calm. "He cheated on me, Kaki. He fathered another woman's child—his first wife's child. I had been as good as an aunt to this child for almost eight years, I had been friends with his first wife even longer … (her voice shook, words filled with air) "but they must have been laughing at me behind my back all that time." She sat, eyes filling, cheeks glistening, shoulders trembling, head bowed, lungs filling and emptying with short quick breaths, hands clasped so tightly in her lap they turned red. "For almost as long as I was married they were laughing at me."

Kaki covered Farida's hands with her own. "Oh, my dear, I'm so sorry. I'm so sorry."

"*That*'s what happened with Horace if you must know. He's a swine and a bastard and I've been the stupidest woman for not seeing it sooner. If you must know what happened, *that*'s what happened. I didn't want to tell anyone, nobody knows, not even Darius—but, there you are, now you know."

"Oh, my dear Farida, I do wish you had told me before."

"Why? What difference would it have made?"

"Perhaps none, but perhaps also all the difference in the world. It never helps to harbor a difficult secret, and it always helps to be in possession of the facts. At least, now, it begins to make more sense."

"Kaki, if you're going to tell me I was on the rebound and all the rest of it, I know all about that. Don't think I haven't given it a great deal of thought myself, but it's not like that. This is the real thing. I feel it so deeply, I can't question it."

"Actually, if you *have* been thinking about it then maybe that is enough—but that is not what I meant. That's not what I was going to say."

"What, then?"

"All this secrecy, it made me think about your Xerxes Uncle. Remember him?"

Xerxes Bamboat was her mother's sister's husband, a scrawny man with a goatee, now long dead, but barely in her life even when alive because he hailed from the Batlivala side of the family, whom even her mother ignored once she became a Cooper. "Yes, of course, I remember him. We used to call him Bamboat the goat."

Kaki's smile was wry. "That wasn't very kind, was it?"

Farida flushed. "Sorry. We were just kids. What did we know?"

"Anyway, yes, him. He was a homosexual. Did you know that?"

"Xerxes Uncle was gay?"

"I suppose that is what you would call him today—but, yes, your Xerxes Uncle was gay. The only reason I mention him is that he came to see me once about a man. He said he was madly in love. He talked about him as you have talked about Darius. I don't say he was on the rebound—in fact, I don't think he was—but of course his affair was also a big secret, and that is why I thought of him again just now. I think whenever there is secrecy the stakes get so much higher, don't they? It suddenly becomes two against the world, putting so much more pressure on the relationship to be perfect that it invariably fails—it almost *has* to fail. Your Xerxes Uncle's partner killed himself finally, jumping from his fourth floor flat, and Xerxes came to me for a talk shortly after that."

Farida wasn't surprised, recalling the continual line of visitors drawn to Kaki's reputation for generosity and compassion, particularly from the Batlivala side of the family.

"He was completely hopeless, wanted to kill himself also, following his lover's example. Sometimes, I think the only reason he didn't was out of revenge. He said if he killed himself they would have won."

"They? Who they?"

"The family, his wife, society—but he didn't want to give them the satisfaction. He said he wanted to make their lives as miserable as they had made his. Poor man, he was so miserable. I felt so sorry for him, but there was nothing I could do except listen—and soon after that, he died."

"A car accident or something, wasn't it?"

Kaki nodded. "Motorcycle, actually—but I always wondered if it wasn't some kind of wish fulfillment. He was so lost. You know, of course, losing yourself in love means only that you are lost."

"Kaki, do you think I'm lost?"

"Oh, my dear, I couldn't say. It's not for me to say. It could be a mix of so many things: Horace, your last miscarriage, all this secrecy, wanting meaning in your life, yearning for love—even the semblance of love, which becomes so romanticized in these cases. When you talk about the love of popular songs and romantic fiction and all the rest of it, I don't know what to think except that you are projecting your reality into fantasies—and that gives me reason for pause."

Farida said nothing, but seemed to be listening, wiping the wetness from her face.

"The trouble is the more secretive an affair the more seductive it becomes, until the secrecy becomes more important than the affair itself. The affair even becomes disappointing because it has such an enormous fantasy to fulfill."

"But if the affair is made public?"

Kaki shrugged. "That opens a whole new can of worms, doesn't it?"

"Then what is the answer?"

Kaki shook her head. "I don't know. I wish I could tell you. I don't think there is anything wrong with what you are doing—except that society disapproves, and that is a huge obstacle to overcome. If it is anyone's fault, it is the fault of society for being so rigid about who it is permissible to love and who it is not—only a man and a woman, the man usually older, sometimes quite a bit older, and able to take care of his wife, and the woman is usually prettier than the man is handsome. No allowances are made for older women and younger men, or rich women and poor men, or Parsis and Hindus—or Muslims, or Christians—or, why not, gay men?"

"And gay women?"

"Of course, gay women—but that is how society is. Anything outside the norm is simply unacknowledged. Exclusion is the worst punishment."

The missionary position and no other, Farida wanted to say, but kept silent, only smiling at the thought. The cassette player reached the final cadence of the "Grand Waltz" and snapped itself off.

Kaki smiled back, misunderstanding Farida's smile. "Then there are the single people—such as yours truly. I was determined not to marry just for the sake of marrying, or just to have children—but that is not something you can explain to most people. They think the key is to get married—and then make the best of it. It wasn't that I didn't want to get married, but the opportunities I had were simply not the opportunities I wanted."

"What opportunities did you want, Kaki?"

"My dear, I was just like you. I wanted love, I wanted to be madly in love, and I wanted my lover to be madly in love with me. It happened only once, a long time ago, before you were born, before your mum and dad were married—years before. I was very much in love with someone. He was actually a couple of years younger than me, very handsome—at least, I thought so—with the profile of a Valentino—but he was poor. That didn't matter to me. I never thought twice about giving him money—in fact, I gave him huge sums—for his relatives, I thought, but then I found out he had been spending it all at the track. I forgave him, of course, but I could never trust him again. It took me a long time to get over him—you might say, since I never married, that I never got over him, but I can't say I regret my choice. I never wanted to marry for company—for company, I had friends. Besides, one person always dies before the other—and then what is the other supposed to do for company? Marry again, just for company? It seems like an awful lot of work for a very small return. If I was going to marry, I wanted it to be for love, but after that incident I was too wary even to fall in love."

"Oh, Kaki, I'm so sorry."

Kaki laughed. "Oh, my dear, don't be. It was *such* a *very* long time ago—but for the longest time people thought there was something wrong with me because I was so determined not to marry for the sake of marrying. Unfortunately, it's not a defensible position, not in our society—but sometimes when I would be asked, entirely innocently, why I never married, I was so tempted to ask them why they weren't divorced, especially when the spouse might have been a famous heel or a shrew."

Farida laughed. "Kaki, why didn't you ever tell me about this man?"

"Oh, my dear, it really was such a very long time ago—and what would have been the point? Everything really did turn out for the best. You see, now I'm not even sure that I would have been happy marrying for love. It was Proust's novel, *Remembrance of Things Past*, that made me see love in a completely different light. Have you read it?"

Farida shook her head. "Too long, too wordy."

"You may be right, but you should read at least the first book, *Swann's Way*, the story of the love between Odette de Crecy and Charles Swann. Odette is a prostitute, a vulgar woman with little or no breeding—and Charles, the son of a stockbroker, with the most refined upbringing, falls in love with her—*madly* in love." Kaki smiled. "And do you know why?"

Farida shook her head again.

"Because she resembled a woman in a painting by Botticelli. Now Charles, being as refined as he was, loved the painting, and imagined Odette was the woman in the painting come to life. *That* was why he fell so madly in love with her. In psychology it's called transference—and I realized I had done a similar thing myself. I thought this man I was so madly in love with looked like Valentino, and I had transferred my girlish crush for Valentino onto him as if he were Valentino himself." She shrugged. "After that I was even more wary about falling in love. It really is a very unconscious and blind way to live, isn't it?"

Farida frowned. "When you put it like that, maybe."

"By the way, Charles and Odette finally married because they had a child—and they lived miserably ever after."

Farida's frown deepened. "But then what does it all mean? We all need love, we all need to be loved, don't we?"

"Yes, of course, we all need to be loved. We all need to feel that we are more special than anyone else to at least one other person in the world—and sometimes we scheme and manipulate and do all kinds of nefarious things to get people to love us the way we want to be loved—which is, of course, entirely the wrong way to set about it, and it invariably backfires."

"But, then, again, Kaki, what is the answer?"

"It's no big secret, Farida. The difficulty is putting it into practice. The way to be loved is to be loving—selflessly loving, without expectation of return. A loving person is a loved person, and a loved person is a loving person. If you have been loved as a child, it is easier to be loving as an adult—but if you haven't been loved as a child it is imperative to be loving as an adult. It is the only remedy—the only recipe for happiness."

Farida frowned. "Then you agree that it doesn't matter *who* you love, only *that* you love?"

"Well, I wouldn't go that far. I mean, we're not saints, after all. I'm not saying we should martyr ourselves to unlovable people—but, yes, in general, it matters more *that* you love than *who* you love. That is why I say I don't think it is wrong what you are doing, but—"

"But, oh, what a pity?"

"Yes, exactly. There are people who are married to unhappy marriages rather than to each other because they are afraid of being alone—and there are married people who beat each other and unmarried people who love each other. It doesn't take an Einstein to figure out who is right and who is wrong. What does it matter who marries whom, or whether they are even married at all, as long as they love each other? It's not being married that makes the difference, it's the people in the marriage—but we have not advanced enough as a society to understand this. We once had sati, we once had child marriages. At least, we recognize those as part of a medieval past—but there is still no understanding that love is more important than marriage, and I'm not talking about something so very elementary as the love between a man and a woman. I'm talking about love as a way of life. I don't even talk about it among my friends. That would only debase the matter. They would say it was the jealous rambling of an old maid."

Farida frowned, staring at her hands again, still clasped though more loosely in her lap. Gradually she raised her head, revealing a fledgling smile. "Kaki, thank you for talking to me about all this."

"Oh, my dear, you are most welcome. I hope I have been of some help."

"You have, Kaki—but how did you get to be so very wise?"

Kaki's smile could not have been more fully fledged. "Oh, my dear, I don't know about wise, but I do sometimes feel a little bit like good old Jane Marple—you know, of the Agatha Christie books. I don't mean, of course, that I'm any kind of detective, but I think people do her an injustice when they write her off as just a writer of detective stories. I never forgot something Miss Marple once said."

Farida was breathless with attention. "What?"

"She said: *The young people think the old people are fools—but the old people know the young people are fools.*" Kaki's smile took wing seeing Farida smile again. "Do you see what I mean? I don't think there are very many writers with a keener perception of the foibles of human nature. She's no Shakespeare, of course—not a literary writer, not even especially lyrical, but I think she shared his understanding of human nature. Of course, Christie used her understanding to expose murderers, Shakespeare to expose the human soul."

"And you?"

"Me? Oh, my goodness, I just try to do my share, cultivate my own garden. When you live alone, when you haven't too many responsibilities, when you have enough money not to worry, you tend to see things at your leisure, more objectively than if you had a hundred and one things to do—and, of course" (she winked), "people trust me enough to drop by and tell me the most secret details of their lives."

III

Farida was prepared for trouble with various bureaucracies regarding the advent of her art gallery; she had been warned by Ratan among other friends about the delays and bribes (which went hand in hand) and cajoling and handholding that would be necessary to get what she wanted; but she didn't understand the stipulation about needing her mother's permission. Sea Mist was located in a commercially demarked zone, she needed clearance from the Municipal Corporation for the use of the ground floor in a commercial venture, and she sat in the Flora Fountain office of Mr. Narendra Naik, Manager of Municipal Affairs, bewildered by what he had said, but ready to sweet-talk the man, bribe him if necessary, anxious now to jumpstart her project.

The office was a tiny cubicle within a maze of cubicles with a freestanding rotating fan, a desk overladen with files and papers topped with weights, and a single wooden visitor's chair dragged from the hallway by a smiling peon. Mr. Naik had held up his hand as if to stop traffic, holding the peon in place until he had asked Farida whether she wanted something to drink. Farida had capitulated to a Mangola after three polite refusals, realizing she was getting special treatment already, and Mr. Naik ordered tea for himself before waving the peon away with a flick of his fingers, unable all the while to tear his eyes from Farida, smiling no less than the peon.

Farida was accustomed to smiles, whether as a Cooper or an attractive woman or both mattered little, but she had worn a sari to the meeting to show her solidarity with India, and chappals as much for their convenience as not to tower over the great numbers of short men. She also spoke the best Hindi she could remember, knowing her effort would be appreciated despite her faltering tone and Americanized accent, and returned all smiles more broadly than they were given, but Mr. Naik's apparent intransigence made her smile increasingly difficult to maintain. "But I don't understand, Mr. Naik. It is *my* property. Sea Mist belongs to *me*. Why do I need my mother's signature?"

Mr. Naik was shorter than Farida by two inches and had joined hands when they met, shaking her hand only because she had held hers out, a gesture she knew he would find charming and irresistible. He wore a white shirt, sleeves rolled to the elbow in wide cuffs, a thin man with a thick handlebar moustache and thick black rectangular frames on his spectacles. Behind him the visage of a local saint gazed from the wall, haloed in gold and garlanded in marigolds. The peon had returned with a tray holding a tall glass of Mangola misted with condensation and a steaming cup of creamy tea. Farida held the glass with a napkin, wiping the condensation, keeping her fingers dry as she sipped. Mr. Naik poured tea into the saucer to cool, blew on it, slurped loudly, wiped his moustache with his fingers and wiped his fingers on his shirt. "Mrs. Cooper, there is no disputation that you may do as you wish. That is not the point of disputation. But it is your mother's property. Only a matter of getting her signature on some forms—nothing more, I can assure you. Nothing of any momentous concern. Only a formality. That is all."

Farida shook her head, maintaining patience with difficulty. "But you don't understand. It *is my* property, and *my* property alone. If my mother wanted to use it she would need to get *my* permission. It was willed to me by my father who died just recently—di*rect*ly to me, *not* through my mother."

Mr. Naik mimicked the shake of her head, his wide smile patronizing her. "Of course, of course, that is how it is in families. What belongs to one belongs to everyone. Your mother will not mind if you use it—but what this is, is just a matter of declaration, purely for technical purposes. That is all."

His eyes finally left her face, watching instead the papers fluttering under their weights from the breeze of the fan, leaving Farida to wonder if he were fishing for a bribe. "Paise ke baat hai? Is it a matter of money?"

Mr. Naik's smile seemed to dance around his face as his head waggled in figures of eight. "No, no, Mrs. Cooper. Not yet. That will be much later, much much later. Look over here. I have got your whole file over here. See? You have signed it yourself—four times you have signed it."

Farida frowned, seeing her signature in the four places indicated by Mr. Naik's finger on what looked like a contract, taking the pages from him. "What does this mean? What are these papers for?"

"What I have been telling you. Sea Mist was once upon a time your building—but you have given it away to your mother."

A finger of ice touched the back of Farida's neck and traced her spine to the small of her back. She read the form, recalling her night at the Darjeeling with Ratan, singing with the Avengers. Her mother had barged into her room the next morning with papers to sign, and she had signed them too sleepy to read, hoping to build trust between them. She looked up again. "May I have a copy of this to take with me?"

"Your mother already has got a copy."

"I would like another copy for myself."

"But we do not have another copy to give away. Another copy you will have to pay for. It is extra, you see, because you have already got your own copy with your mother. This is extra work for our secretaries. There are only so many carbon copies. We will have to type up a new form just for you. Sixty rupees only—twenty rupees for one page."

Farida gave him the money from her purse, sipped her Mangola, glanced at her watch. "I will wait until the copy is ready."

HER MOTHER WAS LUNCHING AT THE WILLINGDON with friends and wasn't due back until almost three in the afternoon. Farida tried lunching herself, but could only nibble at Sashi's tomato rice, otherwise among her favorite dishes. She ate alone since Kaki had been called to Poona, a matter regarding the Cooper estate, and wouldn't be back for another two days. She had left word with her mother's maid, Suzy, to call her when her mother returned, but went downstairs at once when she heard the Falcon in the driveway. She had read the form repeatedly, unable to make sense of the words though their meaning was clear, understanding what had happened but not why. Her mother unlatched the door to the downstairs flat just as Farida came down the staircase. "Mummy, I need to talk with you."

Persis looked over her shoulder, pushing open the door. "Can't it wait, sweetie? I'm a little tired."

"It won't take long. I just need an explanation—about this." She held the pages high, brandishing them so they crackled.

"And what is this?"

"Some property I thought was mine."

Persis entered the flat, Farida following. "And what property is that?"

"Sea Mist, the building, where I was thinking of having the gallery. It seems it's your building now. I thought it was mine. Is it or isn't it?"

Persis headed for her bedroom, blinkered as a cart horse. "Of course, it's yours, sweetie. You can do what you want with it. Why are you wasting my time like this?"

"Because it seems I need your permission. I need your signature."

"If that is all there is to it, just show me where to sign and I'll sign. I have a dinner to attend tonight, sweetie. I need my beauty nap. I seem to need more of it as I get older." She smiled over her shoulder. "Not something you would understand—at least, not yet. You seem to be doing quite all right with that little friend of yours."

Farida flinched, wondering what she might have heard through the grapevine. She had plans to see *The Graduate* with Darius and Yasmin and Arun the same evening, followed by dinner, but ignored her mother's comment. "Mummy, what I don't understand is why I need your signature at all. Why do I need your permission to do anything with it at all if it is my property? It *is* my property, isn't it?"

Persis reached her bedroom, sat in an upholstered chair to remove her shoes. "What difference does it make, sweetie? What's mine is yours anyway."

A pocket of hot air encased Farida's head. "I don't know about that, but you made pretty damn sure that what was mine became yours, didn't you?"

"Well, now, if you want to get technical about it, I suppose I did—but just show me whatever you have to sign and I'll sign it. I'll be glad to give you permission to use the premises for your little gallery. There, you couldn't ask me to be more fair than that, could you?"

Farida's arms grew rigid as pokers by her side. "Mummy, I just don't understand how you could do such a thing."

"What do you mean? What did I do?"

"You got me to sign something over to you under false pretenses. How *could* you?"

Persis shrugged, walking barefoot to draw the curtains, darkening the room. "Really, sweetie. No need to get melodramatic. What difference does it make who owns the building if you can still use it as you please?"

The pocket of air shrank around her head. She was sick of people telling her not to be melodramatic. "Why did you do it, then, if it makes no difference?"

"I didn't know if you were going to stay in Bombay, go back to Chicago, get married again—God knows what, have affairs?" She smiled to herself, falling on her back into her bed. "This way, whatever you do, the building is safe—for you as well as for me. Otherwise, who knows what you might have done with it. You're too much like your father in that respect, sweetie, filling your time with frivolous things and careless about important things. Look at how you just signed it away. Supposing it had been someone else and not me? Then what would have happened? At least, this way, you still get to use the premises—just as if they were your very own."

"I signed it away, Mummy, because I trusted *you*, my *mo*ther! Who should I trust if not my *mo*ther? My God, Mummy, I can't even believe we're having this conversation."

"Oh, so now, all of a sudden, when it suits your argument, I'm your mother."

Farida paused, bewildered. "What do you mean? Of course, you're my mother."

"Yes, of course, that's what you say now, but I can't recall the number of times I've heard you bragging about having two mothers as if one wasn't enough."

"Oh, Mummy, what a thing to throw in my face now! As if it were my fault that I was sent to live with Kaki! I really think you should have got over all that by now. If anything, it was *your* choice. I had nothing to do with it—and you know it. Really, what a thing to say!"

Persis stretched her limbs, rubbing her feet together. "It wasn't my choice any more than it was yours—but you could at least be more considerate now that your father is no longer with us. Don't you suppose people will talk about why you still live upstairs when there's no need?"

"Oh, Mummy, come on! We have been through this so many times. I can't imagine people saying anything about it that they haven't said already years ago."

"No! The situation is different now that your father is dead. There is no reason for you to live upstairs anymore—except your own personal preference. I have made that clear to you many times, but it doesn't seem to make any difference."

"For God's sake, Mummy! What are you saying? That this is some kind of revenge because I won't live downstairs?"

"It's not revenge, sweetie, but there are things beyond our control. There are consequences to all actions. As you sow, so shall you reap. That is a law of nature. I don't do what I do for revenge, but because under the circumstances there is really nothing else for me to do."

"So now you're blaming God for your revenge. Mummy, that *is* my home, upstairs with Kaki. It's what I know, what I'm familiar with, where I spent my childhood—but there's really no need to go into all that now. It's ancient history. I just don't understand why you have done this now of all times. I wish you had at least asked me first."

"When did I ever get anything I asked for, sweetie? You see, you have to look out for yourself—and you're just no good at that. If you want something badly enough you have to go out and get it. You learn how to get what you want—by *not* getting it one time too many. *Then* you change. I don't know what went wrong between you and Horace—but you know, and I know, that you will be more careful who you marry in the future—*if* you marry again at all. I really don't see the point in it myself. It's not as if you're going to have children or anything—at least, at this point, it seems rather a moot possibility, wouldn't you say?"

"Mummy, the point here is that you took my choice away from me. That is the *only* point. Everything else is a red herring. How could you do this?"

"Now, Farida, we've been over all this already. If you want me to sign something for the use of the premises, I'll be happy to sign—but, really now, I'm tired. I don't know that there is that much more to be said about this."

Farida's hands closed into fists, crumpling the pages she held. "I just don't understand how you can be so selfish."

Persis smiled, turning on her side away from Farida. "People who live in glass houses …"

Farida stamped her foot. "I swear, Mummy, sometimes you make me so mad I could scream."

"Oh, for heaven's sake! If it makes you feel any better, be my guest. Scream your head off for all I care. I understand it's all the rage in America, primal therapy or something, screaming like children when they can't get what they want."

Farida surprised herself as much as her mother, drawing a deep breath, letting out a long piercing shriek, carrying the shriek with her as she stamped across the room slamming the door behind her. Suzy came running from the interior of the flat, but stopped as if she'd hit an invisible wall when she saw her mistress's daughter. Farida seemed not even to see Suzy, striding toward the exit, slamming the front door behind her as well.

SHE HAD BARELY REACHED HER BEDROOM before the telephone rang and Sashi knocked on her door. "Bai, Katrak-seth is on the telephone."

"Tell him I will call him later."

Sashi pushed open the door. "Bai, he call two times also in the morning."

Farida realized she would have to deal with Dhun Katrak sooner or later, and perhaps her current mood would give her courage for what had to be done. "Tell him I will be there in two minutes."

She had advanced the Chopin cassette to the start of her conversation with Dhun in anticipation of just such an occasion, and took the cassette player to the telephone. "Hullo, Dhun."

Mr. Katrak couldn't have been more convivial. "Hullo, hullo, Farida! How are you? Finally got through. So difficult to get hold of you."

"Yes, well, you know how it is. The gallery is taking up a lot of my time."

"Of course, of course! That is what I am calling you about. When should I come to see you … you know, what we had discussed, about the plan? Almost any time would be good for me. You just tell me what time is good for you and I will come."

She was surprised by her own coolness. "Actually, Dhun, I don't think I will be needing your help after all—but thank you very much all the same. Very good of you to offer, and I'm sorry to have taken up so much of your time."

There was a brief pause before he picked up the conversation again, hurrying as if she might otherwise hang up. "Arré, but hang on a sec, I say. There is also that other matter."

"What other matter?"

"You know—what Jagdish Kapur saw."

Her imperturbability remained undisturbed. "What about it?"

His conviviality was clearly strained, his tone more cajoling. "Come on now, Farida. You know what I am talking about. No need to be so crude as to say it out loud."

"Is it more crude to say it or to do it?"

The very consistency of her tone seemed to change his abruptly to exasperation. "Farida, I don't know what has changed, but at this rate you will only force me to tell my wife about the whole thing. It won't go well for you. She is not as understanding as I am."

Farida maintained the precision of her tone. "Dhun, I too have something to show your wife—and I don't think she will be very understanding about it either. I would advise you to mind your own business in this matter or it might not go so very well for you."

"What do you mean? What have you got to show my wife?"

"This!" She held the mouthpiece of the telephone to the speaker of the cassette player and pressed the PLAY button.

... In my day I would have wished for his luck—any redblooded boy would have wished—but for his mamma it is a different story, no? He is still her bachchu, her baby. For her sake, no other reason, we need to come to an understanding ...

... Why get mixed up with boys at all? Why not take the oak from which the acorn fell? Why take the sapling when you can have the trunk? We are all sophisticated now, we Parsis. We understand a man's needs ...

... She is sophisticated enough not to worry about what she doesn't know. After all, who are we hurting? Nobody. Why make a fuss? Live and let live is what I say ...

Farida lifted the receiver again to her face. "I want to say only that Darius knows nothing about this and you are not to say a word—or to do anything to stop him or discourage him in any way. Otherwise, I will make sure your wife gets a copy of the cassette. Do you understand?"

He was silent so long she almost asked if he was still there, but heard instead an intake of breath so sharp it was a whistle. "You bitch! You bloody scheming bitch!"

The receiver slammed in her ear like an exclamation point to his words. Farida smiled, distanced enough already from the event to imagine someone else lowering her own receiver to its cradle.

THE PARADISE RESTAURANT ON COLABA CAUSEWAY was long and narrow, cash register in front, booths for four hugging the long walls. Arun had chosen the restaurant for a particular item on the menu unavailable elsewhere—also for its proximity to the Strand where they had just seen *The Graduate*, so they wouldn't need to hunt again for a parking space. Ceiling fans spun like helicopter blades, Herb Alpert piped from the loudspeakers. Darius and Farida faced Arun and Yasmin, the women sitting by the wall, Arun offered Camels all around, lighting them for everyone. Farida combed the menu, exhaling a long white plume. "They seem to have everything: steaks, cutlets, biryani—even spaghetti."

Arun grinned, shaking his head, letting his cigarette build ash in the tray. "Coo coo ca-choo, Farida-bai. Remember what I said. Tonight we surrender to Temptation."

Yasmin peered over her menu, blowing a plume toward the wall. She knew Farida wouldn't mind the double entendre, but Arun was surely asking for trouble quoting the song. They had enjoyed the movie though the premise had cast a pall now challenged by Arun, and as much as Yasmin had enjoyed the movie she had also been shaken by its premise, to think such things happened, a mother so spiteful she could have rivaled Cinderella's. She shook her head, indicating disapproval of Arun's comment. "Once more, Farida, we have to ask you please to excuse Arun. He doesn't know what he's saying."

Arun laughed. "Arré, who do you think you are? Jesus Christ? Forgive him, Father, he knows not what he does? I'm just saying the food here is great, even the conventional fare, but we are here for one thing and one thing only: Temptation—in Paradise!" He had explained earlier. They could get steaks and chops and biryani anywhere, but no other restaurant in the world served Temptation—certainly not one calling itself Paradise.

Darius kept his face in the menu, also gauging Farida's reaction. "It's Cisco's favorite song of the moment. He bought the record in London. I must say it's pretty good, the whole damn album."

Farida glanced sidelong, noting he too had skirted the issue though he had mentioned the song. She saw him now continually with different eyes, wondering how it might have been had he been older, had there been no secrets between them, had he known about the exchanges between her and his father, had she met him without the baggage of Horace when she might have been less vulnerable— wondered also how the movie had affected him. "I agree, great album, great song—but what a bitch!"

Yasmin seemed scared for a moment. "Who?"

Arun winked at Farida, elbowing Yasmin. "Who do you think? She was chikna, na? Not like that little whitebread daughter of hers— but maybe we should ask Darius?"

Darius grinned. "Ya, she was chikna—daughter was also chikna, but she was more."

Farida smiled, blowing another plume. He was being kind, he couldn't have preferred Mrs. Robinson to her daughter, but she was accustomed to his kindness. He was a kind boy, he would be a kind man, that was what mattered, not the difference in their ages, not anything except how they treated each other. If nothing else, money allowed you to live your life with impunity, but as Kaki had warned the disapproval of society was a huge obstacle. It had driven Anna Karenina to her worst and weakest self. Darius had reassured her, offered to leave his family, but that seemed too dire. "She may have been more chikna, but I liked the way the movie ended."

Darius nodded. "Of course, but only because they were in love. If he had been in love with Mrs. Robinson it would have been a different story." He looked at Farida, for which she was grateful.

Yasmin nodded vigorously, anxious to fill whatever cracks Arun might have contrived. "Of course, love is what makes the difference— always. The climax was, I thought, just heartrending."

Arun laughed, raising his arms in a V. "E-LAAAINE! E-LAAAINE!"

Yasmin slapped his thigh. "Shut up, you!" She shook her head at Farida. "No sensitivity. That is his problem. It still gives me goose pimples."

The waiter took their order: four Temptations and soft drinks. Following a brief silence, during which all four blew more plumes into the air, Arun picked up the conversation again, no longer boisterous, speaking surprisingly reasonably. "I say, Farida, it was a good thing you were with us, you know. Things might not have gone so smoothly otherwise."

The others looked at Arun, but only Yasmin spoke. "Why? What do you mean? What would have been different?"

Arun grinned and Yasmin knew she had been baited again. "Arré, Yasmin, I thought for sure you were going to tell them you were eighteen before they even asked. I thought we were all going to get kicked out with you—except, not you, of course …" (he turned to Farida) "not with your mature look."

The movie had been rated For Adults Only, requiring all patrons to be eighteen years old, making Farida the only eligible candidate. She had worn her hair in a ponytail to seem closer in age to her company, and Yasmin hers in a beehive to look older. Yasmin looked so much skinnier next to Farida, especially with both in miniskirts, that she had doubted herself more than the boys, Darius svelte in blue jeans and shirt, confident with Farida on his arm, Arun unflappable as always in a blue kurta, but she just smiled, refusing to rise to Arun's bait. "What nonsense! I have got into the Strand before. It's the easiest theater of all to get into."

Darius nodded, explaining to Farida. "The Regal and the Excelsior are also not so difficult. Then comes the Metro and New Empire, but most difficult is the Eros. I think people have got kicked out of the Eros more than out of any other theater."

Arun grinned at Yasmin. "Ya, right, even a chimpanzee could get into the Strand."

Yasmin didn't hesitate. "Ah, so that's your secret? They thought you were a chimpanzee?"

"If I were a chimpanzee, Darius better be on his guard. Chimps are polygamous."

Darius grinned. "I could take a chimp any day. No sweat."

Arun shook his head. "Don't be too sure. They are very strong. They could tear a child apart like a chicken."

Yasmin made a face. "What a thing to say—and how do you know such a thing?"

"I read it in a book."

Darius shook his head. "What a lot of bullshit! I still say I could take a chimp."

Arun shook his head. "Arré, Darius, chimps are pretty violent creatures in the wild. What do you think? They just sit around and play drums and ride bicycles like in the movies?"

Yasmin grinned, but Farida sighed. "What a lot of squabbling. Such a bunch of juveniles you all are. I think I'm beginning to understand what Arun meant by my mature look."

The dispute turned to laughter, the waiter brought their drinks, Farida toasted the evening, Darius toasted good company, Arun Mrs. Robinson, and Yasmin chimpanzees, setting them all laughing again.

The waiter brought the Temptations: chicken breasts marinated in a tomato sauce, encased in dough, and baked so they emerged from the oven as small loaves of bread. The three looked from their loaves to Arun, Farida the first to speak. "Looks like we could just pick it up and eat it with our hands."

Arun nodded. "No argument, you could—but appearances are deceptive …" (he grinned) "as it should be with Temptation—toasty on the outside, gooey on the inside. I suggest using a knife and fork."

They sliced into their loaves, releasing currents of steam, falling into raptures over the aroma, blowing on the morsels, careful not to burn their tongues, in raptures again over the texture and taste, Yasmin the first to comment. "Super idea, Arun. Why did you never tell me about this place before?"

"Cyrus Taraporewalla only just told me about it. He lives here—you know, in Cusrow Baug."

Darius grinned. "You know, I just had an image of myself tearing this chicken apart like a chimp would tear a child apart."

Yasmin wailed. "Come on, Darius. Not you, too. Not while we are eating."

Darius persisted. "Arré, what do you think? The chicken tore itself apart? Someone had to do it. All I'm doing is talking about it."

Farida found herself suddenly critical, surprising no one as much as herself. "Yes, yes, but what is the point of talking about it, especially when you know how it upsets your sister? Let's talk about something else."

Darius turned to Farida, eyebrows raised, but said nothing. She had never lectured him. Yasmin was no less surprised, but hardly as upset as Farida implied. Arun looked from Darius to Farida before focusing again on his Temptation. "So, Darius, who do you think would win in a fight? Lion or tiger?"

Darius replied without hesitation, glad for relief from the awkwardness. "Lion, definitely."

Arun recognized even a silly conversation was preferable to silence. "Wrong! Tiger!"

"I bet if I had said 'tiger' you would have said 'lion.'"

"No, I know this for a fact. I read it in a book."

"You can't believe everything you read in books."

"Depends what books you read. Check it out for yourself. For one thing, tigers are bigger. For another thing, they're not lazy, like lions. Tigers get up on their hind legs to fight so they can use both forepaws to attack, but lions keep at least three paws on the ground at all times— just sheer laziness. Also, the lion's mane gets too easily tangled in a fight, also makes the head so much heavier—also, most of the time, the lionesses do the hunting. Lions just wait for the dinner bell."

Yasmin interrupted, squealing with delight. "Just like a man!" She looked at Farida for corroboration, but Farida said nothing, not even to change the subject, afraid to prove a wet blanket again, more upset than anyone else with her outburst, but pros and cons raged in her head. The conversation was juvenile—but, more importantly, she was socializing with the children of a man she had blackmailed that very morning. She had come to Bombay to give herself time to figure out what she wanted, but wanting Darius as she did she had waved aside time as she might have a nanny—or a conscience.

"I say, Farida, are you all right?"

Darius had stopped eating, eyes soft with concern, hand under the table squeezing her knee. The others were staring. She was glad for his squeeze, especially after she had behaved badly, and shook her head, kissing his shoulder. "Sorry, I must have drifted off. It's been a long trying day. Sorry."

Darius squeezed her knee again. "It's all right. About the gallery?"

She nodded. "Among other things."

"You want to talk about it?"

She hadn't lied about her day. She could have told them about the interview with Mr. Naik, she could tell Darius about the contretemps with her mother, but she could tell no one about the conversation with Dhun Katrak. "I would like to, but not now. Maybe later?"

"Of course."

Dinner concluded pleasantly, if artificially, each of the four careful not to offend the others. They had been invited to a party at the Banker house on Napean Sea Road, but drove straight to Blue Mansions instead in deference to Farida who remained silent for most of the drive, casting a pall as well on the others. It was half past eleven when the jade Fiat reached the portico. Darius opened his door. "Come on. I'll walk you upstairs."

He wanted to give her a chance to talk away from the others, but Farida surprised them again, remaining seated. "Darius, would you stay with me ... just a little while? I don't want to be alone."

"Of course. I'll just drive them to the party and come back—or you can come with us just for the drive if you want."

"Couldn't Yasmin drive? I'll drive you home later myself, but I'd rather not wait. I really do have something on my mind."

Yasmin almost jumped out of her seat. "Of course, I can drive—and I can come back later, after the party, for Darius, if you want."

Farida looked at Darius. "Would that be all right? She wouldn't even need to come back. I'll drive you home myself."

Darius hesitated. "Mum and Dad don't like Yasmin to drive."

Arun said nothing. He didn't drive, and pleaded that between his driver and driving friends he didn't need to drive. Yasmin spoke, still bouncing in her seat. "I have my license. What is the point of it if I'm not going to drive, and if I'm not good how am I going to get better if I don't drive?"

Farida kept her eyes on Darius. "It's a very small distance, not even five minutes."

Darius pursed his lips, recognizing the impossibility of his position: dictating what Yasmin should do in deference to their parents while sleeping with Farida himself. "Actually, better if she comes back, better if we return home together."

Farida turned to Yasmin. "All right. Anytime after one o'clock—if that's all right with you? I'll leave the front door open so you won't need to ring the bell." She turned back to Darius. "Okay?"

He shrugged. "Yeah, sure. I guess so."

Farida meant to tell Darius what she had learned at Mr. Naik's office that morning, but once they were upstairs all other matters seemed secondary. They knew the first order of business without uttering a word. Darius may not have known what was wrong, but knew how to fix it. Farida knew the fix was temporary, but better than nothing, a permanent fix beyond her capacity for the present. Barely minutes after leaving the car they were in bed, sure of themselves as they were with no other activity.

All things had their seasons, infatuation no less, and looking ahead she could see only the skeletons of bare trees. Darius had been the first to pay her the attention she had needed, and she had proven all too human, falling as if to a pull of gravity. Her dilemma remained: how to incorporate developments with Darius to enlarge rather than diminish their world.

In the timeless interval that followed, their activity grew less feverish, Darius on top, remaining inside her, barely moving, buoyed as if on a bed of water, lips in conjunction, when he raised his head, his voice soft with bewilderment. "Farida, crying? Why?"

She maintained a smile, but tears streamed past her temples. "Whatever happens, my darling, remember I love you. Don't ever doubt I love you." Her voice broke into little pieces as if she were afraid to say more. She brought her hands forward, caressing his face, cupping his chin.

She pulled him forward to kiss him again, but he resisted the pull, his face wrinkling with concern, his voice deep with reassurance. "I don't doubt it, but I don't know why you have to say it. What's wrong? Tell me."

She shook her head, still smiling, still crying, pulling him forward again, raising her head when he continued to resist, kissing him again before laying her head back on the pillow. "I don't know, my love, but I'm afraid. I don't know why, but I'm afraid. I shouldn't be, but I'm afraid."

Her fear was palpable, eyes wide, lips parted, but as he bent to kiss her fears away the doorbell rang and her eyes widened farther, mouth dropping open. It was past one o'clock, when the sound of a pin falling was clear as a gong, and a doorbell screamed in the night like a siren. He glanced at the clock on the nightstand. "Must be Yasmin. I'll tell her we need more time."

Farida's eyes narrowed. She said nothing, but slowly shook her head and he knew she was right. Yasmin would not have rung the bell, she knew the door was unlocked, she had only to turn the knob. In that moment, a clammy hand gripping his underbelly, he understood her fear. As if to corroborate Farida's claim the bell was followed by an insistent knocking, loud in the night as hammers on the door, followed by a voice. "*O*pen this door! Da*ri*us, are you *there*? *O*pen this door!"

Darius jumped off Farida, climbing into his clothes. "Oh, shit! It's my mother!"

"Jesus Christ!" Farida jumped up as quickly, reaching for her robe, no longer afraid, preferring the sudden moment of reckoning to long moments of uncertainty.

His mother got suddenly louder as she discovered the door unlocked and barged into the sitting-room, footsteps clumping through the echo chamber of the night. "DA*RI*US! I *KNOW* YOU ARE THERE! COME ON OUT, WHEREVER YOU ARE!"

The clacking of his mother's slippers was punctuated by the shuffle of bare feet, the amplified crack of a switch flooded the sitting-room with light, visible under Farida's door in a line of yellow. "Bai, what is it? What you want? Farida-bai is gone to sleep."

Darius squeezed Farida's hand. "I'm going out. Don't be afraid."

She conjured a smile, wiping her eyes dry, returning his squeeze. "I'm not—not anymore."

He opened the door, squinting against the light, stepping into the sitting-room, speaking calmly. "Mummy, here I am. What is the matter? Why are you here?"

Sashi stood by the door, her hand still on the switch. His mother was initially still, caught it seemed unexpectedly in a spotlight, disbelieving what she saw, but darted forward to embrace him. "Darius! Oh, my Darius! Thank God you are all right! I was so afraid. Thank God you are okay!"

Darius was too bewildered to move, hands frozen in midair, not touching his mother, not even to push her away. "Why shouldn't I be okay? We were just waiting for Yasmin. We thought you were her."

"You let her drive? You know how we are about that and still you let her drive?"

Farida spoke, framed in the doorway to the bedroom. "It wasn't Darius's fault. He was going to drive them to the party, but I wanted him to stay. *I* asked her to drive."

Mrs. Katrak pushed Darius aside. "*You? You* told her to drive? *You* gave her permission?" She reached Farida in three quick steps, slapping her before anyone could stop her. "*Who* gave you the right? *Who* do you think you are?" She slapped her again. "You think because you are a Cooper you can do what you want? You think you can get away with murder?"

Farida stumbled backward from the assault, a handprint pale on her cheek, and fell heavily to the floor on her back in the bedroom, her robe flying open.

Dhun Katrak seemed spurred by her nakedness to deliver a series of kicks in the matter of a moment to her stomach, doubling Farida on her side on the floor. "Bloody *bitch! Who* do you think you are? *Bay*sharram *shame*less *bitch*!"

Darius leaped into the bedroom, pulling his mother back by the shoulders, almost lifting her off the floor. "Mummy! What is the *mat*ter with you? Have you gone *mad*?"

His mother stared at him, pointing at Farida curled on her side on the floor like a question mark. "*Yes*, I have gone mad! *She* has made me mad! Sly conniving swine of a woman! Whore from hell!"

She kicked Farida in the rump, so quickly and repeatedly her foot was a blur before Darius grabbed her by her waist, lifted her bodily, and thumped her down hard in the sitting-room. "Mummy, what are you *say*ing? Have you gone com*plete*ly stark raving *bonk*ers?"

She twisted loose, shouting to keep him at bay, wagging her finger in his face. "Lay hands on your *mo*ther? For *her*? Have you got no more shame than *her*?"

"Mummy, what the *hell* do you think you are doing?"

"*You* are asking *me*? *You* are asking *me*? Your sister is *dead!*" The silence that followed seemed to contain a deeper silence. When Dhun Katrak spoke again she seemed to speak from that deeper silence, her voice a whimper, without power, without hope. "She is dead, Darius. Our Yasmin is dead." The voice was brittle, words breaking into pieces as she uttered them. Her cheeks were damp, shining in the light of the chandelier. Her legs turned to ribbons and she clung to her son, whispering in brief uncontrollable gasps. "Her fault, Darius—it is all *her* fault—that bloody bitch in heat. Can't you see that?"

Darius drew back his hands, wishing it seemed not to touch his mother, wishing her not to touch him. He jerked himself away and she fell to her knees, still reaching for him, but he took another step back, refusing to be part of the drama. His voice was a hush. "What do you mean? What are you saying?"

She remained on her knees, raising her hands, palms upward, in a mute and mocking appeal, but when he kept his distance she got up, seating herself on the sofa, staring at the floor. "Accident—near the consulate. Daddy is with her. They took Arun ... Breach Candy."

"Arun? He ... also ..."

She shook her head. "By now, who knows?"

Farida had remained on her side on the floor, still uncovered, as one dead herself. Darius kneeled beside her, covering her again with her robe, squeezing her arm. "Farida, are you all right?"

His mother called from the sofa. "Why do you care so much about her? What about your sister? What about me?"

Darius ignored his mother. "Farida, are you okay? Please say something."

He caressed her arm, bending to kiss her, but she shook her head, shook off his arm. "Go to your mother."

His face grew pale. "Tell me first if you are all right. Tell me you are all right."

She shook her head again. "Go to your mother. Your place is with your mother."

His mother called from the sofa. "She is all right. Come on. We should go. Nothing to do here. Daddy is alone."

He continued to ignore his mother. "I have to know. Tell me if you are all right. Everything else can wait."

Farida's voice grew more resolute, even impatient. "Of course, I am all right. Go to your mother. She needs you, not me."

His mother called again. "Of course, she is all right. She has too much money not to be all right."

Darius leaned over to kiss her again and again she moved away. He whispered. "I'll be back as soon as I can."

Farida moved into a sitting position, her back against the bed, careful to keep herself covered. "Don't be foolish. Your place is now with your family."

"You are more important to me. I love you."

She would not look at him. "You are talking like a child. Go now. Go back to your family. This is your chance to be a man. Make the most of it. Go."

His voice was breathless. "Farida …"

She wouldn't look at him. "*Go!*"

His mother got up. "Come on, Darius. Daddy is alone. We should go to him."

Darius ignored his mother, frozen by Farida's repeated commands to leave.

"Come on, Darius. Enough damage you have done."

"We have done nothing wrong."

"Nothing wrong? What do you think? I don't have eyes? I can't see? You think the whole world is blind?"

Darius got up, addressing Farida again, speaking quickly. "I *will* be back. Count on it."

Farida remained on the floor, her back against the bed, as Darius and his mother walked the length of the sitting-room. Sashi locked the front door behind them and returned to the bedroom. "Bai, you want something? Tea?"

Farida shook her head, but changed her mind. "Glass of water, please, Sashi. Thank you."

"Yes, bai." In the time it took Sashi to bring the water Farida got up to sit in one of the club chairs in the sitting-room, her knees and feet together, arms crossed in her lap, staring apparently sightlessly ahead. Sashi placed the glass on a coaster on an end-table by her side. "Anything else, bai?"

She looked up at Sashi's anxious tone, shaking her head. "No, thank you. Go to sleep, Sashi. Nothing more to be done for now."

"Yes, bai."

A half-moon shone on the garden. Farida didn't need to stand to see how it looked. The sound of the sea was enough to evoke the beach, the picket fence demarkating the Cooper property, the flagstoned path in the garden leading to the fountain spouting from the fairy's wand, the patio of fairy lights during the parties hosted by her parents, Strauss waltzes on the gramophone, guests in smart gowns and uniforms, the women flamingos, men emperor penguins, her father by the gate fixing a sprig of bougainvillea behind Flora Diver's ear, sparking the chain of circumstances driving her to Chicago and Horace, bringing her back again to Kaki. It was all so very simple, *the way to be loved is to be loving*, but with all her advantages she had still failed.

She remained seated and still until the grandfather clock tolled three. She returned then to her bedroom to pull on a pair of jeans and an old shirt she left untucked. The shirt, once her father's, had served in her childhood as pajamas without bottoms during sleepovers, and was still large enough to cover her like a sack. Walking to the front door she found Sashi curled on the floor, around the corner from the sitting-room, waking apparently from sleep at the sound of her steps. "Bai is going out?"

"Sashi, go to your room. You don't have to sleep on the floor."

Sashi smiled, wiping sleep from her eyes. "Bai needing something? Bai needing the car? I can call Dev on the telephone."

Her brother, Dev, their driver, lived in Tardeo in a flat the Coopers had helped attain for his family, a wife, two daughters—and Sashi's daughter. Sashi, long estranged from an alcoholic husband, little desiring another man, stayed with them on her days off and holidays. A neighbor had a telephone whereby Dev could be summoned within thirty minutes. Farida shook her head. "No, I'm just going for a walk."

"Where you are going, bai?"

"Not far—just Breach Candy."

Sashi seemed unsure what to say next. "Bai will be back soon?"

Farida nodded, softened by her concern. "Not to worry. Bai will be back soon."

Stepping outside the gate she skirted the villages of the night, a proliferation of charpoys alongside the road, some bearing two, sometimes three, entwined bodies each, while across the wall lay Coopers, alone in their beds, in mansions large enough to house colonies.

She passed Mafatlal Park where she had promenaded as a child chaperoned by her ayah of the moment. She passed Sophia College Lane, the scene of the first party with Darius, the day she had met Arun and Cisco among others. She passed Breach Candy, her kindergarten school, among other childhood haunts, Bombelli's, Chimalker's, Reader's Paradise (her favorite sweetshop, toyshop, bookshop), all within ten minutes of leaving Blue Mansions. Approaching the consulate she slowed her pace, not knowing what to expect, afraid what she might see, seeing finally just what she might have expected, the jade Fiat on the side of the road, a concertina of a car, the driver's side not even that. She muttered prayers from her childhood she thought she had long forgotten when she was interrupted by a voice from a nearby charpoy. "Accident, memsahib."

She didn't turn, but nodded. "Kya hua? What happened?"

The person raised himself from the charpoy. "Bus coming. Girl driving, dead. Boy, hospital."

Farida was crying again. She could hardly talk. "Thank ..."

The person was at her elbow, holding out his hand, palm upward. "Memsahib, baksheesh?"

Farida turned to see a stooped old man, salty stubble on a gaunt face, mouth twisted in the familiar rictus of pleading, but she had brought no money with her and shook her head, patting her pockets. "No money. I have got no money."

The old man's mouth twitched as if he had been cheated, but he repeated himself as if he hadn't understood. "Memsahib, baksheesh? Two days, memsahib, I have not eaten."

Farida pursed her lips, hating to turn away, having no alternative, when she saw someone walk determinedly toward them. "Bai, you are all right?"

Sashi had followed. "Sashi, have you got any money?"

Sashi delved into a little bag she had tucked into the waist of her sari. "Fifteen rupees, bai. Too much for him."

"It will do. Good thing you came." Farida gave the money to the beggar.

Sashi's tone was indignant. "Bai, why?" She screwed her face, raising her chin, hand in a fist, thumb to her mouth, mimicking a drunk.

Farida nodded. "I know. Come, let us go."

IV

Farida slept much of the next two days, visiting once more the site of the accident on the first evening, but not finding courage to visit Arun in the hospital until the second evening, afraid of whom she might meet, afraid of Arun himself under the circumstances, finding him finally (strangely, comfortingly) in the N. B. Cooper wing of Breach Candy Hospital, his mother, his mother's younger sister, and his own younger sister, seated in dumb attendance, three plump brown sorrowful women. Arun's legs were in casts, but he seemed otherwise unhurt, sitting up in the hospital bed, even apologizing for his company. "Good to see you, Farida-bai. Thank you for coming. Pay no attention to these sad sacks. Darius's mum was here yesterday and I think she infected everyone she met—maybe the whole hospital. You know how she is, bloody bitch of a woman."

"Arun!" Mrs. Sarkar seemed more shocked than disapproving, staring at her son as if he had said as much about her.

Arun only grinned, ignoring his mother. "You know the best bloody thing about this stupid business? I can say what I bloody well want, when I bloody well want, how I bloody well want, without fear of retribution. If anyone says anything, I'm bloody well sick. What are they going to do? Stupid fucking bastard that I am, I can't be held responsible for what I say. I tell you, Farida-bai, it is the most liberating feeling, being a fucking cripple."

Farida understood, squeezing his hand, recalling something she had learned in a course in psychology. Language was a way to release rage, evoking outrage in those who heard. "You always spoke your mind, Arun. You didn't need this."

"Not like this, yaar. Never like this. Too bad Yasmin had to be her daughter, but hard to feel sorry for that old sow—always with her snout in everyone's arse." He paused, his mouth drooped at the corners, and for a moment Farida thought he might cry—but he raised his chin, pursed his mouth and spoke defiantly. "She didn't think I was good enough for Yasmin, you know, being a Hindu and all that—but she never stopped talking. Parsis are the best people, the most openminded, the most philanthropic, the most this, the most that. They have built hospitals and colonies and factories and schools, on and on and on—but it's just false pride, you know. People who can only talk about their past are like potatoes. The best part is under the ground."

Mrs. Sarkar's voice was tentative behind them. "Don't excite him too much. Not good for him to be too much excited."

"Shut up, Mummy! This is the best conversation I have had since I've been here. If anyone has excited me too much it's that goddam mother of Darius's, but you never said anything to her. If you don't want me to be excited just keep that bitch away."

His aunt smiled apologetically, speaking no less placatingly than Mrs. Sarkar. "I say, really now, Arun, that *is* a bit much. So much bad language!"

"Look, all of you, if you don't want me to get so bloody excited, just don't talk to me. Just let me have a good conversation for a change with my friend."

Farida turned to the family. "He doesn't mean it—just a difficult time, you know."

The aunt nodded, the younger sister smiled, Mrs. Sarkar seemed bewildered. When she turned back to Arun he was grinning. "Arré, Farida-bai, I was only kidding. You know it and I know it. What does it matter if nobody else knows it?"

Farida shook her head. "Arun, I want to say I'm sorry. I'm so sorry. You were just a bystander in this whole mess. If I had just gone to the party, or if I had just let Darius drive, none of this would have happened." She lowered her voice not to be overheard by the women behind. "If only I hadn't been so damn selfish myself."

"Arré, Farida-bai, don't be sorry, not your fault—and don't let anyone tell you different—not even Yasmin's fault. You'd be surprised how well she can drive—could drive—but that bloody bus driver ... must have been fucking drunk or something. Just bloody swerved right into—" He stopped speaking, suddenly losing breath, taking the glass of water his sister brought wordlessly. "Thank you, bibi." He turned back to Farida as if there had been no interruption. "Nothing anyone could have done. Don't flatter yourself it's your fault. You are not that powerful."

"But if not for me ..."

"Look, if you are going to talk like that, then I don't want to fucking talk to you either. Using that kind of logic you have to go a lot further back. For want of a nail and all that. Might as well say if not for God."

His mother spoke again, scandalized again. "Arun, no blasphemy, please! Not at a time like this!"

"Then who do you think? The devil did it? And if so, why do you suppose God didn't stop him?"

His mother shook her head, subsiding again. Farida squeezed his hand again. "But I *have* given Mrs. Katrak a lot to be upset about. I can't even begin to say how much."

Arun sighed. "Arré, Farida-bai, this is very disappointing, but you are just like a woman—blaming yourself because others blame you. Don't let yourself be fooled. Darius's mum was upset long before any of this. It is just her way, her default, being upset—because she is herself not a Cooper or a Tata or a Godrej or something—only a Katrak. Don't think she didn't know about you and Darius right from the start. It took a crisis to make her true nature come tumbling out like all the troubles from Pandora's box, but that nature was there from the start. You didn't make her like that. I'm telling you, yaar, don't let them snow you."

"I wish I could believe you."

"Arré, believe, believe! I shall lose faith myself if you do not believe. If anyone has a right to be upset it's me, not them, and I'm not upset—at least, not with you."

"I don't understand why not."

"Arré, just look at me. I am a lucky fellow to be alive. Fractures heal, only a matter of time. I could be home even now, but they are keeping me for tests, x-rays—might have concussion, maybe something else, but I don't think so. Just a safety measure, you know."

She shook her head, disagreeing.

"Besides, you are the prettiest sight I have seen since the last time I saw you." He grinned at her mouth dropping like a drawbridge. "I told you, no, I can bloody well say what I want—the advantage of being a bloody cripple."

She shook her head, grinning finally herself. "I swear, Arun, I don't know whether to hit you or kiss you."

"Arré, a kiss, a kiss, by all means, a kiss."

"What about your mother?"

"What about her? I'm asking for a kiss, not poison."

"Maybe before I leave, if you behave yourself—if you are nice to your mother."

He shook his head. "I swear, Farida-bai, the things a fellow has to do just to get a kiss from you." Minutes later, saying goodbye, Farida kissed his cheek. "Arré? Just on the cheek? What is this?"

Farida couldn't help smiling. "Yes, just on the cheek. What do you think? I'm going to kiss all your little booboos? That would take the rest of the evening."

He smiled as she left and a smiling nurse greeted her in the corridor. "Very good for him, you were. Trauma patients, always angry—from burns, amputations, multiple fractures—so mad they are all the time, at everyone—groping, you know, for phantom limbs, phantom lives, forever lost."

Farida nodded. "I think I understand. Yasmin."

"Yes, exactly! From what they are telling me I can say the same. Yasmin!"

SHE HAD WALKED TO THE HOSPITAL, and on her return found Darius sitting on the front steps, his bicycle leaning against a wall in the lobby. She had left the hospital grateful Arun would be all right, more cheered by him than he by her, but she wasn't ready yet to see Darius again. His face was gaunt as she might have expected, but also fearful. Her instinct was to comfort him, but she refused to indulge her instinct: it had plunged her too often into a sea of troubles. She had fled Horace and Chicago to gain time and distance, grant herself a reprieve, only to learn she couldn't run away from herself: she had succumbed again to her instinct. She needed now in greater quantity what she had needed then, more time, more distance, a major extension of the reprieve. Then she had been the sole casualty, now she had made casualties of others, performing a kind of communal retribution. *Those to whom evil is done do evil in return*, but not necessarily to the evildoers, and in the blindness of her fury against Horace she appeared to have lashed out, however involuntarily, at the Katraks, for which transgression she had yet to reap the consequences. Such were the conclusions she had drawn from her long hours in bed since the accident, making it impossible for her to return Darius's tentative smile. "Hullo, Farida."

She frowned. "Hullo."

His mouth twisted into a shallow arc, his eyes receded. "I said I would be back."

She climbed the steps past him into the lobby, her voice cold in passing. "Yes, so you did."

He could not have said what he had expected, but her lack of concern recalled his fear when she had repeatedly commanded him to go to his mother. "I tried to call, but Sashi said you were asleep, not to be disturbed."

"I know." She had instructed Sashi not to disturb her, not for anyone.

"I couldn't come before. The funeral is tomorrow. We had to make arrangements, put notices in the papers—"

She stopped, her hand on the newel of the staircase, looking over her shoulder. "You will pardon me, I'm sure, if I can't make it."

The formality was worse than the brevity. He opened his mouth to say he understood, but trading formalities would only exacerbate their strangeness. His mouth was dry. "Farida, did I … do something wrong?"

She didn't look back, climbing the stairs. "You have to ask?"

He followed her up the stairs, afraid suddenly he would lose her once she entered the flat, and spoke quickly stating his case. "Farida, nothing has changed—between us, I mean. If anything, I feel closer to you."

She fished in her bag for keys as if the task required all her concentration. "Maybe nothing has changed for you. For me, everything has changed. I don't understand how it can be the same for you."

He could see she was fishing for time and his words softened with reverence. "Farida, I love you. That has not changed. I want to apologize for my mother."

She could not speak at once, a golf ball lodged in her throat, and continued to rummage for time in her bag. "Does your mother know you are here?"

The arc of his mouth tightened. "Why should I care about that?"

"Maybe for the same reason we should have cared from the start."

He shook his head, speaking slowly, wanting to impress clearly what he said. "We had no reason then and we have no reason now.

Farida, there is no reason for anything to change between us. We have done absolutely nothing wrong."

She sighed. "How many times have we said that? We keep saying it as if to convince ourselves—but who are we fooling? Look what's happened. It *has* to mean something." She found her keys and singled out the key to the door. "For me, everything has changed." She looked at him, key in hand, ready for insertion. "I don't think you should come in."

"Can't we even just talk?"

"I thought that's what we were doing." She remained still in the silence that followed, speaking finally more conciliatorily. "Darius, I don't have time. I have to meet Kaki at VT. She's returning by the Deccan Express. I have things to do."

He could think of nothing to say, but neither could he leave. Finally, he blurted what was on his mind. "You said you loved me."

"I did."

She might have meant she had loved him once, she might also have meant she had only *said* that she loved him, but slowly the implication spread: either way, she was saying she no longer loved him.

"I meant it."

The implication thickened and he began slowly to lose air, wrinkling into age before her eyes, appearing like a balloon a week after the party. She let herself into the flat, shutting the door in his face, scurrying to her room, wishing no one, not Darius, not Sashi, to witness her own disintegration, the sudden distortion of her face, engraved in a mask of despair, head sunk in rounded shoulders, making her seem a large egg on legs. She fell on her bed, burying her head in pillows to muffle her sobs, her body wracked by involuntary tremors. She needed time to think, but what was Darius to do while she was thinking, so young a boy whom she had aged so quickly?

SHE EMERGED AN HOUR LATER FROM THE FLAT to find him still on the landing huddled in a darkening corner. "Darius, you are still here?"

He seemed unaware, until she spoke, waking with a start, glancing at his watch, sounding as disoriented as he looked. "Sorry. Didn't realize the time."

He wiped his cheeks, soft and damp, hurriedly with his hands. His eyes seemed larger for glistening in the dim light of the landing, lit from a high window by the fading sun. She could have lit the staircase light, but took pity on his appearance. "Darius, what are you doing here still?"

He got up too quickly, almost losing his balance, legs stiff with disuse, speaking slowly. "Sorry. Didn't mean to inconvenience you. Just … lost track … but I'm going."

His voice remained thick, and whatever he said, wherever he looked, the large black glistening eyes remained full of rebuke. She couldn't let him pass. "But why are you here still?"

Her repetition of the question perplexed him. She could see he was leaving, but delayed his leavetaking, standing in his way, asking why he hadn't already left. She had shut the door in his face pleading time was short, but talked now as if time had expanded. She had washed, changed clothes, appeared fresher than he could imagine; in his cramped unwashed state he felt like a leper in her presence; but he answered then as she had wished, saying what she wished to hear, for which response she had repeated her question. His mouth twisted into a rictus similar to the beggar she had met on the night of the accident, asking it seemed for something she could no longer give, a prize she had snatched as precious as a child. "Where should I go? I have nowhere to go. I don't want to be … anywhere else."

She wanted to hold him, tell him she loved him, but she had given him too much false comfort already. Until she knew better what she wanted herself she didn't want to give him even a glimmer of hope. "Darius, there is nothing for you here anymore. There is no reason for you to come here anymore."

In that moment he felt like her toy, dandled like a doll in her lap, spun like a top, pulled back and forth like a yoyo. He was struck by the cruelty of her words so casually making a fool of him. He had been mystified since the night of the accident, but she had behaved mysteriously even before his mother's appearance, and he felt newly stupid for the time he had spent moping on her landing when his sister better deserved his allegiance. Her behavior proved his parents increasingly wise. His arms, bowed by his side, weighted by fists, bulged with veins and muscles straining it seemed to hold him back as he walked threateningly toward her. A sound escaped his lips like a hiss and he walked so close she could feel the heat from his body, but he passed without touching her, halting only when he was midway down the stairs, looking up with a hand on the banister, the other twitching by his side. He walked again in a compass of confidence, even his voice was steady. "Farida, I don't know what went wrong. I'm sorry, whatever it might have been, but I'm beginning to think mummy was right. Who do you think you are treating me like some kind of machine you can turn on and off as you please?"

She realized immediately how greatly she had miscalculated. Her comfort may have been false, but falsities were sometimes kinder than the truth, and kindness had its own merit. Besides, giving comfort she gained comfort herself. Her throat swelled, too full for speech, and she held open her arms instead, but he jerked himself into movement as if he had been paralyzed, turning his back on her to continue his descent, suddenly giving her back her voice. "Darius, don't go!"

He turned again, hands twitching. "Farida ... I don't understand. I just don't understand."

She shook her head, barely able to speak. Tears poured in sheets down cheeks dry barely moments ago. "I don't ... either. Just come here ... please."

Her sudden changes of heart remained confusing, but he realized she was at least as much a pawn in the game as himself, both of them played by a giant puppet-master. "Crying? Why?"

Her arms remained open. "I have done almost nothing but cry and sleep for the past two days—even before that."

"But why? There is something I don't know?"

"There is plenty—but afterward. For now, just come. Let me hold you."

He climbed the stairs to the landing again and her touch replaced the wood and stone of his frame with light and air. They held each other, once more a single entity, heads on each other's shoulders, unmoving until the landing was black with night. "You have to meet the Deccan Express?"

She nodded. "It's always late."

"Still. Kaki might be waiting."

She nodded again, wiping her eyes with her handkerchief, smiling shamefacedly. "Darius, I am so sorry. I have embroiled you in a mess of my own making and I don't know what to do about it. I want to talk to you about this, but I don't know what to say. I need to think about it, but I don't have time just now. I don't have the right to ask you, but may I call you in about a week? I meant it when I said I loved you— but I don't know what that means. It's only a feeling."

She had said it again, spoken in the past tense, ambiguously about love, but he was more fortified than before. "Better call Cisco for now. He will get the message to me. Let it ring once and hang up—you know, like we did before—just in case Dr. Jones is around. Cisco will understand."

She smiled, nodding, glad he was thinking ahead as well.

V

The Naaz was perched so precariously on the side of a hill it might have been cantilevered, but from the upper of its two storeys afforded one of the finest views of Bombay, in particular of Marine Drive, the wide crescent of roadway holding back the sea, an electric arc of gold by night. The café was perfectly situated for its proximity to Hanging Gardens and Kamala Nehru Park.

Farida sipped from her Mangola, Ratan his coke, both snacking from a plate of samosas with tomato sauce between them. It had been Ratan's suggestion to absorb some outdoor atmosphere with appetizers before heading for dinner at the Excelsior where sizzling steaks were served in iron dishes inlaid in wood, and Farida had been only too grateful for the diversion. Ratan was not a man of consequence, not by a long stretch, but his solicitude and long acquaintance made him a safe and comfortable companion. It even comforted her to pierce his pretense of worldliness, so often on display as it was now. He sighed, tapping ash over the railing onto the side of the hill. "So, what's up, old girl? Your mum says you've been pretty glum these days."

"My mum? Don't pay any attention to her. She only sees what she wants to see. I'm quite all right, thanks."

"No, no, she said you were quite angry about that building, Sea Mist, where you were going to have your gallery. She said you were no longer interested in the space. Why not?"

"Arré, Ratan, just let it go. That is between her and me, nothing to do with you. We'll work it out. We'll muddle through as we always do."

"But are you going to have the gallery or no?"

She shook her head. "I don't think so after all."

"But why not? Your mum wants you to use the space as if it were yours. Why all this pettiness about who actually owns the place? I mean, she has to look after her own interests, doesn't she? There isn't anyone to help her anymore, now that your dad's gone."

"Ratan, I really don't want to talk about it."

"But just tell me, no, as a friend? It won't hurt to talk about it. Might even help."

Farida wondered how much her mother had said, whether she had admitted to tricking her into signing the building away when she had enlisted him to bat for her. Kaki knew the whole story and Farida planned to tell Darius, but Ratan was hardly as disinterested a party as he would have her believe. He imagined, wrongly as always, that by patching matters between her and her mother he might win her deeper affection. "Ratan, I *reeeal*ly don't want to talk about it. Please, let's just drop it."

Ratan lost his smile. "You know, Farida, you were not like this before. You used to tell me everything."

"What nonsense, Ratan. Don't flatter yourself. When did I ever tell you everything? In some ways, I swear, you are just like Mummy. You see only what you want to see."

"I take that as a compliment. Your mum is a farsighted woman. I have the greatest respect for her."

Farida might once have been amused—but no longer. Ratan wore his dignity like a pig a tiara, a dolphin a tutu, or a hippo blue jeans. "Make sure you let her know. I'm sure she will be delighted to hear it."

"Arré, Farida, no need to be so damn sarcky—doesn't become you. If I'm not being too presumptuous, I must say that boy has had a very bad effect on you. Now don't look at me like that. Everybody knows. In these matters Bombay is a village—most definitely Bombay society. I mean, no one is mad at you, don't get me wrong. They just think you've gone a little ga-ga after your marriage broke up and your dad died and all that. Nothing that can't be fixed by meeting a good Parsi fellow your own age."

"Like you, you mean?"

"Why not?"

"Arré, Ratan, that boy, as you call him, is someone I love. That doesn't mean anything to you?"

"Arré, but, Farida, see, even you—you called him *some*one you love, not a *man* you love. Means something, no, that he is still a boy? What does a boy know about love? He was taken by you, very understandable—and you were in a vulnerable state, also understandable. No one is blaming anyone. This too shall pass, everything passes. That is all I am saying. I think you should at least think about it."

Farida pursed her mouth so her lips turned white. "He may not be a man chronologically, Ratan, but in important ways he's already more of a man than you."

Ratan sat back, blanching as if he'd been slapped. "I say, that's a bit sharp, don't you think—especially when I was only trying to help?"

"The only person you are trying to help, Ratan, is yourself—and sharp or not, it's true—but I don't expect you to understand. You have led such a sheltered life you have no idea what it means to live outside the Cooper cloister. You have never *nee*ded to be a man. Everything is always done for you—but that is not necessarily a good thing. It leaves you too helpless in the world, a man without skin."

"Arré, I don't understand what has brought this all about, but I have quite enough skin for my needs, thank you. I may not be able to change a tire or fix your latrine or grow a field of cotton or barley or turnips or what have you, but what is the need of such things? If I could do all these things then what would the people do who make a living doing such things? As it is there is a fine balance: I have the money; they have the services. It is this American thinking of yours that is the problem. Everyone wants a big house, but the husband spends all his time in the office paying for the house, and the wife spends all her time cleaning the house. What is the point of owning a house if you can't enjoy it? People should not be allowed even to buy houses unless they can afford maids. Otherwise, what are the maids going to do?"

There was a comical logic to what he said and Farida listened silently.

A sly grin stole over his face. "In any case, I say, what about you?"

"What about me?"

"You have been just as sheltered, if not in a Cooper cloister then in a Fisch cloister—but, of course, you are a woman, and for a woman it is acceptable to be sheltered—even better. A woman who can fend for herself is all very well, but what is the point? She only makes a man feel useless."

Farida sighed, long and deep, recognizing the merit of his complaint. Whatever she had accomplished, it had been underwritten by either Coopers or Fisches, neither of whom she wished to acknowledge. "There is something to what you say, Ratan, but I am too tired to discuss it."

He spoke conciliatorily. "All right then, let's forget it. Let's start again. I am willing to forgive and forget."

"Start what? Forgive what? As if there were something going on between us. You can be such a silly man sometimes, Ratan, I swear."

"*Me?* A silly man? *Me?* You are the one having your way with little boys and *I* am a silly man? Don't you think you owe me an apology?"

Farida pursed her lips again. "You're just being silly again, Ratan. An apology for what?"

"For one thing, I must say you speak very freely to me. It's not always so pleasant, you know, but I put up with it because you are my cousin—and I like you so much—but I must say you can sometimes be quite insulting. The thing is I don't think you realize it, and that's why I don't mind so much."

Farida slurped the dregs of her Mangola through her straw. "You are right, Ratan. I *am* sorry. I *do* take advantage of you, and I shouldn't. It is a bad habit I have got into because you have always been so accommodating, and I shall break it, I promise—but if you don't mind too much I would like to go home. Suddenly, I'm not so hungry anymore. A sizzler would be wasted on me in my present condition."

"Oh, come on now, Farida. We will have a good time and you know it."

She shook her head. "No. I'm very sorry. I am probably taking advantage of your good nature again, but I would really rather not."

Ratan leaned forward across the table. "Farida, you *know* you will feel different once we are there. You *know* you will."

Farida looked around for the waiter. "Ratan, please don't tell me how I will feel. I'm quite capable of knowing myself."

VI

Darius stood on the corner of Warden Road and Napean Sea Road at nine in the evening as arranged, waiting for Farida to pick him up. She had chosen the time for shelter in the dark, but her concern remained less that they might be recognized, more that she communicate clearly what she had to say.

She saw him first as she turned the corner. Despite the crowd of pedestrians he seemed to stand alone, head turned skyward, seemingly in prayer. She was about to honk the horn when he saw her, appearing in that moment to grow taller, his face brighter, dimples and cleft deeper than she remembered. He looked in the window, opened the door, got in. "Hullo."

"Hi." She smiled, squeezing his arm, and for a moment it seemed nothing had changed between them, but she turned her face to the road when it seemed he might lean across the seat to kiss her. "How have you been?"

His smile faded as he faced the road as well, reminded once more that things were no longer the same. "All right."

"What did you tell your parents?"

"They think I'm with Cisco, taking a walk."

"Hmm, okay. I'm not sure where we should go. In some ways it seems we are back to square one, not wanting to be seen together again."

She forced a small laugh at the irony, but he could not have been more serious. "It really doesn't matter to me. I don't care what anyone thinks, least of all my parents. If anyone has behaved badly, it's them—certainly, my mum."

His dad had behaved no less badly than his mum, but he was not to know. She wished neither to condemn nor condone the Katraks. Her concern was neither their behavior nor Darius's, only her own, her culpability in the matter. She had planned to park alongside Marine Drive before she said what was on her mind, but found small talk impossible already. "It's not their fault, Darius—and it's not your fault either. *I* should have known better all along, but I was too proud."

"Proud? Of what?"

She took a deep breath. "There are many things about this that you don't know, Darius, that I need to tell you. I'm not trying to excuse myself, what I did was inexcusable—"

"Nothing doing, Farida. Don't talk rubbish. You did nothing I didn't want you to do—nothing! If anything—"

She shook her head, interrupting. "No, please, Darius, let me finish. This is not easy, but I owe you at least this much. I want you to understand what happened—at least, as well as I understand it myself—then you can talk."

He sat back, eyes again on the road, as were hers, and lit a cigarette. "All right. Sorry. I won't interrupt again."

By the time she was finished he had smoked six cigarettes. They were parked at the south end of Marine Drive, the Chevrolet as still as the eye of a storm, cars speeding by on the right, hawkers and strollers on their left, parents with prams, friends in twos and threes and fours, arm in arm, walking with bicycles, walking with dogs, walking with transistor radios, singing Hindi film songs, munching chana-singh from paper cones, children screaming and running in circles. Beyond the pedestrians the sea raged against land whipped from its grasp, the Marine Drive reclamation, pounding continually the giant concrete tetrapods holding it at bay, drenching at high tide the closer strollers with surf.

True to his word Darius didn't interrupt, but when she finished he crossed his arms. "Farida, I understand what you are saying, I understand your reasons for everything, but it makes no difference to the way I *feel*. If you *feel* the same way, I think we can still make it work. Why should reasons make a difference? What matters is how we *feel*. If we feel the same, we can make it work."

He was staring at her, but she crossed her arms as well, staring again out of the windshield. "If that is what you think, then I haven't made myself clear enough. What I'm trying to say is I was too proud for my own good. I didn't want to admit I had been torched by what happened with Horace. I wanted to pretend I could carry on as if nothing had happened. I hate to say it, Darius, but I think I might have involved myself with you just to prove to myself that I was fine. I didn't need Horace. I didn't need anyone. I could get what I wanted on my own. Do you see what I'm driving at? Do you understand what I'm trying to say?"

She had told him about Horace and Ginger, the miscarriage she had induced, her state of mind when she had arrived back in Bombay, apparently so gay despite the death of her father, everything except the role of his own father. He uncrossed his arms, dropping his gaze, dropping his voice. "Do you mean to tell me … are you saying you never really …"

"No, Darius, of course not. The feelings were genuine—still are—but they were based on a very rocky foundation—not the kind on which to build a life."

"May have been rocky to start, but we can make it firm now. May have acted unconsciously before, but we can act consciously now."

Farida winced, taking a deep breath. "That is what I thought I was doing."

In the silence that followed she could hear his breathing over the other surrounding sounds.

"Darius, how can I put this plainly? You made me feel young again, as if the years with Horace had not been wasted. You gave me back my life. I felt I deserved happiness after what Horace had done, and when you gave me the chance I just grabbed it without thinking— but what I did was to make you my whipping boy."

He looked up. "Very willing whipping boy!"

"No, not at first! Remember? I was so pushy, I was so relentless—I was shameless." She shook her head. "I came all the way from Chicago to think through my problems and look what a muddle I've made of it."

"A muddle? Is that what you call it?"

She winced again, took another deep breath. "I'm sorry. I'm not explaining myself at all well, but I'm only beginning to understand myself. It was something Ratan said to me the other day. I was on my high horse, as I always am with him, always *proud*. I had the cheek to accuse him of living a sheltered life—I practically accused him of not being a man, of always having everything done for him. He said, to his credit as I see it now, that I was just like him—and he's right. We are very different people, but in this one matter we are exactly alike. We have both always been taken care of in one way or another—and I'm not so sure it is a good thing."

"But you are a *woman*! You *do* need to be taken care of!"

Her eyes widened and she bit back her first words. Lacking experience of the world, he had provided the conventional response. She had nothing against convention except when it precluded other options, most particularly the one she had yet to find for herself, more easily found in the anonymity of Chicago where she was just Farida, if anything handicapped by solitude, her color, and lack of antecedents, than in Bombay where she would always be first a Cooper. She had determined that she would strike out on her own in Chicago, refusing all assistance, financial and otherwise, from the Coopers and Horace, becoming finally her own woman, whatever the cost. She had money saved, she had experience in market analysis, she was confident of a job—but didn't want to set long-term goals. Once she had set herself up independently in Chicago she would know what to do next. The difficulty was telling Darius. She took another deep breath. "Well, that is certainly the conventional attitude—but for whatever reason conventional ways haven't worked for me and I no longer even want them. I have to find my own way, but it wouldn't be fair to tie myself to someone else when my own future is so uncertain."

"But it doesn't *have* to be uncertain."

"But it *is*."

"I don't understand you. I don't understand what you're trying to say."

"I'm not sure myself, but I think I want to go back to Chicago after all."

"What about your gallery?"

She had told him about her mother's duplicity, the immediate cause of her ill spirits on the night of *The Graduate*. Wanting the gallery as much as she did she had considered accepting her mother's offer, but decided finally she wanted no part of such strong-armed generosity. "It's not my gallery. It's the Cooper gallery. My mother only proved what I should have known all along. Sea View is a Cooper building, it is not my building, I did nothing to earn it. I want to do something finally that I can call my own. I wish I knew what it might be—but whatever it is I want to do it on my own, and it will be easier to do it on my own in Chicago."

He seemed to shrink into himself, face drooping like wax. "Sometimes, you know, the conventional ways are best."

She wished to comfort him, but restrained herself from more than squeezing his hand. "For some people, yes. Maybe for you, but not for me. I think I might have been running away from something when I came to Bombay, and I need to go back to Chicago and face it, whatever it may be."

He let his hand lie limp, refusing to return her pressure. "Maybe you're running away from something now? Maybe you need to face something in Bombay?"

She didn't want to tell him she no longer wanted the kind of love they had shared, it would have been too cruel, but it wasn't healthy to be dependent upon the presence of another for happiness. Kaki was right: silly love songs and romance novels only perpetuated the myth that such love was real and true and desirable, but what was indicated more than anything else was desperation, an impoverished soul seeking reassurance, correlating the intensity of love with worth. It worked like a drug and she had infected him with her own subterranean need. She was confident time would give him perspective, but her present task lay in convincing him of her affection, while discouraging his hope. "You may be right, but that's not good enough for me. I have to find out for myself."

He pulled his hand away. "I think that's very selfish of you."

She put her hand back first in her lap, then crossed her arms again. "Then I'm selfish, but I don't know how else to be—and you're well rid of me."

He said nothing, recognizing she no longer cared for the argument—more, that he had run out of arguments himself, but refused to acknowledge it.

Farida turned the key in the ignition. "I think we should be getting back. I don't think your parents are going to believe you are still walking with Cisco."

She tried making conversation on the way home. His responses were monosyllabic, rendering her silent as they passed Chowpatty, but as they drove along Hughes Road, ready to turn at Kemp's Corner to Warden Road again, he spoke into his lap. "Farida, I can't bear the thought of never seeing you again."

Tears sprang unbidden to her eyes. "I do think it might be for the best."

His head shook from side to side, apparently involuntarily. "I can't ... No." His breath came in deep gasps as if he were drowning. "I *have* to see you again. I *have* to." She was too full of air herself to speak, but he managed to control his own breath. "I don't want to be a nuisance, I really don't. I don't want you to change your plans—but at least while you are in Bombay I *have* to see you. We can just go for a drive, nothing more, like we did today—but I *have* to see you. At least one more time I *have* to see you. Otherwise, I tell you, this much I know, I won't be able to bear it. I don't know what I will do. It is all just a … a little too sudden."

She didn't have to see him to know; the trembling tone betrayed his tears; glistening cheeks as common now in her life as air. She was barely able to speak herself, but repeated continually, almost to herself. "Of course, my love. Of course, of course. I'm so sorry. Oh, my love, I'm so sorry. Of course."

PERCY FABER AND A WOMAN IN FULL

A nd then what happened?"

Farida lay in the crook of Percy's shoulder in bed, one arm bent like a wing between them, the other across his torso, idly handling his penis, combing his pubic hair, happily inhaling their post-coital tang, Percy's sweat mingled with her own. "We only met twice in Bombay after that. I like to think it gave him some closure, to know we met at his request, not to shut him out completely after I had led him such a dance. I would have met him again as often as he wished, but he seemed to see the wisdom of it after that himself—not to meet again, I mean. I think it even helped that I had decided to come back to Chicago. It made the parting easier—as if I were leaving Bombay, not leaving him. I don't know how we would have managed if I had stayed in Bombay."

"I thought you said he came to Chicago?"

"Yes, he did. That had always been his plan, even before we met, to study architecture at the IIT, and that was what he did—but not right away, almost a year and a half later. His parents knew I was here, of course, and almost prevented him from coming—but he prevailed." She had never told Darius his father had propositioned her, attempted to blackmail her, but she imagined his guilt and the cassette recording had kept him from resisting Darius too strenuously, perhaps even encouraged him to persuade his wife to relent. "I knew he was coming. Kaki had written to me … just in case, I suppose—but I didn't get in touch, I didn't think it wise—but he called me during his sophomore year. He was getting married."

"Ah!"

"I was glad to hear it, particularly that he was marrying an older woman—and a Hindu." She smiled, scratching Percy's belly. "I felt I had had *some* influence over him, and a good one, though I suppose his parents are very likely still swearing at me—not to mention the more orthodox Parsis. Bicharo bagri gayo, the poor fellow got spoiled— meaning me, of course. I had spoiled him forever for a good Parsi girl."

Percy laughed, but his question revealed his concern. "You have no regrets?"

She shook her head against his shoulder. "You have to remember this was all a very long time ago, Darius got his Master's long before you and I even met, but by then I had started writing *Indian American*. I had lost interest in just about everything else. It's funny how a vocation focuses your attention. It made me realize what was important—a bit like having a baby, I suppose" (she laughed), "except when you're having a baby everyone wants to help, but when you're writing a book they think there's something wrong with you—until, of course, it's published."

Percy sensed her regret then, though not the regret he had imagined. "I think I might rather wish to have written a book myself—I mean, don't get me wrong, I'm very proud of my kids—but I suppose every choice implies a road not taken. No point grumbling."

Farida spoke with more resolution. "And I'm not! I really was glad for the wife he chose—five years older, also an architect, in the graduate program." She grinned. "I told him I had always known he would go for a younger woman."

Percy laughed. "I can just see you telling him."

Farida smiled. Darius had been sweet on the telephone, confessing he had loved and missed his sister, but for those first months he had missed Farida more, and she had thanked him for letting her know; confessing further that if not for her he might not have married an older woman, and she had thanked him again for his confidence, glad to have affected him finally to a positive end. "They invited me once to dinner and we had a lovely time. All things considered, we couldn't have ended on a higher note. Her name was Priti Das—and she was like her name, a pretty woman, but also so much more. Her family had been active in the freedom movement, very unorthodox—cultured, educated, imaginative—friendly with the Nehrus and Gandhis. Her grandmother had run away from home to escape an arranged marriage. I must say he did very well for himself."

He had also revealed that his mother had wished to prosecute Farida, but to his surprise his father had taken up the cudgels in her defense saying they had no proof, they could never compete against the Cooper lawyers. Farida had smiled, understanding Mr. Katrak's concern immediately, but said nothing. Percy nuzzled her hair. "They do seem to have resisted the stereotypes." They were in accord on the subject: the Fifties model of man as breadwinner and woman as breadmaker had surrendered to the double-income family, but the relative standing of men and women had not changed, not even in the Eighties. The woman's income remained subsidiary to the man's, a wife still sought her identity in her husband's profession, secretaries and schoolteachers lived the lives of architects and engineers, therapists and office managers the lives of lawyers and bankers and physicians, a woman making $20,000 married a man making $35,000, a woman making $75,000 a man making $125,000—nothing the matter with the model except when it preempted other models. *Why not*, she had said, *a woman bringing home the bacon for her man to cook?*

Farida nodded vigorously against his shoulder. "They certainly did!"

"If you don't mind my saying so, so have you."

"So have I what?"

"Resisted the stereotypes. It takes courage to go against the grain."

Her voice softened. "I don't know about that, but I think I learned something about courage from Alma. She was scared of hospitals, a timid woman, very much the little woman of the Fifties—but in the end she was forced to be courageous. I thought about that old saying: Some are born to greatness; others have it thrust on them. It was the same for Alma with courage. She wasn't born to it, but she showed a great deal in the end. She knew she was going to die, she was continually in pain, but still she smiled, never complained."

The chores she had performed, fetching Alma's paper and mail, groceries from the Jewel, errands to the bank and post office, had begun as pleasures, but the span of a year had made her resentful of the demands on her time, most especially when the hospice had shirked its responsibilities knowing she would pick up the slack. She recalled Alma had tired of caring for Homer in his last days and chosen not to attend the funeral, not even to stand by his sickbed once he was dead, absenting herself entirely from all proceedings—and she had done the same. She had sat with her friend through a score of attacks, one image rising above the rest: she had let herself into the apartment once to see Alma like a ragdoll in her armchair, hands limp between her knees, shoulders slumped, head fallen, face of wax, flat as cardboard. She might have been blown in through the window by a tornado for the way she looked, a woman of dust and straw and waste-paper. Farida's cheeks had sheeted with tears at the sheer brutality of the sight.

On the final morning she had called Farida and Farida had arrived in time to see her on her sofa taking her last garroting breath. Her lower jaw had fallen like a drawbridge, leaving her mouth open. Farida had lifted her jaw with a finger, marveling at her skin, still as fine as a rose petal, but the hinge of her jaw no longer functioned. She understood the body was already no more than a shell, and sensed the spirit of Alma hovering over her shoulder. She had called the hospice and abandoned her friend to their care, unsurprised that more than anything she felt gratitude and relief. She had mourned her friend while she had still been alive. "It got me thinking. Why wait to be dragged into the arena? Why not enter with your head held high? If she had found the courage for surgery she might have been alive today."

Percy nodded, but remained intent on his point. "She might, and not to take anything away from Alma—but I'm talking about a different kind of courage—going against the grain."

Farida laughed. "I was lurching more than going against the grain."

He seemed not to hear and she understood his concern better when he spoke again. "I mean, you do appear to have run the gamut of men—going from Darius, seventeen years younger, to me, fourteen years older."

There was admiration in his voice and she had run the gamut more than he knew, but the details of the more casual affairs after her return to Chicago would make him uncomfortable, her refusal (some might say her inability) to commit in the aftermath of Horace and Darius, and she didn't elaborate. More to the point, she had lost all desire to invest too much of herself in any man, and given up even the affairs when she had begun to write in earnest; given up cigarettes for the health benefit, the economy, the discipline, also dining out, entertainment in general, reducing her life to essentials. She had taken the job at Telesurveys, she had enrolled in the Master's program at Lincoln State University, she had Rohini whose family she had adopted as her own, she had two or three other friends she met less frequently, and she had her work. With Horace she had run the gamut of the conventional social marriage, with Darius the wild romance many women fantasized about, with subsequent anonymous men the anonymous affairs some women also fantasized about, but she had come to Percy with a fuller maturity, a greater understanding of what she wanted, and of all she had to offer, only beginning to understand what Kaki had said: *A loving person is a loved person, and a loved person is a loving person.* That had always been Percy's way and she wanted to make it hers, but it had taken her so very long to recognize what he seemed always to have known. Kaki had added: *If you have been loved as a child, it is easier to be loving as an adult—but if you haven't been loved as a child, it is imperative to be loving as an adult.* "You're the same age as Horace. Does it bother you?"

He laughed. "Heaven forbid! I may be old, but I am not yet in my dotage. More than anything else, where you are concerned, I am grateful—and full of wonder for what is happening to me."

"You paid a heavy price."

She was talking about the accident and he knew it. His left hand had been shattered, two ribs broken, from a car ploughing into his side when he had driven through a red light, but Farida's attentions in the aftermath, her allegiance divided between him and Alma, had mended more than his body. "It was worth every second, if that's what it took."

She didn't like to be reminded. "You had me long before that. I was just too dumb to know it." She snuggled closer, putting a finger to his lips. He had been unsure after they had returned from the hospital whether to proposition her or to propose, and pitying his indecision she had taken matters in hand rather than endure the embarrassment of a proposal she would have refused.

He had learned quickly, asking after their first lover's kiss, preparatory to stepping into his bedroom: *Is this what you want?*

Yes! Do you want more?

Not if you don't!

I don't, not for now—but please don't misunderstand. I haven't slept with anyone in a long while.

I'm flattered.

Don't be. If I had found a man like you I might not have waited so long.

I'm even more flattered.

She wondered later if she had baited him or just wanted to keep her options open, but they had said no more about it, she busy with the galleys of *The Long Sunset,* followed by a visit to London for the release of the novel to which she had invited Kaki, taking her on a motor trip later through Scotland and Ireland, and bringing her finally to Chicago to meet Percy. Even her Master's had come through, though not without a great deal more red tape. "Not just dumb, but stupid for so long. I don't want to be stupid anymore. I *want* to grow old. I want to grow old in the best way—and I can't think of a better way than with you."

Percy kissed the top of her head. "So, what are your plans for today?"

She smoothed soft commas of white hairs on his shoulder. "Mostly to proof those galleys." The English publication of *The Long Sunset* had been followed by an American, also a French translation, reviews and sales had been respectable, and *That in Some Big Houses* had been accepted for publication by Butterworth & Blanding, leading to her move to a larger apartment in the bedroom of which they now lazed. "You?"

Turning sixty-six, Percy had retired from the Mandalay Market to devote himself to a new pastime: cookery. The dinners he prepared for as many as a dozen and more of his friends at a time had greatly enhanced his social standing, as had Farida's continual presence beside him. It had also helped exercise his arm and leg. "Not much—which leaves me plenty of time to cook dinner. My place, Chicken Monaco, six o'clock, tonight?"

"Sounds lovely." She kissed his cheek. He knew how well she liked his Chicken Monaco. "Thanks."

II

Percy had lived a quiet life since Erica's death, visiting sons in San Francisco (playing proud grandfather to the piano prodigy) and New York (no less proud of the track star), and parents in Ely (both in their nineties, long retired from the chemist shop). He had been grateful for attention from Chicago friends, if not always receptive, particularly during the months following the obsequies. He remained attractive to women of a certain age, but their overtures had surprised and appalled him. He realized rituals of courtship had changed during the time of his marriage, but he had found the more enterprising women immodest and alarming, at once taking him for granted and begging his pardon for doing so, apparently unsure themselves of the new etiquette.

With Farida the association had begun avuncularly. He couldn't say when he had first imagined in her more than a colleague, more than a friend—perhaps not before she had made her intentions clear herself, perhaps when she had first revealed her two files of desperately burgeoning correspondences, perhaps also during their very first interview when he had decided to give her a second chance—but he had not been sure until after the accident. She had seemed too mired in herself for her own good, for anyone's good, but all she had needed was a chance to prove herself and the accident had given her just that. He was fortunate to have escaped with just a smashed hand and she had spent every spare moment by his bedside, assisting as no one else in his physical therapy. She had also come to know members of his family when they visited, all of whom were grateful to her and full of admiration for him: the patriarch was doing better than they could have imagined.

He removed two salads from the refrigerator, poured a dressing of his own creation into a gravy boat, checked buttered noodles and peas simmering on the stove, and added cream to chicken simmering in butter and basil and sherry in a skillet. She had brought a bottle of Chardonnay which they had opened. He could see her hands in the pass-through, setting the table with dishes and silver and wineglasses and a candelabra as if she had been mistress of the house for years. She had worn a sari (blue with a darker blue choli) because she knew he liked her in saris though it was cold and a mist hovered outside. She seemed entirely at ease though preoccupied, gazing periodically out of the dark glaze of the twenty-second storey window toward the lake.

Having set the table Farida placed Mendelssohn's *Midsummer Night's Dream* on the turntable and stood by the window gazing. Sometimes the mist was heavy enough to grip the building like a fist, but tonight it was light, revealing the cityscape through a veil, a water-color of Chicago, brightening increasingly with light as the night deepened. Nearby highrises glowed like giant chandeliers, jewels in the night, constellations in deep space. She smiled: as a painter she might have rendered just what she saw, but as a writer she would need to avoid the confusion of images, she would need to pick among chandeliers and jewels and constellations. Chandeliers and jewels were perhaps too bright for mist, but not constellations, clouds of vapor and steam and light, betokening perhaps the birth of stars—betokening her own birth finally as a woman in full after fifty-three years.

They had not discussed marriage, but appeared to have settled into a partnership no different. She would marry Percy gladly if he wished, or live with him, or live in an adjoining apartment. She had grown to like her solitary life, even to be jealous of her space, but Percy was not the man to crowd a house, an apartment, or even a room.

The tinkle of a fork hitting a wineglass drew her from her reverie, Percy calling her to dinner, and her face glowed like the constellations of highrises outside as she answered his call.

AFTERWORD

I was in highschool in Bombay (where I was born and raised), when one of my classmates dated one of the teachers. He was trim, handsome, smart, 17; she was lovely, vivacious, talented, 34. Like all the boys, I envied his good luck, as did the teachers. Even the headmaster fumed at one point: "What does she *see* in that boy?!!" I never learned the true nature of their association, but there was a great deal of smoke and like the others I imagined a conflagration underneath.

Many years later, after I had made my home in Chicago, after I had published my first novel, *The Memory of Elephants*, and was casting around for ideas for new books, I recalled an image of the two of them walking side by side. There was no handholding, there were no yearning glances, but what had impressed me was the confidence with which the boy walked. In his place, I might have fidgeted, bounced on my feet, cast continual sidelong glances to make sure I wasn't dreaming, but he walked as if they were peers. That impression stayed, but recalling the image I no longer envied him. Instead, I asked a variation of the headmaster's question. What might have happened to make her initiate such an affair? Whatever his appeal, he was half her age. The answer to the question led to a new novel, *A Woman Madly in Love*, published in India by Roli Books in 2004. It received excellent reviews, some of which I have blurbed for this edition, but I grew unhappy with the story. It ended well for Farida Cooper, but she remained essentially narcissistic and I didn't know how to resolve that until I had an experience with an elderly woman living in my building, the Alma of the novel.

I was working then on TRIO (my book about the Schumanns and Brahms, the first draft of which grew to 1,800 pages) and home most of the time. After meeting on the elevator a few times, she invited me to visit for hot chocolate and pastries. I got in the habit of visiting her, watching TV, and chatting over pie ala mode (key lime for me, strawberry rhubarb for her) and soft drinks and ice cream among other delicacies. She was 93 years old and a couple of years or so after we met she suffered a heart attack. The doctors gave her three weeks to live unless she underwent surgery. She didn't want surgery, she'd lived a long and happy life, but staying on the fifth floor was too weak to leave her apartment to collect her newspaper, mail, and groceries everyday, even for just those three weeks. I offered to manage her chores and she gave me the key to her apartment. (Another tenant, a woman, managed her laundry.)

The three weeks bled into more than a year during which time I lost count of the number of heart attacks she endured, some lasting moments, others up to three hours. There was little I could do except hand her syringes of morphine to ease the pain, hold her hand, and offer moral support while she moaned and sweated and sank into her sofa.

It was an extraordinary experience, at once prurient and profound and I realized this was the experience Farida needed to make her a fuller person. I made notes of what I saw and wrapped the episode into the fabric of *Woman*, accounting for this revised version, now titled *Portrait of a Woman Madly in Love*.

Strangely, I was a man writing the life of a woman, supposedly fictitious, but I found myself understanding better than ever Flaubert's bon mot: "Madame Bovary, c'est moi." Farida is descended from a long line of heroines not unlike Emma Bovary (Anna Karenina, Isabel Archer, Lily Bart, Edna Pontellier), women a little too pleased with themselves for their own good, and like her forebears she pays a price—as I paid a price for my own head too swollen for my own good in my younger years.

II

A friend once invited me to read from one of my novels at a party. During the dinner which followed I was seated beside a young academic with a doctorate in English. He congratulated me on the reading, which he was good enough to say he had enjoyed, before the conversation devolved into shoptalk about literature. The academic pronounced with a grin of complicity that the University of Michigan at Ann Arbor was one of those old-fashioned universities which imagined Authorial Intent still meant something.

The surprise was not that I took umbrage (as an author I could do no less), but that he was too dimwitted to recognize that an author might do no less. He was not a stupid man, it takes more than stupidity to earn a doctorate in English—but steeped as he was in the theoretical fads of the day, and eager as he was to display how deeply he'd been steeped, he was able to parrot the fashionable chestnuts with glee, though unable to question their veracity. Similarly, a Barnes & Noble manager once piped at another dinner that she NEVER paid any attention to what an author might mean, but interpreted every work to suit herself.

That is her privilege, and I don't say an author should wield her intent like a weapon; Authorial Intent is not the last word on the subject; different readers must read the same passage differently, for no reason other than that they bring different associations to the reading, and a writer takes that for granted as a physicist takes gravity; but a reader ignores an Author's Intent at her peril. If a reader reads only to confirm her own beliefs she does no more than run in circles, no more than deepen her rut—as all too many literary theorists have all too often done. The problem is not merely what theorists say, but their inability to say it clearly, allowing for easy weaseling out of tight corners. Take for instance the following sentence (if you may call it a sentence): "Moving by this Foucauldian intuition we might say that academic US feminism names social-constructionism as 'anti-essentialism,' and polarizes it against 'nature' because, briefly, this is how their discursive formation de-fangs Marxist-materialist radicalism." The sentence could be read to mean the moon is made of goats and butter. I won't divulge the identity of the writer because identity is beside the point; the point is the meaning of the words—but the person is an eminent theorist, and unfortunately not alone in such eminence.

As an author, my concern is with having something to say and saying it clearly, if not memorably. I may not always succeed, but that is my intent. I do not say an author's reading is the only reading. I do say it should be considered and understood and debated, and the skinnier the line between an author's intent and a reader's comprehension the more successful the communication, the more successful the work. Multiple readings such as Derrida provided of multiple texts may be ingenious, but that doesn't make them any less false, any more ingenious, than Shaw's spelling of fish: G-H-O-T-I ("gh/f" from "enough," "o/i" from "women," "ti/sh" from "ignition"). Significantly, Shaw tucked his tongue well within his cheek, but not even Derrida's acolytes know the whereabouts of Derrida's tongue, and Derrida's defense of the deceits of Paul de Man (adulterer, swindler, Nazi, and doyen of deconstruction at Yale among other things), lays to rest any rational doubts regarding his objectivity—for many his perspicacity, despite his undeniable brilliance.

This is not the place to revisit old arguments. I found the best palliative to the pollutions of theorists in Keith Windschuttle's *The Killing of History* and John M. Ellis's *Literature Lost*. Windschuttle and Ellis forward the necessary arguments more ably, clearly, convincingly, and knowledgably than I can, and I recommend their books highly to anyone further interested in the debate.

Conversations with professors on Deconstruction brought forth widely divergent responses. One called it "obfuscatory," another said she simply avoided it, another said it was pointless unless followed by a *re*construction, another that she found it funny and never took it seriously, another de*fen*ded it by saying it was going out of fashion!! Whatever the argument, a grounding in Theory is required of students pursuing doctorates in English, however nonsensical some professors may find it—and persons such as Farida Cooper find themselves cheated of the chance for a doctorate because they refuse to abide by what many consider nonsensical coursework—and without a doctorate they are cheated of the chance to teach at university levels, however expert they may be at subjects unrelated to Theory—most glaringly, Literature.

The theme of Qualifications Versus Experience is nevertheless secondary in *Portrait of a Woman Madly in Love*. The primary theme is Love (or its lack) and its variations: love between parents and children, friends and lovers, husbands and wives. The theme of Love may not require the same explication as that of Theory, but Love as a theme is ballyhooed in academia in Saul Bellow's memorable phrase as "a school thing, a skirt thing, a church thing." Bellow was talking about Poetry, but the rationale is the same for Love. As a postcolonial professor once argued about one of my novels: it's not political, and if it's not political it doesn't matter. She went on to confound her own argument by saying that EVERYthing was political: if you were apolitical that was a political statement in itself—but the corollary seemed to escape her, that if everything was political then nothing was political. At bottom, of course, these are bullying tactics—reducing all arguments to a dichotomy and forcing a choice, the better to control the agenda. This is how autocracy works, how dictators are born, whether in universities, corporations, or countries.

In part, the contemporary run on postcolonialism is a bid for relevance as much as a bid for grants, a call for socioeconomic importance that

Literature appears to have lost. It is no longer enough to say Literature holds a mirror to ourselves, even to our souls: that requirement appears to have been preempted by the pop psychologies of the day. Instead, Literature reasserts its relevance by leapfrogging into the realm of such subjects as history, sociology, and ethnography—but such leapfrogging sidesteps the heart of the matter. Are the Marxist, feminist, and postcolonial literatures, for instance, literature because they meet the challenge of the eternal verities, because they show us the consequences of the choices we make, or because they forward Marxist, feminist, and postcolonial agendas? In brief, are they studied because they are Marxist, feminist, and postcolonial, or because they are Literature? In the best of all worlds they are both, but all too often the adjectives (Marxist, feminist, postcolonial) overwhelm the noun (literature).

The difficulty arises because at heart all literature is propaganda. The measure of the literature is the measure of the skill with which it forwards its propaganda—or, as E. M. Forster put it, how well the author can bounce the reader into accepting what he says—or, as Flannery O'Connor put it, how well the author can make the reader look the other way before hitting her over the head with a baseball bat.

All of which brings me back to the theme of Love. There is no more important theme, no more important propaganda—a theme deserving continual rejuvenation for no reason other than that it repays the thoughtful reader in her life and work. It is also a word continually traduced, misunderstood, and manipulated—and so common a theme that it has become invisible. The final scene in the book between Kaki and Farida is hardly the most complex or dramatic I have written, but it may well be the most profound. It is hardly the final word on love, but I would hate to see it discounted simply because it is not overtly political. If you want history, read a history book; if politics, a book on political science; and if you are a pedant, by all means, criticize a novel for not being a history book, or a book on political science, or whatever else you had no right to expect from a novel not written to your specifications—but the reader does both reader and writer an injustice when she attempts to read her own agenda into the writer's work: more helpful by far to ask what the writer is saying, and then measure how effectively she's said it.

It may be no more than a game of patience. The wheel of literature is as round as that of history or political science or any other subject. What is down today ascends tomorrow, and what is up descends. Specialization is the greater problem, professors forwarding their own agendas against the greater good because they know no better, and university curriculums more concerned with being contemporary than universal. My work fits comfortably in the postcolonial pocket, and some will say I have no axe to grind, but *Portrait of a Woman Madly in Love* was discounted for many unfathomable reasons, once by an agent looking for ethnic novels because it wasn't ethnic enough (not postcolonial enough, not Third World enough, not enough poverty-chic—neither, ironically, unfortunately, was it American enough). That is as ridiculous a reason as any for declining a manuscript, but it is also a different debate (whether a novel matters for its quality or its content), and I will save it for another time.

GLOSSARY

Arré: exclamation of surprise
Ayah: nanny
Baat: story, matter, talk
Baba: boy
Bai: madam
Bachchu: baby
Bagri gayo: got spoiled
Baksheesh: alms
Baysharram: shameless
Bewaquoof: fool
Bibi: sister
Bicharo: poor fellow
Charpoy: rope bed
Chikna: sexy (slang)
Chowkidar: watchman
Chalo: let's go
Falanu-dhiknu: this and that
Four-twenty: crazy (slang)
Ghati: lower-class, uneducated
Godown: store room
Gujarati: the language and people
  of the state of Gujerat
Lafran: problem, hassle, mess
Matka: earthenware pot to keep
  water cool

Memsahib: madam
Navroz: Parsi New Year
Paise: money
Papeti: Parsi holiday
Patrel: leafy, juicy, pulpy, spicy
  snack
Pukka: ripe, pure
Sahib: sir
Samosa: deepfried snack with
  vegetarian or non-vegetarian
  filling
Seth: sir
Shikara: a canopied Kashmiri boat
  resembling a gondola
Thero: wait
Yaar: filler word, interchangeable
  with "man," "like" (slang)

Boman Desai was bound for a career in market analysis when a chance encounter with Sir Edmund Hillary, his first hero, turned him back to writing. He had his first break when an elegant elderly woman submitted half a dozen of his stories for publication to *Debonair* (in Mumbai)—all of which were published, but the woman vanished and her identity remains a mystery to this day. His second break came when another elegant elderly woman, Diana Athill, published his first novel, *The Memory of Elephants*. Desai is best known for that novel, published subsequently by the University of Chicago Press, and for TRIO, *a Novel Biography of the Schumanns and Brahms* which was awarded the Kirkus star and listed among their Best Books of 2016. The book was subsequently transcribed into an opera, *Clara*, and may now be seen on youtube. More recently, he published *A Googly in the Compound* (a novel of the Raj), its plot ranging from 1910 to 1945, from rural Navsari to cosmopolitan Bombay to 1930s London to wartorn Burma and Mesopotamia, both world wars playing a role in the plot. Desai has won about a dozen awards and taught fiction at Truman College and Roosevelt University (both in Chicago), and the University of Southern Maine. He is also a musician and composer, with among other things a symphony and piano concerto to his credit (though yet to find performances). You may learn more about him at bomandesai.com. He may be reached at boman@core.com

T R I O

THE SCHUMANNS
AND BRAHMS
(A NOVEL BIOGRAPHY)

BOMAN DESAI

It is perhaps Boman Desai's greatest achievement that the great composers of the Romantic Age appear as full-bloodedly as if they might have been his neighbors.

ZUBIN MEHTA

Boman Desai

A GOOGLY IN THE COMPOUND

a novel of the Raj

The tiger cub grows as dangerous as
the British Raj for India. Both have
tasted blood and both demand more.
Desai spins a fascinating story of Parsi
bloodlines, romance and intrigue,counter-
pointed by the events that made WWII
such a watershed in the history of both
India and the world.

Anjana Basu

A family's long-simmering tensions boil over during a trip to the old
homestead in this literary novel.... The result is a wide-lensed meditation
on power dynamics—within countries and within families.
—*Kirkus Reviews*

DANA AWARD FOR BEST NOVEL OF THE YEAR

The Elephant
Graveyard

A Moby Dick for Elephants

Boman Desai

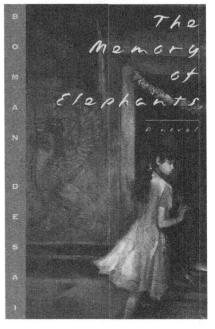

The
Memory
of
Elephants

A novel

BOMAN DESAI

Excerpts from

TRIO
A Novel Biography of the Schumanns and Brahms

The trio comprises three musical geniuses: Robert and Clara Schumann and Johannes Brahms. Clara married Robert with whom she fell in love when she was just sixteen, though it meant challenging the iron will of her father who wished her to marry an early or count, certainly not an impoverished composer. The Schumanns had eight children and Robert's greatness as a composer was never in doubt, but he was also mentally ill, attempted suicide, and finally incarcerated himself in an asylum where he died two and a half years later.

Johannes Brahms entered the picture shortly before the incarceration and fell deeply in love with Clara, but was just as deeply indebted to Robert for getting his first six opuses published within weeks of their meeting. Clara was forbidden to see Robert in the asylum because the doctors feared she would excite him too much. Brahms became a go-between for the couple, ferrying messages to and from, but both loved Robert too well to abuse his trust. Brahms learned instead to associate deep love with deep renunciation—and, coupling this love with early experiences of playing dance music for sailors and prostitutes in Hamburg's dockside bars, he became a victim to the Freudian conundrum: Where he loves he feels no passion, and where he feels passion he cannot love.

Firmly grounded in fact, the book unfolds like a novel, a narrative of love, insanity, suicide, revolution, politics, war—and, of course music.

FIRST EXCERPT

The rule in Paris was to play first at soirees, and if and when the newspapers mentioned you to follow up with a concert. Her uncle arranged for invitations to soirees and the first at which Clara played, the Princess Vandamore's, was notable as much for what happened as what did not. The chambers were upholstered, hung with tapestries and portraits, stuffed with porcelain, figurines, vases, cups, and stuffed animals and birds; dogs had the run of the rooms as did parrots and canaries—as, to Clara's delight, did a monkey, with whom she shook hands, though Wieck warned that she could not trust such an animal not to bite—alongside princes, ambassadors, and priests arrayed in their finest. Wieck shook his head in disbelief; the French were children pretending to be adults; how Bonaparte had conquered Europe he would never fathom.

A young man approached the piano for which Wieck was relieved, more comfortable listening to music than making conversation, particularly in French. The man was short, stooped, and frail, his eyes were heavylidded, and the long fair hair covering his ears was exquisitely combed. He smiled, appearing to enjoy himself, but looked beyond the walls and once he sat at the piano he appeared beyond the weal of the world himself. Wieck, more concerned with seating himself comfortably, paid little attention until the man began to play, one note in the high treble, so clear and commanding that Wieck became still. A configuration followed, more single notes, first descending, then ascending, but what a configuration! With an uncanny use of the pedal he had blended the individual notes into one great blooming undulating chord.

Clara gripped his wrist with a whisper. "Chopin!"

SECOND EXCERPT

He sighed, sitting again at the piano. Willy wouldn't be back until late in the evening and he was faced with the prospect of the long day ahead. He had work to do on the *Zeitschrift* and the *Fantasiestucke* he was writing for Robena, but he sat at the piano instead, doing nothing—or so it appeared, but something was spinning in his head that he needed to let out and he could let it out only on the piano.

He couldn't explain how it worked: had he not pined for Clara there would have been nothing to release; had he not sat motionless at the piano there would have been no conduit for release. He couldn't have said how long he sat, but something congealed in the time, the red blood, the hard bone, of the new composition, a strident melody, roiling harmony, interspersed with tender interludes, pulled from the collision of the thunder outside, the purr of the rain, and the noise in his head. He held his hands over the keys and under them the landscape of his nerves, blood, and bones sprang to life, little kingdoms growing under his fingers.

THIRD EXCERPT

On March 7, 1897, a shrunken Johannes Brahms, suffering from cancer of the liver, attended a performance in Vienna of his Fourth Symphony.

The symphony glides so smoothly into its first theme that the listener finds himself deep in its wake before he realizes it has even begun.

The second movement showcases a plaintive melody hovering around a single note like a hopeless lover. A friend had said that only Brahms could have written that symphony, and even Brahms had had recourse to certain locked chambers of his soul for the first time – but he had finally run out of locked chambers.

At the end of each movement the conductor turned to Brahms's box to acknowledge the composer, the audience stood, and the composer stood to acknowledge the downpour of applause, knowing the symphony would not otherwise commence.

With the conclusion of the symphony, the downpour swelled to a monsoon, all eyes turned to the tiny man, hollows in the back of his neck, skin discolored to bronze, trembling with tears, the auditorium awash with light and color in his blurry eyes.

Twenty minutes later the emaciated old composer still stood, the audience still applauded.

He was tired, but remained standing, clinging to the rail, buoyed by the love in the hall, wishing no more to sit or to leave than they, his lovely Viennese, wished to let him go, their eyes no less damp than his own, cheeks no less bright, manly beards aglitter with tears like diamonds, all of them knowing it was the last time they would be seeing one another.

He died less than a month later, but what remained – the residue, the essence, distillate of his life, gold from straw – remains impervious to fang and claw, at once the heart of the riddle of life and medicine for the heart.

Excerpts from
A GOOGLY IN THE COMPOUND
A Novel of the Raj

The Sanjanas planned to enjoy the tiger cub and surrender the adult to the zoo, but no plan had been made for the adolescent. The family is breakfasting in the compound of their bungalow when the cub gets its first taste of blood from a cut on Sohrab Sanjana's hand. Also in attendance are Daisy (Sohrab's English wife, married when she was stranded by WWII in India); Rustom (Sohrab's brother, back from the war in Burma); Dolly (their mother, afraid the rivalry between her sons might erupt into violence echoing the rivalry between the two brothers she had married in succession); and Phiroze (Dolly's second husband, younger brother of her first). Their story spans the years from 1910 to 1945, and the globe from rural Navsari to cosmopolitan Bombay to 1930s London to wartorn Burma and Mesopotamia.

FIRST EXCERPT

The crowds had thinned when many British and Indians had turned west, some in the party suggesting they too should turn west, but Stilwell had continued north, transferring loads from sedans to trucks when the terrain had proven too rough for sedans, and from trucks to jeeps when they'd had to ford a stream and sacrifice most of the trucks. They'd had one narrow escape already. Taking two wrong turns they had lost miles when they couldn't afford to lose yards, and having corrected their path they had stopped to confirm their direction and found themselves overlooking a valley of roiling humanity.

At first it resembled nothing so much as a large snake coiling and uncoiling, but grew worse as details came clear: gray-uniformed Chinese dragged a Burman from the cab of his truck, slapped him with a pistol, bloodying his face, breaking his nose, commandeering his truck; blond Britishers struck unarmed families with the butts of their guns for bags of rice; tall gaunt Punjabis with long black beards snatched food from toothpick children; tribespeople looted bodies of the dead; heat waves magnified the disaster like a glass; the smell rose to grip them like a giant hand; someone fired a rifle, someone replied with a tommygun, then came screams, then more gunfire, then silence, first to fall were first to be trampled, women and children the fairest game of all.

They had hurried back to their convoy to find families of skeletons, grey with dust, holloweyed and leatherskinned, foul with shit and blood and flies, beyond the shame of their nakedness, crawling and rising from the ground, cracked cups and broken bowls in outstretched hands, babies sucking from dry dugs, children picking grains of rice from piles of shit. Stilwell had walked into the midst toward his jeep, shouting his concern out loud. "Hold it! Don't give them anything or we'll be mobbed! Crank up and get moving and don't stop for anything!" They had started engines, honked horns, and hurried away.

SECOND EXCERPT

Alphonse took two steps forward. He was close enough to touch Victoria when he steadied the gun, took aim again, and fired. In the wake of the blast there was once more the howling of monkeys, the screeching of fowl in the forest, but in the compound there was only a wide white silence, the sentient stillness of cemeteries awaiting the advent of ghosts, followed by an awful vibration riding the air, sweeping the grounds like a grating, atomizing all it swept, the savage roar of the tribe of tiger, Victoria erupting in an orange flame as if the ground were a bed of lava.

THIRD EXCERPT

"It was on Christmas Eve, the Turks attacked our makeshift fort, and Rajan … at one point … he simply threw himself at me. I didn't understand, I hadn't seen the shell whistling its way toward …" Phiroze was once more speechless. Rajan had thrown him on his back and spreadeagled himself to cover him like a second skin—before growing suddenly weightless. His back had ripped open releasing fluids coagulating around Phiroze, encasing him in a gelatinous mold. He had tried to hold Rajan close, tried to hug him, but he had hugged bones, a ribcage clawing his chest, a skull like a lover's head lolling over his shoulder. The smell of shit was overpowering, but in that moment of sacrifice everything pertaining to Rajan became sacred, and he had breathed the odor as if to make it part of himself, wallowing in the clay that had once been his friend.

Phiroze swallowed, but still could not speak. Daisy squeezed his hand again, gripping and rubbing his arm, seeming to understand what he couldn't put into words. "My God, Phiroze, I'm so sorry. I'm so glad ... I'm so grateful you're still here."

He shook his head, eyes glistening, speaking again though his voice still trembled. "I am the one who is sorry. All this happened so long ago, more than thirty years—and here I am, an old soldier, blubbering like a baby."

Excerpts from
THE ELEPHANT GRAVEYARD:
A *Moby Dick* for Elephants

Myrtle Bailey's death in the circus ring clouds the lives of 5 people and one elephant: Hazel (her daughter, chief elephant handler); Brown E (a clown, once Hazel's lover); Dinty (her husband, once a contortionist); Jonas Frank (proprietor of the circus); Spike (her son, ghost narrator of the story); and Hero (blackest elephant in the world, oiled to blackness to grab attention during the dreary years of the Depression). Their fortunes are tied to those of the Blues, a black family: widowed mother Maudine; Royale (favored son, hair of ginger, skin of peach); Elbo (born elbowfirst); and Prize (for Surprise, Elbo's unexpected twin who came tumbling after). Amid the sawdust and spangles, the jitters and jangle, erupt scenes both horrific and exotic: a king cobra loose in a Chicago penthouse; a black boy trampled to death in a Toledo citysquare; slaves riddled with smallpox left on West African riverbanks awaiting crocodiles; a white elephant in musth (testosterone overdrive); a striptease on elephantback. Multiple thrills and zaniness mingle with meditations on slavery, circusing, the afterlife, and the ivory trade. A *Moby Dick* for elephants, *The Elephant Graveyard* is as rich with elephantalia as its predecessor was with whalology, as informed by Melville's incantatory prose and philosophical concerns, and attempts to understand why bad things happen to good people.

FIRST EXCERPT

As juggler and tumbler I might have been counted among acrobats, but as a bullman not even among joeys. I was barely above ponypunks and dogboys in the circus dungeon, while Eileen hovered among clouds drifting past turrets and towers. Each of us did flips and tumbles, but mine were on the broad back of Hero, the blackest elephant in the world, and hers on the thundering rump of her Andalusian, Andromache, the difference between performing in the middle of a plain and the middle of an earthquake—and differences there were more and plenty. For starters, she was a celebrity, flashed on the posters, tycoons gave her diamonds, beer barons gave parties in her honor. I couldn't compete.

As luck would have it I didn't have to compete. She knew better what to do with coals smoldering in the basement than I did. She invited me into her trailer one lazy Sunday afternoon in Wilmington, Delaware (we played different towns every day of the week, resting on Sundays). I lacked grace, I lacked gravity, I lacked authority; I lacked emeralds and other glittering flowers; I lacked the means to make them available; but though my face was as smooth as a girl's my appetite was more rapacious than that of the most heavily bearded man, my stamina that of a stallion. I marveled at my fortune, the girth of her thighs, each thick as a hydrant. I appeared and disappeared at her pleasure, asked no questions, and said little, not because I had little to say but because I didn't want to reveal how little I knew about the world, how littlesuited we might be for each other.

SECOND EXCERPT

Elbo didn't move, but could see from where he lay on his back that he was at one end of a long room with cages on each side mounted three feet above the floor. A doorway stood at the far end of the room and he prayed to reach it safely, prayed the cages were locked, but couldn't find the courage even to move. He felt safe only as long as he didn't attract attention. Even behind bars, the tiger on high, chin tufted in a Vandyke, one gleaming fang overhanging a furry lip like that of a crocodile, appeared as regal and menacing as a sphinx, as if he could reach Elbo anytime he chose by extending one dangling paw.

Elbo could have lain there until someone found him, but he was no more enthralled about the prospect of another term in jail at the end of his adventure, and plucked courage finally to slide on his back, imperceptibly as possible, toward the door.

The first move, the most difficult, attracted the most attention. Something touched his knee and he kicked reflexively sending it clattering as loudly as a motorbike through a mausoleum, the object he had picked and tossed through the window, a blowtorch. The tiger erupted with another jackhammer roar, three inch claws raking the air inches from his face, other cats nudging the bars of their cages, grunting and growling and puttering like tractors. Elbo would have been no more terrified had the Great Sphinx itself cracked out of its stone death to roam the plains of Ghiza. Had he not been on his back he might have fainted again, but when the tiger failed to touch him he slid again toward the door, moving in infinitesimal increments, as if he were running a gauntlet between the cages, as if he were on a tightrope though there was plenty of space between the cages along the center of the room.

THIRD EXCERPT

The elephant was more grey than white with salmon highlights, but its hair was white contributing, more than its pigmentation, to the illusion of whiteness even by night. Three-foot tusks, curved like scimitars, gleamed like pearls. The eyes were midnight blue, not the common pink of albinos. Long lashes fluttered, feminine and flirtatious.

The ammoniac smell of piss was predictable, but another smell of rot and sewage grew stronger: musth. The elephant was rutting for females in estrus, black liquid seeped from gashes in its temples appearing like makeup running in rain. The abundance of testosterone made it an impossible animal for the most experienced of mahouts, but facing the elephant was no mahout with the metal claw of an ankus, but a man with a machinegun—Quint—and off to the side, where the tall timbered wall of the boma met the ground, fallen on her flank, frozen with fear and shock, lay Mercedes.

Excerpts from

THE MEMORY OF ELEPHANTS

When Homi Seervai, a whiz kid from Bombay, is dumped by his first love in Aquihana, Pennsylvania, he invents the Memoscan, a machine designed to scan his brain to make a record of its memories. Isolating the memory traces covering his time with his inamorata, he sets the Memoscan on a repeat cycle to relive continually the most ecstatic hours of his life. Unfortunately, the machine goes haywire, dipping into his Collective Unconscious, the Memory of Mankind, including his own racial, familial, and ancestral memories. Seeing the dead and the living juxtaposed in a jigsaw of history and biography, he imagines he is going crazy—but, instead, as he comes to realize, he is only beginning to live, his first love no more than a flicker in the panorama of possibilities that beckon him into new life.

FIRST EXCERPT

Let me be clear: It wasn't a movie as much as a single scene, a single scene which I had played repeatedly through the memoscan—at first, and for countless times, successfully, to its conclusion —but, increasingly, the memory disintegrated into hallucinations. Yes, hallucinations. There was no other explanation. Back in the room, I saw naked Candace; back outside, camelbacked Arabs; back and forth, back and forth, Candace and Arabs, Arabs and Candace, both hostilely glaring at me. When the images began to merge, my command finally slipped and I surrendered to the madness. The lips of her vagina grew larger, more wrinkled, grey, an elephant's trunk and tusks emerged from the folds, elephant ears sprouted like wings on her back. I think that was when I started to scream.

What was happening? A vagina was flying on elephant ears, dragging trunk and tusks behind. Worse, I saw the dead (Bapaiji, Granny, Dad) and the living (Mom, Jalu Masi, Sohrab Uncle, Soli Mama, Rusi, Zarine—Myself!) as if they were acting out the scenes of their lives by my bedside. Worst of all, I saw armies, hordes and phalanxes of warriors, Arabs and Iranis, on foot, horseback, camelback, elephantback, engaged in battle, showers of descending arrows, a constant swarm of adverse activity as might be witnessed when rival ant colonies or galaxies collide. The fantastic merged with the real, the ancient with the modern, naked Candace, airborne on elephant ears, mounted on an elephant's trunk and tusks, split into a hundred similar images, and the flight of Candace angels soared to meet squadrons of flying monkeys approaching from the distance. The landscape was littered with rhinestone jackets, gold ballet slippers, blue miniskirts, and red panties, all to the accompaniment of a relentless atonal symphony. No wonder I felt in terror of imminent insanity.

SECOND EXCERPT
They were not far when they heard Dhunmai call. Adi threw everything into his sack and jumped into the tree, Bapaiji on his heels. They didn't mind being found together, but didn't want to give Dhunmai the satisfaction of finding them. Too late they realized they'd left one of Adi's whittling knives on the ground. Behind Bapaiji, in the thick foliage, hung the tails of three monkeys. She would have ignored them; there were hundreds of monkeys in the trees, tails hanging like furry brown ribbons; but not this time. She grabbed all three tails and yanked—hard. The idyll of the forest was slashed as if by lightning: the monkeys shrieked oop-oop-oop-oop, setting other monkeys shrieking, birds screaming, a wolf howling in the distance as if it were night; and woven into their screams, as brilliantly as the centerpiece of a peacock's fantail, was Dhunmai's screech as she turned and ran. The monkeys continued to shriek, oop-oop-OOP-OOP-OOP-OOP!!, baring their teeth, whooping around Bapaiji and Adi as if the trees had suddenly grown too hot to touch. Bapaiji bared her own teeth, whooping back. Adi laughed so hard he fell out of the tree; when Bapaiji reached to catch him he pulled her down with him; the fall knocked the air out of them and they choked, unable to stop laughing.

THIRD EXCERPT

The summer came to an ugly end: Penny, descending the schoolbus, flaxen hair flying as she turned her head for a final (too prophetic) goodbye, flashing her last big happy sweet last lover's smile before the rush across the street to meet Erica, her English speaking ayah whom she called Nanny; a screech, a thud, a scream, Miss Bean (responsible for the children on the bus) shouting, "Do not look. Nobody is to look out of the window."

How does a six year old cope with the loss of his sweetheart? He puts himself in quarantine, he lowers his resistance, he searches out toxins as if they were grail, he dreams of a reunitement (pupal angels cocooned in a Hansel and Gretal heaven). In the two years that followed I contracted mumps, jaundice, chicken pox, typhoid, two kinds of measles, three kinds of flu; I underwent a second tonsillectomy, an appendectomy; I had yet to run through cholera, small pox, tuberculosis, and whooping cough, but something I read and someone I met so exposed the selfindulgence of my quarantine that even the most benighted eyes (mine) began to see.